ROMANTIC TIM...
NEW YORK TIMES BESTSELLING
AUTHOR CONNIE MASON!

GYPSY LOVER

"Mason's romances are always a feast for readers seeking a passionate, exciting story peopled with larger-than-life heroes who take your breath away."

THE PIRATE PRINCE

"A legend of the genre, Mason delivers a tried-and-true romance with a classic plot and highly engaging characters."

THE LAST ROGUE

"A delight…. This is a must read for Mason fans."

SEDUCED BY A ROGUE

"Another wonderful story filled with adventure, witty repartee and hot sex."

THE ROGUE AND THE HELLION

"Ms. Mason has written another winner to delight her fans who want sexual tension that leads to hot explosion, memorable characters and a fast-paced story."

THE LAIRD OF STONEHAVEN

"[Ms. Mason] crafts with excellence and creativity… [and] the added attraction of mystery and magic. [The reader will] enjoy the facets of the supernatural that permeate this wonderful love story."

LIONHEART

"…Upholds the author's reputation for creating memorable stories and remarkable characters."

THE DRAGON LORD

"This is a real keeper, filled with historical fact, sizzling love scenes and wonderful characters."

THE BLACK KNIGHT

"Ms. Mason has written a rich medieval romance filled with tournaments, chivalry, lust and love."

Other books by Connie Mason:

GYPSY LOVER
THE PIRATE PRINCE
THE LAST ROGUE
THE LAIRD OF STONEHAVEN
SEDUCED BY A ROGUE
LIONHEART
A LOVE TO CHERISH
THE ROGUE AND THE HELLION
THE DRAGON LORD
THE OUTLAWS: SAM
THE OUTLAWS: JESS
THE OUTLAWS: RAFE
THE BLACK KNIGHT
GUNSLINGER
BEYOND THE HORIZON
PIRATE
BRAVE LAND, BRAVE LOVE
WILD LAND, WILD LOVE
VIKING!
SURRENDER TO THE FURY
LORD OF THE NIGHT
SHEIK
ICE & RAPTURE
LOVE ME WITH FURY
SHADOW WALKER
A PROMISE OF THUNDER
PURE TEMPTATION
WIND RIDER
THE LION'S BRIDE
SIERRA
TREASURES OF THE HEART
MY LADY VIXEN

A Knight's Honor

Connie Mason

LEISURE BOOKS NEW YORK CITY

A LEISURE BOOK®

November 2005

Published by

Dorchester Publishing Co., Inc.
200 Madison Avenue
New York, NY 10016

If you purchased this book without a cover you should be aware
that this book is stolen property. It was reported as "unsold and
destroyed" to the publisher and neither the author nor the publisher
has received any payment for this "stripped book."

Copyright © 2005 by Connie Mason

All rights reserved. No part of this book may be reproduced or
transmitted in any form or by any electronic or mechanical means,
including photocopying, recording or by any information storage
and retrieval system, without the written permission of the
publisher, except where permitted by law.

ISBN 0-8439-5463-9

The name "Leisure Books" and the stylized "L" with design are
trademarks of Dorchester Publishing Co., Inc.

Printed in the United States of America.

Visit us on the web at www.dorchesterpub.com.

Prologue

Mariah of Mildenhall entered her husband's bedchamber, pleased to find him awake. He appeared in better spirits than she had seen him in several days.

"Mariah, my dear, come sit beside me," Edmond said, making room on the edge of the bed for her.

"You seem in good spirits today, husband. Are you feeling better?"

Edmond of Mildenhall, a gaunt, elderly man with kind eyes, sighed. "We both know I am nearing the end of my life."

Mariah grasped his hand, her voice fraught with concern. "You cannot give up, Edmond. You must live. What will I do without you?"

"Think you I do not know what my death will do to you? I am an old man, Mariah, a very sick one. I would have died long ago if you had not come into my life. You were but a child placed under my guardianship when I was already an old man."

1

A tear slipped down Mariah's cheek. "I love you, Edmond."

"I know you do, but as a father." She shook her head, refusing to look at him. He held up a hand. "Nay, do not deny it. I wed you to save you from being given to the husband the king had chosen for you. I knew the man and his reputation for cruelty well, and could not bear to see you abused. You were but fourteen when we wed, still a child."

"Now that I am one and twenty, I still love you."

Edmond reached out a bony hand and caressed her satiny smooth cheek. "Thank you for that, little one. But we have more practical things to talk about. The last physician I consulted gave me only a year or two before my heart gives out, if I spend most of my days in bed. Edwina, the healer you put such store in, agrees with him. Lying in bed is not something I enjoy."

"What do you wish to talk about?" Mariah asked, though she had a good idea. Her future looked bleak indeed.

"My brother Osgood has his sights set on Mildenhall. Since I have no heir, he will claim it once I have drawn my last breath. I do not want that to happen. Mildenhall is your home, the only one you have known since your parents' death from the fever that swept through England when you were a wee lass of seven."

Mariah stared at her hands.

"I know what you are thinking, Mariah. The times I've bedded you during our seven-year marriage have been few. I knew I needed an heir to keep Mildenhall out of my brother's hands, but each time I bedded you, I felt I was committing a mortal sin. You were more daughter to me than wife."

"Do not worry about me, Edmond. Concentrate on getting well. I will still have a widow's portion."

"'Tis not enough. You would have to leave Mildenhall, perhaps find another husband. But my worst fear is that Osgood will force you to wed his son."

Mariah blanched. "I would never wed that despicable lecher."

"He could petition King Henry for approval, and then you would have no choice. Our warrior king might look favorably upon Osgood's request because of my brother's reputation as a fierce knight."

"You're frightening me, Edmond. I am but a woman, who must yield to laws made by men. I am neither weak nor bird-brained, yet I am not allowed to inherit my home unless I have a male heir. 'Tis unfair."

"Life is unfair, my dear, especially so for a woman. There is only one solution. I waited until I felt strong enough to speak to you about this. You must present me with an heir."

Mariah looked at her frail husband, a man who rarely left his bed, a kind man who would do nothing to hurt her; a man who considered her the daughter he'd never had. She wondered how he expected to accomplish the miracle of producing a child.

"Do not look at me so, Mariah. You know I am incapable of bedding you."

"Then how—"

"Listen to me, sweet child, listen carefully. I would find no fault with you if you found an honorable man to give you a child. There must be someone in Mildenhall you fancy."

"Edmond! How could you suggest such a thing?"

3

"After I am gone, you will have no one to protect you. A son would secure Mildenhall for you. If you had one, not even Osgood or the king could force you to leave."

She shrank away from him. "I cannot."

He grasped her hands. "Do you love me, Mariah?"

"You know I do."

"Then take a lover and give me a son."

"I cannot," she repeated.

Edmond sank into the mattress and closed his eyes, weary unto death. But he couldn't die and leave Mariah just yet. Poor Mariah. A woman as young, as beautiful and full of life as his wife deserved better than the hand fate had dealt her.

Except for a few brief couplings he'd managed once she had reached seventeen, he hadn't touched her despite his need for an heir. Over the years, Mariah had become his beloved daughter, one who had never known desire or experienced passion with a virile man.

"You didn't answer my question, Mariah. Is there no man among Mildenhall's knights you fancy?"

Mariah shook her dark head. "I took vows, Edmond. Sacred vows."

"The sin is not yours when a husband cannot function as a man, and hasn't for many years. Do not naysay me until you have considered my proposal. A male heir would solve both our problems."

Mariah had watched Edmond wither before her eyes. How she loved this dear old man. She would do anything for him. Anything except betray him. Even if she did as he asked and took a lover from among the castle's knights, her sin wouldn't remain a secret for long. It would be impossible to hide the truth from the inhabitants of Mildenhall, and Osgood would have reason to doubt his brother's ability to sire an heir. Osgood was a cruel man; he wouldn't rest until he ferreted out her lie.

"All this talk has tired you," Mariah said, pressing a kiss on his papery cheek. "We will discuss this later."

"Please think about what I have said," Edmond rasped as Mariah let herself out of the chamber.

Chapter One

Norfolk, England, 1414

Sir Falcon of Gaveston whistled a happy tune as he traveled along a deserted roadway through a forest in a part of Norfolk he had traveled only once before. A fortnight ago he had become betrothed to a wealthy maiden whom King Henry had promised him for his bravery at the battle of Agincourt in France. Henry's ten thousand archers had shattered the French knights, and Falcon had ridden at Henry's side, one of the king's own knights.

Rosamond of Norwich was an heiress who would bring him the wealth and land he yearned for. As a third son and landless, Falcon had to make his own way in life, earn his own keep and find a way to obtain a piece of England to call his own.

After meeting Rosamond, Falcon had decided that Henry had chosen well for him. The heiress had proved to be a raven-haired beauty who had found him as favorably disposed as he had found her. Marriage to Rosamond wasn't going to be difficult; the fervent kisses they had shared during stolen moments alone had been more than satisfactory.

If Rosamond appeared frivolous, Falcon blamed it on her youth. Though her flirtatious manner with other men did not please him, he felt confident in his ability to tame her wild ways. All in all, the visit had gone well. The terms of Rosamond's dowry had been ironed out between him and Rosamond's father, the Earl of Norwich, and the wedding was set for a fortnight hence. Rosamond and her father planned to travel to London, where the wedding would take place in the king's own chapel.

Falcon was a happy man. The land and small fortress that would be his upon his marriage earned a good profit from crops and sheep. Aye, Falcon's life couldn't be better right now.

The tiny village where Falcon hoped to engage a room and a meal at an inn lay ahead. It was growing dark. Shadows began to lengthen, casting the forest in near darkness. A prickling at the back of Falcon's neck made him wish he had not decided to travel alone. But since his visit to Norwich was of a personal nature, he had left his men and squire behind in London.

A rustling of leaves made his horse perk up his ears and skitter sideways. Falcon patted his neck and spoke soothingly to him, but the animal refused to settle down. Deciding that his faithful palfrey knew something he didn't, Falcon reached for his sword. A moment later pandemonium broke loose.

Two burly men dressed in rags and wielding cudgels dropped from the trees, knocking him from the saddle. These were the brigands whom Lord Norwich had warned him about, Falcon thought in a moment of clarity. They lived in the forest, attacking and robbing travelers foolish enough to be caught alone on the road after nightfall.

Falcon rolled to his feet and drew his sword, preparing to defend himself. He realized his was a losing battle when he saw several more men materialize from the forest and surround him. Falcon fought fiercely, with uncommon valor, but he was one man against many. He managed to wound two men and kill another before he was brought to his knees and dealt a crippling blow to the head by a bandit who had managed to creep up behind him while he fought off a vicious frontal attack.

Falcon fell senseless to the ground, unaware of the blows falling randomly, one after another. When the leader finally called a halt, Falcon lay bruised and battered beyond recognition. As a final insult, the bandits stole his valuables, ruthlessly stripped off his clothing and left him lying naked and vulnerable in the dirt. Taking Falcon's horse with them, they melted into the forest, leaving the king's knight unconscious and close to death.

Falcon lay in the middle of the road throughout the night. His body was discovered shortly after sunup by a cotter on his way to Mildenhall Castle to deliver produce.

The cotter, a husky man of middle years, drew his donkey cart to a halt, leapt down and cautiously approached the naked man. After a moment's contemplation, he nudged Falcon with his foot. "Are ye dead, then?"

A tormented moan answered his question.

"Well, then, what am I going to do with ye?"

No answer was forthcoming. "I suppose I can take ye to the castle since I'm going that way. If the ride in the back of my cart don't kill ye, mayhap old Edwina can fix ye."

The cotter lifted Falcon's broken body into his cart and covered him with a horse blanket. Then he climbed onto the driver's bench and plodded off toward Mildenhall Castle.

"Milady, a cotter has just brought a wounded man to the castle," Sir Martin, Mildenhall's steward, informed Mariah. "He'd been badly beaten and left in the forest for dead."

Mariah looked up from the silver she had been counting. "Where did you put the poor man?"

"I had him carried to a guest room in the solar. I hope that meets with your approval."

"Did you summon Edwina?"

"Aye, though I fear he is beyond the healer's help."

Mariah lifted her skirts and hurried toward the winding stone staircase. "I shall go to him immediately."

"Wait!" Sir Martin called after her, but she paid him no heed. He followed in Mariah's wake, his tunic flapping about his knees.

Mariah entered the chamber and came to an abrupt halt. The man lying on the bed was naked and bleeding from numerous cuts and bruises. His muscular body, honed biceps, powerful torso and sturdy legs were those of a warrior. Obviously, the man was well acquainted with death and violence.

Huffing and puffing, Sir Martin rushed into the chamber behind Mariah. "Milady, I tried to warn you. The man was brought in as you see him before you."

"Has he spoken? Do you know who he is?"

"Nay. He said naught to the cotter and naught since he reached the castle. Think you he will die?"

9

Connie Mason

"I do not know. Return to the hall and wait for Edwina. Bring her to me as soon as she arrives."

Sir Martin's eyes settled on the naked man. "I cannot leave you alone with him."

"A man in his condition can do me no harm. Go, Sir Martin."

Mariah approached the bed. The poor man hadn't moved since she'd arrived in the chamber. Her breath caught; he was a masterpiece of hair-roughened bronze skin pulled taut over rippling muscles. As she reached for a coverlet and started to ease it over him, her gaze settled on a part of him she had refused to look at when she first entered the chamber.

Never in her life had she seen a male as magnificently endowed as the man lying in the bed. Since she had never seen her husband naked, she'd had no idea a man's male part could be so fascinating. Shaking such wicked thoughts from her head, she drew the coverlet over the stranger's battered body and gazed into his bruised countenance.

Mariah couldn't tell what the man looked like, for his face was swollen and covered with purple and yellow bruises. His eyes, ringed with black, were sunken into their sockets, and his chin was covered with day-old stubble as black as the hair on his head. She hadn't even touched him, and yet, inexplicably, she was stirred.

Mariah was still staring at him, wondering about the color of his eyes, when a bent old woman carrying a basket over her arm hobbled into the chamber.

"Who is he, milady?" Edwina asked as she approached the bed.

"I know not," Mariah replied. "The poor soul took a fearsome beating. Apparently, he was set upon by bandits.

They stole everything he owned and left him for dead. If he had a horse, it, too, was taken. We'll have to wait for him to awaken to learn his name. Can you help him?"

"Depends on how badly he's hurt. Step aside, milady, while I tend his wounds."

Mariah backed away, unwilling to leave until she knew if the man would live. Something about him reached inside her in a way she had never experienced before. She closed her eyes and willed him to live. If will alone would make him well, he'd be in excellent health right now.

"I need hot water, milady, and clean cloths."

"I'll see to it," Mariah said, slipping from the chamber. Mariah sent a maidservant to fetch hot water from the kitchen, and then she headed to her chamber for cloths she kept in a cupboard for her personal use.

Edmond was awake and sitting in a chair before the hearth. Cedric, his personal servant, stood nearby, waiting to help his master into bed. Edmond looked up when Mariah entered. "Sir Martin just informed me that a wounded man was brought to the castle this morning."

"Aye, he's in dreadful shape. Edwina is with him."

"A young man?" Edmond rasped with more animation than Mariah had noted in a long time.

"I think so, though 'tis hard to tell. He was beaten and left for dead on the road. We won't know who he is until he can speak."

Mariah retrieved the cloths she had come for and turned to the door.

"Keep me informed," Edmond called after her.

Edwina was bent over her patient when Mariah returned. The hot water had already arrived, awaiting the cloths Mariah brought.

"How is he?" Mariah asked.

"Still alive," the old woman answered.

"Has he spoken?"

"Naught but groans have come from his mouth."

Mariah watched as Edwina bathed the man's face and searched his head for wounds.

"Ah," Edwina said.

"What did you find?"

"A lump the size of a goose egg." She cleansed the blood from his wound and applied salve. "Judging from the color of his bruises, he has lain unconscious and unattended for hours, mayhap all night. If he doesn't wake up soon, I hold scant hope for his survival."

"What of his other injuries?"

"The man must be made of iron. I could find no broken bones despite the battering he took, though he may have injuries that I cannot see." She shrugged. "Other than apply salve to his wounds and feed him an infusion to ease his pain, there is naught I can do for him. We will have to wait and see what happens."

Edwina worked diligently over the man, soothing his hurts with marigold salve and mixing a potion that she dribbled into his mouth to ease his pain. "I will return later," she said as she collected her herbal concoctions and returned them to the basket. "Have a maidservant sit with him. Tell her to fetch me should his condition change."

"I will sit with him myself," Mariah said. She pulled a chair up to the bed and settled into it as Edwina slipped from the chamber.

Mariah studied the man's face as she kept watch, wondering who he was and what he was doing in these parts.

Mildenhall was so remote that few visitors arrived at their gates, and certainly no one in this poor man's condition. Was he a traveler on an important mission? A husband returning to his wife and children? A knight about his business?

Mariah sighed and closed her eyes. Staring at the man wasn't going to make him well.

"Water—"

Falcon awoke in pain—brutal, pounding pain. His body, his head, there wasn't a part of him that didn't hurt. His body demanded water, but his swollen lips refused to voice his needs. He tried again but didn't recognize the sound that came from his mouth.

"Don't try to speak." The voice was soothing and female. "I'm going to lift your head so you can drink. You must be parched." A woman's soft breasts cradled his head.

Falcon felt a cup pressed to his lips. Water trickled down his throat. It tasted like the nectar of the gods. When the cup was empty, she lowered his head. He managed to peel his eyes open and peer through gummy, swollen slits at the woman bending over him.

"Am I dead?" he croaked.

She smiled, bathing him in warmth. This had to be heaven, he thought.

"You are alive, sir."

Unless his eyes were deceiving him, which was a distinct possibility, the woman smiling down at him was beautiful beyond belief. Hair the color of a golden sunrise, held in place by a circlet of silver, cascaded over her shoulders in a spill of pure magic.

"How can I be alive? Are you not an angel?"

Mariah's answer was forestalled when Falcon's head lolled against the pillow and he became unresponsive. Seized by panic, she felt for a pulse in his neck, heaving a sigh when she found one.

Mariah returned to her chair, smiling when she recalled his words. He thought her an angel.

The chamber was dark but for the dim light from a single candle when Falcon next opened his eyes. The woman was still with him, sleeping with her head resting on the bed. Who was she? Her bright hair beckoned him. He tried to raise his hand to brush a stray strand from her forehead and failed. What had happened to him? He had struggled awake from a nightmare, where monsters were attacking him, but that was all he recalled.

He closed his eyes and slept again.

It was full daylight when Mariah stirred and lifted her head. She was more than a little startled to see that the man was awake and staring at her.

"How do you feel?"

"Like I rode full tilt into a stone wall," he rasped. "Do you know what happened to me?"

"We think you were beaten and robbed by bandits who travel in groups and live in the forest. They left you for dead in the roadway."

Falcon closed his eyes, trying to recall the attack that had left him close to death. His mind was blank. No remnants of his earlier nightmare remained.

"Where am I?"

"Mildenhall Castle. Are you thirsty?"

"Aye." Mariah held a cup to his lips, and he drank

thirstily. She rose. "I'll fetch some broth, you must be hungry."

No answer was forthcoming. He had fallen asleep again. Mariah tiptoed from the room.

Time had no meaning for Falcon. Each time he awakened, either the golden angel, an old crone or a manservant who saw to his personal needs was in the chamber with him. He recalled being fed water, broth and something vile-tasting. Of all his shadowy visitors, it was the golden angel whose presence he craved—she of the stirring voice and gentle hands.

Falcon's head never ceased aching, even as his body's hurts began to heal. His brain was so scrambled he could recall naught of what had happened prior to his waking up in a strange bed. He didn't even know where he belonged.

One day, despite his befuddled brain, Falcon decided it was time to get out of bed and test his legs. He sat on the edge of the bed until his head stopped spinning and then pushed himself to his feet. He wobbled, found his balance and took a step. When he didn't fall flat on his face, he took another, and another.

While Falcon tested his legs, Mariah sat in her husband's chamber, discussing the wounded man.

"Is he young?" Edmond asked.

"I believe so. Though his face is still somewhat swollen, he has the body of a young man."

"Is he comely?"

Mariah shrugged. "It's difficult to tell, but I believe his face will be pleasing to look upon once the swelling recedes."

Edmond's eyes narrowed thoughtfully. "How fortunate that he should come to us now."

Mariah bristled. "Do not even think it, Edmond. We have no idea who this man is. He may have a wife and children awaiting him somewhere. He could be a common criminal."

"Do you think he is a criminal?"

"Nay," Mariah admitted. "I would describe him as a fighting man, mayhap a soldier or knight."

Edmond struggled to his feet. "I wish to see the man who has captured your fancy."

"Edmond! I have done no more than care for a man near death."

He resumed his seat. "Forgive an old man's musings, my dear. Find out his name. Perhaps I know his people."

When Mariah entered Falcon's chamber a short time later, she found him leaning against the bedpost, panting as if he'd just run a great distance.

"'Tis too soon for you to be out of bed," she scolded. "You must remain in bed until Edwina says you are well enough to leave it."

"I cannot regain my strength if I lie in bed all day. There is someplace I need to be, though I cannot name it."

"The only place you need to be right now is in bed. Let me help you."

"I can help myself. Turn away, lady; I am unclothed."

As if suddenly aware of Falcon's state of undress, Mariah turned her back.

Slowly Falcon eased his way into bed and pulled the coverlet up to his waist. "You can turn around now."

Mariah turned. "Are you hungry?"

16

"Famished. How long have I been here?"

"Seven days."

His eyes widened. "Seven days? Truly?"

The swelling around his eyes had receded, and for the first time Mariah saw their color. They were golden and compelling, not dark as she had imagined. Distracted by her discovery, Mariah took a moment to recall his question. "Truly, sir."

"You called me sir. Do you not know my name?"

"You have yet to provide one."

Falcon stared at her. "I was hoping you could tell me."

Mariah gasped. "What are you saying?"

His eyes glowed with desperation. "I recall naught before the moment I woke up in this bed. I hoped you could help me remember."

Mariah shook her head, saddened by his plight. "I have never seen you before you were brought to the castle, grievously injured and near death. Mayhap your head injury resulted in a temporary loss of memory. I have heard of such a thing happening. I'm sure you will remember in time. I will consult with Edwina about your memory loss."

Disheartened, Falcon sank against the pillow and closed his eyes. "Whenever I try to think, my head feels as if a thousand demons are bedeviling me. Of what use am I? I can't even use the chamber pot without help."

"I'll send a manservant to help you. Do whatever it is you need to do while I fetch you something to eat."

"Wait! I have a question."

Mariah turned away from the door. "What is it?"

"Who are you?"

"I am Mariah of Mildenhall."

The door opened. Edmond tottered in, assisted by two servants. They eased him into a chair and left to await him outside the chamber. He studied Falcon for several minutes, then smiled.

"Edwina said you would live, and she was right."

"Who are you, sir?" Falcon asked.

"I am Edmond, Earl of Mildenhall."

"Forgive me for not rising, my lord. Your daughter tells me I have been the recipient of your hospitality for several days."

The old man's eyebrows lifted. "Ah, yes, my *daughter* Mariah. 'Tis a sad thing to be widowed so young."

Mariah shot her husband a warning look. "Edmond—"

Edmond held up his hand. "Please, Mariah, I wish to speak to the young man. What is your name, sir?"

"I was hoping someone here could tell me," Falcon answered.

"Can you not remember?"

"Nay. I feel as if I should be somewhere but cannot recall where. Do you know me? Can you tell me my name?"

Edmond shook his head. "I have never seen you before, so 'tis safe to say you are not from these parts. Do not worry, lad, you are welcome at Mildenhall while you regain your memory. Besides, Edwina tells me it will be weeks before you are able to travel. I pray you will accept our hospitality while your mind and body heal. It would be remiss of me to send you away without a memory."

"Thank you, my lord," Falcon replied in a voice made hollow with despair. Not knowing his name or origins was a humbling experience.

"Forgive me for cutting my visit short, but as you can

18

see, I am not a well man." Edmond held out his hand to Mariah. "Come, daughter, I would have a word with you in my chamber."

Mariah kept her silence until Edmond was settled in his bed and the servants dismissed.

"Whatever were you thinking?" she demanded, rounding on him. "You deliberately lied to . . . to . . . Oh, I don't even know what to call him."

"Call him a miracle sent by God to save us, to save you. That young man is a maiden's dream."

"I am not a maiden. I am a wife. Your wife."

Edmond shook his head. "I have never been a true husband to you. Let me die in peace. Give me an heir to save Mildenhall and carry on my name and title."

"Do not push me into this, Edmond, I beg you. If I did what you asked, I could have a daughter, and then where would I be?"

"That young man I just saw will give you a son."

"How do you know that?"

"Some believe Edwina is a witch. I do not believe in witches, but I do believe she can see things others cannot. She knows how desperately I need an heir, and told me the nameless man in the bed will give you a son."

"No one but God can determine that," Mariah insisted.

"You know Edwina's predictions have proven true in the past. Why are you being so obstinate about this?"

"Because what you suggest is a sin."

Edmond closed his eyes. "Leave me," he said wearily. "I will die soon and cannot bear the thought of Osgood forcing you from your home or into an intolerable marriage with his son."

Mariah hesitated a moment before taking her leave. Instead of returning to the sickroom, she went to the chapel to pray for guidance. She had never disobeyed her husband in all the years of their marriage, but what he wanted her to do went against God's law.

The chapel was a peaceful place this time of day. Mariah knelt on the wooden kneeler, folded her hands and began to pray. To her dismay, her mind kept wandering to the man with no memory, the man whose golden eyes were filled with confusion and pain. Little by little his face had returned to normal, revealing a ruggedly handsome visage that would turn any woman's head.

His body proclaimed him a fighting man. Was he a knight? Was someone he loved even now looking for him? Did he have a wife? A betrothed? She had to admit he was magnificently put together, and wondered what it would be like to have a man like that in her bed. Looking at him set off all kinds of wicked thoughts inside her head. She stirred restlessly, her body making her aware of feelings that were strangely arousing. Strange because she'd never had them before.

She prayed harder.

"You seem troubled, my child."

Startled, Mariah looked up at Father Francis, the resident priest. "I didn't hear you, Father." She concentrated on her clasped hands, embarrassed to be caught thinking impure thoughts in a holy place.

"You were lost in prayer, my lady." He gazed at her, as if he himself were deeply troubled.

Father Francis had come to Mildenhall many years ago; he was here when she had arrived to live with Edmond. Though he was old and not as spry as he used to be, his keen intelligence and sharp eyes missed naught that went on at Mildenhall.

"I just spoke with Lord Edmond, Lady Mariah."

Mariah's attention sharpened. She watched him with trepidation as he began to pace back and forth in front of her. "Is something wrong, Father?"

"Lord Edmond told me about the stranger Edwina is nursing back to health."

"What did he say?" *Surely Edmond didn't tell him what he wants me to do, did he?*

"We discussed the possibility of Lord Edmond's dying without an heir, and what it would mean to you."

She clutched her throat. "Dear Lord, what did he tell you?"

The priest swung around, his brown robes swirling about his skinny legs. "Everything."

She hid her face in her hands. "Oh, no. You must forgive Edmond! He is worried about me and Mildenhall. I did not for one moment countenance committing such a grave sin."

Father Francis continued his pacing. "Edmond is right about many things. Osgood is a cruel man. Our people will not fare well under his guidance." He whirled to face her. "Mildenhall will fall into ruin."

He fell to his knees beside Mariah. "God forgive me," he implored. "Never have I been so challenged in my faith. What Edmond suggests is a sin, yet I cannot condemn his reasoning or fault his judgment, for it is sound. Mildenhall needs an heir to survive, and Edmond cannot give you one."

Mariah leapt to her feet. "I must go."

"I will pray on this dilemma," Father Francis said, waving her off.

Mariah all but ran out the door. Had the world gone mad? How could a man of God condone adultery? Yet . . . yet, the priest had all but encouraged her to seduce the nameless man who had come to them. A laugh caught in her throat. As if she knew how to seduce a man. Her steps slowed. Would he welcome her attention should she offer it?

Edwina hailed Mariah in the great hall. Mariah stopped and waited for the healer. "What is it, Edwina? Is there a problem with your patient?"

"Nay, he is progressing well, milady. I just left him. He asked about you. He wanted to know how your husband had died."

"What did you tell him?"

"Naught. 'Tis for you to decide whether or not you will make the sacrifice for Mildenhall."

"Aye, it *is* my decision, my sacrifice," Mariah agreed. She walked away, her mind in turmoil. Without realizing where she was headed, she found herself climbing the stairs to the solar and entering the injured man's chamber.

Falcon was restless. He had asked Edwina for a looking glass. She had brought him a silver tray, polished to a high sheen. He had gazed upon his face for the first time and seen a stranger—a man with no past and no future.

Earlier today, a manservant had scraped the hair from Falcon's face. He had hoped he would recognize his face without hair. A familiar feature, mayhap. He had seen naught but a man with odd golden eyes, dark hair, twin slashes of black eyebrows and generous lips. Though his nose was somewhat long, the dimple in his chin softened his harsh features.

He had found a scar above his left eyebrow and another to the right of the dimple. And he didn't remember how he'd come by either of them! Earlier he had discovered scars on his left thigh and right knee. The only thing he could deduce from his findings was that he was a fighting man, which would also account for his muscular build.

Falcon had never felt more alone or desperate, or at least he thought he hadn't. And then Mariah entered the chamber, bringing sunshine and warmth, chasing away the fear that threatened to consume him.

"Edwina said you were asking questions about me."

A corner of his split lips lifted into a half smile. "Whenever you are with me I feel better," Falcon said. "Stay awhile and talk to me. Tell me about yourself."

Though she feared she was making a mistake, Mariah sank down into a chair. "What is it you want to know?"

"Your father said you were a widow. How long ago did your husband die?"

Mariah should stop this charade now. "A few months ago."

"How did he die?"

How? "A . . . hunting accident. Please, I don't want to talk about him."

"You must have loved him very much."

Mariah sought a way to change the subject and found it. "We should give you a name until you can remember your own. Do you have a preference?"

His brain scrambled for memory, found only terror and empty spaces. He shook his head.

Mariah cocked her head and tapped her lips with a fingertip. Falcon felt a stirring he knew was not new to him. Aye, this golden-haired, blue-eyed angel stirred him, made him feel alive and eased his fear.

"You are beautiful, lady," he murmured, unable to help himself. "Your husband was a lucky man."

"I . . . I suppose. We were talking about your name. What shall I call you?"

A sense of angry impotence filled him. *He didn't know!* His mind was as blank as a newborn babe's. He sent her a look fraught with terror.

Mariah's heart ached, unable to bear his pain. "Until you regain your memory, I shall call you Sir Knight. Now you should rest, and I have duties to attend."

He grasped her hand. "Nay, do not go. When I am alone, I am consumed by demons."

How could Mariah refuse? "Very well. I will stay for a little while."

Chapter Two

Mariah perched on the edge of the bed. Who was this man? She knew he was feeling terror—anyone would in his situation. It must be frightening to look at your own face and see a stranger, or to have your memory completely erased. Though she felt attracted to him, that attraction hadn't lessened her sense of right and wrong.

"What are you thinking?" Falcon asked.

She blushed and looked away, relieved that he could not read her mind.

His gaze swept over her. She was wearing a blue gown today, a color that closely matched her eyes. The neckline was modest, but it did naught to disguise the lush curves of her breasts.

"Why are you looking at me like that?" Mariah asked.

"You are fair to look at. Are you sure we have never met before?"

"Aye, Sir Knight, I never set eyes on you until you were brought to Mildenhall. Perhaps I resemble your mother, or wife."

Falcon looked away, as if searching for something familiar. "Nay, I am sure my mother is not fair like you, and I feel no connection to a wife. Although . . ."

"What?"

He shook his head. "I am confident I am not wed."

Reaching out, he stroked her cheek. She pulled back as if stung.

"Forgive me, I had no right."

Mariah dragged in a calming breath. What was wrong with her? The burning sensation that lingered where Sir Knight had touched her was a new one. His innocent caress raised bumps on her skin. She felt heat rise to her cheeks, then spread downward to private places.

"Lady Mariah, are you all right?"

"I am fine, Sir Knight."

Falcon didn't think she was fine. She looked flustered and breathless. Had his touch done that to her? Touching a woman felt natural to him, as if he had done this and more in the past. He felt a stirring in his loins and suddenly realized something about himself. He was a sexual creature who enjoyed women.

How did he know that?

"Did you remember something?" Mariah asked.

"Aye." He touched her cheek again, only this time he trailed his fingers over her chin to her throat, and then drifted lower, outlining the curve of her breast. "Caressing you made me recall that I am accustomed to touching women and being touched by them."

She stared at him. Was he attracted to her? Or was he the kind of man who used women to sate his lust and discarded them at will? Could a man with no memory feel lust?

She stood and backed away. "I'll check on you later."

"I need something to wear. If I don't leave this bed soon, I will never regain my strength. Perhaps if I leave this chamber, I will encounter something or someone to trigger my memory."

Mariah took measure of his length and the width of his shoulders. "Sir Martin's nephew is about your size. His clothes should fit you well enough. They won't be fancy, but you should find them adequate. If Edwina approves, I'll send someone up to help you to the hall for the evening meal."

Falcon sent her a lopsided smile. Her breath hitched. The man was so devastatingly handsome, she could well imagine women offering themselves to him just to see him smile. Her wicked mind wondered how it would feel to be made love to by a young man. Would a man of his size and strength be a rough lover? A selfish one?

Mariah had felt naught but mild disgust the few times Edmond had bedded her during their seven-year marriage. She had been too young to know that pleasure could be had from the act. After, Edwina had told her that women did indeed find pleasure in coupling, but Mariah remained skeptical. There was naught about Sir Knight that disgusted her, however. Could he give her the pleasure she'd been denied all these years?

Flustered, Mariah left the chamber. If she continued this line of thinking, she'd be tempted to use Sir Knight to get the heir she and Edmond needed.

Mariah sought out Edwina. She found the healer in Edmond's chamber. "Are you feeling ill, Edmond?" Mariah asked worriedly. "I had thought you much improved."

Edmond sent her a weak smile. "I am as usual, my love. How is our guest?"

"Eager to leave his bed. I told him I'd consult with Edwina and find him some clothes if she approved. He's anxious to regain his strength."

"What say you, Edwina?" Edmond asked.

"He is still weak, but I have no objection if he wishes to leave his bed."

"Does he give any sign of regaining his memory?"

"Nay," Mariah answered, "but I think it will return in time. Even now he experiences brief glimpses of his past. He believes he is unmarried because he feels no connection to a wife."

"That is a good sign." Edwina nodded sagely.

"He wants to take his evening meal with us in the hall."

"I doubt he can manage the stairs on his own," Edwina warned.

"I know. I'll send someone to help him."

Falcon tried out his legs and found they held him up better than the last time he had attempted to stand. He gazed down at himself and grimaced. He had so many bruises, there was scarcely a place on him that wasn't purple, yellow or a combination of both. He did feel stronger, however, and his appetite had improved.

Falcon looked forward to dining with his host and the people of Mildenhall tonight. He held high hopes that someone would recognize him and give him his past back. Falcon took several tentative steps and felt strong enough to pace the chamber. So far, so good, he thought. It wouldn't be long before he could leave Mildenhall to search for his identity.

That thought brought another. Mariah. Each day he became more and more attracted to her, as if pulled in her direction by invisible strings. His healing body had become aware of her in the most elemental way. After their encounter today, he realized that he wanted her sexually. Though skittish for a widow, she seemed as intrigued by him as he was by her.

What was he going to do about Mariah? Did he dare insult her father by bedding her? Was he capable of performing sexually? He had no idea if he was a good lover. He didn't believe he had it in him to be a rough lover, or a selfish one. One thing he knew about himself was that he loved women, and some deeply ingrained instinct made him believe he wouldn't leave the widow Mariah wanting.

Just as the sun began to set, a servant brought clean clothing for Falcon. Falcon donned the plain white shirt, brown hose and unadorned doublet without complaint, despite a dim memory that he was accustomed to richer attire. He wiggled his bare toes and wondered if he'd have to appear in the hall barefoot.

His question was answered when Mariah appeared with a pair of woolen stockings and soft leather boots.

"The fit might be a little snug, but they should do," she said, eyeing his bare feet.

"Thank you," Falcon said as he pulled on the stockings and pushed his feet into the boots. "Actually, they fit very well. Whose are they?"

"They belong to Edmond. He no longer has need of them."

"Edmond? You call your father by his given name?"

Lies—how she hated them. "Sometimes, but I mean no disrespect by it."

Falcon stomped the boots on the floor and stood. "I'm ready."

Mariah stepped back, admiring the way the hose hugged the long muscles of his legs. Though plain and without fancy trim, the doublet seemed to enhance his manly physique. Forcing her gaze away from the splendid male standing before her, she opened the door, admitting two husky servants. "Chad and Horace will help you. 'Tis a long way down to the hall."

Falcon hated feeling helpless, but he acquiesced. One day soon, he vowed, he would negotiate the stairs and much more by himself. By the time he reached the bottom landing, Falcon was glad he had Chad and Horace to lean upon. Mariah led him to the high table, where he sank most gratefully into a chair. Servants began bringing out food from the kitchens almost immediately.

"Isn't your father joining us?" Falcon asked.

"He rarely takes his meals in the hall anymore," Mariah replied.

"May I visit him after the meal?"

"I see no harm. But you mustn't tire yourself."

Falcon devoted himself to the excellent meal, eating as much as his diminished stomach would hold. While he ate, he gazed at each face in the hall, searching for someone familiar, someone who might recognize him. He saw naught but strangers, and by the curious looks he received in return, he could tell he was unknown to them. The puzzle that was his life deepened.

After the meal, Mariah led Falcon to Edmond's chamber in the solar. Edmond welcomed him warmly and dismissed Mariah with a wave of his hand. Though reluctant to do so, Mariah left the men alone. When she returned later, she found them engaged in a game of chess.

"Your father beat me," Falcon said. "I must have lost my knowledge of the game along with my memory."

Edmond sent him a sharp look. "Can you remember naught of your past?"

Falcon's golden eyes assumed a haunted look. "Sadly, I remember naught, though at times brief images flash through my mind. Unfortunately, they do not remain long enough for me to identify them. One recurrent image is that of a bird."

"A bird?" Mariah repeated. "What kind of a bird?"

"I know not. But I feel the bird is the key that will unlock my memory. Tomorrow I intend to go outside and test my theory. Perhaps I shall see a bird that will jog something in my mind."

"Do not overtax yourself, Sir Knight. I am not eager to lose you as a guest. Nor is Mariah, I vow. She leads a lonely life."

"Are you ready to return to your chamber?" Mariah asked before Edmond said something to embarrass her.

"Aye. Perhaps Lord Edmond will consent to another game of chess tomorrow."

"Any time, lad, any time," said Edmond, beaming. "Mariah, since I am confined to my bed, why don't you show Sir Knight around when he feels up to it?"

"I'd like that," Falcon said, rising. "I wish you good night, my lord."

"I will summon Chad to help you mount the stairs," Mariah said.

"Nay, do not," Falcon demurred. "I can manage with your help."

Mariah hesitated. She no longer felt comfortable with

this virile male. Her experience with any man other than her elderly husband was very limited.

"Help Sir Knight to his bed, Mariah," Edmond urged. "Go on with you now—our guest must be exhausted after his first excursion out of bed."

Mariah sent Edmond a disgruntled look before placing an arm around Sir Knight's narrow waist and guiding him toward his chamber. She knew what Edmond was trying to do and didn't approve. Sir Knight placed an arm around her shoulders. Her knees trembled, but she managed not to stumble.

The heat of his body surrounded her in a blanket of warmth. She felt as if she were melting. What was wrong with her? There were men aplenty at Mildenhall—why didn't any of them affect her like Sir Knight?

"Are you all right?" Falcon asked. "Am I too burdensome for your narrow shoulders?"

"I . . . am fine. We're almost there."

But she wasn't fine. She was beginning to feel things she shouldn't; beginning to look upon Edmond's plan to gain an heir with favor. Mariah had always longed for a child. Having a babe with this magnificent man would be an answer to all her prayers. Mildenhall would be safe from Osgood's clutches, and she would have a child to love after Edmond was gone.

They reached the guest chamber. Sir Knight halted before the door. He maneuvered her until her back rested against the wall and leaned into her. In the flickering light provided by a wall sconce, his golden eyes gleamed with wicked intent.

"What are you doing?"

He rested his forehead against hers. "You intrigue me,

lady. Touching you is not enough. I'm going to do something I've been thinking about since I first laid eyes on you. I'm going to kiss you."

He gave her no chance to protest as his mouth covered hers. His lips were warm and soft; she yielded, unable to resist the tempting taste of him. Only when his mouth hardened and she felt him lick along the seam of her lips did she become alarmed.

"Open your mouth, Mariah," he whispered against her lips.

Her lips parted. "Why?"

He thrust his tongue into her mouth, showing her without words what he wanted. Mariah's heart slammed against her chest. What was he doing? With the wall at her back, she couldn't escape Sir Knight's passionate kiss. She could only feel . . . and taste as he kissed her more thoroughly than she ever dreamed a man could kiss a woman. When he touched her breast, she nearly jumped out of her skin.

For the first time in her life, Mariah felt desire stirring in that secret place between her legs. Long ago Edwina had tried to explain passion to her, but Mariah despaired of ever experiencing that emotion. She knew love—the kind of love she felt for Edmond—but that was far different from what she was feeling now. She knew it wasn't love; it was an emotion far more powerful.

She wanted it to go on forever.

But all good things must come to an end. Sir Knight broke off the kiss and gave her an apologetic smile. "I want to take this further, but I fear I cannot until I am strong enough to do both of us justice."

It took a moment for Mariah's addled brain to assimilate his words. When she finally understood, her cheeks bloomed a rich red. She shoved herself away from the wall and scooted around him. Her fingers flew to her lips. "This cannot be. I am mar . . . a widow."

Falcon looked unconvinced. "You said your husband died months ago."

"Aye."

"Why aren't you wearing black?"

She gazed down at her green gown. "I . . . my husband had an aversion to black; he wouldn't want me to wear mourning forever."

"Have you taken no lovers since his death?"

The high color drained from her face. "Nay, I would never—"

"Then I will be the first, but not until I am up to the challenge. Until then, lady, I bid you good night."

Mariah stared at the closed door, her temper rising, her fists clenched. What made Sir Knight think she wanted him in that way? Had that single kiss sent him a message she hadn't intended? Or had he read acquiescence into her response? Unwilling to delve too deeply into her emotions, she turned and fled.

Falcon barely made it back to bed. His first foray out of his chamber had left him exhausted. Or was it the kiss that had weakened him? He had been truthful with Mariah. He was in no condition to take his desire for the beautiful widow any further than a kiss.

He pulled off his boots and lay down fully clothed, folding his arms behind his head. What kind of man was he? he wondered. Obviously he was not timid, nor was he inexperienced. Kissing had come naturally to him. Had he taken it further as his body demanded, he knew he would have given a good accounting of himself despite his lingering weakness. Making love was something a man didn't forget.

Before sleep claimed Falcon, he vowed to exert himself more each day, until his strength had returned to its former level of endurance. And perhaps, along the way to recovery, his memory would return.

In the darkest part of night, Falcon jerked upright from a nightmare. Sweat poured down his face in rivulets, soaking his shirt. If the dream was a window into his past, he wanted naught to do with it. The cries of wounded and dying men rang in his ears. He saw himself wielding a sword, visiting death and destruction upon a nameless enemy.

Next he saw himself lying on the ground, being pummeled near to death by men wielding cudgels. Then he woke up. His head pounded, and he couldn't drag in enough air to fill his lungs. Sucking in deep, shuddering breaths, Falcon managed to calm himself and think more clearly.

Had he remembered something about himself? Had he actually experienced the battles of his dreams? Mariah called him Sir Knight, and the flashbacks he'd been having seemed to confirm her belief that he was a warrior.

Sinking down into the mattress, Falcon closed his eyes and drifted back to sleep. He didn't awaken until Chad arrived with a pitcher of water and shaving equipment.

"Can you manage by yourself?" Chad asked.

"Did your mistress send you?"

"Aye." He took note of Falcon's rumpled clothing and

asked, "Shall I take your clothing to be refreshed? It shouldn't take long. 'Tis early, and we won't break fast for another hour."

"I was so tired last night I didn't take time to undress. If I'm to be presentable, it would probably be best to have my clothes sponged and pressed."

Falcon peeled off his shirt, doublet and hose and handed them to Chad. He felt stronger this morning, more like himself, whoever that might be. He was attempting to shave when Edwina entered the chamber. He dove for the coverlet to cover himself.

Edwina cackled to herself. "No need for that, Sir Knight. I've seen you without a stitch on before. How do you fare after your first day out of bed?"

"Well enough. I need to regain my strength so I can search for my identity."

"Do not be hasty," Edwina warned. "Give your body and mind time to heal."

"I had a nightmare last night," Falcon revealed. "I dreamed I was in the middle of a battle, wielding a sword. Then the scene shifted and I was lying on the ground, being pummeled with cudgels. I woke with sweat pouring off me and fighting for breath."

"Did none of that jog your memory?" Edwina asked.

He shook his head. "Are you here for a reason?"

"Aye, I wanted to see for myself how you are doing after sitting through the evening meal."

"It fair exhausted me, but I had to start somewhere. Lying in bed is driving me mad."

Edwina peered at him. "You look well enough. Lord Edmond asked me to check on you."

"Lord Edmond appears to be a good man. Is he as sick as he looks?"

Edwina nodded gravely. "Aye, he has been ill for a long time. His illness progresses to a natural conclusion. There is naught anyone can do for him."

"Poor Mariah. She will be alone when her father dies. How long does he have?"

"A week, a month, a year—'tis in God's hands. Lord Edmond's greatest fear is that Mariah will be left to the mercy of his scurrilous brother and greedy nephew after his death."

"I do not understand."

"'Tis simple enough. Without a male heir, the earldom and all it entails will pass to Edmond's brother, Sir Osgood Fitzhugh."

"Sir Osgood Fitzhugh," Falcon repeated thoughtfully.

"Do you know the name?"

"The name sounds familiar. I will think on it."

Edwina left when Chad returned with Falcon's clothing. Falcon finished shaving, dressed quickly and proceeded with great care down the staircase to the hall. Men and women, some whom he recognized from last night, were already seated at long tables set up in the hall. A servant escorted him to the high table. Mariah joined him a short time later. She barely acknowledged him.

Platters of food began to arrive. Falcon helped himself to eggs, ham, kippers and cod. Another thing he'd learned about himself was that he had a healthy appetite, in more ways than one.

"How is your father this morning?" he asked Mariah around a mouthful of eggs.

Connie Mason

Mariah, he noted, concentrated on her food instead of looking at him. "There is no change."

"I'm sorry about his poor health. He is very old. I'd be grateful to live past middle age."

Mariah shot him a quelling look.

"Did I say something wrong?" he asked.

"Nay, 'tis just that I am concerned about Edmond's health."

Edmond again, not Father. Strange, but he had heard of stranger things, if he could remember them. "I thought you might be angry with me."

Mariah gazed at him then, studying his features. His face was no longer swollen, revealing the handsomest man Mariah had ever seen. His golden eyes held a hint of amusement, reminding her of the stolen moments of intimacy they had shared last night. She had tried to forget, but how could she when she could still feel the softness of his lips against hers and the roughness of his tongue thrusting in and out of her mouth?

"I'm not angry. But you shouldn't have taken liberties."

"Why not? You are a widow, not a nun. I thought our attraction was mutual."

Mariah hated living a lie. She wanted to blurt out that Edmond was her husband, but if she did and lost her one chance of having a son, Mildenhall would cease to exist as she knew it after Edmond's death. For Edmond's peace of mind and for the people of Mildenhall, she must seduce Sir Knight for the child he could give her. And it had to be soon, before he regained his memory.

Last night Edmond had spoken to her at length about the future of Mildenhall. He had impressed upon her that her future and the future of those she loved rested on her shoulders. Long after she had retired, she realized that her sacrifice wouldn't be a sacrifice at all. In fact, if the kiss she'd shared with Sir Knight last night was any indication, she would find pleasure in his arms.

Falcon pushed back his plate. "Would you like to show me around, Lady Mariah? I'd like to start with the grounds."

Mariah scraped back her chair. "Are you sure you feel up to it?"

"I need to stretch my legs. I am a man accustomed to pushing my body to its limits."

"How do you know that?"

"'Tis merely a feeling. Just like the feeling that tells me this isn't the first time I have suffered wounds to my body. It is, however, the first time I lost my memory because of them."

They walked from the hall into the sunshine. Falcon blinked, raised his head and savored the fresh air. Mariah pointed out the various buildings in the inner bailey and what they were used for. Everything Falcon saw looked familiar. He realized that he had been inside or lived in a castle much grander than this at one time. He could name every part of the fortress, from the portcullis to the crenellations topping the parapet.

"Are you tired yet?" Mariah asked.

"Nay, I wish to see the stables."

"You won't find your horse there."

"Nevertheless, I want to see how familiar I am around horses."

"Very familiar, I suspect."

The stables felt like home to Falcon, a place where he felt comfortable. After admiring the horseflesh in Lord

Edmond's stable, he left with a sense of belonging in this kind of environment, and a belief that it was only a matter of time before he knew where he fit in. Meanwhile, there was Mariah, a woman who intrigued him more with each passing day.

Sometimes she looked at him as if she wanted something from him. If it was sex, he would happily oblige, once he felt strong enough to make it good for both of them. He had almost reached that point now.

Falcon did not return to his bed that day, for he felt strong enough now to remain upright for long periods. That night after the evening meal, he played chess with Lord Edmond while Mariah looked on. During the following days he practiced at swordplay with Sir Maynard, the captain of Mildenhall's guards, and proved himself a capable swordsman. Now that Falcon's strength had returned, he hoped to heal his memory, and remaining hidden away at Mildenhall wouldn't do that for him.

One day Falcon asked Mariah to take him to the cotter who had found him.

"Very well," Mariah agreed, "but I doubt you will learn anything from him. You can choose a horse from Edmond's stables."

Mariah had proven correct. The cotter told him naught that he hadn't already learned from Mariah and Edwina. Then he asked Mariah to take him to the place where he had been found. After asking directions from the cotter, Mariah and Falcon started off to search for Falcon's past.

When they arrived at the place described by the cotter, Falcon dismounted. He stood in the middle of the roadbed, searching for something, anything that would jog his memory. He looked around him, at the dense forest lining either side of the road. His brow furrowed in concentration as an image flashed before his eyes. But it fled, vanquished by a crushing pain in his head.

A groan ripped from his throat; he clasped his head between his hands, trying to fight the agony that threatened to consume him.

"What is it?" Mariah asked as she leapt from her horse and came to his aid.

Falcon wagged his head from side to side. "There was something—I almost had it but I lost it. The pain—damnation, why can't I remember?"

"Does your head still hurt?"

"Like the very devil."

"Come, there's a place nearby where you can rest until the pain goes away. Follow me."

Leading their horses through the trees, Mariah guided Falcon to a grassy bank beside a babbling brook. Falcon dropped to the ground and rested his head against his crossed arms, waiting for the pounding to stop so he could think clearly.

He lay back on the grass, staring at fluffy clouds floating aimlessly across a blue sky. If he never regained his memory or found his place in the world, of what use was he? What if his memory never returned?

He glanced at Mariah and found her staring at him. "What are you thinking?" she asked.

He studied her lovely face. The pain in his head had subsided, allowing him to see Mariah clearly. She was beautiful, kind and intelligent. Perhaps he should concentrate on what he had here and forget his past. Mildenhall was not a bad place to live, and he truly liked

41

Mariah's father. He wondered if he could make a life at Mildenhall.

With Mariah.

"I'm thinking I'd very much like to kiss you. The first time whetted my appetite for more."

"Your head—"

"The pain has passed. It only comes when I try to remember. Mayhap I should make new memories." He extended his hand as if in supplication. "Will you help me, Mariah?"

A day hadn't passed that Mariah didn't think about that first kiss she had shared with Sir Knight. It had been like naught she had experienced in her twenty-one years. So how could she resist another taste of heaven?

She took his hand and knelt beside him. She knew it was wicked of her to want Sir Knight's kisses when her husband lay ill in his bed, but she craved more out of life than tending an old man. She wanted to know pleasure, and she wanted a child.

Edwina believed that Sir Knight would regain his memory one day, and that meant he would leave. She could almost bear his leaving if he gave her a babe to love.

Sir Knight reached up, curled a hand around her neck and eased her over him. His body was hard, his face stark with a need she had never seen before on a man's face. Their lips touched, meshing together as their bodies melded. Icy shivers raced down her spine as his hands grasped her bottom and pulled her up snugly against his loins. Mariah had never felt anything to compare with the hard ridge of his sex pressing against the soft place between her thighs. A small sigh hummed through her mouth as he prodded it open with his tongue and pressed inside.

She closed her eyes, surrendering to the sensations tumbling one upon another. He brought his hands around to her breasts, tweaking her nipples through the material of her gown. A strange wetness pooled between her thighs as his hands and lips worked their magic on her. Her hips rocked against him of their own accord, as if riding to some unknown melody. At that moment she would have done anything he asked of her.

Sir Knight broke off the kiss. Mariah murmured a protest. "You're very good at this," she said breathlessly.

"I am, aren't I?" His lightheartedness dissolved as he lifted her away from him and sat up.

"Did I do something wrong?" Mariah asked. "Was I too bold?"

"Too bold? Oh, nay, sweeting. This place is too dangerous for what I have in mind."

He helped her to her feet, brought her against him and kissed her hard. "Come to me tonight," he whispered against her lips. "Let me finish what we started."

Chapter Three

Wearing naught but a chamber robe over her nakedness, Mariah sat curled up in a chair, staring into the dying embers in the hearth. The hour was late; the castle had settled down for the night, and the servants had long since gone to their beds. While Edmond slept soundly in the adjoining chamber, sleep was far from Mariah's mind.

Come to me tonight, Sir Knight had said.

That she even considered going to him surprised Mariah. His kisses had tempted her, made her aware of what she had missed in her marriage. Not that she regretted marrying Edmond. She loved him dearly. By his own admission, however, he didn't think of her as a wife, and bedding her had made him feel guilty, as if he were committing a sin.

Mariah tried to convince herself that going to Sir Knight's bed was a sacrifice she was only considering to save Mildenhall. But she was no fool. She wanted Sir Knight, not just for the son she needed but for herself. She wanted his passion. If she was to experience passion only one time in her life, she wanted it to be with Sir Knight.

Mariah heard the chapel bell toll Matins. As if in a daze, she rose and left the solar, irresistibly drawn by Sir Knight's promise of pleasure. No one saw her; no one heard her footsteps whispering along the corridor. She paused before Sir Knight's closed door, fearing she was making a mistake but unable to retreat now that she had come this far.

Falcon lit another candle when the first one sputtered out. Would Mariah come to him? he wondered for the hundredth time since he'd left to seek his bed. Besides recovering his memory, making love to Mariah was what he most wanted . . . needed . . . craved. Mariah was an enigma. Her seductive innocence appealed to him. She seemed refreshingly unaware of her own sexuality. It was clear to him that she was a stranger to passion. Even her kisses had been childlike, until he had shown her how one's tongue came into play in a passionate kiss.

It was late, past Matins. Falcon feared that Mariah would not come to him. He should have finished what he had begun in the woods earlier today instead of worrying about their safety. But he would never put Mariah in danger. Nor would he have pursued her if she had been married instead of a widow. He didn't know how he knew that about himself, but he did. He was learning that he had lived his life by a code of honor.

A faint noise in the corridor caught his attention. He strode to the door and pulled it open. Mariah stood on the threshold, looking frightened and uncertain. He pulled her inside and closed the door.

"You came," he whispered. "I was beginning to think you wouldn't."

"I . . . couldn't help myself."

He hugged her against him. "I'm glad. You won't be sorry, I swear." He led her toward the bed and pulled back the covers.

He loosened the belt holding her robe together and pulled the edges apart, gasping when he realized she wore naught underneath but satiny skin. He pushed the robe off her shoulders; it fell to her feet in a puddle of silk.

"God's nightgown," he whispered, awestruck by the vision standing before him. Candlelight painted her body in varying shades of gold. "Words cannot describe your beauty. I have never seen its like."

"How . . . how can you say such a thing when you cannot remember the women in your life?"

"I may not remember, but my eyes tell no lies." She backed away. "You're not shy, are you, Mariah? 'Tis not as if you are a virgin."

"I have been with no man but my husband."

"He is dead," Falcon said harshly. "If you cannot forget him this night, then leave now, for I want no other man in our bed, not even a dead one."

Mariah caught her breath. Was Sir Knight angry? She had come this far, she could not leave now. Even though she wanted this night for herself, she must think of Mildenhall and the son she needed to secure the holding for her people. She had never seduced a man, but if that was what it took to convince Sir Knight that he was the only man she wanted, then so be it.

"Make up your mind, Mariah," Falcon challenged. "Can you forget your dead husband when I make love to you?"

Mariah sidled up to him and wound her arms around

his neck. His torso was stunningly bare; his thin hose did naught to conceal the engorged ridge of his sex.

"I promise I won't leave you with child, if that's what you're worried about."

Mariah blinked. "'Tis of no consequence, for I am barren," she lied.

"Are you certain?"

"Aye. Edwina has said it is so. 'Tis you I want, Sir Knight, you and no other."

"Then prove it."

Mariah stared at him. She hadn't the slightest idea what he was talking about. She knew naught about seduction. Though she lacked a maidenhead, she had never really been made love to.

"Kiss me," Falcon urged.

Mariah moved erotically against him, her fingers tangling in the silken curls at his neck, still damp from his bath. She raised her mouth to his.

Sir Knight's mouth slammed down on hers. There was no gentleness in his kiss. It was hard, demanding, unrelenting. He prodded her mouth open with his tongue; she opened for him and he plunged inside. Lightning shot through her as he laved her mouth with his tongue, igniting the embers of passionate longing she had suppressed all these years. She dug her fingers into his shoulders, struggling for balance. His skin was surprisingly soft to her touch, yet underneath she felt his muscles harden and flex.

She inched closer, crushing her breasts against his chest. His arms snaked around her waist, hugging her close as he kissed her mouth, her eyes, her cheeks, her chin. And then his mouth found her breasts. Unexpected thrills surged through her as Sir Knight's tongue circled a nipple with hot, lazy strokes. Part of her mind marked every stroke of his tongue while the other part wondered what he would do next. She had never imagined a man's touch could arouse this kind of need in her.

His mouth left her nipple; he scooped her into his arms and placed her on the bed. He stood over her, watching her as he stripped off his hose and tossed them aside. Mariah glanced at the thick length of his manhood and felt her cheeks heat. It rose hard and high against his stomach from a nest of black curls. She had seen his manhood before but never like this.

He lowered himself to the feather mattress and rolled on top of her. Mariah felt a moment of panic but quickly pushed it aside. Apparently, Sir Knight knew precisely what he was doing, and she thanked God for it.

His mouth found her breasts again, sucking hard on each nipple in turn, until they pebbled into aching buds. She bit her bottom lip to stifle a groan. He pressed an open kiss to her stomach, searing her skin with his tongue. Her mouth went dry. Alarm swirled in her belly when his mouth didn't stop there but continued on a downward path. Her senses had been unprepared for what he did next, and she suddenly realized that she was too inexperienced for this virile man.

"Please," she whispered.

"Aye, sweeting, I aim to."

He spread her legs with his shoulders. Cool air teased her open flesh. Suddenly she felt exposed, shy. But there was more. To her utter humiliation, Sir Knight bent his head and flicked his tongue across her sex. She bucked; he chuckled and held her in place as he found the tender nub between her thighs and sucked it between his lips. Sensation soared. Tremors raced through her core. She cried out.

He raised his head. "Did you like that?"

"Nay! Aye! I don't know. Anything that feels that good must be sinful."

He lowered his head and pressed his tongue inside her womanhood. She arched, gasped and tried to push him away. He looked up, watching her, sweat glistening on his forehead.

"Did your husband not kiss you there?"

"Nay, he would never—"

"A pity," he sighed, moving up her body. "We shall save that for another time."

He began kissing her again, her mouth, her breasts, her tender nipples, driving Mariah mad with wanting. She had never felt like this before. She burned, she couldn't catch her breath. Hot blood gushed through her veins, heating her from the inside out. Color bloomed on her cheeks as Sir Knight's hand drifted between her thighs. He opened her and plunged a finger inside. In and out, in and out, until she feared she would explode. Something momentous dangled out of her reach, but she didn't know what it was or how to seize it.

"Sir Knight . . . please." She wanted . . . she wanted . . . what? She didn't know what to ask for.

He moved up her body. "Do you want me now?"

"Aye."

"Where do you want me?"

She blinked but didn't hesitate. She'd have to be made of stone not to know precisely where she wanted him. "I want you inside me."

Bracing his hands alongside her, he lowered himself until he lay fully atop her. His member, hard like granite and hot as a flame, pressed into her inner passage. She heard herself moan.

Falcon paused. "You're tight . . . too tight."

Mariah had naught to say to that.

He pushed inside another inch, her wetness smoothing his entry. She held her breath. He bucked his hips, thrust forward and filled her. He was inside her, deep, full, stretching her. For a moment she feared she would tear. But of course she did not.

"Damnation," Falcon hissed from between clenched teeth. "If you weren't lacking a maidenhead, I would swear you were a virgin. Did I hurt you?"

"Only a little and just for a moment. Don't stop."

Their bodies were pressed together and slick with sweat as Falcon began to move. If he had done this before, and he knew he had, it had never been like this. Naught within his realm of understanding had ever felt this good.

He flexed his hips, thrusting his manhood in and out of her wetness. Mariah grasped his buttocks and arched upward, taking every turgid inch of him into her wet core.

She writhed, sobbed and rocked with agonizing rapture. The intense pleasure was almost too much for her to bear.

"Sir Knight," she cried. "Please. I know not what is happening to me."

"Trust me," he grunted. "I will not leave you wanting."

He continued thrusting and retreating, driving her, pushing her until she could stand it no longer. Pressure built; and then it happened. Her muscles contracted, she spasmed, heat flooded her core, and she screamed. He continued pumping into her, panting, crying out as he emptied himself inside her.

Naught but harsh breathing filled the chamber. While Falcon had a vague memory of having lain with other women, he knew that what he and Mariah had just experienced was unique and precious.

Mariah stirred beneath him. Fearing he was crushing her, he pulled out and settled beside her.

"That was . . . I cannot describe it," Mariah murmured. "I have never felt anything like that before in my life. What did you do?"

"You are very good for my pride, lady," Falcon said, grinning. "I made love to you. When you mated with your husband, did he give you no pleasure?"

Mariah shook her head.

"Then he did not deserve you," Falcon observed. "I am glad I am the first to unleash your passion."

Falcon thought she looked so adorable all rumpled, her lips swollen from his kisses, that he wanted her again. He decided he must have been without a woman a very long time to be so greedy, and so ready.

He turned Mariah toward him; she went willingly into his arms. Then he began to make love to her again, using his hands, his mouth and his lips to arouse her. When he lifted her on top of him and told her to ride him, he knew by her puzzled expression that this, too, was another pleasure her husband had denied her.

"Ride you?"

He spread her legs so that she straddled him. Then he lifted her slightly and pushed her down onto his swollen cock. She gasped. He smiled. Grasping her buttocks, he began to move her up and down until she learned the rhythm. She proved an apt pupil. Soon she was riding him like a bucking bronco, bringing them both to a shattering climax.

After that they slept. Mariah woke to the church bell announcing Lauds. Sir Knight was sleeping soundly beside her. She studied his face in the flickering candlelight, wondering how many women he had made love to before learning to do it so well. She smiled. Asleep, he looked very young and very vulnerable.

But he was a strong man. He had survived injuries that lesser men would have succumbed to. And she knew—*knew*—he would hate her if he learned she had lied to him and used him. Edwina had predicted a son would come of her coupling with Sir Knight, but if it did not, she would always have this night to remember. And God willing, there would be other nights like this one before Sir Knight left.

Mariah rose without waking him, donned her discarded robe and returned to the solar. Edmond was still sleeping. She wasn't going to tell him about this night, or any others that might follow. Only if she conceived would she confess her sin. Until then, she fully intended to savor the pleasure Sir Knight gave her.

Falcon began to feel as if he belonged at Mildenhall. During the day he trained with Mildenhall's knights, proving his worth as an experienced swordsman. He ate all his meals at the high table with Mariah and either played chess or just conversed with Lord Edmond when the old man felt up to it. But the nights belonged solely to him and Mariah.

She came to him at Matins, sometimes left at Lauds,

but more often than not lay with him until Prime, when the castle inhabitants began to stir. As far as Falcon was aware, no one knew about their nightly trysts. The passion he and Mariah shared within his chamber was without compare. The only thing stopping him from asking her to wed him was his lack of memory.

One night, as Mariah lay sated in his arms, he couldn't recall how long he had been Lord Edmond's guest and asked Mariah.

She thought a moment, and then said, "You were brought here on a Saturday, the day cotters bring produce to the castle. Since then, four Saturdays have come and gone."

Falcon reared up. "That means I've been here well over thirty days. Has no one come looking for me?"

"Nay, but we are a remote holding and seldom have visitors."

"Has no one heard rumors about a missing knight?"

"If they have, word hasn't reached us yet. Are you so anxious to leave us?"

"I need to know who I am and where I belong, Mariah."

The conversation came to an abrupt halt when Falcon turned to Mariah and began making love to her. Thinking about his missing past made him edgy and uncomfortable, but making love to Mariah made him forget for a short time that he was a man with no name, no past and no future.

Two days later, Falcon was heading out to the training field with his borrowed sword when Mariah intercepted him. "You've been training every day. Would you like to do something different today?"

He sent her a lopsided grin. "That depends on what you have in mind."

She laughed. "Behave, Sir Knight. Come with me to the mews. You haven't visited there yet."

A buzzing began in Falcon's head. "The mews?"

They turned in the direction Mariah indicated. "You haven't seen Edmond's falcons. He takes great pride in them. I thought we might take them out today. There's a peregrine Edmond is particularly fond of. He used to love to hunt. Do you—"

Falcon stopped in his tracks. The buzzing in his head grew louder, and devils began dancing in his brain. He shook his head, trying to dislodge the pain.

"Sir Knight, what is wrong? Are you ill?"

Falcon stared at Mariah. "What did you call me?"

"Sir Knight. 'Tis what I always call you."

The buzzing turned into a roar. Holding his head, he fell to his knees. His breath seized, and in that breathless moment he remembered his name and everything else about himself.

Mariah dropped down beside him. "Shall I summon Edwina, Sir Knight?"

He looked up at her, unfocused, disoriented. But out of the pain came illumination. "Do not call me Sir Knight. I have a name."

Air exploded from Mariah's lungs. "What just happened?"

He rose slowly, shakily. "I know who I am. I remember everything. The attack, where I was headed and where I had come from. I am one of King Henry's knights. I fought with him in France and earned his praise. My name is Falcon of Gaveston and . . . and . . . God's teeth!

My betrothed is waiting for me in London. We were to be wed over a fortnight ago. I must bid your father good-bye and leave immediately. Pray God Rosamond is still waiting for me."

Stricken, Mariah searched his face for a hint of the man she knew as Sir Knight, her lighthearted lover. But that man was gone, replaced by a stranger. The moment he had remembered his name and past, his face had changed, hardened. He had his own life and purpose now, and she meant naught to him.

Not that she ever could have been anything to him. She had Edmond, and Falcon had Rosamond.

"You must love Rosamond very much," Mariah dared.

Falcon shrugged. "I hardly know her. The king chose her for me as payment for my years of faithful service to England. He promised to find me a wife who would bring me land and wealth. As third son, I've had to make my own way in life. The only way I can have enough money to provide for a family is to marry an heiress. Rosamond is perfect for me."

He turned to leave, unaware of Mariah's breaking heart. She followed him into the hall and trailed him up the stairs to the solar. They found Edmond sitting in a chair near the window, a blanket tucked around his legs.

"Mariah, Sir Knight, how did you know I was lonely? Sit down and make an old man happy."

"I know who I am," Falcon said without preamble.

Edmond stared into Falcon's eyes. "Aye, I can see a difference in you. Pray, do not keep me in suspense."

"I am Sir Falcon of Gaveston. My father is the Earl of Gaveston. I am a knight in King Henry's service."

Edmond stroked his chin. "I should have known you

were one of Gaveston's lads by the color of your eyes. I've always admired your father's golden tiger eyes. I knew him many years ago."

"Sir Falcon is betrothed, and his bride-to-be is waiting for him in London," Mariah revealed. "He is anxious to leave."

"We will miss you, Sir Falcon," Edmond said sadly. "Feel free to bring your bride to Mildenhall for a visit. Mariah will make you both welcome, will you not, my dear?"

One look at Mariah was all it took to remind Falcon of what he was leaving behind. He would never forget their nights of unbridled passion, the closeness that had grown between them. But as much as he might desire it, he could not remain at Mildenhall now that he knew where he belonged and with whom. He would always remember Mariah. How could he forget her? If not for his commitment to Rosamond and the king, he could remain here forever and be happy.

But his duty lay in another direction, and he never shirked his duty. "May I borrow a horse, my lord?"

"Of course, take any mount you fancy. Consider it a gift."

"Thank you. Mariah, might I have a private word with you?"

Mariah followed him out the door and into the corridor. "I'm sorry, Mariah."

"Don't be," she said brightly. "I knew you would regain your memory one day. As your body healed, so did your mind. Now you know where you belong, and it isn't here."

How could she sound so cheerful when it was killing

him to bid her good-bye? "I will never forget you. I will always think of you with affection." He brushed a tear from her cheek.

"We were never meant to be, Falcon. You have your life and I have mine."

"I'd best be on my way."

"Aye. I wish you and your betrothed many years of happiness."

He stroked her cheek with the back of her hand and then let his arm drop back to his side. Mariah wanted to cringe away. His touch felt like that of a stranger, even though she knew him as intimately as a woman can know a man.

"Farewell, Sir Falcon."

Falcon stared at her for the length of a heartbeat, and then walked away. He wanted to kiss her good-bye but knew it wouldn't be the right thing to do. Everything had changed the moment he reclaimed his identity. Falcon of Gaveston had had many women, he remembered that. But Mariah was more than just a woman he had bedded and discarded. Mariah was . . .

A woman he had to forget if he hoped for happiness with Rosamond.

London hadn't changed in his absence, Falcon thought as he entered the city. He headed directly to Whitehall, expecting to find Rosamond waiting for him. The first person who recognized Falcon nearly fainted at the sight of him.

"You're supposed to be dead," Sir Albert Melrose croaked when he recovered his aplomb. "We searched for you from Norwich to London and back again. Where have you been?"

"Lost in a fog," Falcon said dryly. Falcon and Sir Albert were comrades in arms but had never been friends. The knight was too full of himself for Falcon's liking. "I'll explain after I see the king."

"You'll have to go to France to see him," Sir Albert replied. "He left with his army two days ago."

"Why are you still here?"

He sent Falcon a sly smile. "I just recently married. The king gave me leave to escort my wife back to our estate. I plan to join him in France at a later date."

Apprehension churned in Falcon's gut. "What lady did you wed? Do I know her?"

"Aye, my bride is Rosamond of Norwich."

Falcon glared at him, his face stony, his eyes darkening from gold to murky brown. A muscle at his temple twitched, the only sign that he'd heard Sir Albert's words. "You lie!" he hissed. "Rosamond is *my* betrothed."

"You're supposed to be dead, remember? Once the search was called off, I offered for her and her father accepted. You're not the only knight who longs for a piece of England to call his own. My bloodlines are as good as yours; the Earl of Norwich saw no reason to return home without a husband for his daughter and asked Henry to sanction the marriage."

Falcon lunged at him. He might have killed Sir Albert had Rosamond not appeared at that moment. "What are you doing to my husband? Take your hands off him, sir!"

Falcon turned at the sound of her voice. Rosamond staggered backward. "Falcon! This cannot be. You are dead."

Falcon gave her a mocking bow. "As you can see, my lady, my death was grossly exaggerated."

Beyond speech, Rosamond merely stared at him.

"What happened to you?" Sir Albert asked, keeping well out of Falcon's reach.

"I was attacked by bandits and left for dead. I awoke hours later at Mildenhall Castle, severely injured and without a memory."

"Mildenhall Castle? I've never heard of it," Albert mused.

"'Tis off the beaten path, but it could have been found had the search for me been more thorough. Who was in charge of discovering my whereabouts?"

Albert cleared his throat. "I was. After a sennight, we concluded that you had been attacked by bandits after you left Norwich. We believed you'd been slain, and your body devoured by wild animals."

"How convenient for you," Falcon sneered.

"Even the king was convinced you were dead," Rosamond interjected.

Falcon's gaze sought his former betrothed. "Did you even wait a sennight to marry after I went missing? Did you even mourn me?"

"Pray do not speak to my wife in such a demeaning manner," Albert charged. "If you wish to challenge me, do so and I will select my seconds."

Falcon's mouth settled into a grim line. "I will not lower myself by dueling over a faithless damsel. I will leave immediately to join the king in France."

Turning on his heel, Falcon strode off, hurt and disillusioned by the shabby treatment he had received from his king and his friends. He no longer had a betrothed; the land he had been promised had been yanked from under him by a quirk of fate. He felt lost and without direction.

Briefly he considered returning to Mildenhall and claiming Mariah. But he discarded the notion as soon as it was born. He could not offer for any woman; he had naught to offer. Furthermore, he suddenly realized that he was fiercely angry at the Earl of Mildenhall and his daughter. Why hadn't Lord Edmond sent someone to London to find out if a knight had been reported missing? The earl's failure to do so was unforgivable. Falcon had lost a wife and an estate because of Edmond and Mariah's negligence.

Falcon left Whitehall, fury and disappointment burning deep in his gut. He had a great deal to accomplish before he sailed to France. He had to let his family know that he was alive, and after that, he needed to collect his squire, who had charge of his war chest, and find out if he had enough money to outfit himself for battle.

Rosamond and Albert could go to the devil, for all he cared. What he yearned for now was a sword in his hand and someone to fight until the anger drained out of him.

Chapter Four

London, five years later

The court at Whitehall had been in a jubilant mood since a victorious Henry and his army had returned from France two months earlier. With the forces of the French King Charles VI defeated, the triumphant Henry had forced Charles to recognize him as his heir. That had been a great day for England, a cause for prolonged celebration.

But once King Henry returned to London, he immediately became immersed in affairs of state. Petitions awaited him, many too complex to act upon without further investigation. To those petitions Henry assigned advisors to act in his stead. After giving one such petition considerable thought, he sent for Sir Falcon of Gaveston.

When Falcon received word that the king wanted to see him, he hoped the reason was that Henry had found another heiress for him to wed. Five years hadn't erased the bitterness he harbored at losing Rosamond and her lands to Sir Albert. And it still rankled that his supposed death had been so easily accepted by everyone, even his family.

Nor had Falcon forgiven Lord Edmond and his daughter for neglecting to seek information about him when he turned up at Mildenhall without a memory. But much could be forgotten and forgiven if Henry found him another heiress. Falcon still yearned for land to call his own, but only the king could grant it.

Falcon paused before the king's privy chamber to compose his thoughts and slow his racing heart. He hadn't felt this kind of excitement since he'd helped Henry win French lands for England. There was still more to be accomplished, but for the time being, the battles were over.

A guard opened the door; Falcon strode inside. He found Henry alone with his secretary.

"Ah, Falcon, come in, come in."

Falcon approached the king and bowed. "You wished to see me, sire?"

"Aye." Henry gestured toward a chair. "Sit down; you tower over me like some great bird of prey."

Falcon perched on the edge of a chair, too nervous to be comfortable. Though he knew the king well, he felt more at ease riding beside him in battle than sitting beside him in his royal chamber.

"As you know," Henry began, "I have been inundated with petitions and matters of state since my return."

"I am well aware of your duties to the Crown, Your Majesty."

"Aye, and it just so happens that you can help me."

"Me, sire?"

"Indeed. In fact, I can think of no one more suited to handle this particular matter for me."

Falcon's spirits fell. "I thought . . . I hoped you had found an heiress for me."

Henry dismissed Falcon's words with a wave of his hand. "I am still assembling a list of eligible heiresses for you to choose from. While the search continues, a matter at Mildenhall needs attention—attention I have scant time to devote myself to at this time."

Falcon's heart pumped furiously. "Mildenhall, sire?"

"Aye. I remembered that you are familiar with Mildenhall and its inhabitants and thought of you immediately. I want you to go to Mildenhall and investigate a problem that has arisen there. You are to act as my surrogate and have the power to resolve the problem as you see fit. I will not dispute your decision, however you decide."

Dismay stole Falcon's ability to speak. He had no desire to return to Mildenhall and Mariah. Though he'd tried to forget, he had thought of Mariah often during the past five years. Indeed, he recalled everything about her worth remembering. The softness of her skin, the sky blue of her eyes, her passion, her lush red lips, the silkiness of her inner thighs—naught escaped his memory. She was probably wed by now, he thought. But even if by chance she was still single, she wasn't for him.

To Falcon's knowledge, Mariah possessed neither land nor wealth, for after her father died, the uncle she despised would inherit. Though it wasn't right, it was the law of the land.

"What say you, Sir Falcon?" Henry prodded. "I will give you ten knights of your choice from my own army to help resolve the chaos at Mildenhall."

Falcon's heart lurched. Was Mariah in danger? "Perhaps you should explain precisely what I am to do at Mildenhall, sire."

Henry grew pensive. "During our sojourn in France, the Countess of Mildenhall gave birth to a son, although I don't recall precisely when. Then, some time ago, Lord Edmond passed on to his reward."

Falcon sent Henry a startled look. Though he regretted Lord Edmond's demise, something did not ring true to him. "There is no Countess of Mildenhall. There is only Lord Edmond's daughter."

"I beg to differ, Falcon. I attended the wedding myself. Though the girl was young, she did indeed became Edmond's wife."

Confusion warred with logic inside Falcon's brain. "I saw naught to convince me that Lord Edmond had a wife. I never encountered the countess during the weeks I lived at Mildenhall."

Henry shrugged. "By your own admission, your brain wasn't working right. Trust me, Falcon, Lord Edmond had a wife, and that wife bore him a son before his death."

Falcon couldn't imagine the frail old man he had come to know being vigorous enough to sire a child. "I assume there is more to the story."

"Indeed. Sir Osgood Fitzhugh and his son Walter have questioned the legitimacy of the child. They claim Lord Edmond had been bedridden for years and was too ill to bed his wife. They accuse the countess of taking a lover and passing the child off as Lord Edmond's heir."

"I don't know Sir Osgood very well, but I suspect he is eager to claim Mildenhall for his own."

"Aye, you have the right of it. I cannot grant Osgood his wish without investigating, and that's where you come in. I cannot take the time to travel to Mildenhall to sort this out. I have been away from London and my duties too long to leave at this time."

"I had hoped to visit my family," Falcon hedged.

"I received a petition from the Countess of Mildenhall, asking for help. It seems that Sir Osgood has taken up residence in the castle, claiming to be Lord Edmond's legal heir. She also claims that Sir Osgood is pushing for a marriage between her and Walter."

From what Mariah had told him and what he knew about Osgood and his son, Falcon guessed the match would be pure hell for the poor countess. But for the life of him, Falcon couldn't recall a countess. How could that be possible?

"I will provide you with documents giving you authority to act in my name. I want you to investigate Osgood's claims against the countess and make a decision based on your findings. A great deal is at stake, Falcon, and the power is yours to determine who is lying and who is not. Mildenhall is small by most standards, but from what I recall of the holding, it is not poor and provides a comfortable income."

"From what I know of Osgood, he will do everything in his power, even lie, to secure the land for himself and his son. Lord Edmond's daughter held him in low regard."

Henry stroked his chin. "I don't remember Sir Edmond's daughter. Perhaps she was born on the wrong side of the blanket before his marriage. But that's neither here nor there and should have no bearing on your decision."

Falcon had never considered that Mariah might be illegitimate. He did wonder, however, why he had never seen the countess. Had his brain been more addled than he'd thought?

"You know Mildenhall and its people, Falcon. Do this for me and I will be forever in your debt."

"Are you sure you're willing to trust my judgment, no matter whom I decide for?" Falcon asked.

The king shrugged. "I leave it entirely in your hands. I simply do not have the time for this. You have never failed me in battle, and I know you won't fail me now. I trust that after a thorough investigation your decision will be fair and unbiased."

Falcon wondered if he could be unbiased when it came to Mariah's welfare. He tried one last time to pass the task to another.

"What about Sir Gordon? Could he not do as well as I?"

Henry stared at him. "I suppose he could, but he isn't looking to wed an heiress; you are. If you want a quick solution to your landless state, I suggest you accept this mission. Handle this matter for me and there might even be a title in it for you."

A title! Falcon had been determined to gain land of his own, but a title had always seemed too far out of his reach. But the moment the king had hinted at the reward that could be his, Falcon knew he would accept. Seeing Mariah again might be difficult, but they had been naught more than brief lovers fated to be parted. Five years had passed since he'd left Mildenhall; Falcon held mixed feelings for the woman who had saved his life but done naught to help him find his identity.

Falcon looked the king in the eye and said, "I will do it, sire. How can I refuse when you tempt me with a bride and a title?"

"I knew you would agree!" Henry crowed. "You have taken a great load from my shoulders. I am much in demand since my return to England. While you pack your belongings and select the men to accompany you, my secretary will prepare a document, which I will sign and seal, giving you absolute authority to rule in my stead concerning the disposal of Mildenhall."

Falcon rose. The king waved him off. As Falcon strode from the privy chamber, he wondered what he had gotten himself into.

Mildenhall, one week later

A strange feeling overtook Falcon when the spires of Mildenhall Castle came into view. Memories he had relegated to the back of his brain began pushing to the fore. He pictured Mariah as she was the first time he had seen her. He'd thought her an angel, and that he had died and gone to heaven.

"You weren't jesting when you said Mildenhall was remote," said Sir John, one of the knights accompanying Falcon.

Falcon turned to look at his friend, glad that he wasn't alone, like the last time he had traveled this road.

"Travelers rarely come this way," he acknowledged. "No visitors arrived during the weeks I spent in Lord Edmond's keep."

Falcon led the party of knights out of the woods into the clearing surrounding Mildenhall. The portcullis was lowered, which Falcon thought odd. Then he gazed up and saw faces looking down at him from the parapet.

"Raise the portcullis!" Falcon shouted.

"What do you want?"

"Let me in and I will tell you."

"Identify yourself."

Falcon's squire raised the pennant, prominently displaying a red falcon, with wings extended, on a field of blue.

"I am Sir Falcon of Gaveston. I bear documents from the king for the occupants of Mildenhall."

"I'll fetch Sir Osgood," the man replied, turning away.

"It seems we are not welcome," John mused.

Falcon's horse pranced restlessly beneath him. Falcon patted his neck, murmuring comforting words. The wait seemed interminable but in reality was of short duration. The next voice Falcon heard was that of Sir Osgood, who appeared at the portcullis with his son.

"I was expecting the king. What are you doing here, Falcon of Gaveston?"

"I am the king's chosen representative, here to investigate the situation at Mildenhall and make a decision on my findings."

"You?" Osgood screamed. "What gives you the authority to come here and judge me?"

"My authority comes from the king, and I have documents to prove it. Open the portcullis. I would meet the countess and investigate the charges of adultery you have brought against her."

"Mildenhall is mine," Osgood asserted. "I intend to wed my son to the countess despite her infidelity to my brother so that she and her bastard will have a home." He smiled. "I am not without a heart."

Falcon eyed Osgood with a hint of derision. Short and stocky, Sir Osgood was a fierce knight known for his cruel ways. He showed no mercy, gave no quarter. In manner, his son appeared an exact replica of his father, down to the sneer that curled his thick lips. They differed only in their size. While Osgood was short and stocky, Walter was tall and husky.

"I will be the judge of that," Falcon said. "Open the portcullis. To disobey me is to disobey the king."

Osgood nodded to Walter, who moved off to do his father's bidding. Moments later the portcullis began to rise, groaning a protest as it opened completely. Falcon rode forward, his men falling in line behind him. Once in the courtyard, Falcon dismounted and waited for Osgood to join him.

"Welcome to Mildenhall, Sir Falcon," Osgood said. "But the keep is not new to you, is it? I heard you spent time here when your brains were addled and you knew not who you were."

Falcon sent him a startled look.

"Oh, aye, did you think I didn't know? The story of your memory loss was quite amusing. Pity you lost your intended bride and her generous dowry."

"My men are hungry and tired," Falcon said curtly. "Shall we postpone this conversation for later?"

"Of course," Osgood said quickly—a little too quickly. "Bring your men inside. I'm sure Sir Martin can find food and beds for your party."

Falcon fell in step behind Osgood as he climbed the stairs to the keep. He was somewhat apprehensive at seeing Mariah again and wondered if she remembered him. He had neither seen nor contacted her in five years, though she was seldom far from his thoughts despite his best efforts to forget her.

What really intrigued Falcon was meeting this countess whom he had not met in all the weeks he had spent at Mildenhall. A smidgeon of something he didn't even

Connie Mason

want to consider worked its way into his brain. What if . . . Nay, it didn't even bear thinking about. No one could be that devious, that scheming. Mariah had had no reason to lie to him. Somewhere in this keep there existed a countess who had petitioned the king for help.

The wide oaken doors swung open. Falcon strode into the hall he remembered so well, even after five years. He heard a strangled sound and turned to find the cause. His gaze found Mariah.

Her stunned expression spoke volumes. Apparently, she wasn't pleased to see him at Mildenhall. Their gazes met and clung. The years dropped away and he became Sir Knight again, Lady Mariah's lover. He took a step toward her, saw her cringe, and forced himself to back off. Something was definitely wrong. Mariah seemed frightened of him. Had she been intimidated by Osgood and his son?

"Lady Mariah, greetings," Falcon said.

Mariah slanted a worried glance at Osgood and acknowledged Falcon's greeting with a nod.

"Lady Mariah and Edwina cared for me when I arrived at Mildenhall more dead than alive," Falcon explained. "I owe my life to them."

"How fortunate for you," Osgood drawled. He motioned to Sir Martin, who was hovering nearby.

The steward approached Falcon, greeting him warmly. "Welcome back, Sir Falcon."

"Sir Falcon and his knights require food and accommodations," Osgood said curtly. "See to it."

Martin slanted Osgood a look that Falcon had no difficulty interpreting before the steward nodded and left to do Osgood's bidding. Apparently, Osgood and his son were despised by the inhabitants of Mildenhall.

Falcon glanced at Mariah, who still hovered near the hearth. What in the world was going on?

"Please summon the countess so we can discuss the reason for my visit," Falcon suggested.

Walter's shaggy eyebrows shot up. "What is there to discuss? The countess committed adultery and passed the boy off as Edmond's legitimate heir. My father is the rightful heir of Mildenhall. But I assure you, Sir Falcon, the lady will not stray once she is my wife. All traces of rebellion will be beaten out of her."

Osgood clapped Walter on the back. "This is my son Walter, in case you haven't guessed."

Falcon acknowledged Walter with a curt nod. "Please summon the countess. I wish to meet her."

Osgood spun around to survey the hall, found Mariah and called for her to join them. As Falcon watched Mariah approach, her dragging steps and wary expression set off warning bells in his head. She stopped in front of him, refusing to look at him.

"For some unknown reason, Lady Mariah," Falcon said, "Sir Osgood is reluctant to produce the countess. Would you fetch her for me?"

Osgood glared at Falcon through narrowed eyes. "What trick is this, Sir Falcon? The Countess of Mildenhall stands before you, and well you know it."

Falcon stared at Mariah as if seeing her for the first time. His intuition had tried to tell him what his mind refused to believe. Mariah was Edmond's wife, not his daughter, Falcon realized. She had used him, lied to him and . . . God's bones! Had Edmond encouraged her to bed him, or had the earl been too ill to realize what was going on under his very nose?

Falcon had never felt the inclination to shake a woman senseless before, but now the powerful urge pulsed through his blood like wildfire. His hands clenched and unclenched as anger surged through him; his heart pumped riotously against his ribcage. What had she done?

"*You* are the countess?" he growled menacingly.

She looked up at him, her eyes silently pleading with him to understand. "Forgive me, Falcon," she whispered.

"What's this?" Osgood asked suspiciously.

"Naught that concerns you," Falcon replied. "I wish to speak privately with you and the countess. I carry a missive from King Henry you will both want to read."

"We won't be disturbed in the solar," Mariah said.

"Agreed," Osgood said. "Walter should be included since he is to wed Mariah."

"I will not wed Walter!" Mariah defied. "If the king decides in Sir Osgood's favor, my son and I will leave Mildenhall."

"You are without funds," Walter taunted.

Mariah did not flinch beneath the intensity of his gaze. "I am *not* without funds. I have my widow's portion. But thus far King Henry has given no indication he plans to turn my son and me out of our home and install your father as the new earl."

Falcon listened to the exchange with an air of detachment. Though his anger was beginning to ebb, he still had a great many truths and untruths to sort out before he could make an informed decision. Was Mariah's child a bastard as Osgood claimed? Or had Lord Edmond rallied long enough to bed and impregnate his wife? If Mariah had lied to him, she most certainly could lie about the paternity of her child.

They reached the solar. A young nursemaid sat on the floor near the hearth, playing toy soldiers with a small lad. Mariah seemed startled to see her son in the solar and took a protective stance near him, shielding him from view.

"Becca, please take Robbie to the nursery," Mariah said.

Becca picked up the child and trotted off before Falcon got a good look at the boy who might or might not be the new earl.

Osgood and Walter took the only two comfortable chairs in the solar, leaving a bench for Falcon and Mariah to share.

"Very well, Falcon, you may speak freely. What are the king's wishes regarding Mildenhall?"

Falcon removed the missive from his pouch and offered it to Osgood. Osgood dithered a moment, then asked Falcon to read it aloud. Falcon smothered a grin. Apparently, neither Osgood nor his son could read.

Falcon unrolled the parchment and made known the king's wishes. When he finished, Osgood jumped to his feet. "'Tis ludicrous! The decision should not be yours to make! You are neither king nor nobleman. You are in no position to investigate my claim. Mariah's child is a bastard, I tell you!"

"That is for me to decide," Falcon replied. "The king will stand by my decision." He rose. "Excuse me; I'm going to join my men in the hall."

Falcon strode from the chamber, leaving a stunned audience behind.

* * *

Mariah took advantage of the lull to rush after Falcon. She caught him at the bottom of the stairs. "Sir Falcon, please tarry a moment. I wish a private word with you."

Falcon's fierce expression brought her to an abrupt halt.

"You lied to me," he accused. "What did you hope to gain?"

A son. "Can you not forgive me and undertake this matter with an open mind?"

"Why should I forgive you? You could have sent word to London and learned my identity long before it came to me. I lost a promising future as a landowner because of your failure. I lost a bride and the dowry that came with that marriage. Thanks to you, I am still a landless knight."

He hadn't married his Rosamond! "Why did you not find another heiress?" she dared.

"I was so angry and confused by everything that had happened to me that I left immediately to join King Henry in France. But I expect to have a bride soon. By the time my assignment here is completed, Henry will have found several heiresses for me to choose from."

"I am sorry, Sir Falcon. Is it your intention to turn my son and me out of our home? Sir Osgood doesn't deserve Mildenhall. He forced his way into the keep and made unfair demands upon my people."

Falcon stared at her. Mariah flinched beneath his scrutiny. How had the passionate lover she had once known become this cold, uncompromising stranger? Pray God he never learned that Robbie . . . Nay! Robbie belonged to her; no one was going to take him from her.

"My assignment is to learn the truth and make a decision based upon my findings." He turned his golden eyes on her. They were filled with shadows. "You told me you couldn't conceive. You lied to me about being a widow. What else did you lie about? Was Lord Edmond aware of your deception? Did he condone it?"

Mariah glanced behind her, saw Sir Martin approaching and said, "We cannot talk here." She edged away as Sir Martin reached them.

"Mariah, wait!" Falcon called.

She strode off without looking back.

Mariah's heart was beating so loudly she feared Falcon would hear it. Why did he have to show up now? Once he'd learned she was Edmond's wife and not his daughter, he had treated her with contempt. And who could blame him? She *had* used him, but there was more to it than that. Her feelings for Falcon had run deep. His hasty departure without a proper good-bye had devastated her.

She had no idea what had gone wrong between Falcon and Rosamond, but obviously he blamed her for his loss. Now here he was again, at a time she'd least expected him. He had been sent to Mildenhall to act as adjudicator. In whose favor would he decide? How could she keep Robbie away from him? Once Falcon learned the truth, he would hand the earldom and demesne to Osgood. Oh, what a tangled web she and Edmond had woven. Her sins were coming back to haunt her.

Falcon hated her. Would he hate her son as well?

Mariah saw Edwina in the hall and hurried over to her. "What is it, lass?" Edwina asked. "What has Osgood done to you?"

"'Tis not Osgood this time, 'tis the king," Mariah gasped. "He sent Sir Falcon to investigate Osgood's claim that Robbie is illegitimate." She shook her head. "I am lost, Edwina. Robbie and I will be deprived of our home. What am I to do? My widow's portion cannot support us forever, and I refuse to wed again."

Edwina led Mariah to a chair. "Sit down, child. Sir Falcon strikes me as a sensible man."

"He hates me, Edwina. He knows I lied to him and sinned against Edmond."

"With Edmond's approval," Edwina reminded her.

Mariah shook her head. "It matters not. I should start making plans to leave. I shudder to think how the people of Mildenhall will fare under Osgood's heavy hand."

"Do not give up yet, Mariah. Falcon cared for you once, I saw it plainly."

"Five years ago Falcon was a different man. He had no past, he remembered naught. I took advantage of his situation; I seduced him for the son I wanted from him. It was wrong of me, and now I must pay the penalty."

"Pah! Stop this talk. The Mariah I know and love would not give up without a fight. You must seduce Falcon all over again. Make him see how wrong it would be to turn you and your child out of your home."

"If I tell him the truth about Robbie, he will accuse me of stealing a part of him. All these years I believed Falcon was wed to Rosamond. I mourned his loss and missed him dreadfully. But I had his child, and that gave me hope for the future. My son is my life, Edwina. Think you Falcon will take him away from me?"

"Not even a battle-hardened warrior would be that cruel. I will think on this," Edwina promised. "Meanwhile, make Sir Falcon welcome."

Edwina left, and Mariah slipped off to the nursery. Robbie looked up from his play and grinned at her when she entered the chamber. Thank God the lad looked more like her than Falcon, Mariah thought. But for his golden eyes, his features were all hers. And the soft hair covering his head was blond, not black like his father's. Let Falcon think what he liked; she'd never admit that Robbie was not Edmond's child.

"How old is the lad?"

Mariah glanced toward the open door, where Falcon leaned against the jamb, watching Robbie at play. Although Robbie had just turned four, she lied, shaving a year off his age. "He just turned three."

"Though I know naught of children, I would guess he is big for his age."

"Edmond was a large man before his illness."

Falcon glanced at Robbie, who was eyeing him curiously, and asked Mariah to join him in the corridor, where the lad couldn't hear. Mariah obeyed him with marked reluctance. Falcon closed the door behind them.

"Do you still claim Lord Edmond is the lad's father?"

"I do. 'Tis the truth."

"So you say, but I've been lied to before. What did you hope to gain by claiming that Lord Edmond was your father?"

"A virile lover," Mariah whispered, and realized it was not a lie. "A man whose skin did not sag, a young, vigorous man who made me feel like a woman for the first time. You did that, Falcon. Your loving brought something to my life that I lacked."

Falcon snorted. "Whom did you turn to after I left? Osgood told the king that Edmond was incapable of performing in bed."

Mariah stared him in the eye and said, "Osgood wasn't

in bed with me and Edmond when Robbie was conceived. Robbie is Edmond's son."

Falcon winced. The thought of Mariah in bed with Edmond made his stomach churn. "That is something I have yet to prove." Turning on his heel, he stalked off.

Chapter Five

When Falcon slid into a chair at the head table that night to partake of the evening meal, he noticed that Osgood issued orders to the servants as if he were already the Earl of Mildenhall.

Falcon rose when Mariah entered the hall. Osgood also rose and seated her in the vacant chair between himself and Walter. Falcon saw how distasteful the seating arrangement was to her and decided to do something about it.

"Lady Mariah," he said, leaning across Osgood. "Change places with Sir Osgood so that we may speak privately during the meal."

"Now see here, Falcon," Osgood growled. "Who gave you the right to countermand my orders?"

"The king," Falcon drawled. "Until I deem otherwise, Lady Mariah is still the mistress of Mildenhall. Her wishes should be respected, and I can tell from her expression that she does not wish to sit between you and Walter."

Mariah stood, her expression grateful as Osgood, his ill humor apparent, exchanged places with her.

"Mariah is my betrothed," Walter protested. "You have no right to separate us."

"I am *not* your betrothed," Mariah protested as she slid into the newly vacated chair beside Falcon. She leaned toward Falcon and whispered, "Thank you."

Nodding, Falcon turned his attention to his meal. Mariah ate sparingly, he noted, and realized she must be feeling uncomfortable after the lies she had told him.

"Does your conscience bother you?" he asked in a voice only she could hear.

Mariah glanced up at him. "Why should it?"

"You lied to me. Which one of Mildenhall's knights did you sleep with after I left? I am not stupid, Mariah. Lord Edmond was not capable of bedding you."

"Sir Falcon, if you intend to turn me out of my home, tell me now so that I may prepare for my departure."

"I haven't been here long enough to investigate Osgood's charges or reach a decision." He took a bite of venison, chewed slowly and swallowed. "Tell me, do you truly intend to refuse Walter's proposal?"

"Aye. I can tolerate neither Walter nor his father. If you hand Osgood the title, it will destroy Mildenhall. Osgood will run the estate into the ground. He thinks he can force me to wed his son, but he cannot. Father Francis will not perform the ceremony if I am unwilling."

"Perhaps you should rethink your position. At least you would not have to leave your home if I decide in Sir Osgood's favor."

Mariah looked up at him then. Her pain was easily discernible from her expression. Falcon experienced a jolt of guilt but refused to let it hinder or influence his investigation.

"You must do what you have to do, Falcon," Mariah said quietly. "I know how you feel about me, so why torment me?"

Falcon's dark brows shot up. "Torment you? Nay, Mariah, I merely seek the truth. God knows there has been little enough of that at Mildenhall."

Mariah scraped back her chair. "Excuse me, I must see to my son."

Falcon watched her walk away, remembering their nights of unbridled passion. He had promised her naught and left without a backward glance, but he had not forgotten her. He had to forcibly prevent himself from following her to her chamber, tossing her on the bed and thrusting himself inside her.

"She's a tempting piece," Osgood said. "Walter is eager for the match."

While Falcon had been woolgathering, Osgood had moved into the chair Mariah had vacated. "I hadn't noticed," Falcon lied.

Osgood laughed. "Tell that to someone who will believe you. I saw the way you looked at her. Something happened between you while you were at Mildenhall. Did you bed the bitch?"

"You have a nasty mind, Osgood," Falcon drawled.

Osgood leaned closer. "Would you like Mariah in your bed for the length of your stay?"

Falcon nearly leapt at Osgood's throat but contained himself. He wanted to see where this conversation was going. "How do you propose to manage that, and what must I give you in return?"

"You know what I want. Give me the earldom."

"What makes you think Mariah will have me? And what will Walter say about sharing the woman he hopes to wed?"

"Walter doesn't have to know. This is between you and me—a gentlemen's agreement, so to speak."

"What if Mariah refuses?"

Osgood grinned. "She will agree. All I have to do is threaten her son. She dotes on the little bastard."

Falcon's anger rose swiftly. A man who threatened a child was without honor. "I have no proof that the lad is illegitimate."

"Bah! You are a fool if you think my brother sired the brat. And Edmond was a bigger fool to accept the boy as his heir."

"Ah," Falcon mused. "So Lord Edmond acknowledged the child, did he? I was wondering about that. In fact, that was to be my first line of investigation. Thank you for clearing up the matter."

Osgood jumped up so fast his chair crashed backward to the floor. "This conversation is beginning to bore me. Go ahead, conduct your investigation, but know this. I *will* have Mildenhall and Walter *will* have Mariah. Your opinion means naught to us."

"I represent the king. Think again if you believe my opinion carries no weight."

"Walter, 'tis time to retire," Osgood ordered as he charged off. Like a puppy, Walter shoved past Falcon and followed Osgood from the hall.

Falcon wondered if Walter would still idolize his father if he knew Osgood had just offered him the woman he intended to wed.

* * *

Mariah settled Robbie down for the night and returned to her chamber. One of the maids had built up the fire and left several candles burning for her. She found her brush, sat down on a stool and began to brush her long golden hair.

Things weren't going at all well for her. She had hoped the king would give her problem his personal attention and rule in Robbie's favor. Never had she expected Falcon to turn up at Mildenhall and expose all the lies she had told.

Mariah seriously considered leaving Mildenhall for good. If she was frugal, her widow's portion would last until she found a position as nursemaid or governess. She knew Edwina would come with her to mind Robbie if she asked. Fleeing an intolerable situation was far better than wedding Walter and watching Mildenhall fall into Osgood's vile hands.

Mariah didn't hear the door open, but her keen senses warned her that she wasn't alone. She rose and turned toward the door, expecting to see Edwina. It wasn't Edwina.

"Walter! What are you doing here?" She backed away as he strode forward. "Get out!"

"You had best be nice to me, Mariah," Walter drawled. "You want your bastard to reach manhood, do you not?"

Mariah's hand flew to her throat. "How dare you threaten my son!"

"Now, why would I do that? I just want you to be nice to me. We'll be man and wife soon, so what's the harm in anticipating the nuptials?" He stalked toward her.

Mariah put the bed between them. "I will never marry you, Walter. You're as heartless and vile as your father. If you don't leave, I'll scream."

Walter laughed as he lunged for her. He missed. "You *will* lie with me if you value your son."

Mariah began to shake. She would die if anyone hurt Robbie. But letting Walter bed her was unthinkable.

Walter made another grab for her and this time caught her skirt. He began reeling her in like a fish on a hook. She screamed, but the sound was quickly stifled by Walter's meaty hand. His fingers dug into her face so hard, Mariah knew they would leave bruises. But that didn't keep her from fighting back.

The hall was empty but for Falcon, Sir John and Sir Martin. They lounged before the hearth, sharing a pitcher of ale before retiring to their separate quarters.

"This is the first chance we've had to talk since my arrival, Sir Martin," Falcon said conversationally. "Tell me, what do you think of Sir Osgood?"

"Sir Osgood!" Martin spat. "The people fear him and his son. They arrived over a month ago and claimed rights to the keep and its people. Lady Mariah had been expecting Sir Osgood to invade the keep and dispatched a letter to the king, asking his help in establishing young Robbie's right as Earl of Mildenhall."

Falcon stroked his chin, aware that what he was about to ask was presumptuous and personal. "You've been steward at Mildenhall a long time, have you not, Sir Martin?"

Martin immediately became wary. "I have been Mildenhall's steward these past twenty years."

"Do you believe Osgood's claim that Robbie is illegitimate?"

"Lord Robbie was born during my lady's marriage to Lord Edmond," he said.

"That is not what I asked," Falcon pressed.

Martin chose his words carefully. "Lord Edmond acknowledged Robbie. Never say *you* believe Osgood's charges."

Martin's words startled Falcon. "'Tis too soon to make a judgment."

"Lady Mariah was devoted to Lord Edmond," Martin said staunchly.

"Did you know that your lady originally told me Lord Edmond was her father? Why is that, do you suppose?"

Martin shrugged. "You will have to ask my lady."

"I did, but she was evasive. I intend to learn the truth of the matter before I leave Mildenhall."

Falcon rose and stretched. "'Tis late, I'm for bed."

John swirled the ale in his tankard and drained it in one gulp. "'Tis time I retired, too."

"Sir Knight, Sir Knight, you must go to Lady Mariah immediately! She needs you."

Edwina rushed up to Falcon, frantically pulling on his arm.

"Why must I go to her?"

"She is in grave danger."

Falcon grew immediately alert. "What kind of danger?"

"I saw Walter sneaking up the stairs to the solar. He has no business there; his chamber lies in another direction. I fear he intends my lady harm."

Falcon raced toward the stairs, taking them two at a time. John sprinted after him. Falcon heard a muffled scream and burst into Mariah's chamber in time to see Walter pressing her down onto the bed, one heavy hand over her mouth, the other raising her skirts.

Walter must have heard the door open for he called

harshly, "Get out of here! Can't you see the lady and I want privacy?"

Falcon could tell by Mariah's struggles that she wasn't the one wanting privacy. With a roar of outrage, he launched himself at Walter. Grasping Walter's doublet, he pulled him off of Mariah and flung him across the chamber, where he landed at Sir John's feet. When he started to rise, John pressed his sword against Walter's throat.

Falcon was too concerned about Mariah to care what was taking place behind him. She had rolled up into a ball on the bed, her hands covering her face. "It's all right, Mariah," he soothed. "Walter won't hurt you again; I'll make sure of it."

Mariah peeked at him through shaking fingers. "Falcon?"

"Aye, Mariah." He perched on the edge of the bed. "Did he hurt you?"

She turned toward him, clutching frantically at his shirt. "He wanted, he tried . . . Thank you for coming to my aid."

"Thank Edwina. She alerted me to trouble."

He noted the bruises on her face, the perfect imprints of Walter's fingers, and cursed. He touched her cheek, turning her face to the light. "Did he do that to you?"

"He tried to keep me from calling for help."

Falcon whipped around, turning the full potency of his rage on Walter, who still lay on the floor beneath John's sword.

"Let him up," Falcon hissed.

John raised his sword; Walter scrambled to his feet. "This is none of your business, Falcon. This is between Mariah and me."

"I'm making it my business. But first—" he glanced over his shoulder at Mariah. "Did you invite Walter to your bedchamber?"

"Nay! He entered without my permission and attacked me."

"Attack is a harsh word," Walter mumbled, his bravado returning. "I was merely exercising my right as Mariah's betrothed. She opened her legs for other men besides Edmond. Why should I be denied her favors?"

"I am not your betrothed," Mariah denied vehemently.

"Be careful what you say, Mariah," Walter warned. "Your future and that of your son depend on my father's goodwill."

Spinning on his heel, Falcon delivered a stunning blow to Walter's chin. He fell heavily to the floor, holding his jaw and groaning. "Not another word," Falcon growled. "John, escort Walter to his quarters and station a guard outside his door. I want Osgood and his entourage escorted from Mildenhall at first light. They are no longer welcome here."

"You cannot do that!" Walter howled, rising unsteadily to his feet. "Mildenhall belongs to us."

"That's for me to decide," Falcon replied. "Rest assured your father will be informed of my decision when my investigation is completed and I have reached a decision. I will inform him about his expulsion from the keep as soon as I am free here.

"John, inform Sir Maynard that he's to rally Mildenhall's knights in case Osgood refuses to comply with my orders and tries to make trouble."

John grinned as he prodded Walter from the chamber. "It will be my pleasure to relay your message."

Falcon closed the door behind John and Walter and turned back to Mariah. She was sitting on the edge of the bed, watching him closely.

"Thank you," she whispered. "He threatened to hurt Robbie if I didn't . . . do as he wished."

"Neither Walter nor Osgood will harm your son."

Falcon crossed to the pitcher, poured water into the basin and wet a cloth. Then he returned to the bed and sat down beside her, turning her face toward him and carefully pressing the cloth to her bruises.

"Are you sure he didn't . . . ?"

"Nay, he did not."

Relief swept over Falcon. As they stared at one another, something stirred between them, something hot and potent and immediate. Memories he preferred not to address flooded his mind and body. Were her kisses still wildly tantalizing? he wondered. Would her body melt into his if he pulled her into his arms and kissed her? Would her passion be as stunning as he remembered?

He lowered his head, unable to resist the lure of her soft lips. She raised hers, stretching to meet his mouth. Their lips touched briefly, parted. He tasted her breath, knew he should leave but couldn't bring himself to move. He urged her into his arms and drew her against him. Mariah's gaze met his, as if asking for something he wasn't prepared to give.

"We cannot become lovers again, Mariah," he warned. "I am here to make an impartial decision."

"Aye," Mariah whispered.

But Falcon failed to heed his own warning as his lips moved over hers, tasting, savoring. He felt her breasts swell against his chest, felt the thudding of her heart, and felt his cock respond in a predictable manner. He had promised himself that this wouldn't happen again, had been confident that his attraction to Mariah had waned with the passage of time.

There was a great deal about Mariah and Edmond that Falcon didn't understand, and Mariah had been no help in explaining the lies she had fed him. How could he want a woman he neither understood nor trusted?

"I am sorry, Falcon," Mariah murmured, as if reading his thoughts.

"So am I," Falcon replied. He drew back slightly. "I must go. I need to inform Osgood that he is leaving at first light." But he didn't move.

"You won't let them hurt Robbie, will you?"

"Your son is safe, Mariah." They were sitting so close together he could feel her heat surround him; his own heat pulsed hotly in his groin. His cock stirred restlessly, wanting, needing.

Mariah tried to draw away but his arms refused to release her. They tightened around her. Then he did what he had wanted to do since he'd set eyes on her again. He kissed her, hard, sweeping his tongue inside her mouth and probing roughly. It was a fiercely wild kiss, a kiss meant to punish as well as please. Falcon's feelings were so confused where Mariah was concerned that he couldn't control the emotions pummeling him.

He brought his hand around to fondle her breast, heard her moan and knew that the only thing preventing him from pushing her back into the mattress, flinging up her skirts and thrusting himself inside her heated core, was his duty to the king.

The king! Honor demanded that he do Henry's bidding.

Groaning, Falcon broke off the kiss and set Mariah away from him. "I won't let you do this to me again."

Mariah thought his words unfairly harsh. Aye, their coming together five years ago had been seduction, but Falcon had wanted her, too. Their loving had been mutual, something they had both wanted and both needed. Aye, she had lied to Falcon, but he had left her for Rosamond without a backward glance. He hadn't returned to Mildenhall because he wanted to see her again—nay, he was here on the king's behalf. If Henry hadn't promised Falcon an heiress once this duty was completed, he wouldn't be here now. She meant naught to him and never would.

Anger fueled her resolve. She would not let Falcon into her heart again. He was not Sir Knight. She rose and gave him her back. "Go, Falcon, I am fine. Complete your investigation as soon as possible and leave Mildenhall. If you choose to give my husband's holding to Osgood my son and I will leave immediately. You care naught for me; you never have."

Falcon stood and reached for her, dragging her back into his arms. "We are not strangers, Mariah."

She gazed into his eyes. "Aye, we are. I do not know you, Sir Falcon. The man I knew as Sir Knight, the man I took as a lover, was naught like you." She touched his face. "He was sweet and kind, a man I . . . grew to admire."

"That was a long time ago. Sir Knight would not have bedded you had he known you were married, and neither would I. I respected Lord Edmond. Naught you can say will convince me that he encouraged you to bed me."

Mariah refused to speak ill of Edmond. She had loved him dearly. He had been her closest friend. If she had her way, Falcon would never learn that bedding him had been Edmond's suggestion.

"I told you my reasons, and they have naught to do with Edmond. I wanted to be loved by a young man, and you showed up at the right time. 'Tis as simple as that."

"Why turn to me and not one of Mildenhall's knights?"

"I did not want any of Edmond's men in that way."

"But you wanted me? I'm trying to understand, Mariah, but you are making it difficult."

Mariah shrugged and stepped away from him. He dropped his arms and let her go. "You were a stranger, that's why I chose you for my lover. I knew you would regain your memory and leave, and so you did. No one knows about us but Edwina. That's the way I want to keep it."

"Your child—"

"Is mine," Mariah said fiercely. "Mine and Edmond's. He acknowledged Robbie before he died."

A burning began in Falcon's gut. "Who did you sleep with after I left, Mariah?"

"No one but Edmond," Mariah maintained.

The burning burst into flame. "Are you sure the lad is not mine?" The notion that he had sired Mariah's son had been in the back of his mind since he'd arrived at Mildenhall, but he had kept it imprisoned within his brain. The question had come spewing forth before he could stop it.

"How dare you suggest such a thing? Robbie is Edmond's, and that's all I'm going to say on the subject. Leave me alone, Falcon of Gaveston. I've had enough aggravation tonight to last a lifetime."

"Aye, you have," Falcon agreed softly, "and I'm sorry for it."

Falcon bowed, turned and walked away. It wasn't what he wanted to do, but what he had to do. If he had a choice, he would throw caution to the wind and make love to Mariah all night and into the morning. But he was a knight who took duty and honor seriously.

Falcon strode through the great hall and climbed the stairs to the wing where Osgood and his son were quartered. A guard, one of Falcon's knights, guarded Walter's door.

"All is quiet, Falcon. I don't think we will hear any more from Walter tonight."

"What of his father, Sir Dennis?"

"I have heard naught from Osgood. He must be sleeping."

"Stay alert, Dennis. I'm going to wake Osgood and inform him that he will be leaving Mildenhall at first light."

Dennis drew his sword. "You can count on me."

Falcon walked past Walter's door and stopped before the next. Dragging in a deep breath, he clenched his fist and pounded on the thick panel. He heard a rustling inside, and then Osgood flung open the door.

"What do you want? What must a man do to enjoy a good night's sleep in this keep?" He was naked, his thick body showing signs of going to fat.

"I'm here to inform you that you and your entourage will be leaving at first light tomorrow."

"What in the hell is that supposed to mean? You can't tell me to leave. I belong here."

Falcon drew himself up to his impressive height, towering over Osgood. "If you don't leave of your own accord, you will be forcibly escorted from Lord Edmond's land."

Osgood reached for his sword, frowning when he realized he was naked. "I demand to know the reason behind your sudden decision to ban me from Mildenhall. Did that bitch Mariah get to you? Did she offer her body in exchange for a decision in her favor?"

"You've got it all wrong, Osgood. Your son attacked Mariah tonight in her chamber. If Edwina hadn't alerted me, he would have brutally raped her."

Osgood had the temerity to laugh. "Mariah is Walter's betrothed. No harm done if they want to anticipate the wedding."

"Mariah wasn't willing," Falcon growled.

Osgood shrugged. "She would have been if you hadn't interfered. There's no need for all this fuss. Leave them to hash out their differences and everything will work out to our mutual satisfaction. I'm sure the king will be pleased to know that Mariah will be looked after when you declare me Edmond's heir."

"Nay, Osgood Fitzhugh. I've considered this from every angle and decided that you and your entourage must leave Mildenhall. From what I've heard, you came here and took over without an invitation."

"Mildenhall is mine, I needed no invitation!" Osgood snarled. "Mariah's brat has no legal right to the earldom."

Falcon ignored Osgood's protestations. "You will be escorted from the keep at first light tomorrow." He turned to leave, then spun around to face Osgood. "By the way, there's a guard at Walter's door. I want no more trouble tonight."

The door slammed in his face.

"He did not take it well," Dennis said.

Falcon shrugged. "It matters not. He has disrupted the household with his overbearing presence."

"Have you decided in Lady Mariah's favor, then?"

"I have decided naught. I haven't been here long enough to reach a decision. Good night, Sir Dennis."

Falcon found his chamber, stripped, washed and climbed into bed. He fell asleep almost instantly. He awoke before dawn to the pounding of footsteps and clatter of weapons. Leaping from bed, Falcon pulled on his hose and boots, grabbed a shirt and had one arm in the sleeve when there came a frantic knocking on his door.

"Open up, Falcon! Something terrible has happened."

Falcon recognized John's voice. When he flung open the door, he heard wailing coming from the solar. "God's bones, what is it?"

"Osgood and Walter are gone, and so is Lady Mariah's son. They sneaked away like thieves in the night. Robbie's nursemaid was knocked senseless. Though still groggy, she awakened and alerted Lady Mariah. A short time later we found Sir Dennis lying unconscious before Walter's door."

"Is he badly hurt?"

"Nay, but he'll have a headache for a while."

His face grim, Falcon poked his arm in his other sleeve and reached for his weapons, strapping them on as he strode from his chamber. "Alert the troops. We'll leave as soon as I speak to Lady Mariah."

Falcon didn't look forward to facing Mariah. He knew

the kidnapping of her son must have devastated her and wished there was something he could have done to prevent the tragedy. He blamed himself for failing to place more guards at Osgood's door, and securing Osgood's men under lock and key for the night. Falcon knew Osgood had a cruel streak, but he'd never thought he would kidnap an innocent child.

Falcon found Mariah in her chamber, surrounded by Edwina and her maids. She was sobbing disconsolately. Falcon shooed everyone but Mariah out the door.

Mariah blinked at him through swollen eyes. "'Tis your fault! You promised to protect Robbie. Now he is gone, and I'll never see him again." She rocked back and forth, her sobs heartrending.

Falcon knelt before her, taking both her hands in his. "Mariah, I placed Walter under guard. I never expected this of Osgood."

"He said he would hurt Robbie if I refused to marry Walter," Mariah wailed. "You promised . . . You promised . . ."

Guilt weighed heavily on Falcon. "I meant it, Mariah. And I'm going to make another promise. Robbie will be returned to you safe and sound."

Falcon prayed his promise wouldn't prove an empty one. The thought of a vulnerable child like Robbie in Osgood's hands twisted his insides.

"Where would Osgood take Robbie? I need some idea where to look for him."

"Osgood lives in a small manor that came to him upon his marriage to Martha. 'Tis located near Southwold."

"Osgood has a living wife?" That was news to Falcon.

"Aye. He also has a daughter. Elizabeth remains unwed because Osgood refuses to grant permission to suitors unless he is paid a hefty sum for the privilege of wedding her."

Falcon rose. "I will find him. Trust me to bring Robbie back to you." He strode toward the door.

"Wait! I'm going with you."

"Nay, you will remain here, where it is safe. The ten men I brought with me will accompany me. Your men will remain at Mildenhall. I spoke with your captain of the guards last night. Sir Maynard is a good man, he will protect the keep in my absence."

"Nay, I need to be with you! What if Robbie's release depends on my promise to marry Walter?"

"You will *not* wed Walter under any circumstances," Falcon snarled. "Trust me to return your son to you. I'm wasting time here, Mariah. The sooner I leave, the sooner I can bring Robbie back to you."

Suppressing a sob, Mariah threw herself into Falcon's arms and pulled his head down for her kiss. She kissed him hard, showing her desperation without words. He hardened instantly, but before he could return her kiss, she pulled away and grasped his shirt front.

"Bring Robbie home, Falcon. Bring him to me safe and sound."

Chapter Six

Mariah stood before the window, watching Falcon and his men ride through the portcullis. Once she was certain they were well on their way, she grabbed her cloak and raced down the stairs to the kitchen to pack food for her journey. When she returned to the hall, Edwina halted her flight.

"Where are you going, Mariah?"

"I'm going to follow Falcon. Robbie will need me after his frightening experience. Please, Edwina, do not try to stop me."

"Nay, I won't stop you. But have a care, Mariah. Falcon knows what he is doing. Do not interfere. Trust him to find Robbie for you."

"I do trust him, but Robbie needs his mother." So saying, she strode past Edwina and out the door. Sir Maynard didn't question her right to have her mare saddled or to leave, for he was busy elsewhere. She rode unchallenged through the portcullis, pleased to find it in a raised position. She had no idea Edwina had fetched Sir Martin, who immediately dispatched two guardsmen to follow her.

Mariah rode through the day, keeping well behind Falcon, stopping for naught but to rest her horse and drink from a stream. When hunger pangs gnawed at her, she nibbled on bread and cheese. At nightfall, Mariah knew she could push her horse no further and would have to stop soon. Her one consolation was that both Osgood and Falcon would also have to stop for the night. Mariah could not stop worrying about Robbie. Had his captors thought far enough in advance to bring food for him? Her son had a healthy appetite.

Mariah was looking for a spot to stop for the night when she heard a screech. The hair rose on the nape of her neck; she reined in her horse, waiting, listening. Then she heard it again. No animal she knew made that sound. Mariah had heard that same cry so many times she recognized it immediately as a child's cry.

Robbie!

Mariah slid from the saddle, peering through the tangle of shrubs and trees in the direction from which she had heard the sound. The cry came again. Once she had identified the screech, naught in this world would keep her from going to her son. Not even the thick forest that lined both sides of the road.

Mariah tied her horse's reins to a low-hanging branch near the edge of the road. She might have to leave in a hurry and wanted easy access to her horse. Then, taking a deep breath to steady her nerves, she entered the forest, using Robbie's crying to guide her.

She came upon them suddenly; Osgood, Walter and six of his dozen or so mercenaries were lounging around a small fire. She slipped behind a tree, her gaze searching for Robbie. When she saw him, her heart nearly stopped.

He had been wrapped in a blanket and tied with a rope, to prevent him from wandering off, she supposed.

Mariah's anger exploded when she saw his pitiful attempts to wriggle free. She wanted to go to him immediately, to soothe him, to let him know that his mother hadn't abandoned him. Aware of her vulnerable position, she crouched down and waited for the right time to act.

Robbie lay several feet away from the main group of men. Mariah wondered why they had dared to build a fire, why Falcon had missed them and she had not.

"Can't you keep that brat quiet?" Osgood hissed to his son.

"He's hungry, I suspect. We should have brought some food with us."

"There was no time."

Walter glanced at Robbie, who was hiccupping between sobs. "I could gag him. Or better yet, let me kill him."

"Don't be stupid; that would defeat our purpose. The boy has to stay alive for our plan to succeed. Splitting up was a brilliant move," Osgood crowed. "While Falcon is chasing after the men I sent ahead, we'll double back to the keep."

Walter grinned. "With Robbie in our possession, Mariah will realize how easily we can hurt the brat and agree to marry me. Once Mariah is my wife, Mildenhall will be legally ours no matter what Falcon decides."

Osgood clapped Walter on the shoulder. "'Twas my plan to wed you to Mariah long before Edmond breathed his last. I wanted to leave naught to chance or King Henry's whim. Once you and Mariah are wed, it matters not whether I am Edmond's heir. You will get Mariah with child as soon as possible. When she gives you a son, we will get rid of Robbie. After he joins his maker, I will become earl and you my heir. Mildenhall will belong to our branch of the family into perpetuity."

"The wedding will be accomplished before Falcon returns, just like we planned," Walter gloated. "He won't be able to do a thing about it."

Mariah heard every word. If she hadn't chanced upon Osgood and Walter, Osgood's dastardly plan probably would have worked. She peeked around a tree at Robbie. He had cried himself to sleep. He must be terrified, and there was naught she could do about it.

"The brat is sleeping," Walter announced.

"We should get some rest ourselves." Osgood got up and stomped out the fire. "I want you well rested for your wedding night."

Walter guffawed. "I'll plow Mariah so thoroughly she won't be able to walk for a sennight." He rubbed his crotch. "I get hard just thinking about rutting between her white thighs."

They soon parted, each curling up in a blanket near the mercenaries, who had already settled down for the night. Mariah feared she would go mad waiting for the men to fall asleep. Fortunately for her peace of mind, the men were tired and fell asleep quickly. Mariah waited until the sound of snoring filled the small copse before creeping from her hiding place.

At first her legs refused to work. She had crouched in the same position so long her muscles had stiffened. After stretching her limbs a few minutes, she began crawling cautiously toward Robbie. She moved slowly, careful not to snap a twig, holding her skirts so they wouldn't rustle.

Robbie didn't awaken as she scooped him into her

arms, turned and picked her way through the forest toward the road where she had left her horse. The poor tyke was so worn out he barely stirred, except for an occasional sob that shook his tiny chest.

Mariah flinched every time she stepped on a twig, waiting for a hue and cry from Osgood's camp. All was quiet. Fortune surely smiled on her. Mariah quivered with anticipation as she spied the road through the trees. That was when Robbie awakened and stared at her through huge, frightened eyes.

"Mama?"

"Be quiet, darling," she whispered. "I'm taking you home. But you mustn't make a sound. If you do, the bad men will come after us."

Robbie continued to stare at her but remained silent as Mariah reached the road, and ran straight into the arms of two men. She was on the verge of screaming when a sliver of moonlight revealed the faces of Chad and Horace, two of her own guardsmen.

"My lady, thank God you are well. We came upon your horse and were about to enter the forest to find you."

"What are you dong here?"

"Sir Martin ordered us to follow you," Horace informed her.

"Mama, I want to go home," Robbie whispered.

"Hush, darling, you'll be home soon."

"You have Robbie?" Chad exclaimed when he realized the bundle Mariah held was her son. "Where is Falcon?"

Mariah snorted. "Following a false trail. I'll tell you all about it when we reach Mildenhall. Horace, take Robbie on your horse and ride as fast as you can to the keep. I'll be right behind you. Chad, find Falcon. Tell him Osgood's mercenaries are setting a false trail for him, and that Robbie is safe."

Chad rode off immediately while Horace mounted and held out his arms for Robbie. Mariah removed the rope binding her son but left the blanket in place to keep him warm. Then she handed him to Horace.

Robbie protested until Mariah said, "You know Horace, darling. He's going to keep you safe."

"Are you ready, my lady?"

Mariah mounted with the help of a nearby stump. "Aye, Horace. Don't spare the horses. We must reach safety before Osgood's camp awakens and he finds Robbie missing."

They rode the rest of the night and into the day, stopping briefly near a stream to drink and feed Robbie the last of the bread and cheese Mariah had brought with her. Around midday, she took Robbie up on her own horse for the remainder of the journey. He wound his arms around her neck and nestled his towhead into the space between her shoulder and neck, gaining comfort from his thumb stuck firmly in his mouth.

They reached Mildenhall near dusk. Once they rode through the portcullis, Horace ordered that the gates be lowered and not raised for anyone but Falcon and his party. People rushed out from the keep to greet them when they reached the courtyard.

Mariah spotted Becca hastening toward her. "Take Robbie, Becca. He's dirty, hungry and thirsty."

Becca took Robbie from Mariah's arms and carried him into the keep. Mariah slid from the saddle and collapsed the moment her feet touched the ground. Then she knew no more.

* * *

During the time Mariah had been rescuing Robbie, Falcon had called a halt for the night. He knew he was gaining on Osgood's party, but his men and horses were tired and needed a short respite. Though Falcon knew he would catch up with Osgood on the morrow, he feared that Osgood might hurt Robbie in the meantime. That thought had kept him going, pushing horses and men mercilessly to catch up. He had promised Mariah he would bring Robbie home safely, and he wouldn't countenance failure.

Falcon scanned their surroundings, hoping to find a campsite. He had no sooner dismounted than he heard the sound of hoofbeats pounding along the road they had just traveled. "How many men does it sound like to you?" he asked John, who had come up to join him.

"One horse, one man," John replied.

"I agree. It could be someone from Mildenhall. We'll wait for him here."

They didn't have long to wait. The horseman appeared a few minutes later, a mere shadow beneath the waning moon. He reached Falcon and skidded to a halt. Falcon grasped the reins, noting that the horse was foaming at the mouth and panting. The rider wasn't in much better shape.

"It's Chad, one of Mildenhall's guardsmen," John cried. "What's amiss, man?"

Falcon's heart was thumping so fast he feared it would leap from his chest. "Has something happened at Mildenhall? Is Lady Mariah all right?"

Chad fought to catch his breath.

Fearing the worst, Falcon grasped Chad's doublet in his fist. "Tell me."

"My lady found Robbie," Chad said breathlessly. "She and Horace are returning to Mildenhall as we speak. My lady sent me to tell you that Osgood set a false trail for you."

"How does she know that? Where and how did she find Robbie?"

"I do not know the details," Chad replied. "Edwina encountered Lady Mariah leaving the hall shortly after you rode through the portcullis. She intended to follow you. Edwina informed Sir Martin, and he sent Horace and me to follow her and make sure that she came to no harm. We found her some distance behind you; she had Robbie with her. Somehow she had stolen him away from Osgood and Walter; that's all I know."

"Mariah followed us?" Falcon all but shouted. "Is the woman crazy?"

"Like a fox," John observed. "She found her child on her own and sent someone to inform us that we are following a false trail. What do we do now?"

"Since there's naught to gain by continuing forward, we shall establish a campsite, rest here tonight and return to Mildenhall on the morrow. After this latest fiasco, Osgood deserves neither the earldom nor Mildenhall. Relay my orders to the men, and station guards near the road. Osgood and Walter are behind us. No telling what they'll do now."

John nodded and departed. "Follow me, Chad," Falcon said. I want to know everything you can tell me about Lady Mariah and Robbie."

Chad followed Falcon to a fallen stump. They both sat heavily, saddle-weary and exhausted. Chad spoke first. "Lady Mariah had no idea we were following her. As we rounded a bend, we saw her horse cropping grass at the side of the road. She had tethered him to a branch but was nowhere in sight."

"Did you follow her?" Falcon asked.

"Not right away. She might have gone into the forest to relieve herself, and we didn't want to disturb her. She had been riding hard for some time."

"Did you see aught of Osgood or Walter?"

"Nay, we neither saw nor heard anything; we never suspected they were near. We believed they were ahead of you. But my lady had been in the forest so long, we began to fear that something had happened to her."

"So you followed her," Falcon guessed.

"Nay, we intended to, but she returned for her horse before we could carry through. To our utter astonishment, she had Robbie with her. My lady and Horace returned immediately to Mildenhall while I pressed on to inform you of the latest developments."

"That's it? That's all you know?"

"Lady Mariah feared Osgood would discover Robbie missing and give chase; there was no time for a lengthy explanation."

"Damnation! How could one woman rescue a child when ten men could not?" He clapped Chad on the back. "Get some rest. We return to Mildenhall at first light."

Osgood's camp was in disarray the following morning. He went into a rampage when he learned that Robbie had disappeared. He stomped around in a rage, sending Walter and his men scurrying in all directions to search for the missing boy. After long hours of fruitless searching, Osgood was of the opinion that the child had been dragged off and eaten by a wild animal, though there was no proof to support his theory.

"What are we going to do now?" Walter complained. "We've lost our leverage and with it, the earldom. We should have left the brat sleeping in his bed, for we gained naught by taking him with us. Think you Falcon will look kindly upon your suit after what we have done?"

Osgood paced away and then spun around. "The boy could not have wandered off. He was wrapped up and tied with a rope. I tied him myself."

"We were all sleeping," Walter maintained. "It's as you said, a wild animal dragged him off to its lair."

Osgood shuddered. "'Tis not the end I had planned for the boy, but it will do."

"Are we to return to Southwold, then?"

"Nay! I have no wish to endure the company of my wife and daughter. We'll take ourselves to London and petition the king in person for Edmond's title and lands. We shall inform Henry that Mariah's son is dead. Everything is working out better than our original plan."

"You're forgetting one thing," Walter reminded him. "We are responsible for the brat's death."

Walter's words seemed to deflate Osgood. "Perhaps we'll reach the king before word of Robbie's demise. They'll be mourning him at Mildenhall and won't think to notify the king. The lapse will give me time to plead my case before the king in person. Henry needs to know that Edmond could not have sired a child in his condition."

Falcon and his men returned to Mildenhall the following day, tired, dirty and hungry. The portcullis clanged down into place as soon as the last man had passed through.

Falcon strode into the hall and called for ale. His throat felt like a desert.

Smiling broadly, Sir Martin joined him. "Welcome back, Falcon."

"Where is Mariah? Is Robbie well?"

Martin lost his grin. "Robbie is well and none the worse for his ordeal. Mariah, on the other hand . . ."

Falcon's heart skipped a beat. "Is something wrong with Mariah? Tell me, man."

"Rest easy, Falcon. Mariah is merely saddle-sore and exhausted. Edwina ordered her to bed. Robbie's kidnapping and rescue wearied her nearly beyond endurance."

Falcon decided to bathe before looking in on Mariah. He stank of horse and sweat; his ripe odor offended even himself. Deciding to forgo food until later, he ordered a tub before he climbed the stairs to his chamber. An hour later, clean and feeling more like himself, Falcon made his way to Mariah's room. Edwina opened the door to his knock.

"Sir Falcon," Edwina greeted. "Mariah was beginning to worry about you."

"How is your mistress?" Falcon asked, glancing over Edwina's shoulder at the bed. "Is she awake?"

"She'll be relieved once she learns you've returned safely. She's awake, so you may as well go in. I imagine you'll have questions for her."

Falcon's face hardened as Edwina slipped into the corridor and shut the door behind her. He couldn't help feeling anger. Mariah had left the keep after he had ordered her not to. What if things hadn't worked out as they had? What if Mariah had been hurt?

"If you're going to stay, come here where I can see you," Mariah said.

"Are you sure you're up to company?"

"I'm fine. 'Tis easier to obey Edwina than argue with her, though I must admit to being a wee bit weary."

Falcon strode to the bed, fully intending to issue a stinging rebuke, until he saw Mariah; her face was pale, her eyes rimmed with dark shadows. He stopped in his tracks.

"You *are* ill!"

Mariah struggled to sit up. "I assure you my malaise is temporary. I was in the saddle too long without sleep or respite. But I'd do it again for Robbie."

Falcon perched on the edge of the bed. "You should not have left the keep; you placed yourself in grave danger." Without conscious thought, he reached out and stroked her cheek. "Are you well enough to tell me what happened?"

She nodded, turning her head into his caress. She wanted him to keep touching her, but he dropped his hand. After gathering her thoughts, she began talking. She told him everything that had happened, from the moment she'd left Mildenhall up to the time she snatched a sleeping Robbie from under Osgood's nose.

Halfway through the telling, Falcon stood and began pacing. When she finished, his expression held a note of disbelief. "How could you hear Robbie crying when I did not?"

"There were ten men and horses in your party. The pounding of hooves would have masked his cries. I was but one rider—a mother who recognized her child's crying."

"You should have ridden for help."

"Nay, I should not have. I did what was necessary. I heard Osgood and Walter talking while I waited for them to go to sleep. They intended to double back to Mildenhall while you were chasing the men he sent ahead to lay a false trail. Once he returned, Osgood would have used Robbie to force me to wed Walter. It would have worked, for I would have done anything to save my son. When you returned, the deed would have been done, and Mildenhall would belong to Osgood and Walter no matter what your decision regarding the earldom."

"Damnation! The man is a true villain, using a child to gain his own ends. How is Robbie?"

"I'm told he's well, but I haven't seen him since we returned. I'm worried about him. Would you look in on him when you leave here to make sure I'm not being lied to about his health?"

"Of course."

Mariah gazed up at him. He was staring at her lips, and for a moment she was reminded of Sir Knight, the man who at one time could not get enough of her kisses. She closed her eyes, picturing them together, imagining his hands on her, loving her. Color tinged her cheeks, and she shook her head to clear it of arousing thoughts. Falcon was not Sir Knight. Falcon was a man who cared naught for her.

"What are you thinking?" Falcon asked. "Your eyes are closed. Am I tiring you?" He started to rise. "Perhaps I should leave you to your rest."

Mariah stopped him with a hand on his arm. "Don't go . . . please."

Falcon settled back on the edge of the bed. "Do you have any idea what Osgood might make of Robbie's disappearance?"

"Nay, I wondered about that myself. Do you think he'll return to Mildenhall?"

"I shouldn't think so, but I doubt we've seen or heard the last of him." Falcon's thoughts turned inward. "Mayhap Osgood thinks that Robbie was dragged off by wild animals."

Mariah sat up, a look of horror on her face. "What if Osgood believes Robbie is dead? What would his next move be?"

"If it were me, I would take myself to London to present my petition to the king. Robbie's death could change everything. Osgood would become Edmond's legal heir."

"But Robbie isn't dead!"

"I know. I'll dispatch a messenger to apprise the king of Robbie's continued well-being."

Mariah flopped back against the pillows, her color returning. "May I assume you are no longer considering handing the earldom to Osgood?"

Falcon remained silent a long time . . . too long. "Falcon, please tell you aren't going to take Robbie's inheritance from him."

"After Osgood's trickery, I cannot in good conscience rule in his favor." He stared at Mariah, as if searching for answers. "But before I take my decision to the king, I want you to tell me the name of Robbie's father."

Mariah went still, returning Falcon's look without flinching. "I already told you. Edmond is Robbie's father."

Grasping her shoulders, Falcon brought her to him nose to nose. "You lie! We both know that's impossible. Are you incapable of telling the truth?"

"Falcon, stop it! You're hurting me."

Immediately Falcon's fingers gentled as he pulled her into his embrace and held her close. "Forgive me,

Mariah. Imagining you with another man drives me mad. I find it difficult to forgive you when your lies have cost me so much."

"You're thinking of Rosamond," Mariah whispered. "I'm sorry. I confess I was unfaithful to Edmond, but only with you."

Falcon wanted to believe Mariah but couldn't. Though Osgood was no longer in the running for the earldom, Falcon was determined to learn the truth about Robbie before he left Mildenhall. His mouth settled into a grim line, but anger was difficult to maintain with Mariah in his arms. When he'd first learned Mariah had rescued Robbie, he had been worried and angry at the same time.

Mariah stared into the intensity of Falcon's mesmerizing golden eyes and lost the ability to think. His expression . . . He looked at her with desire, but how could that be? Moments ago he was angry and accusatory, but now . . .

He looked like Sir Knight the lover—her lover.

The weight of Falcon's hand slid over Mariah's breasts, then over her belly. She tried to pull away, but he would not allow it. Raw, untamed heat shot through her veins. She glanced up at him; his lips were curled into a dangerous smile. Sir Knight was gone, replaced by Falcon, the fierce warrior and king's emissary.

"Falcon, release me."

"Do you remember how it was between us?" Falcon murmured against her lips.

"I've tried to forget," she replied truthfully. "I never expected to see you again. After you returned from France, you made no effort to contact me."

"There was no reason to," he said, an impatient edge to his voice. "I needed a wealthy heiress, not the penniless widow you led me to believe you were."

Her eyes flashed defiantly. "Did you think about me at all? Did you think about our time together after we parted?"

In a rash moment of truthfulness, Falcon confided, "After we parted, I burned for you in a way I've never burned for any other woman, and there have been plenty of them since you."

His fingers tightened on her shoulders. "I am a man of honor, Mariah. I did not put horns on Edmond by choice." His touch turned into a caress. "But now that you're a widow in truth, there is naught to stop us from continuing where we left off. We can be lovers until I return to London."

Mariah wrested free of his embrace. "You speak of honor. What honor does becoming your mistress bring me?"

Leaning into her, Falcon nibbled her ear, kissed her throat, her neck. He released the ties on her shift, bared her breasts and kissed them. "Had you possessed a modicum of honor, you would not have lied to me about your relationship to Edmond."

"How long must you punish me for that? Did my explanation not please you? You wanted me, Falcon, and I wanted you—'twas as simple as that." She tried to push him away. "But I no longer want you. I have Robbie, and he's all I need."

He pushed her back against the pillows, trapping her beneath him. Her breath caught in her throat.

"You're lying, Mariah. The look in your eyes, the

catch in your breath when I touch you, they all tell me you want me."

He kissed her breasts again, with a boldness that made Mariah's breath hitch. His tongue wrought magic upon her tender nipples, and she could do naught but savor the pleasure he bestowed. Heat simmered within her. No man had touched her since Falcon, and her need could not be contained.

Why this man? she wondered. She had been widowed a long time. She could have taken to her bed any man she found attractive. But she wanted no one except Falcon, and he had been lost to her, or so she'd thought. Never in her wildest dreams had she believed she would see Falcon again in this life.

But she didn't want him like this, a man driven by equal parts of anger and lust. Mariah regretted using Falcon, but it had been necessary. What she hadn't known was that she would develop strong feelings for him. Apparently, any tender feelings Falcon held for her had disappeared the day he had regained his memory. His purpose now was clear and simple, she thought. Falcon wanted vengeance for her deceit.

"Why are you doing this? You hate me," she said.

His thumb traced the outline of her nipple. "I don't know. My feelings are confused right now. I felt as if I had been betrayed when I arrived at Mildenhall and learned I had bedded Lord Edmond's wife."

"I've already apologized for that."

"On the other hand, I was mindless with worry when I learned you had followed me into danger," Falcon continued. "You could have been killed, and Robbie along with you."

Falcon lowered his head and suckled her nipples.

She tried to push him away. "Someone might come in."

Falcon raised his head, scrambled off the bed and locked the door. He shed his doublet, shirt and boots and slid into bed beside her. His hair was still wet from his bath, Mariah noted, and his skin smelled of soap and his own special scent, one she remembered so well.

"No one will bother us now. Raise your arms so I can remove your shift."

Mariah began to have second thoughts despite the hot blood surging through her body. "Is this wise, Falcon?"

"Probably not. Are you going to stop me?"

She should, but oh, she was desperate to feel Falcon inside her again. Desperate for his touch; needing his kisses. After Falcon had left her five years ago, she had been bereft. If she had not discovered herself with child, she would have become an empty shell after Edmond died. Though Robbie had given her life new meaning, something was still missing from it. That something was Robbie's father, the man who must never learn he had given her a son.

She raised her arms. Falcon stripped off her shift. Giving her a wicked grin, he set his lips against the taut skin of her stomach, licking and nipping between kisses. Locking his hands about her hips; he shifted lower, spreading her thighs with his shoulders, wedging himself between them.

Her fingers clenched in his hair. He felt her drag in a breath as he bent his head and set his mouth on her weeping core.

"*Falcon!*"

She uttered his name on a muffled scream. Smiling to

himself, he licked, probed, then settled in the cradle of her thighs to savor her fully, tracing the swollen folds with his tongue. He found her secret nubbin erect and swollen beneath its hood and gently sucked it into his mouth.

He pushed her closer and closer to the edge, until her fingers curled into claws and her hips tilted, mutely offering herself to him. He opened her with his fingers, probed her entrance and penetrated her with his tongue.

He savored her soft cries, gloried in her passion as she fractured and broke apart. The moment she quieted, he rose, stripped off his hose and—

There came a knock on the door. "My lady, Robbie is asking for you."

"Becca," Mariah whispered weakly. "I must answer her."

Falcon looked at his pulsing erection and said, "Tell her to return in one hour."

"But Robbie—"

"Can wait."

When Mariah hesitated, Falcon straddled her, positioned his hands on the bed on either side of her, spread his thighs and nudged her entrance with his cock. "Tell her," he whispered urgently.

"Bring Robbie to me in an hour," Mariah instructed the nursemaid. "I'm . . . I cannot entertain him right now."

Falcon's expression was pained as he teased her entrance with his cock.

Then he drove himself in to the hilt.

Chapter Seven

Mariah cried out his name and arched wildly beneath him. She had despaired of ever feeling Falcon inside her again. Though she believed anger was fueling his lust, she didn't care. Naught mattered but finding pleasure with the only man she had ever wanted sexually.

"Aye, call my name," Falcon moaned, driving deeper. "I've never forgotten how my name sounds on your lips when you shatter."

He closed his eyes to better absorb the sensation of her heated sheath yielding and then clamping around his erection, her feminine flesh pulling him deep inside her and squeezing tight. He wanted to plunder, to let his primitive instincts take over, but he did not. He was not now and had never been a selfish lover.

He stilled, heard her panting breath in his ear, felt the thudding beat of her racing heart. He lifted his head and gazed down at her. Her glittering gaze was fixed on him, her lips swollen, slightly parted. He bowed his head, kissed her, moving his cock in and out in slow, measured thrusts while his tongue mimicked the rhythm in her mouth.

He broke off the kiss, saw her eyes close as she whispered, "Please."

"Please what?"

She licked her lips. "Faster, harder, please."

He would have grinned but couldn't; his features were taut with restrained passion. He took a deep breath, locked his hips in place and thrust harder, deeper, faster. He groaned against her mouth. The fire was still there, just as he remembered. His mouth covered hers; her tongue tangled with his, taking the kiss deeper, feasting, savoring.

Adrift on a sea of erotic sensation, caught by the invisible links forged by their previous association, Falcon gave his racing passion full rein. When he heard Mariah cry out and felt her arch beneath him, his restraint suffered a swift surrender. With a feral roar, he erupted, plunging deep, his seed exploding from his body into hers. He was grateful for the stone walls that held the sound of his pleasure inside the chamber.

Mariah felt the wet warmth of his seed surge deep in her belly, briefly aware that he could leave her with another babe. If that happened, the child would be as welcome as Robbie had been, even though she knew that Falcon would leave her, just as he had before. He would forsake her for an heiress, one who would bring him the land he yearned for.

His weight left her as he rolled onto his back. "Falcon—"

He made a slashing motion with his hand. "Nay, do not

say anything. I am deeply ashamed. You were ill and exhausted and I took advantage of you. I've compromised my honor." He rose and began to dress.

The question she needed to ask burned on her tongue. "Why did you make love to me just now?"

He yanked on his hose. "I lost my head. Lust does strange things to a man. It can warp his brain, rob him of logic and steal his honor. It can leave him weak and confused."

He looked away, his voice ripe with self-condemnation. "When I came in here, I merely intended to rebuke you for following me into danger. I had no intention of making love to you." He spun around to face her. "But lust, laced with memories of the past, can turn the best of intentions."

"You remembered how well matched we were as lovers," Mariah guessed.

Falcon's laugh held little warmth. "Aye, that and more. But when all is said and done, your lies still stand between us." His gaze swept over her, cool, assessing. "Tell me, Mariah, did Lord Edmond know what we were doing behind his back?"

"Does it matter?"

"It does to me."

Mariah clamped her lips tightly together.

"Very well, keep your secrets."

Falcon strode to the door and flung it open. He collided with Robbie, who fell on his backside and began to whimper. Falcon swept the boy into his arms and attempted to comfort him.

"There, there, lad, you're not hurt, are you?"

A fat tear rolled down Robbie's cheek as he stared at Falcon with large golden eyes.

"Did you come to see your mama?"

"Aye, I want to see Mama," Robbie replied. Clearly he was entranced by the large man holding him, and a little frightened.

"I'll take you to her, but you have to stop crying."

As he stared at the lad, a jolt of recognition shot through him. But try though he might, he couldn't recall who the child resembled. Perhaps he saw Mariah in him, for the boy had his mother's coloring and blond hair.

Robbie's tears stopped. Falcon wiped them away with his thumb and carried him to his mother. He placed the child on the bed and stepped back, watching as he leapt into his mother's arms.

"Does Robbie stand for Robin or Robert?" Falcon asked.

"Robert. 'Twas my father's name."

"My father's name, too," Falcon said.

Mariah appeared stunned. "Truly?"

"Truly. 'Tis a common enough name."

"Oh, my lady," Becca said from the doorway. "Robbie slipped away from me. I hoped I'd find him here."

"He's fine, Becca. Sir Falcon found him in the corridor and brought him to me. You may leave him with me for a while."

Slanting a shy smile at Falcon, Becca took her leave.

"What are you looking at?" Mariah asked when she noted the way Falcon was staring at Robbie.

Falcon shifted his gaze to Mariah. "The lad resembles you in many ways, but I do not see Lord Edmond in him.

Yet there is a familiarity about him that has naught to do with you."

"Haven't you something better to do than stand here and ask questions?" Robbie's paternity was the last thing Mariah wished to discuss.

"I won't intrude on your privacy," Falcon replied as he prepared to leave.

Robbie, however, had other ideas. Scrambling over his mother, he gazed up at Falcon and said, "You're very tall."

Falcon couldn't help smiling at the rambunctious lad. "Would you like to ride on my shoulders?"

"Robbie, no," Mariah chided. "Sir Falcon must be about his duties."

"I've never seen anyone as tall as Falcon, Mama. I'd like very much to ride on his shoulders."

"Up you go, Robbie," Falcon said, plucking the boy from the bed and placing him on his shoulders. Robbie squealed in delight.

"I believe Robbie is fascinated by the view from your great height," Mariah said. "You may put him down now."

Falcon lowered Robbie onto the bed, ruffled his fair hair and took his leave. He returned to his own chamber, found quill and ink and penned a missive to the king, informing him of Robbie's well-being and Osgood's treachery. Then he found Jamie, his squire, and sent him off to London with an escort of two seasoned knights.

Once that was taken care of, Falcon descended the stairs to the great hall, accepted a mug of ale from a servant and dropped onto a bench before the hearth, soaking up the warmth. The day was raw and damp, a harbinger of fall, and the chill seemed to seep through the stone walls.

Sir John and Sir Dennis joined him. "What was that all about?" John asked. "Why did you send Jamie to London with an escort?"

"Jamie is carrying a missive to the king. The escort is to make sure he reaches Whitehall safely."

"Are we to remain at Mildenhall?" Dennis asked.

"Aye. I explained the reason in my letter to Henry," Falcon informed him. "Once we leave Mildenhall, there's naught to stop Osgood from returning and doing Robbie harm."

The two knights accepted tankards of ale from a servant. "Are you convinced, then, that Robbie is Lord Edmond's son?" John asked.

Falcon stared into his ale. "I am convinced of naught but the rightness of choosing Robbie over Osgood and Walter. I cannot in good conscience leave Mildenhall to a man who would harm a child or force a woman. Lord Edmond was a good man, and 'twas common knowledge that he did not want Osgood to inherit."

They drank in silence for a time, and then John asked, "How long did you stay at Mildenhall while you were incapacitated?"

"Several weeks. Why?"

John and Dennis exchanged knowing looks. "That was five years ago, wasn't it?"

"Aye, more or less."

John cleared his throat. "How close were you and Lady Mariah during your stay? You seem well acquainted. Perhaps—"

"Robbie is but three years old," Falcon said sharply, "conceived well after I left."

"So you do admit to bedding the lady," Dennis said.

"Enough!" Falcon growled. "I admit naught." He drained his mug. "The men are growing soft. Exercises will commence in the training field at dawn tomorrow."

Falcon strode off, intending to saddle his horse and take an invigorating ride before dark. He had a great deal to think about. A quarter hour later, he ordered the portcullis raised and rode away from the castle toward the ridge of low hills rising behind Mildenhall.

Falcon had no idea what had possessed him to make love to Mariah today. Or why he had been so worried about her after he learned she had taken to her bed following her ordeal.

Though they had been brief lovers five years ago, there was naught between them now. They had both known he would leave once his memory returned. He was dismayed by his overwhelming need to make love to Mariah today. She had lied to him and used him, and still he wanted her. It was as if a bond had been forged between them five years ago, a bond he was not certain he welcomed.

Falcon rode to the top of the ridge, then wheeled his horse to stare down at Mildenhall. Its towers rose against a damp sky like sentinels of ancient gods. Lord Edmond had taken good care of his lands; even the village had prospered under his guidance. Despite the surrounding forest and remoteness of the demesne, there was plenty of rich land available to raise crops and graze animals. With Mariah to guide Robbie during his formative years, the land should prosper under the young earl.

Despite that knowledge, Falcon couldn't help wondering about Robbie's father. He understood why Mariah wouldn't trust him with the man's name. Falcon was, after all, the king's emissary, sent to investigate Robbie's legitimacy.

Truth to tell, Falcon was inclined to agree with Osgood about Robbie's illegitimacy. Lord Edmond had been too ill to sire a child.

Until Osgood and Walter had shown their true colors, Falcon had been undecided in regard to the earldom. He no longer harbored doubts. Osgood was undeserving, and Robbie, whether or not he was legitimate, was an innocent in all this. Mariah was the guilty one, if guilt were to be placed. It was clear to Falcon that Mariah had slept with a man other than her husband to get an heir for Mildenhall.

Even more disturbing were his confused feelings for Mariah. Apparently, five years hadn't been long enough for him to forget her. His lust for her was as strong as ever. When he'd learned that Mariah was Edmond's wife during the time of their brief affair, his anger had been stunning, while at the same time her reason for bedding him had fed his male pride. She had wanted him because he was young and virile. But was that the only reason?

What else had she lied to him about?

Robbie . . .

Falcon's own knights had voiced suspicion about his relationship with Mariah during his stay at Mildenhall. Wouldn't Mariah tell him if Robbie was his son? He laughed aloud at that thought. Mariah delivered naught but lies.

When a light rain began to fall, Falcon returned to the keep. He had enjoyed the cool, damp air, but his brain was still muddled regarding Mariah. He had made one decision, however. Naught good could come of making love to Mariah again. The farther he kept away from the countess and her lies, the better.

Whitehall, London

Osgood and Walter were kept cooling their heels in King Henry's reception chamber for two days before they were finally granted an audience.

Henry glowered at Osgood through narrowed lids as his subject bowed and waited for the king to acknowledge him.

"I thought you were at Southwold," Henry groused. "What brings you to London?"

"I am the bearer of sad news, sire," Osgood said, assuming a gloomy expression. "Young Robbie of Mildenhall is dead."

The king half rose from his chair. "Dead, you say? Did you kill him?"

"Majesty, you do me a grave injustice. I am not a monster given to killing children. The lad wandered away from the keep and was carried off by wild animals. That makes me Lord Edmond's sole surviving heir."

"Why did I not hear of the lad's death directly from Mildenhall?"

Osgood shrugged. "They are still grieving, sire. Perhaps no one thought to inform you."

Henry stroked his chin. "Sir Falcon should have notified me immediately. 'Tis not like him to delay news of such import."

"Nevertheless, the boy's death changes everything.

There is no longer a reason to stop me from claiming Edmond's title and lands. Mildenhall comes to me by right of inheritance."

Walter stepped forward. "I would ask a boon, sire."

Henry waved his hand. "Ask away."

"I wish permission to wed Lord Edmond's widow."

"Is the widow willing?"

Walter cast a sidelong glance at his father.

"Lady Mariah has little choice in the matter," Osgood answered for his son. "If she does not agree, she will lose her home. Walter is willing to wed her despite her infidelity to my brother."

"I will sleep on this matter and give you my answer tomorrow."

"Forgive me, Majesty, but what is there to think about? The matter is straightforward. I am Edmond's legal heir."

"You dare much, Sir Osgood," Henry warned. "Off with you now. My chatelain will admit you to my privy chamber tomorrow, after I have sorted through everything you have told me."

Osgood was clearly upset as he and Walter bowed and left the chamber.

"Summon my secretary," Henry ordered after they were gone.

He thrummed his fingertips on the arm of his chair as he waited. He would not take Osgood's word without confirmation from Falcon, but if the young lad was indeed dead, Osgood's claim was valid and had to be honored. As for Walter's wish to wed the widow, he would leave that up to the lady. A widow was usually given more latitude than a young virgin in choosing a mate.

Henry's secretary bustled into the chamber. "You sent for me, sire?"

"Aye, Becker. Has a messenger arrived from Mildenhall?"

Becker nodded. "Aye, sire, a missive from Sir Falcon arrived with his squire this very day. I intended to bring it to your attention following your audience with Sir Osgood."

"You have it with you?"

"Indeed, sire." He removed a rolled parchment from his belt and presented it to the king.

Henry read it quickly, spat out a curse and asked a guard to fetch Falcon's squire. Jamie arrived shortly.

"You are Sir Falcon's squire?" Henry asked.

"Aye, sire. I am Jamie of Dunhurst."

"Very well, Jamie of Dunhurst. I need a few answers from you. When you left Mildenhall, how was Robbie of Mildenhall's health?"

"Hale and hearty, sire. The lad was kidnapped by Sir Osgood but has since been returned safely to Mildenhall."

"Did Sir Osgood bring him home?"

Jamie looked affronted. "Nay, sire. He was rescued by his own mother. I'm sure he meant the boy harm."

"Thank you, Jamie. You may return to Mildenhall after you have eaten and rested. Before you leave, I will have a reply ready for you to carry back to Sir Falcon."

The king was ready for Osgood the following day. A missive was already on its way to Falcon, and now he had but to dole out punishment to Osgood.

Osgood and Walter arrived at the appointed hour. By chance, Lady Rosamond happened to be in the privy chamber with several other ladies and courtiers when they arrived. Since they were not asked to leave, they listened avidly to the conversation between Osgood and Henry.

Osgood wore a look of complete confidence when he strode into the privy chamber. He was convinced that naught stood between him and Mildenhall. All that Edmond possessed would be his, and Walter would have the woman he'd lusted after.

"Come forward, Osgood of Southwold," Henry directed.

Beaming, Osgood approached the throne and bowed. Walter followed on his father's heels.

"So," the king intoned. "You are your brother's sole surviving heir."

"And after me there is Walter," Osgood replied.

"Hmmm. Are you certain young Robbie is dead?" Henry probed.

"As sure as I am standing here, sire."

"After you were dismissed .yesterday, I received a missive from Mildenhall." Osgood stiffened, his eyes sliding away from the king. "It appears the lad you claimed had been killed by wild animals is alive and thriving."

Osgood's face turned pasty white. "Nay, it cannot be! Falcon lies."

"Many untruths have been told, but not by Falcon. The message bearer confirmed the little earl's continued good health."

"The little earl? Sire, surely you cannot mean that. The boy is a bastard. His mother cuckolded my brother."

"If that were true, Falcon would have informed me of his findings to that effect." He sent Osgood a stern look.

"Falcon wrote that you kidnapped the lad and carried him away from the keep in the dead of night."

"The charges are false!" Osgood exclaimed. "Mariah has seduced Falcon to her will. Aye, the witch has taken him to her bed."

"Do you know that for a fact, Sir Osgood?"

Osgood stammered incoherently, gesturing wildly as he searched for an answer.

"'Tis just as I thought, Sir Osgood," the king said. "You are the liar. I know not why you reported the young earl's death when you had no confirmation. Wishful thinking, perhaps?"

For once, Osgood was silent. He must have realized he was treading on dangerous ground.

"I have no doubt that you kidnapped the young earl, and that you planned his death either now or at some point in the future. Because you have fought bravely for England, I am inclined to be lenient this once. Your punishment shall be banishment from London. Return to your manor forthwith and tend to your own hearth and home. You are not to return to London or show your face at court until I deem your exile ended."

"When will that be, sire?" Osgood dared.

"I know not. You will be the first to know when I do decide. Get out!"

A feminine voice rang out. "Sire, might I have a word with you before Sir Osgood leaves?"

"Lady Rosamond, can this not wait?"

"Nay, sire, I beg you to grant me a moment of your time. What I wish to speak to you about concerns Sir Osgood."

The king gave a weary sigh. "Very well, you may approach and say your piece."

Rosamond hurried forward, made her curtsey and said, "What I have to say is private."

"Private, lady? More private than this?"

"Aye, sire, I beg your indulgence."

Henry glanced about the crowded chamber and ordered everyone out but Sir Osgood and Walter.

The chamber cleared quickly.

"What is it that must be said in private, and how does it concern Sir Osgood?" Henry asked curtly. "Keep in mind that I have little patience for frivolous matters."

"Have you found an heiress for Sir Falcon to wed?"

"I have several in mind but lack the time to pursue the matter." He eyed her narrowly. "What are you getting at, Lady Rosamond?"

"I am an heiress and a widow, sire. If you recall, my husband died serving England. I have both wealth and extensive lands that came to me upon my mother's death. Once my father passes on, his title will die with him, for there are no male heirs. If Falcon is looking for a title, he would be the logical choice to become Earl of Norwich once he becomes my husband."

"The prospect of wedding you to Falcon does have merit," Henry agreed. "You were betrothed to Falcon before he lost his memory, were you not?"

"Aye, sire, so our marriage makes perfect sense. When do you expect Falcon to return to London?"

"His missive indicated that he has no plans to return any time soon." He slanted a look at Osgood, who was too far away to hear. "Falcon fears that leaving Mildenhall and the young earl unprotected will invite trouble. He will return once he is certain Osgood no longer presents a danger to the boy and his mother."

"I heard what Sir Osgood said about Falcon and Mariah of Mildenhall becoming . . . close. If I am to become Falcon's wife, I should like to go immediately to Mildenhall and apprise him of our betrothal. Since Sir Osgood is traveling in that direction, perhaps he could escort me to Mildenhall."

The king considered Rosamond's request carefully. "I have no intention of forcing Falcon into a marriage he does not want. He has served me too well for that. But if he agrees to the match, it could prove advantageous for all."

"Does that mean I have your permission to travel to Mildenhall?"

"Aye. Are you sure you wish to travel in Sir Osgood's company?"

"If you charge him with my safety, I'm sure he will be most careful of my person lest he anger you more than he already has."

"You have the right of it, my lady. I will not be lenient if he offends me again."

Henry motioned Osgood forward. "Sir Osgood, Lady Rosamond has need of an escort to Mildenhall. Since it won't be too far out of your way, she has asked to be allowed to travel with you and your party. I promised Falcon an heiress, and Lady Rosamond has suggested herself. Since I have no objection, Lady Rosamond wishes to reach Mildenhall as soon as possible." He sent Osgood a stern look. "See to it that naught happens to her along the way."

"Thank you, sire," Rosamond simpered.

"Give Falcon my best," Henry said, happy to solve two

problems at one time. He waved them off. "Go, then, all of you."

Osgood and Walter bowed themselves out of the chamber. Once in the main reception hall, they turned and headed for the door, anxious to leave before the king changed his mind and levied a stiffer punishment.

"Sir Osgood, you are going too fast!" Rosamond chided. "I cannot keep up with you. Do you plan to leave London immediately?"

"'Tis what Henry wishes."

"My trunk is packed. I have been waiting for the right moment to seek the king's permission to travel to Mildenhall. I will have my trunk placed in a cart and fetch my maid. One of your men can drive the cart for me so that I may ride my palfrey."

"Why do you wish to wed Falcon after I just informed the king of his involvement with Lady Mariah?"

"I was betrothed to Sir Falcon before he lost his memory. When he did not show up for our wedding, Father wed me to Sir Albert. My husband died over a year ago in France; when I learned the king was seeking a wealthy bride for Falcon, I wanted him for myself."

A sly grin spread across Osgood's face. "You want Falcon, do you?"

"Aye, and I think he still wants me despite taking Lady Mariah for a lover." She preened for Osgood's benefit, showing her charms to best advantage. "I can offer Falcon wealth and land and much, much more."

"I would be happy to give you escort, lady. If you can pry Falcon from Mariah's clutches, perhaps she will turn to Walter for solace."

Mildenhall

When Jamie returned from Whitehall with the king's answer to Falcon's missive, Falcon wasn't pleased with Henry's leniency regarding Osgood and his son. With Osgood still on the loose, Falcon could not leave Mildenhall vulnerable to the villain's plotting.

Robbie was a small child, and Mariah hadn't the experience to handle Osgood and Walter should they decide to ignore the king's decree and attack Mildenhall. Sir Martin was loyal, and so were the castle guardsmen, but too few knights remained to defend the keep should Osgood launch an attack.

In his letter, the king had given Falcon permission to remain at Mildenhall for the time being. He decided he would do so.

In order to keep himself occupied and his thoughts from dwelling on Mariah, he began training with his men. He saw Mariah only in passing and at the evening meal, which was fine with him.

During this time, Falcon decided to question the priest and Edmond's personal servant concerning Edmond's ability to sire a child during his extended illness. The priest had been evasive, and so had the servant.

After mulling over the situation, Falcon abandoned his investigation. He saw no point in proving or disproving Robbie's legitimacy, for the lad had become the new earl by default. If Falcon continued this line of questioning, he realized, he would be doing Robbie a grave disservice. As for Mariah, his feelings remained confused. Though she had lied to him, used him to suit her needs, he still wanted her.

Falcon was in the courtyard one misty day when a guard alerted him to visitors approaching the castle. Curious, Falcon walked to the portcullis and peered through the bars. Since casual travelers rarely came this way, he couldn't guess who the visitors might be.

"'Tis Sir Osgood and his party," a guard on the wall walk called down to him.

The party reached the gate. "You are not welcome here," Falcon announced. "I understand the king banished you from London and court."

"Before I left London, the king ordered me to escort your lady to Mildenhall," Osgood replied.

"My lady?" Falcon repeated.

Lady Rosamond detached herself from the main party and rode forward. "Greetings, Sir Falcon," Lady Rosamond said. "I hope you are as pleased to see me as I am to see you."

"Rosamond!" Falcon gasped. "What brings you to Mildenhall?"

"You do, Sir Falcon."

"Behold your betrothed," Osgood crowed.

Osgood's laughter lingered in the air as he wheeled his horse and rode away, leaving Rosamond and the small cart bearing her trunk and maid behind.

Chapter Eight

"God's bones, Rosamond, what do you here?" Falcon asked, a mixture of surprise and annoyance coloring his words. "And why, pray tell, were you traveling with Sir Osgood? The man is a disgrace to knighthood."

"Invite me inside and I will tell you," Rosamond said archly. "'Tis discourteous of you to keep me standing here."

Falcon ordered the gate raised and stepped aside. "Forgive me, I wasn't expecting you."

Rosamond indicated the cart that Osgood had abandoned when he'd left. "Kindly summon someone to help my maid and drive the cart bearing my trunk to the keep."

Falcon issued orders to one of his men, who immediately handed the maid down, climbed into the cart and took up the reins. Then Falcon helped Rosamond dismount and escorted her and her maid to the keep and up the stairs into the hall. A tense silence prevailed as those milling about turned as one to watch the dark beauty stride into the hall on Falcon's arm.

Mariah saw them enter and went utterly still. Though

she did not know the woman's identity, Mariah's instincts told her the haughty beauty meant trouble. Remembering her manners, she approached the lady to wish her welcome.

"I am Lady Mariah, Countess of Mildenhall," she said, summoning a smile she didn't feel. "I bid you welcome."

Rosamond sniffed disdainfully. "I am Lady Rosamond, widow of Sir Albert of Melrose, daughter of the Earl of Norwich."

Mariah stiffened. *Rosamond.* 'Twas a name she knew well. Falcon would be wed to her now had he not lost his memory.

"What brings you to Mildenhall, my lady?" Mariah asked when she noted the size of Rosamond's trunk as it was carried into the hall. "You have traveled some distance out of your way if you are journeying to your father's keep in Norwich."

"My throat is parched and I am exhausted from my journey up from London," Rosamond said, ignoring Mariah's question. "I will be happy to explain my presence once I am made comfortable."

"Forgive my lack of hospitality," Mariah replied. "Falcon, please escort Lady Rosamond to a comfortable chair before the hearth while I take her maid into the kitchen and fetch something for Lady Rosamond to eat and drink."

Osgood's parting words before he had left Rosamond at the gate kept resonating through Falcon's mind. What did they mean? Was Rosamond really here to claim him as her husband? Did she have the king's blessing?

Once Rosamond was made comfortable, Falcon asked, "When did your husband die? I wasn't aware of it."

"Albert died in France nearly a year ago. I'm not surprised you hadn't heard about it, for he died of a fever, not in battle. I've been in mourning and only recently returned to court."

"I'm sorry for your loss," Falcon said. He hesitated a moment, then asked, "What did Osgood mean when he said he was delivering my bride to me?"

Rosamond favored Falcon with a coquettish smile. "Osgood spoke the truth. You wanted me once, Falcon, but unforseen circumstances came between us. Now that I am free to wed again, our match can proceed. I am still a wealthy woman, for my dowry was returned to me after Albert's death, and the lands left to me by my mother are still mine. I have everything you want in a wife."

Mariah returned, followed by a servant carrying a tray laden with food and drink. Rosamond helped herself to ale, cheese and bread. After quenching her thirst, she looked up at Mariah and asked sweetly, "What think you, my lady? Does a match between me and Falcon not make sense? The king seems to think so."

The stricken look on Mariah's face made Falcon want to place a hand over Rosamond's mouth to silence her. But the lady wouldn't be silenced.

"I have wealth and land, everything Falcon desires from a marriage," Rosamond purred. "He wanted me once, and now that I am available again, naught stands in the way of a match between us."

"Why did the king not mention this to me before I left London?" Falcon wanted to know.

"Henry hadn't considered it until I approached him, but I believe he would have gotten around to seeing me as a mate for you sooner or later. He is newly returned to England after a long absence and had more important things on his mind. Everyone knows he's been looking for an heiress for you to wed, so I reminded him that I am available and willing."

Falcon's eyes narrowed. "Are we to wed by the king's order?"

Rosamond hesitated.

"The truth, lady, for I have but to send a message to the king for verification."

Rosamond sighed. "Though he did not order us to wed, he hoped you would find the match appealing."

"So the choice is mine to make," Falcon said.

Rosamond smiled up at him, her eyes promising untold delights. "Aye, but I hope to convince you of the rightness of it. Do you remember how well we dealt with one another when we were betrothed?"

"Aye, I remember. But I also recall how quickly you wed another when I failed to show up for our wedding."

Rosamond shrugged. "'Twas Papa's doing. When the search parties returned without you, we all assumed you were slain by bandits and eaten by wild animals. Sir Albert immediately offered for me. Papa deemed it a good match and saw no reason to wait. I had naught to say about it."

Falcon glanced at Mariah, saw her staring at Rosamond and wondered what she was thinking.

"I will have a chamber prepared for you, Lady Rosamond," Mariah said. "Is your stay to be a lengthy one?"

"That depends on Falcon," Rosamond purred. "If you have a resident priest, we can be wed immediately and leave Mildenhall for London to receive the king's blessing."

Falcon did not answer immediately. He needed time to think before committing himself to Rosamond, even though marriage to the wealthy heiress would gain him everything he had ever desired. He would no longer be a landless knight. It was difficult to forget, however, that she had waited less than a fortnight after his supposed death to wed another.

"I need time to think," Falcon said.

Rosamond voiced her displeasure with Falcon's answer. "What is there to think about? The match is a good one." She turned her glittering gaze on Mariah. "What say you, Lady Mariah? Do you not agree with me? Falcon has made no secret of his desire to wed wealth and acquire land through his bride."

Mariah lifted her eyes to Falcon, eyes shadowed by an emotion Falcon found difficult to read. "Falcon is his own man. He will do as he wishes." She turned away. "Excuse me; I must see to your lady's chamber. Let me know if you require the services of Father Francis."

"Mama! Falcon!" Robbie spied his mother from across the hall, ran toward the group and skidded to a halt before her. Mariah scooped him up and carried him away from Falcon and Rosamond.

"So that's Lady Mariah's bastard," Rosamond said disparagingly.

An unaccountable anger made Falcon turn on Rosamond. "The boy's name is Robbie, and I have yet to prove his birth is anything but legitimate. If you continue to refer to him as a bastard, I shall have to ask you to leave."

"Sir Osgood swears that his brother was too ill and too old to get his wife with child," Rosamond argued.

"Sir Osgood is an immoral man with an evil tongue. Believe naught of what he says."

"If you believe the child to be legitimate, why are you still here? Could it be Lady Mariah who keeps you at Mildenhall? Sir Osgood told me she is your mistress."

Falcon muttered a curse beneath his breath. "What keeps me at Mildenhall is Lady Mariah's need for protection. I do not trust Osgood. Once I leave, there is naught to stop him from riding roughshod over Mildenhall. And the king cannot spare men at this time to come to Mariah's aid. The bulk of his army is protecting England's borders from the Welsh and the Scots."

"Do you deny that Lady Mariah is your mistress?" Rosamond prodded.

"I cannot believe this conversation is taking place, lady. Norwich is but a day's ride from here; perhaps you should remove yourself to your father's keep and await my answer there. I will provide an escort for you."

Rosamond rose to her diminutive height. "Nay, Falcon, I will await your answer here. I am weary; I should like to rest."

Mariah returned just then. "Your chamber is being prepared as we speak, my lady, and your maid awaits you there. Allow me to show you the way."

Falcon watched the women leave, his mind spinning with confusion. Why hadn't he jumped at the chance to wed Rosamond? At one time he had been eager to wed the dark beauty. He still needed a wealthy bride and he still wanted land to call his own. Rosamond could provide both.

Sir John joined Falcon as he contemplated this surprising turn of events.

"You look befuddled, and I don't blame you," John said. "What brings Lady Rosamond to Mildenhall, in the company of Osgood, of all people?"

"Apparently the king is promoting a match between Rosamond and myself. Osgood told Rosamond that Mariah is my mistress, and she decided to come to Mildenhall to lay the proposal before myself."

John choked back a laugh. "It must be nice to be sought after. You could do worse than Lady Rosamond."

"Henry has left the decision of whether or not to wed her to me."

John's eyes widened. "Never say you're thinking of refusing."

Mariah reentered the hall; Falcon followed her with his eyes. "I haven't made up my mind."

John threw up his hands. "What is there to decide?" His gaze followed Falcon's. "Ah, I see. 'Tis Lady Mariah you desire. You are a fool, Falcon. Lady Mariah can bring you naught but trouble. Osgood will never let this matter between them rest."

"What do you suggest, John? That I wed Rosamond and leave Mildenhall unprotected? That I abandon Mariah and her son to Osgood's machinations?"

"Henry will intervene if Osgood continues to harass Lady Mariah."

Falcon shook his head. "You know that is not true. Henry's army is spread too thin to come to the aid of a widow of no importance."

"I wonder," John mused. "You and Lady Mariah have a history together. She saved your life, though you appeared none too grateful when you first arrived at Mildenhall."

"'Tis a long story, John. Mariah lied to me. I did not know the truth until I returned to Mildenhall. Nevertheless, she *did* save my life. My honor will not allow me to leave Mildenhall while the lady needs protection."

"Are you sure that's all there is to it?"

Falcon stiffened. "Your questions are beginning to annoy me. I would be better served if you joined the men on the training field. Your expertise with a broadsword is second to none."

Sending Falcon a wry look, John took his leave.

A few minutes later, Mariah approached him and cleared her throat.

"Your betrothed has been made comfortable," she reported. "Will you be wed here or at Norwich?"

"I have yet to agree to the marriage," Falcon growled, his mood deteriorating from bad to worse.

"According to Lady Rosamond, there *will* be a wedding. She was quite adamant about it."

Falcon chose not to reply.

"You would be a fool not to wed her, Falcon. She was your first choice, and wedding her now is still to your advantage."

Falcon's gaze met hers, held, and then he looked away. "You're right, of course. I am a lucky man. But do not rush me into marriage when my work here is far from done. Once I am certain Osgood has resigned himself to losing Mildenhall, I will leave."

Mariah's mouth dropped open. "You will stay, even though you despise me for lying to you?"

"I do not despise you, Mariah. I loathe what you did, but I don't hate you. All I've ever wanted from you is the truth."

Mariah lowered her head. Falcon would never hear the truth about Robbie from her lips. The truth could cost her Mildenhall and her son. She couldn't take that chance.

"Think you Lady Rosamond will accept your decision to remain at Mildenhall?"

Falcon shrugged. "She can wait at Norwich if she so desires. Wedding plans, if there is to be a wedding, will be deferred until I decide Osgood and his son are no longer a threat to you."

"Lady Rosamond will not like that."

" 'Tis the way things have to be. I will speak to Rosamond and explain the situation."

Mariah wished him luck. Rosamond did not seem to be blessed with patience. She had wed another far too soon after Falcon's supposed death.

Mariah was about to excuse herself when Robbie ran into the hall—he rarely walked when he could run—with his nursemaid trailing behind him. He skidded to a halt before Falcon, raised his arms and said, "I want to ride on your shoulders, Falcon."

"Robbie, nay," Mariah scolded. "Falcon has no time for you."

As if to disprove Mariah's words, Falcon lifted Robbie up and set him on his shoulders. Laughing in delight, Robbie grasped a handful of Falcon's hair to steady himself.

"Go, Falcon, go."

"One turn around the hall and then I have to join my men on the training field," Falcon told the lad.

"You will spoil him," Mariah chided. "He is taking advantage of you."

Falcon sent her a quelling look. "One turn around the

hall can do no harm. I will return him to you directly." Then he took off.

Mariah wrung her hands as she watched Falcon parade around the hall with Robbie on his shoulders. Her son was becoming too fond of Falcon. He was bound to be hurt when Falcon left.

Falcon returned and set Robbie down on his feet. "I will see you at the evening meal," he said as he strode off.

"I like Falcon," Robbie said. "Can I have him for my papa?"

"No, you cannot," a voice from behind Mariah answered.

Mariah spun around. "Lady Rosamond—I thought you were resting."

"Send your bas . . . your son away. We need to talk."

"Go along with Becca, darling. Mama wants to talk to our guest."

"Will Becca take me to watch Falcon train?" Robbie asked.

"I'm sure she will if you ask her."

Robbie skipped off. Mariah reached deep inside herself to summon a smile. "What is it you wish to discuss, my lady?"

"Your relationship with Falcon."

"Our discussion will be a short one then, for there is no relationship," Mariah said evenly.

"Your son seems overly fond of Falcon."

"Robbie is a child; he admires Falcon."

"Do you admire him, too?"

"What are you hinting at, my lady?"

"Sir Osgood claims you are Falcon's mistress."

"Sir Osgood lies. Even the king is aware of his evildoing."

"Still, you kept Falcon at Mildenhall while his brains were addled instead of allowing him to return to London for our wedding."

"Your accusations are false," Mariah corrected. "No one here was aware of Falcon's identity. He could have been a simple peasant, for all we knew. He returned to London the moment he regained his memory. He would have died if my healer had not nursed him back to health."

Rosamond sniffed. "Very well, I will allow you that much. But I give you fair warning. Falcon is mine. Stay away from him. You will no longer make him welcome in your bed."

Anger roared through Mariah, and she clenched her hands to keep from placing them around Rosamond's neck.

"Do you always speak so frankly?"

"Nay, just when another woman is infringing upon my property."

"You are welcome to Falcon," Mariah stated. "He holds me in little regard. Feel free to leave with him whenever you wish." Spinning on her heel, her color high with anger, she strode out the door. She needed a breath of fresh air after her confrontation with Rosamond.

Edwina intercepted Mariah in the courtyard. "Who is that woman?" Edwina asked. "I do not like her."

"Your instincts serve you well, Edwina. The lady is Rosamond of Norwich, Albert of Melrose's widow."

"What does she want here?"

"She has come to wed Falcon."

Edwina snorted. "The woman is daft, Mariah, that wedding will never take place. Falcon will not have her."

Mariah gaped at the healer. "What makes you say that? Rosamond has a great deal to offer Falcon."

"'Tis not enough," Edwina sniffed. "Mark my words, Mariah, Falcon does not want Rosamond."

"But . . ." Before Mariah could voice her question, Edwina hobbled off, cackling to herself.

Mariah shook her head. Though Edwina's ways were strange, she loved the woman dearly. Time would tell if Falcon would have Rosamond.

Falcon returned from the training field well in time to bathe and speak privately to Rosamond before the evening meal. There was a great deal for them to discuss before he made his decision.

A half hour later, Falcon stood outside Rosamond's door. He rapped sharply. The door was opened by Rosamond's maid. Rosamond heard him speaking to the girl and came to the door.

"Falcon, please come in. Have you come to escort me to supper?"

"We need to talk, Rosamond."

Rosamond turned to her maid. "You are dismissed, Leticia. Return to help me prepare for bed." The maid slipped out as Falcon stepped inside the chamber. Rosamond closed the door behind him. "Do you wish to discuss our wedding? Shall it take place at Mildenhall?"

"You take too much for granted, Rosamond," Falcon said. "I am in no position to marry at this time."

Rosamond tossed her dark head, her voice filled with scorn. "It's because of *her*, isn't it?"

"If you are referring to Lady Mariah, then yes, in a way it is because of her. Tell me, Rosamond—do you trust Sir Osgood?"

"I traveled with him, didn't I?"

"Aye, and that surprises me. Osgood does naught unless it serves a purpose. He wants me to leave Mildenhall and is hoping you will lure me away."

"Why do you care? Mildenhall means naught to you. My wealth puts Mariah's widow's portion to shame."

"Mariah hasn't enough men to properly protect Mildenhall. Once my men and I leave, she will become vulnerable to attack. Osgood cares not what the king says. He knows Henry will not bestir himself for so obscure a holding. If Osgood seizes control of Mildenhall and forces a marriage between Walter and Mariah, Henry will not interfere."

Rosamond pressed herself against Falcon, looking up at him from her diminutive height. "Again I ask: Why do you care? You wanted me once, Falcon. I can make you want me again. Do you not remember how sweet our kisses were? I have learned a great deal since those innocent kisses we shared."

Falcon felt her breasts pressing against his chest, heard the promise in her words and wondered why he hesitated. Rosamond was beautiful, passionate and eager to share her body with him. Desire began to build inside him. Wedding Rosamond would be the practical thing to do. He drew Rosamond into his arms and lowered his mouth to hers.

Then, unaccountably, he envisioned Robbie holding his arms out to him, and desire fled. He released Rosamond and stepped away.

"What's wrong?" she demanded. "You were going to kiss me. What stopped you?"

"It isn't the right time," he demurred.

"The time will never be right as long as you remain at Mildenhall. Come home with me. We can be wed in the chapel at Norwich Castle. Papa is ill, Falcon. When he dies, there is no heir for the earldom. The king could very well give it to you."

"We will speak of wedding plans after I leave Mildenhall. Meanwhile, you will continue on to Norwich with an escort I shall provide."

"Nay, I will abide here until you are ready to leave," Rosamond maintained. "I refuse to leave you to that whore and her bastard son."

Falcon grasped her shoulders and gave her an ungentle shake. "I warned you, Rosamond. You are not to speak of Lady Mariah and her son in a disrespectful manner."

Rosamond seized the opportunity Falcon afforded her by wrapping her arms around his neck and pulling his head down for a kiss. Stunned, Falcon felt his lips grow pliant beneath hers, and then he stiffened. It wasn't Rosamond's lips he wanted to kiss, it was—

"Oh, excuse me," came Mariah's voice. "I knocked, but you must not have heard me."

Falcon groaned as he removed Rosamond's arms from around his neck.

"What do you want?" Rosamond snapped.

Mariah was standing in the doorway, her gaze shifting from Falcon to Rosamond. "I was passing by your chamber and wondered if you needed help finding your way to the hall." Her gaze returned to Falcon. "I didn't know you had company."

"Do you always enter a chamber without knocking?" Rosamond said.

"Forgive me. I did knock, and when I received no answer, I thought you were already in the hall and decided to make sure your chamber had been properly prepared. This *is* my home, after all, and I am responsible for the comfort of my guests."

Falcon shook himself free of his languor. "Come, ladies, I will escort you both downstairs."

"You may escort Lady Rosamond," Mariah said. "I want to look in on Robbie first."

Rosamond grasped Falcon's arm, her possessiveness obvious as she sent Mariah a sly smirk. Falcon had no choice but to leave with Rosamond clinging to him. But it was Mariah he watched as she exited Rosamond's chamber.

Confusion swamped Mariah. When Falcon's betrothed had turned up at Mildenhall, she'd felt as if someone had delivered a fatal blow to her. How could Falcon make love to her one day and claim another as his betrothed the next? Following on that thought was another. Falcon, like most men, took what he wanted when he wanted. The promise of Rosamond's wealth would be difficult to give up.

Now that the threat to Robbie's inheritance had been resolved, Mariah decided it would be in her best interests if Falcon and his bride-to-be left Mildenhall. Seeing him with another woman hurt too much, and there was the added risk of Falcon learning that Robbie was his son.

Mariah found Robbie playing contentedly with some toy soldiers Sir Martin had carved for him. Mariah stayed but a few moments, then left the nursery. She closed the door behind her and headed for the stairs; moments later she ran headlong into Falcon. He caught her against him and held her close. In a moment of madness, she melted against him. Then realizing her mistake, she stiffened.

"Why aren't you with Rosamond?" Mariah asked, quickly regaining her senses.

"I excused myself. I wanted a moment alone with you."

"You can release me now."

He held her a moment longer, then dropped his arms. "I wanted you to know that I had naught to do with Rosamond showing up at Mildenhall. It was as much a surprise to me as it was to you."

"So I gathered, but it changes naught. 'Tis obvious the match is a good one. I advise you to leave Mildenhall and pursue the life you've waited for so long."

"I cannot leave yet. I do not trust Osgood. You and Robbie have need of my protection. I told Rosamond as much."

Surprise colored Mariah's words. "You told Rosamond you intended to remain at Mildenhall because we needed your protection? I cannot believe she accepted that."

Falcon shrugged. "I advised her to return to Norwich and await me there, but she refused."

"I'm not surprised. The lady does not like me and fears my influence over you. Little does she know I have no influence over you." Her gaze met Falcon's. "When do you plan to wed?"

"*If*, and I emphasize if, I decide to wed Rosamond, it won't be until I'm certain Osgood will obey the king's order and remain at Southwold."

Stunned, Mariah asked, "You mean you are still undecided about wedding Rosamond? Why do you hesitate? You have no ties to Mildenhall, no reason to offer protection."

"My ties to Mildenhall are longstanding ones. You *did* save my life. If not for you and Edwina, I would have died. Though I cannot fathom why you and Edmond lied to me about your relationship, I still owe a debt of gratitude to Mildenhall. As a man of honor, I cannot leave you and Robbie without protection."

"I release you from your debt," Mariah said. "You have already proven Osgood's charges to be false; naught stands in the way of Robbie's inheritance."

Falcon's eyes narrowed. "Nay, I am not entirely certain Osgood's charges are false. Robbie is the new earl by default. Osgood's evildoing ruined his chances that I would award him this holding." He stepped closer, so close she could feel the heat radiating from his body. "We both know Edmond was incapable of siring a child."

Fear spiraled through Mariah. Would Falcon never give up his search for Robbie's sire? Why was he so determined to seek out the truth when it no longer mattered? What did he suspect?

"Believe what you want, but I know the truth."

"What is the truth, Mariah?" His voice was firm, unforgiving.

Rather than lie, Mariah pressed her lips firmly together, refusing to answer. She had told her household to shave a year off Robbie's age if questioned by Falcon. How much lower could she stoop to keep her secret?

Falcon's fingers dug into her shoulders. "Answer me, Mariah. Who is Robbie's father?"

"Release me! You'll be missed if you don't return to the hall immediately."

Falcon stared at her full, lush lips. He recalled how soft they felt pressed against his, remembered the sweetness of her mouth, and couldn't stop himself from lowering his head and kissing her. The moment his mouth claimed hers, all thoughts of Rosamond and her wealth faded. Naught mattered but the woman in his arms, the woman responding to his kisses, the woman whose body he knew so well.

"What is the meaning of this?"

The strident voice broke them apart. Both turned as one to an irate Rosamond.

"How dare you try to seduce my betrothed!" Rosamond hissed. "Come, Falcon, we shall leave Mildenhall immediately."

"If you leave, it will be without me," Falcon said evenly. "I have not yet agreed to a betrothal between us."

"Oh!" Rosamond cried, angrily stomping her foot. "The whore has bewitched you. She has naught to offer but her body; why do you continue to pursue her?"

Mariah's cheeks flamed; she was embarrassingly aware that Falcon said naught to Rosamond in her defense. She turned and fled.

Chapter Nine

Supper that night was an uncomfortable affair. Rosamond clung to Falcon like a leech throughout the meal while staring daggers at Mariah. Falcon knew Mariah was angry at him and didn't blame her. Things were happening too fast, and making love to Mariah hadn't helped matters. Being with her, inside her, had dredged up memories he had kept buried for five long years.

The one truth he had learned from their coupling was that he still wanted Mariah. His passion for her, despite her lies, had not died. But Mariah was not for him. A woman who would cuckold her husband with Falcon and perhaps others was not the kind of woman he wanted for a wife. Besides that, she would bring naught to the marriage. Little Robbie, when he reached his majority, would inherit Mildenhall and all its assets.

"Falcon, did you not hear me?" Rosamond asked, jerking Falcon from his reverie.

"Forgive me, Rosamond, I have much on my mind. Were you speaking to me?"

"I asked you to escort me to my chamber. I am weary."

Falcon rose, more than happy to end this interminable meal. "Lady Mariah, the meal was delicious," he said to Mariah. "Lady Rosamond is weary and wishes to retire."

Mariah nodded without looking at him. Rosamond swept past Mariah without acknowledging her and, clinging to Falcon's arm, made a grand exit.

They climbed the stairs in silence, but when Falcon would have left Rosamond at her door, she refused to release him. "Come in for a moment, Falcon. I want to know your decision concerning our marriage. If you refuse to wed me, I shall leave and seek a husband elsewhere." She sniffed. "You aren't the only man looking to wed a fortune. I refuse to wait around for your answer when I can do much better than a mere knight."

Though Rosamond's words angered Falcon, he knew she was right. Since it didn't look as if the king was in any hurry to find him a wealthy bride or grant him a title, refusing Rosamond made no sense. John had called him a fool, and he was beginning to think his friend was right. If he didn't accept her proposal, he could lose Rosamond, her lands and quite possibly a title once her father passed on. But if he did accept, it meant he would never see Mariah and Robbie again.

Falcon didn't resist when Rosamond pulled him inside her chamber. She closed the door and leaned against it. "I'm waiting, Falcon. Shall we wed? Or must I seek another husband?"

Caught on the horns of his dilemma, Falcon considered the advantages and disadvantages of marrying Rosamond. In the final analysis, the advantages far outweighed the disadvantages. When images of Robbie and Mariah kept disrupting his thoughts, he firmly closed his mind to them. It served no purpose to dwell on things that interfered with the course he wished his future to follow. His aspirations flew higher than mere knighthood, and marrying Rosamond could help him achieve his goals.

"Very well, Rosamond. I can think of no reason to refuse a match between us. I will wed you in London when I am finished here."

Rosamond frowned. Though she had gotten what she wanted, she wasn't pleased with Falcon's answer. She knew intuitively that remaining at Mildenhall presented a danger to Falcon. He was far too fond of Edmond's widow and her son for her liking.

"If you insist on remaining at Mildenhall to protect Lady Mariah, we shall speak our vows here," she insisted. She pushed herself away from the door and pressed her lush body against Falcon. "I cannot wait for you to be mine. Though I mourned Albert's death, I cannot say I am sorry now, for you and I will finally be together, just as we were meant to be."

"I do not wish to speak our vows at Mildenhall," Falcon demurred. "London is a far better choice, for there the king could attend the ceremony."

When Rosamond realized she wasn't going to sway Falcon, she sought another way to turn him away from Mariah's influence. "Make love to me, Falcon," she purred. "We are betrothed; there is no shame in bedding your future wife. I am willing to wait for a priest to join us, but I see no reason why we cannot join our bodies tonight in celebration of our betrothal."

Falcon searched for but could find no reason to refuse. Bedding Rosamond would be no chore. The woman was beautiful, her body enticing. Falcon had always taken

GET UP TO 4 FREE BOOKS!

You can have the best romance delivered to your door for less than what you'd pay in a bookstore or online. Sign up for one of our book clubs today, and we'll send you **FREE* BOOKS** just for trying it out...**with no obligation to buy, ever!**

HISTORICAL ROMANCE BOOK CLUB

Travel from the Scottish Highlands to the American West, the decadent ballrooms of Regency England to Viking ships. Your shipments will include authors such as CONNIE MASON, SANDRA HILL, CASSIE EDWARDS, JENNIFER ASHLEY, LEIGH GREENWOOD, and many, many more.

LOVE SPELL BOOK CLUB

Bring a little magic into your life with the romances of Love Spell—fun contemporaries, paranormals, time-travels, futuristics, and more. Your shipments will include authors such as LYNSAY SANDS, CJ BARRY, COLLEEN THOMPSON, NINA BANGS, MARJORIE LIU and more.

As a book club member you also receive the following special benefits:

- **30% OFF all orders through our website & telecenter!**
- **Exclusive access to special discounts!**
- **Convenient home delivery and 10 day examination period to return any books you don't want to keep.**

There is no minimum number of books to buy, and you may cancel membership at any time. See back to sign up!

*Please include $2.00 for shipping and handling.

YES! ☐

Sign me up for the **Historical Romance Book Club** and send my TWO FREE BOOKS! If I choose to stay in the club, I will pay only $8.50* each month, a savings of $5.48!

YES! ☐

Sign me up for the **Love Spell Book Club** and send my TWO FREE BOOKS! If I choose to stay in the club, I will pay only $8.50* each month, a savings of $5.48!

NAME: _____

ADDRESS: _____

_____

TELEPHONE: _____

E-MAIL: _____

☐ **I WANT TO PAY BY CREDIT CARD.**

☐ VISA   ☐ MasterCard   ☐ DISCOVER

ACCOUNT #: _____

EXPIRATION DATE: _____

SIGNATURE: _____

Send this card along with $2.00 shipping & handling for each club you wish to join, to:

Romance Book Clubs
20 Academy Street
Norwalk, CT 06850-4032

Or fax (must include credit card information!) to: 610.995.9274.
You can also sign up online at www.dorchesterpub.com.

*Plus $2.00 for shipping. Offer open to residents of the U.S. and Canada only.
Canadian residents please call 1.800.481.9191 for pricing information.

If under 18, a parent or guardian must sign. Terms, prices and conditions subject to change. Subscription subject to acceptance. Dorchester Publishing reserves the right to reject any order or cancel any subscription.

JOIN NOW!

great pride in his ability to please a woman, and Rosamond would be no exception.

"Are you sure this is what you want?" he asked.

Stretching on her toes, she pressed her lips to his. "Very sure, Falcon. I've dreamed of this day ever since you turned up alive after I wed Albert. From the moment I became a widow, I've waited for the right moment to approach the king about a match between us. I want us to make love. Now. This very minute."

Rosamond unbuttoned her bodice, shrugged her shoulders and let the material fall to her waist. She did the same with her shift, baring her breasts to Falcon. Falcon stared at them. They were firm and pert, but they did naught to arouse him.

He did what was expected of him, however. Scooping Rosamond into his arms, he carried her to the bed, praying that his body wouldn't fail him. But to judge from his flaccid cock, it was going to take time to work up desire for Rosamond.

Falcon began unbuttoning his doublet while Rosamond slid out of her gown. She had just reached for the hem of her shift when Leticia walked into the chamber.

"Oh, my lady, forgive me. I . . . I didn't realize—"

"Get out of here!" Rosamond shrieked.

Leticia turned to flee. "Nay, stay," Falcon said. She hesitated at the door. Falcon turned to Rosamond, an apology on his lips. "Another time, Rosamond," he whispered.

So saying, he turned, brushed past Leticia and quit the chamber. Behind him he could hear Rosamond screaming at her poor maid. Was this an example of Rosamond's temper when she didn't get her way? Truth be told, Falcon was glad of the reprieve. Vaguely he wondered if he'd be in the mood to make love to Rosamond when the time came, then pushed that thought from his mind.

Falcon ran into Mariah in the corridor. "Falcon—I thought you had retired."

"Nay, not yet. May I have a word with you in private?"

"What more is there to say?" she asked.

"Not here. Let's go to your chamber, where we can speak in private. I want you to be the first to know."

"Know what?"

"Mariah, please, the corridor is not private enough." Grasping her arm, he pulled her along with him to his chamber.

Once inside, Mariah rounded on him. "What is this all about?"

"I've come to a decision tonight, and I wanted you to be the first to know."

Mariah sank into the nearest chair, lifting her face to Falcon. "You've decided to wed Rosamond," she said before he could speak. "'Tis the logical thing for a man in your position to do. Will you wed at Mildenhall?"

Falcon began to pace. "Nay, the ceremony will take place in London, but not until my duty here is done."

Mariah looked away. "I'd like you to leave as soon as possible. Robbie is becoming too fond of you."

"I vowed to protect Mildenhall from Osgood. I will wait a fortnight. If he causes no trouble during that time, I will leave."

"To whom did you make that vow?" Mariah challenged.

"Myself. I am not without honor, Mariah. You might think otherwise, but 'tis the truth. I never would have made love to you that first time had I known you were Edmond's wife. I owe Edmond for sinning against him. Protecting his home and legacy will assuage my guilt."

"What about your anger?" Mariah asked. "Will keeping your vow free you from your anger?"

Falcon stood before her, more uncertain than ever of his decision to wed Rosamond. His mind told him the marriage was precisely what he desired, while his heart remained unconvinced. Rosamond did not move him emotionally. Falcon had no idea why that should be important in a marriage when most people wed for money and position. Marriages were made for reasons that did not include emotional attachments. Falcon did not require romantic love in a marriage.

Nor was lust necessary in a marriage. He would do his duty by Rosamond; he'd never had any lack of virility, but he hoped she wouldn't demand his love. She had lost the right to be loved by him when she'd wed another so soon after his alleged death. She might claim her marriage to Sir Albert had been her father's doing, but he felt sure she would have been granted time to mourn if she'd really wanted it.

Falcon glanced at Mariah and knew she was waiting for an answer to her question. "I do not know. I cannot describe the rage I felt when I learned you and Edmond were husband and wife instead of father and daughter."

Mariah gazed up at him. "I never meant to hurt you, Falcon. I cannot explain my reason for lying to you; I hope one day you will forgive me."

Falcon reached out to her. He touched her lightly on the shoulder and knew immediately that he was in deep trouble. The breath left him in a rush as heat radiated up his arm. Her indrawn breath told him she had felt the same jolt he had. Groaning, he raised her to her feet and drew her fully into his arms, burying his face against her hair, breathing in the sweet scent of lilac.

"You smell good," he whispered against her ear.

"This is wrong," Mariah warned breathlessly. "You just became betrothed to another woman."

He pulled away slightly, so he could look at her. Candlelight deepened the mystery of her eyes and warmed the curve of her jaw. He let his gaze travel the graceful length of her throat to where her breasts rose and fell beneath her gown. He could hear the soft sound of her breathing. He grew immediately hard, something he had failed to do with Rosamond.

"Do you want me to leave?"

Silence.

"Mariah, did you hear me? Do you want me to leave?"

"It would be best for both of us if you did. What you're contemplating isn't fair to your bride-to-be."

"What we did five years ago wasn't fair to your husband, but that didn't seem to bother you."

Anger stiffened her shoulders, until she realized he was right. She lifted her face to him, intending to tell him to leave, but somehow the words never left her lips. Even if she had to confess her sin to Father Francis tomorrow, she wanted one last time with Falcon. One last good-bye before she lost him to Rosamond. The priest would probably keep her on her knees for days, but it would be worth it.

Falcon took advantage of her hesitation. The chamber throbbed with silence as he lowered his head and claimed her mouth. His tongue probed her lips. The fire between them sprang to life as she opened her mouth to him, meeting his tongue with a sliding motion of her own. They clung together, passion exploding between them as his kiss grew demanding, igniting a response inside her that could not be denied.

The fire blazed out of control as his arms circled her waist, drawing her closer. He kissed her again, feeling inexplicable relief at having her in his arms, knowing she wanted him as desperately as he wanted her.

And she truly did want him. He felt it in her response, tasted it on her tongue as she stretched against him, pressing close. Her hunger was nearly as fierce as his as her lips demanded more and more.

Winding his arms beneath her bottom, he lifted her against him and carried her to the bed. His arms loosened and she slid down his body to her feet. Then he began to undress her, slowly, oh so slowly, piece by piece, adoring her flesh with his lips as he stripped her naked.

"Now you," she whispered, pulling on his doublet.

His golden eyes never left her as he ripped off his clothing and tossed it aside. Once they were both naked, he tumbled them onto the bed, rolling to trap her beneath him, ravaging her mouth with his. When he broke off the kiss, she pushed him onto his back and leaned over him. Her head lowered. Her hair brushed the skin of his thighs. He flinched, uncertain what she intended and praying she wouldn't stop.

His cock rose high and hard, throbbing, begging for her touch. She didn't disappoint him. Her fingers skimmed the underside of his rigid sex. He jerked; caught his breath.

She closed her hand around his erection. "Mariah," he gasped. "You're killing me."

Mariah raised her head and gazed at him. A tantalizing smile curved her lips. "Don't stop me, Falcon, I want to do this. Once you leave, you will have Rosamond while I will have no one."

Lowering her head, she kissed the tip of his cock, plying him with the wet lash of her tongue, a wanton, erotic caress that drove him wild. Her tongue swirling, she lapped and sucked and tasted as shudders shook his body. She traced the head with her lips, licked around and down the long shaft. His entire body went rigid; his fists clenched the sheets as he bowed upward.

Falcon couldn't have denied her even if he'd wanted to. The muscles of his belly clenched; he was naught but a helpless captive to her seductive wiles. He clung to sanity, his breathing increasingly frantic. Equal parts of agony and ecstasy swamped his senses; he feared he would go mad if she didn't stop.

His hands slid into the tangled mass of her hair. "Stop, Mariah, for I can stand no more!"

He caught her, rolled, and brought her beneath him.

The weight of Falcon's hand slid over Mariah's breasts, over her belly, leaving languid heat in its wake. His fingers slipped between her thighs as he kissed her ear, her throat, her breasts, laving her nipples with his tongue, suckling them. Then he traced a burning path of kisses to her navel, finally easing between her thighs.

Lifting her bottom, he lowered his head and kissed her there, between her legs. Heat shimmered though her veins as his tongue sought out her sensitive flesh, delving deep, then laving the tender folds. She heard herself moan as desire built to a blinding crescendo. She was fully aware that this would be their last time together. Heat raged within her, growing hotter and greater than she had ever imagined possible. Nearly insensate with pleasure, she caught his hair in her hands and begged for release. His tongue darted inside her.

Mariah exploded; she feared she would be reduced to a burning cinder as she climaxed violently. Her taut body was still hot and explosive with need as he withdrew his mouth and thrust his turgid staff deep into her quivering center. She arched against him, her fingers digging into the muscles of his shoulders, her breath ragged. His eyes held hers, smoldering, intense. He drove into her harder, faster; she met him stroke for stroke, writhing, straining.

His mouth was on her neck, licking away a trickle of sweat he found there. He loomed over her, the muscles bunching on his arms as he filled her, expanding her, until tiny shudders wracked her body.

Pleasure renewed itself and washed over her in sweeping waves. She cried out. He captured her mouth, their cries mingling as he drove into her one more time, his body shuddering with the force of his climax. Her body was still shivering deliciously when he collapsed beside her.

Mariah drifted to sleep, utterly spent, utterly sated. She had no idea how long she slept, but when she awakened, the chamber was dark and Falcon was gone.

Falcon stared out the window into the dark night. He was a troubled man. Making love to Mariah had been a mistake. He knew he should leave Mildenhall. Leave now, and to hell with honor. He turned away from the window and began to pace. Mariah was a sickness inside him. The only way to cure that kind of sickness was to cut it out. Out of his life and out of his mind and heart.

Rosamond was the woman he was going to wed; he owed her his fidelity. Why, then, couldn't he leave Mariah alone? He didn't love Rosamond, but then he didn't love Mariah either, did he? He wanted Mariah in his bed, yet Rosamond left him cold. Never had he been so conflicted. Though he had a rational reason for wedding Rosamond, he had no idea why he desired Mariah sexually.

He stopped before the fireplace, bracing his hands on the mantel and staring down into the flames. He'd lost his mind, and with it his judgment. He was so completely mired in thoughts of Mariah that he could no longer think clearly.

And yet, leaving wasn't the answer. He sensed there was something here he needed to know, something Mariah was keeping from him. Had he succumbed to Rosamond's urging to wed her too quickly, without considering alternatives? He hated this dilemma. Hated the way Mariah made him feel. Hated how his heart melted when Robbie lifted his arms up to him.

Wearied by his thoughts and having come to no clear conclusion, Falcon undressed and lay in bed a long time before finally falling asleep.

A surprise greeted Falcon the following morning and another that same evening, neither of them welcome. The first occurred at breakfast, when Rosamond publicly announced their betrothal and intention to marry soon in London. Falcon would have preferred to delay the announcement, but Rosamond would not be denied.

The next surprise arrived that evening, when Falcon entered the hall for the evening meal. Osgood appeared at the gate, asking the gateman permission to enter. He was accompanied by his son, two women and several mercenaries.

"I've brought my wife and daughter to visit Lady Mariah," Osgood said. "Please inform your mistress of our presence."

Falcon received the news with mixed feelings. He decided to defer to Mariah's judgment in this and told her so.

"Why is Sir Osgood kept waiting at the gate?" Rosamond asked. "Is he not Lady Mariah's brother-in-law?"

"Why do you champion the man, Rosamond, when you know he does naught without an evil purpose?" Falcon asked.

"He has been naught but good to me," Rosamond shot back. "You and Mariah misjudge the man."

"Even the king is aware of his machinations," Falcon replied, holding on to his temper by a thread. "He kidnapped Robbie in order to force Mariah to his will."

She sent Mariah a sidelong glance. "Mariah could do worse than marrying Walter."

"Do you really think so?" Falcon mocked.

He turned his attention to Mariah. "'Tis up to you, Mariah. Shall you allow Osgood and his party inside the keep?"

Mariah searched his face. "What do you think?"

"How badly do you wish to see Osgood's wife and daughter?"

"They are both decent women, existing as best they can under Osgood's heavy hand. I would not withhold my hospitality, for I have not seen them since they attended my marriage to Edmond."

"You must know that Osgood has his own reasons for bringing them."

"Aye, I know it well, but I cannot deny Martha and Elizabeth."

"Of course you can't," Rosamond huffed. "They are relatives; you must open your home to them."

"The decision belongs to Lady Mariah, Rosamond," Falcon reminded her.

Mariah summoned the captain of the guard with a wave of her hand. "Sir Maynard, tell the gateman to raise the portcullis to Sir Osgood and his party."

Falcon wondered where Osgood's visit would lead. To no good, he supposed, but he would not gainsay Mariah.

A short time later, Osgood paraded into the hall ahead of his party. He halted abruptly when he saw Falcon, and then seemed to regain his composure. His smile did not reach his eyes as he greeted Mariah. "My lady, thank you for welcoming us." He turned to Rosamond. "Lady Rosamond."

"Sir Osgood," Rosamond simpered.

"Sir Falcon," Osgood said with false heartiness. "I assumed you were in London by now. What keeps you at Mildenhall?"

"I have my reasons for remaining," Falcon said cryptically. "More importantly, what brings *you* to Mildenhall?"

"My wife and daughter expressed the desire to visit Mariah," Osgood said smoothly. "Since they cannot be expected to travel alone, it would be remiss of me if I did not provide escort." He glanced behind him. "Martha, Elizabeth, come greet Mariah."

The two women approached Mariah. Both were slim and of medium height. Martha, Osgood's wife, had sad eyes and graying hair. Elizabeth, a woman around Mariah's age, appeared too blond and pretty to belong to Osgood. Falcon had but to look into her blue eyes to glimpse the fear her father inspired in her.

"Welcome to Mildenhall," Mariah said, smiling at the women. "This is Sir Falcon and his . . . betrothed, Lady Rosamond."

The ladies smiled shyly at Falcon and Rosamond. "'Tis good of you to welcome us, Mariah," Martha replied, sending a fearful look at her husband.

"You must be tired and hungry. Come, sit down and sup with us."

The women followed Mariah to the head table, where servants scrambled to add extra chairs for the guests. Once the women were seated, Walter sidled up to Mariah.

"'Tis good to see you again, my lady. I have missed your sweet smile."

Mariah stared at him. "Leave off, Walter. 'Tis not my sweet smile you crave. We both know you want to steal Robbie's birthright."

"You wound me, lady," Walter replied, placing his hand over his heart. "I still want you for my wife."

"I don't want you for my husband," Mariah sniffed. She glanced at Falcon, signaling him with her eyes. He came to her aid immediately.

"Your place is beside your father at the end of the table," Falcon told Walter.

Walter sent him a dark look and huffed off to join his father.

"Thank you," Mariah said.

"What did he want?"

Mariah shrugged. "'Tis not important." Repeating

Walter's words would only delay Falcon's leaving. She had lost her heart to Falcon five years ago and was in serious danger of doing so again. Last night had been her final good-bye to the man who continued to haunt her dreams.

"Mariah . . . about last night—"

" 'Tis already forgotten. Go to your betrothed, Falcon. I wish to visit with Martha and Elizabeth."

Mariah turned to Martha, who had been trying not to listen to the conversation. "Martha, 'tis years since you've visited Mildenhall. Why did you and Elizabeth not come to visit me while Edmond was alive?"

Martha glanced at Osgood before answering. "Traveling is . . . difficult. Osgood rarely allows us to leave Southwold."

Elizabeth gave a snort of disgust. "Tell her the truth, Mama. Tell Lady Mariah that Father keeps us virtual prisoners in our own home. He won't let me marry until he finds someone willing to pay the outrageous sum he asks for my hand."

Martha leaned over Mariah to touch her daughter's arm. "Hush, Elizabeth. Don't let your father hear you complaining. We are here now, though only Osgood knows why, so why not make the most of our visit before he orders us home."

"You and Elizabeth are welcome to stay at Mildenhall as long as you like, Martha," Mariah offered. "Unfortunately, my invitation does not extend to your husband, and I'm sure you know why."

"We understand," Elizabeth sighed. "It would be wonderful, though, to be out from under Father's thumb for a while. Since the king has banished Father and Walter from

London, they have been difficult to live with. Mama and I are happiest when they are in London or off fighting."

The meal progressed. At length, Martha pushed her plate back, glanced once again at Osgood and whispered, "Walter intends to wed you."

Mariah stiffened. "Then he will be disappointed. I do not like your son."

Martha winced. "Walter was a good boy until Osgood took him away. Once I lost influence over him, he turned into someone I no longer know. I am sorry that he has hurt you, Mariah."

" 'Tis not your fault, Martha. Do you know why Osgood brought you here?"

"Nay. I would tell you if I did. I do not understand why my husband does any of the things he does. He is a greedy man."

"Mariah," Osgood called from the end of the table. "It grows late, too late to return to Southwold tonight. May we impose on your hospitality?"

"Your wife and daughter are welcome in my home, but since the keep is already filled to capacity, you and your men will have to camp beyond the walls in the outer bailey. Mildenhall will provide whatever you need in the way of tents and blankets. Take your requests to my steward."

Mariah could tell by the look on Osgood's face that he did not appreciate the arrangements, but there was naught he could do about them. Mariah spoke to Sir Martin, who was hovering nearby.

"Please show Martha and Elizabeth to their chamber, Sir Martin."

Martha touched her hand. "You are kind, Mariah, but I always knew that."

Mariah rose and excused herself. Tonight she intended to sleep in the nursery. With Osgood nearby, she trusted no one with her son but herself. She paused briefly to issue orders to Sir Maynard concerning Osgood's sleeping arrangements. She would leave naught to chance.

Falcon waited until Mariah was gone before rising to make his own arrangements concerning Osgood's party. The moment Falcon quit the hall, Osgood joined Rosamond.

"So, my lady, when is the wedding to be?"

"Soon. We will be wed in London."

"I assumed you and Falcon would be long gone by now. Apparently, Lady Mariah has a stronger hold over Falcon than either of us imagined."

"Falcon has a strong sense of duty and honor. He believes he must stay to protect Lady Mariah from the likes of you."

Osgood threw back his head and laughed. "I wish the lady no harm. I merely want to wed her to Walter. Mayhap we can form an alliance."

Rosamond sent him an interested look. "An alliance? Kindly explain what you mean."

"'Tis simple. You want Falcon and Walter wants Mariah. Once Walter gets a son from Mariah, something unforeseen will happen to her bastard. I will claim Mildenhall and the earldom and everyone will get what they desire. But naught will go as we wish unless Falcon is out of the picture. Take him away from here as quickly as possible, before you lose him to Mariah."

Rosamond nodded. "I shall do my very best, Sir Osgood. Falcon cannot afford to deny me."

Chapter Ten

Falcon escorted Osgood, Walter and his mercenaries into the outer bailey, where tents had been set up for them. Only when the portcullis was lowered, cutting off Osgood from the keep, did Falcon feel that the occupants of Mildenhall were safe from Osgood's machinations, whatever they might be.

Knowing that Osgood was up to no good, Falcon posted extra guards around the perimeter of the keep. As an added precaution, he intended to spend the night at Robbie's bedside, for the lad was all that stood in Osgood's way of inheriting Edmond's title and estate.

The nursery was dark when Falcon entered. As he neared the bed, he tripped over something on the floor. He started to fall, steadied himself, and stepped back, startled, when the figure let out a muffled cry and rose up on its knees. Light entering the chamber from the hallway wall sconce revealed a disheveled Mariah, something Falcon should have anticipated.

"What are you doing here?" Mariah hissed.

"The same thing you are, I suspect—trying to protect

Robbie. You trust Osgood and his family no more than I do. Where are the women?"

"In the other wing. This wing is fully occupied. But don't worry; I'm not leaving Robbie's side tonight. Think you Osgood will depart tomorrow?"

"I know not what's in that man's mind. We must remain vigilant as long as he's here. Are you sure you'll be all right? I can stay if you'd like."

"That won't be necessary. There is no way Osgood can get into the keep without being seen. And I trust Martha and Elizabeth." "Mildenhall would be difficult to defend," Falcon mused. "The walls can easily be scaled."

"Stronger fortifications were never needed. We are too remote and unimportant to warrant more protection than we have now. Mildenhall has no enemies. Until Osgood, that is. But I doubt Osgood plans a siege. He fears the king's wrath."

Though reluctant to leave, Falcon could find no excuse to remain in Robbie's chamber. In fact, if Osgood left Mildenhall without making trouble, Falcon felt it would be safe to return to London. After making love to Mariah last night, he couldn't remain here. He had promised himself to Rosamond, and he had already dishonored his commitment. If he stayed, he knew he would dishonor it again and again. Mariah's hold on him had to be broken.

"Good night, Mariah."

"Good night, Falcon. Sleep well."

Ha! Falcon thought; as if he could sleep with his mind pulled in two directions. He returned to his chamber, dragged a chair to the window overlooking the portcullis and kept watch until streaks of mauve and orange chased away the night. Stretching, Falcon left the window and prepared for the new day, hoping that no more surprises would be forthcoming.

When Falcon arrived in the hall a short time later, men were beginning to bestir themselves. John was already up and waiting for him.

"Will Osgood and his party leave today?" John asked.

"Your guess is as good as mine. I find it difficult to believe he came at the behest of his wife and daughter. 'Tis easy to see they mean naught to him."

John cleared his throat. "Is Elizabeth spoken for?"

"I doubt it. Osgood is asking a steep price for her hand."

"She's a comely maiden," John mused.

"But not for you," Falcon warned.

"Why not? I'm highborn and come from wealth. What if I'm willing to pay the price?"

"Forget her. Heed my words, John, for I love you well. You do not want Osgood as your father by marriage. 'Tis time to raise the portcullis and let Osgood and his men inside the keep to break their fast."

Falcon sat down at the table and accepted a mug of ale from a servant. Mariah joined him a few minutes later.

"Did you get any sleep?" Falcon asked.

"Enough. Will you open the gate to Osgood and his men?"

"I've already ordered the portcullis raised and expect them to arrive momentarily." He paused, then said, "Mariah, if Osgood leaves today, then so shall I. You have loyal men to protect you and Robbie. If I don't go now, I may never leave."

"What . . . what do you mean by that?"

"Mariah, you must know that I—"

"Good morning, Falcon. I rose early in case today is the day we leave for London. You saw for yourself that Sir Osgood means no harm to Lady Mariah. There is no reason to linger here when our wedding awaits us in London. Leticia is packing my trunk as we speak. I can be ready to leave within the hour."

Falcon stood. "Whether or not we leave today depends upon Osgood," Falcon replied. "I intend to send a messenger ahead to inform your father of our impending marriage. He is in London, is he not?"

Rosamond shrugged. "Father was ill when last I saw him in London. I doubt he has the strength to return to Norwich. It matters not if he attends our wedding. I am a widow, capable of making my own decisions. I insist that we leave today. Unless," she said, casting a sly glance at Mariah, "you have a reason for remaining that I am not aware of."

Mariah and Falcon exchanged speaking glances. "There is no reason to remain, Rosamond. You are right, of course. If Osgood leaves today, we shall depart immediately afterward."

Mariah looked away as Rosamond threw herself into Falcon's arms. "Thank you, Falcon, thank you! I cannot wait until we are wed."

Osgood strode into the hall, saw Rosamond and Falcon in an intimate embrace and smiled. When he reached them, he slapped Falcon on the back. " 'Tis heartening to see a young couple in love." He glanced at Mariah. "Are my wife and daughter up yet?"

"Would you like me to check?" Mariah asked.

"Aye, if you please."

Mariah left, and Falcon departed immediately afterward. Rosamond clutched Osgood's arm, urging him to sit down. "You must leave today," Rosamond hissed. "Falcon has promised to take me to London as soon as you and your party depart. Once we leave, you can do as you like with Mariah and Mildenhall."

Osgood sent Rosamond a mocking smile. "You sound as if you hold little regard for the countess."

"Indeed I do not," Rosamond admitted. "Falcon cannot fool me. I know he has bedded Mariah since my arrival, probably more than once. I need to get him away from here, but he won't leave until you do."

Osgood stroked his chin. "I confess I was annoyed to find Falcon still here when I arrived. I brought the women along to gain entrance to the keep, and my ploy worked. But I don't know if I can use that excuse in the future."

"If you remain, so will Falcon. Neither of us wants that. I'm sure you are smart enough to find another way to gain entrance to Mildenhall."

"Without Falcon's protection, Mildenhall will fall to me like a ripe plum. Once I gain control of Mariah's brat, she will agree to anything to save him. Even wedding Walter. Once the deed is done, the king won't interfere. After a year or two, the brat will sicken and die. By then Mariah will have borne Walter a son or two."

"As I said, I do not care what you do once Falcon and I leave. So will you do it? Will you leave today?"

Mariah returned with Martha and Elizabeth in tow. "You wished to see us, Father?" Elizabeth asked.

"Aye, daughter. We will take our leave after you and your mother break your fast."

Dismayed, Martha asked, "So soon? We've barely had time to visit with Lady Mariah."

Osgood sent Martha a fulminating look. "Do not argue with me, woman! We leave today and that's final."

"I'll see that food is brought out immediately and order bread, meat and cheese packed for your journey home," Mariah offered.

Looking sad and resigned, Martha said, "That is kind of you, Mariah." Elizabeth appeared ready to cry.

Sir John lurked nearby, listening to the conversation. He must have heard enough, for he stalked off, his face set with determination. Moments later, he found Falcon in the courtyard.

"Osgood and his party plan to leave after they break their fast," John revealed.

Falcon nodded. "Tell the men to prepare for our own departure. If Osgood meant harm to Mariah and Robbie, he would not leave Mildenhall. Apparently, he fears the king, and that's as it should be."

John hurried off to do Falcon's bidding while Falcon returned to the hall. After he had passed the word around, John found Jamie, Falcon's squire, in the stable and told him to pack Falcon's belongings for the journey to London. He was rounding a corner when he saw Elizabeth sitting on a bench beneath a tree.

"Mistress Elizabeth, is aught amiss?"

Elizabeth lifted her face to John; he could see that she had been crying.

"You're crying! What is it? Has someone hurt you?"

Elizabeth shook her head. "Forgive me, sir, I thought I was alone."

"I am Sir John; we met briefly when you arrived. I was hoping for a chance to speak with you in private, Mistress Elizabeth. Will you tell me what is wrong?"

Elizabeth raised brimming eyes to him. John thought her the most beautiful woman he'd ever seen.

"'Tis naught. I'm being foolish."

John touched her shoulder. "Nay, you do not strike me as a foolish woman. Something or someone is making you unhappy."

"You are very perceptive, Sir John. I'm unhappy because I cannot bear to return to Southwold with Father and Walter. I know not how Mother stands Father's brutality. He's been even worse since the king banished him from London. Lady Mariah is so kind. I wish I could stay with her. But then Mother would be alone and vulnerable to Father's foul moods."

John couldn't help himself. He sat down beside her, reached out and brought Elizabeth into his embrace, gently stroking her shiny golden hair. She didn't resist. As if encouraged by his comforting, she began to weep anew.

"I hate him," she sobbed. "He won't let me wed. There's no way I can escape him. Mama and I are happiest when he is in France with the king or in London."

"Is there someone you wish to wed?" John asked, holding his breath as he waited anxiously for her answer.

"Nay. I know few men. Those who offered for me were discouraged by Father when they couldn't pay the price he asked. I think Father enjoys keeping me under his thumb."

John drew back so he could gaze into her startling blue eyes. "I would wed you, Elizabeth. I would pay the price and take care of your mother."

"You? But you hardly know me."

"Some brides don't meet their husbands until the day they are wed. If you feel as I do, I will speak to Sir Osgood before he departs."

Elizabeth gave him a shy smile. "I would not protest a match between us, for you appear to be a good man. But Father will not allow it. He hates Sir Falcon, and you are his friend."

"Let me worry about that. Osgood is a greedy man, and I am a rich one. My father has accumulated a great deal of wealth, and I am his only son. Just say you will wed me."

"I will wed you, Sir John; I pray that Father will let me go."

John felt like jumping up and down and yelling. He had been taken by Elizabeth since he'd first seen her. Once he'd decided he wanted Elizabeth, he was prepared to pursue her, however long it took.

He drew her close and kissed her, very gently upon the lips so as not to frighten her. When he released her, her eyes were glowing like shimmering stars.

"Return to the keep, sweet one. I'll find your father and lay my request for your hand before him. But first I must speak to Falcon."

Once Elizabeth was gone, John went in search of Falcon. He found him in the courtyard, issuing last-minute orders. "I'm getting married," John said without preamble.

Falcon's mouth dropped open. "If you meant to shock me, you succeeded."

"I came upon Elizabeth; she was crying. She didn't want to return to Southwold with her father. She fears him."

"So you decided to become her knight in shining armor," Falcon mocked.

"I want her, Falcon. I'll do whatever it takes to have her."

"You don't even know her."

"I know enough. Osgood mistreats Elizabeth and her

mother, and I can't allow it to continue. I'm off to speak to Osgood now. Perhaps I can convince him to leave Elizabeth and her mother here with Lady Mariah."

"Good luck," Falcon said. "I'll be there directly to hear Osgood's answer."

Osgood was still in the hall, talking with Mariah and his wife and daughter when John approached him. He paid scant heed to John until John cleared his throat and addressed him.

"Sir Osgood, might I have a word with you?"

Osgood looked him over as if he were a piece of dung. "What is it? I am pressed for time."

"I wish to ask for your daughter's hand in marriage."

Mariah, who was standing nearby, gasped and clapped a hand over her mouth. Martha sat down hard, staring at John as if he had just grown horns. Elizabeth grasped her mother's hand and held her breath.

Osgood threw back his head and laughed. "You want my daughter? You just met her."

"I know enough about her to know I want her for my wife. I'm not a poor man. I know you value your daughter highly, and I am willing to pay any price to make her my bride."

Osgood turned to his daughter. "Elizabeth, you and your mother will find your horses saddled and waiting in the courtyard."

"Father, you haven't answered Sir John."

"I do not intend to. Sir John may be able to afford you, but he cannot have you. I have my sights set higher than a mere knight. The Earl of Barkham has asked for your hand, and I am considering his request."

"Barkham!" John all but shouted. "The man is old enough to be Elizabeth's father. He's already killed three wives and is rumored to have the pox."

"Lies," Osgood maintained, shrugging. "Think you I'd let Elizabeth wed one of Falcon's friends after what Falcon did to me? He made sure I'd never inherit my brother's holding." He saw that his wife and daughter hadn't obeyed him and barked, "Go, both of you! We are leaving immediately."

Elizabeth squared her shoulders. "I'm not going, Father. Lady Mariah has invited me and Mama to remain at Mildenhall for a longer visit."

Osgood's hands clenched at his sides and his face turned purple with rage. "Is that true, Mariah?"

"Of course. I'd be delighted to have Martha and Elizabeth stay for an extended visit."

"They will accompany me home if I have to carry them out by force," Osgood spat. "They will obey me or suffer the consequences."

Walter joined them in time to hear the conversation. "Elizabeth needs a good beating," he said. "I'd be happy to administer it for you, Father."

"No one lays a hand on anyone," Falcon said from behind Osgood. He had heard the altercation and had a good idea what it was about. He turned to Elizabeth. "How old are you, Mistress Elizabeth?"

"Twenty-five," she said, blushing.

"Then you're old enough to make your own decisions. Do you wish to wed Sir John?"

Elizabeth slanted John a tentative smile. "Oh, yes, very much."

"I won't allow it," Osgood thundered.

Falcon ignored him. "Instead of leaving you here with Mariah, we'll take you to London with us. You and John can be married there, with the king's blessing."

"Thank you, Falcon," John said quietly.

"Do you wish to accompany your daughter to London, Dame Martha?"

"You cannot take a man's wife from him!" Osgood roared. "You are not God. Martha belongs to me, to do with as I please. And the king will agree with me. What God has joined together—"

"What say you, Martha?" Falcon interrupted.

"Osgood is right. I shall return home with my husband."

"Mama!" Elizabeth cried. "You cannot mean that."

"Aye, love. You are of age, go with Sir John. He is your future. My life is with Osgood."

She held out her arms, and Elizabeth went into them. She whispered something into her daughter's ear, then moved away. "I'm ready to leave, Osgood," Martha said.

"That's wise of you, wife. Go outside and wait for me."

Her head lowered, she stumbled off. Elizabeth started after her, but John placed a hand on her shoulder, stopping her. "Nay, stay," he urged. "Perhaps we can do something for your mother after we are wed. You still want to marry me, don't you?"

Elizabeth nodded, her gaze riveted on her mother's slumped shoulders.

"You are a monster, Osgood," Mariah hissed. "Edmond was right when he said you didn't deserve to inherit Mildenhall. I feel sorry for your wife. I will not hesitate to offer her shelter should she ask."

Osgood grasped Mariah's arm, jerking her like a rag doll. "Think you I am through with you? Think again, lady."

"Take your hands off her," Falcon said in a voice taut with menace.

Osgood shoved Mariah away from him. She struck a chair and started to fall. Strong hands grasped her waist and brought her against him.

"Do not *ever* touch Lady Mariah again," Falcon snarled.

"Bah! Your whore disgusts me. I cannot imagine why you cling to her when you have Lady Rosamond."

"Get out!" Mariah shouted. "And never return. You and your son are not welcome here."

Grinning as if he knew something they did not, Osgood turned and strode off.

"Are you all right, Mariah?" Falcon asked.

She turned in his arms. "I'm fine. Thank you . . . for everything."

His arms tightened around her. "I'll always be here for you, Mariah. If you need me, you have but to send word."

Suddenly a screech rent the air. "What is *she* doing in your arms? I cannot trust you alone with that woman."

Falcon's arms dropped away. "Behave, Rosamond. I returned to the hall and found Osgood mistreating Mariah. What would you have me do?"

"I would have you keep your hands off her," Rosamond sniffed. "Where is Sir Osgood?"

"Preparing to leave," Falcon replied.

"Why is his daughter still here?"

John tightened his hold on Elizabeth. "Elizabeth is my intended bride, my lady. We will be wed in London."

Rosamond's finely etched brows shot upward. "When did this all come about? Sir Osgood will not allow the match. He told me he had chosen another for her."

"Elizabeth is of age," Falcon explained. "She is free to choose her own mate, and she has found a champion in Sir John."

"Naught good can come of this," Rosamond muttered.

The words had no sooner left Rosamond's mouth than the thunder of hooves announced Osgood's departure. Falcon walked to the door and watched them ride through the portcullis and head west toward Southwold. Mariah joined him.

"Do you think we've seen the last of him?" she asked.

"I have the king's ear. As soon as I reach London, I'll make sure he knows that Osgood needs to be watched. Osgood was excessively bold to return to Mildenhall as he did. He used the women to gain entrance, knowing you wouldn't turn them away. If I hadn't been here, I don't know what would have happened. I'm convinced he expected to find Mildenhall unprotected when he arrived."

"You must leave immediately and tell the king about Osgood's behavior. Mayhap Henry will banish him from England. That would be a blessing to Martha."

"I'll be sure to suggest it," Falcon said. He gazed down at her, willing her to look up at him. She did. "I don't have to leave, Mariah."

"Aye, you do. You have Rosamond. You're promised to her. I'm naught to you."

"You know that's not true." He paused. "Mariah, before I leave, is there anything you wish to tell me? You are holding something back from me, I can feel it. What is it you're not telling me?"

"Naught . . . I—"

"Mama! Falcon! Is Osgood gone?"

Falcon knelt to Robbie's level. "Sir Osgood rode away, for good, I hope."

"I'm glad. He was a bad man. I wish you could stay here with me and Mama."

"Sir Falcon cannot stay, Robbie. He has duties elsewhere."

Robbie stole a glance at Rosamond. "Is *she* his duty?"

"That's enough, Robbie," Mariah said sternly. "You cannot have everything you want."

Falcon rose. "Your son is going to make a fine earl one day, Mariah," he said wistfully.

"Perhaps you will have a son of your own in the not too distant future."

"Perhaps," Falcon said, trying to picture children with Rosamond's features and failing.

Rosamond came up to join them. "I am ready, Falcon. Osgood is gone—'tis time for us to leave."

John and Elizabeth walked hand in hand out the door. A glance into the courtyard told Falcon that the men were already mounted and ready to leave.

"Jamie will help you mount," Falcon told Rosamond. "I'll be there in a moment."

Rosamond looked as if she wanted to protest, but she must have thought better of it, for she flounced off.

Falcon pulled Mariah into an alcove where they

couldn't be seen. "I meant what I said, Mariah. Should you or Robbie need me, send word to the king. He will know where to find me."

Pain settled in Mariah's heart. She knew if she told Falcon that Robbie was his son, he would take their child away for Rosamond to raise. She couldn't bear losing the only person she had left to love. 'Twas best to say good-bye to Falcon now and bear the heartache of his leaving. There would always be a bond between them, no matter where he went or whom he was with.

"I promise to send word to the king should I need help," Mariah choked out.

Falcon nodded. But he couldn't leave her this way. "If by chance you are with child, promise you will let me know."

"To what purpose, Falcon? I will raise your child and love it without reservations should there be one." *Just as I have done with Robbie.* "You belong to Rosamond now; you must think of her and the children you will have together."

"I'm sorry, I shouldn't have—"

"Don't be sorry. I'm not."

Falcon stared at her for a heartbeat before pulling her into his arms and kissing her. Mariah melted into him, kissing him back as if it were the last time she would ever see him, which indeed she was sure it was.

Abruptly he broke off the kiss. He stared into her eyes one last time and then strode off.

Osgood's party traveled only as far as a range of nearby hills. They halted there, out of sight of the keep, until a lookout posted on high ground reported that Falcon and his men had left Mildenhall. Martha, who had been resting beneath a tree, rose and shaded her eyes against the sun.

"What are you planning, Osgood? Please tell me you intend Lady Mariah no harm."

"Don't question me, wife," Osgood snarled. "One of my men will see you home."

"Osgood, please leave Mariah alone. Why are you doing this?"

Without warning, Osgood struck her across the face. She staggered backward, into Walter's arms. Walter promptly lifted her and set her on her horse.

"If you bear me any love, Walter, you'll try to talk your father out of what he is planning."

"I'm not going to hurt Mariah, Mama," Walter replied gruffly. "I'm going to marry her. With Falcon gone, naught stands in our way of claiming Mildenhall."

"Mariah will never marry you," Martha warned. "Besides, Mildenhall belongs to Robbie."

Laughing, Osgood pushed Walter aside. "She'll agree. I intend to use her bastard son to force her to our will. Then once Walter gets a son from her, Robbie will quietly disappear." He slapped the rump of Martha's horse and it shot forward. One of Osgood's mercenaries followed.

"When do we leave?" Walter asked.

"As soon as I'm positive Falcon won't turn back."

"How do we get Mariah to raise the portcullis?"

"Trust me, Walter; I have devised a plan that is foolproof. I kept some of your mother's clothing. One of the smaller mercenaries will don the clothing and pose as your mother. When we reach the portcullis, I'll claim that

Martha became ill and we had to return. Mariah has a kind heart; she'll let us through the gate."

Osgood sent the lookout back up the hill to watch the road.

Four hours later, Osgood's party, which included a woman shrouded in a cloak, returned to Mildenhall. A guard on the wall walk spotted them and gave the warning. Mariah hurried from the keep and climbed the ladder to get a better look.

"What do you suppose they want?" Mariah asked Sir Maynard.

"We're about to find out, milady," he replied.

The group approached the portcullis. Osgood looked up, spotting Mariah immediately. "Lady Mariah, Martha is ill. Please allow us to enter so that your healer can examine her. We cannot continue to Southwold with my wife in this condition."

"When did she become ill?" Mariah called down to him.

"Soon after we left Miildenhall. Look at her—does she not look ill?"

Mariah glanced at the poor woman bent over the saddle, and her heart went out to her. "What say you, Sir Maynard? Shall we allow Dame Martha to enter?"

"I do not trust Osgood," Maynard replied. "I say nay."

"Oh, but look at Martha. She could be desperately ill. I cannot bear to see her that way. Edwina may be able to help her. Order the portcullis lifted so that Martha can enter."

Sir Maynard gave the order as Mariah scrambled down the ladder to await Martha. The portcullis cranked up slowly. Mariah smiled at the cloaked figure as she rode through the gate, her shoulders bent, her spirit apparently defeated.

"Martha, welcome—"

The greeting died in her throat as Osgood's mercenaries surged through the opening behind the ill woman. Stunned, Mariah watched as "Martha" ripped off her cloak and gown, revealing a small but burly mercenary. Osgood leapt down from his mount, grabbed Mariah and ordered, "If you value your life, order your guardsmen to back away."

By now, guardsmen were pouring from the keep, their swords drawn, ready to do battle. Mariah detested bloodshed, could not bear to see her faithful men maimed or slain, so she did as Osgood asked. Though surrendering her keep to Osgood infuriated Mariah, what truly terrified her was Osgood's evil intent toward Robbie. She knew he meant her son harm.

Falcon, I need you, she silently implored. *Please help me*.

Her plea floated upward and sped away on a gust of wind.

Chapter Eleven

Becca heard the commotion in the courtyard and ran to the window. Fear raced through her when she saw the activity below. Sir Osgood had returned; he held Lady Mariah captive while his mercenaries were disarming Mildenhall's guardsmen. Panic-stricken, Becca tried to recall what Lady Mariah had told her about safeguarding Robbie should disaster strike.

Suddenly Edwina burst into the hall. "Pack some clothing for Robbie and yourself while I fetch the lad," the old crone said. "You must leave the keep immediately. Sir Osgood means Robbie harm."

Becca didn't ask questions as she flew to obey Edwina.

"Where are we going?" Robbie asked when Edwina burst into the nursery and announced that he and Becca were leaving.

"Sir Osgood has returned and is up to no good. You cannot remain in the keep, lad," she said in a hushed voice. "You mustn't make a sound. Promise now, for your life could depend upon it."

"Where is Mama?"

"Your mama would want you to be safe. She'll be fine; never doubt your mother's courage or resourcefulness."

Robbie brightened. "Mayhap Falcon will return to save us."

"Aye, lad, mayhap he will. We will pray for that." She glanced toward the door. "Here's Becca—'tis time to leave."

Becca arrived with a satchel filled with clothing. "Give me that," Edwina said. "Bring the lad and follow me."

Cautiously Edwina led them out into the corridor toward the winding staircase. All was quiet below in the hall.

"Hurry," Edwina admonished.

They hastened down the stairs and ducked into the kitchen. The hall and kitchen were both deserted. Apparently, the servants had fled through the postern gate at the first sign of trouble. Edwina hurried Robbie and Becca out the back door and through the kitchen garden.

"Where are we going?" Becca asked.

"Quiet," Edwina said, shushing her.

Edwina stopped before the postern gate, a thick panel that latched from the inside. Osgood might send a man to guard it later, but he was far too busy in the courtyard to attend to it now. The gate was unlatched, proving Edwina's theory that the servants had fled through it. Edwina and Becca worked together to pull the heavy gate open, and then Becca and Robbie slipped through.

"Listen carefully," Edwina whispered. "Go to the alewife in the village; tell her I sent you and what has happened here. Ask her to hide you in her cellar until we can send Robbie to London to seek the king's protection. Can you remember that, Becca girl?"

"Aye," Becca replied. "Aren't you coming with us?"

"Nay, I must stay to help Mariah."

Then, with Becca pulling and Edwina pushing, the gate slid smoothly back into place. Edwina shot home the bolt and returned to the keep.

Meanwhile, Mariah's guardsmen had been disarmed by Osgood's mercenaries.

"Lock the guardsmen and steward in the barracks," Osgood ordered. Then he pushed Mariah into Walter's arms. "Take your betrothed into the hall." He sneered at Mariah. "Walter has something to ask you, Mariah, and you had best give the correct answer."

"I'll give you naught," Mariah said defiantly.

Walter literally dragged Mariah into the hall. Seizing her shoulders, he turned her to face him. "Will you wed me, Mariah of Mildenhall?"

"Nay, Walter. Not now, not tomorrow, not ever."

"You've just made a serious mistake, lady," Osgood warned. He called to one of his mercenaries. "Hugo, fetch Mariah's bastard!"

Hugo headed purposefully toward the nursery. Mariah tried to pull free from Walter's hamlike hands, but he held her fast. "If you harm Robbie, I swear you will regret it. Falcon will avenge him."

"Falcon has a betrothed now. Why would he put himself out for you and your bastard? He will have no time for you now that he has Rosamond."

Mariah saw Edwina sidle into the hall from the kitchen, and hope flared. Elation replaced that slim hope when Edwina nodded and smiled at her. Mariah knew exactly what Edwina was trying to tell her. Robbie was safe.

Squaring her shoulders, Mariah said, "I repeat: I will not marry you, Walter Fitzhugh."

"Do you value your son so little that you would risk his life?" Osgood growled.

"My son *is* my life," Mariah replied.

"Then I suggest you wed Walter with haste. I will send someone to fetch the priest."

Before Osgood could act, Hugo burst into the hall. "The boy is gone!"

Mariah dared a glance at Edwina. A small smile played across her lips.

Osgood yanked Mariah away from Walter and gave her a vicious shake. "Where is he, lady?"

"I know not," Mariah said through clattering teeth. If Osgood didn't stop shaking her, he'd scramble her brains.

"Release Lady Mariah!"

Osgood stopped shaking Mariah as Father Francis ran toward her, his black robes flapping around his skinny ankles.

"Ah, the priest," Osgood said. "You're just in time to perform the ceremony. Mariah and Walter wish to wed."

"Nay, he lies! I have *not* agreed to wed Walter."

"But you will as soon as we find the boy. Walter, see to it. Search every nook and cranny in the keep." He returned his attention to Mariah. "We'll find him, and when we do, his continued good health will depend upon your willingness to become Walter's wife."

Walter left immediately to direct the search.

"And then what?" Mariah dared. "How long will Robbie live after I wed Walter? I put no faith in your word, Osgood. Edmond trusted you not, and neither do I."

"You have no choice," Osgood replied. "I know you, Mariah. You would gladly sacrifice yourself to save your son."

"Aye," Mariah answered. "But perhaps my sacrifice won't be needed. You have to produce Robbie first."

Osgood dragged Mariah to a bench and pushed her onto it. "Ale!" he called. "And food. We've had naught to eat since we broke our fast this morning."

No one answered his call. "Where are the servants?" he demanded.

Mariah shrugged. "If they were smart, they would have fled at the first sign of trouble."

"Fled? How? I replaced your gateman with my own man."

Mariah remained mute. Let him find the postern gate on his own. Had she known what Osgood intended, she would have fled through it herself. She worried about Robbie and prayed that Edwina had found a safe place for him to hide. As long as Robbie remained safe, Mariah would continue to defy Osgood and Walter. What could they do to her? Even if they killed her, Robbie would still be Edmond's heir.

One of Osgood's men drew a pitcher of ale from a barrel sitting near a sideboard and placed it before Osgood. Osgood drank deeply from the pitcher, too thirsty to wait for a mug. Mariah eyed him with disgust as ale dribbled from his chin onto his stained doublet.

A small smile played at the corners of Mariah's mouth as, one by one, Osgood's mercenaries returned to the hall without Robbie. When the last man had reported his failure, Osgood flew into a rage.

Rising, he clenched his fist and punched it into the air. "Search again. There has to be a hidey-hole someplace in this keep where a small boy can be concealed."

The men fanned out again. Osgood grew impatient and began to pace. Hours passed before the men returned empty-handed, much to Mariah's relief. Osgood then ordered the men into the courtyard and bailey, demanding that they search every building within Mildenhall's walls.

Mariah's heart nearly stopped when, after the men left, Osgood noticed Edwina and beckoned to her. "You there, come here!"

Edwina shuffled forward. Mariah tried to send her a silent message to hold firm against Osgood, but Edwina did not look up.

"What will you have of me, Sir Osgood?" Edwina whined.

"It grows late—fetch food for me and my men."

Mariah rose. "Edwina is a healer, not a cook. I will help her."

Osgood pushed her back onto the bench, more roughly than was necessary. "Nay, stay here. I trust you not."

"Then we are even," Mariah said sweetly, "for I have never trusted you."

Osgood blasted her with a daunting look before waving Edwina off to the kitchen.

Father Francis hurried over to lend his support to Mariah. "Have faith, daughter," the priest whispered. "Our good Lord will find a way to resolve this situation. Last time He sent Sir Falcon to us. Perhaps He—"

"Nay, Father. Sir Falcon has no reason to return. We must find our own way out of this coil."

"What are you two whispering about?" Osgood demanded.

"I am but lending Lady Mariah courage," Father Francis said.

"What do you know about her bastard's disappearance, priest? Did you have a hand in it?"

"Nay, I was on my knees in the chapel, deep in prayer."

At length, Edwina arrived with a tray of bread, meat and cheese, which she banged down before Osgood. "If your men wish to eat, they can fetch their own food from the kitchen. I am old and frail and not up to the task you set for me."

She hobbled away before Osgood could stop her.

"Belligerent old crone," Osgood grumbled as he began shoveling food into his mouth.

"Edwina did as you asked. Are your men too lazy to go into the kitchen and find their own food?" Mariah asked.

"What are we supposed to do for a cook?" Osgood whined.

"Perhaps one of your men can manage. You cannot blame the servants for disappearing after your mistreatment of them the last time you occupied Mildenhall. If Sir Falcon hadn't arrived, they would have found a way out of the keep then, too, just as they did today."

Osgood grasped her wrist, squeezing hurtfully. "How did they leave if not through the gate?" He stood, knocking down his chair in his haste. "Of course, there's the postern gate! It slipped my mind. I will post a guard there immediately."

Osgood's foul mood continued as Walter and the mercenaries returned to report their failure to find Robbie.

Connie Mason

"He must have escaped by the postern gate," Osgood snarled. "Walter, place a guard there and lock Mariah in the solar. The rest of you search the village." He sent Mariah a look that did not bode well for her. "We will find the boy, and when we do, you will wed Walter."

Mariah clutched Father Francis's hand as Walter jerked her to her feet.

"Let me go with her," the priest said. "We shall pray together for the Lord's guidance."

Walter looked to his father for instruction.

"Nay, there will be no plotting together. Go back to your chapel, priest, and pray that we will find Mariah's bastard."

Walter herded Mariah up the winding staircase to her chamber and pushed her inside. Then he closed the door, turned the rusty key in the lock and went to join in the search.

Long before Osgood sent his searchers into the village, Edwina had left the keep. Osgood's guard had let her pass through the gate, having recognized her as Mildenhall's healer. Edwina carried a basket over her arm, informing the guard that she carried herbs to aid a cotter's wife who had just birthed a babe.

Edwina hurried as fast as her old legs would carry her to the home of the alewife. "Did Robbie and Becca arrive safely?" she asked anxiously.

"I hid them in the cellar as you requested," Dame Bertha whispered. "The lad is frightened, and who can blame him?"

"I suspect Osgood's men will reach the village soon to search for Robbie," Edwina revealed. "We don't have much time."

"They won't find him," Dame Bertha asserted. "They'll never find their way into the cellar."

"Aye, that's why I sent the lad here. I have a basket of food from Mildenhall kitchens. I'd best see the lad now, before the mercenaries arrive."

Dame Bertha led Edwina to the stillroom, where she brewed her excellent ale. The yeasty smell of fermenting ale hung heavy in the air. The alewife pushed an empty brass kettle aside and opened the trapdoor beneath it. Edwina scampered down the narrow wooden ladder into a damp chamber that was lit by several candles. Robbie was fast asleep on a pile of blankets. Becca, who sat beside him, rose when Edwina appeared.

"What is happening at the keep?" Becca asked.

"It doesn't look good, lass. I brought a basket of food. You're to stay here with Robbie until it's safe to leave."

"What of Lady Mariah? Is she . . . in good health?"

"She was when last I saw her. Osgood doesn't dare harm her, at least not until Robbie is under his control and Mariah is wed to Walter. Once that happens, and pray God it does not, both their lives could be threatened."

"I will pray for all of us," Becca said.

"Be prepared to leave when Dame Bertha fetches you. I will try to arrange transportation to London. Once there, you are to seek out the king and tell him what has happened here." She thrust the basket at Becca. "There's a sack of gold coins tucked in the basket. Use it to provide for Robbie while in London. Though you are young, Becca, I trust you to keep Robbie safe."

"I love Robbie," Becca said solemnly. "I will do whatever it takes to protect him. Lady Mariah and Lord Edmond have been good to me and my family—I can do no less."

Edwina nodded, looked one last time at Robbie and then climbed up the ladder to the stillroom, where Dame Bertha awaited her return.

"When is your next delivery?" Edwina asked, aware that Bertha often sold her ale to surrounding villages and towns.

"My next batch is scheduled to go out tomorrow," Bertha replied. "My husband Malcolm and son Horace drive the delivery wagon and unload it themselves."

"Prepare two empty kegs for the next delivery," Edwina said. "One each for Robbie and Becca. Advise your husband to deliver the lad and his nursemaid to London. Becca knows what to do there."

They discussed arrangements as Edwina helped Bertha close the trapdoor and lug the brass kettle into place.

"I shouldn't be here when Osgood's men arrive," Edwina said. "I must return to the keep before I am missed. Be alert, Bertha. Robbie and Becca must leave soon, before they are discovered. Tell no one they are here."

Falcon's party was well on its way to London when he abruptly halted and glanced behind him. He distinctly heard someone calling his name, but when he looked over his shoulder, no one was there. He had been bringing up the rear, trying to hurry along the cart carrying Leticia and Rosamond's trunk.

Chiding himself for being fanciful, Falcon passed the cart and took the lead from Sir Dennis. Rosamond rode up beside him. "Is aught wrong, Falcon?"

"Did you call me a few minutes ago?" he asked.

"Nay." She looked at him oddly. "I heard naught."

Falcon grunted but wasn't convinced. He had distinctly heard someone calling his name, someone pleading for help.

Mariah.

It couldn't be. His imagination was getting the better of him. Falcon had been uncomfortable leaving Mariah, and because of it, his mind must be playing tricks on him. He lifted his head. The breeze whispering through the trees seemed to repeat the same words, over and over.

Help me. I need you.

Falcon dropped back to speak with his squire. "Jamie, I want you to return to Mildenhall. I have a feeling that all is not well there. Find out what you can and report back to me at my quarters in London."

"Do you suspect foul play?"

"I have naught but my suspicion. Go, lad. I will be waiting anxiously for your return."

Jamie let the rest of the party pass him before wheeling his horse back toward Mildenhall.

"What was that about?" Rosamond asked when Falcon rode up beside her. "Why did your squire turn back?"

"You need not concern yourself with Jamie," Falcon replied. "I but sent him on an errand."

While his answer seemed to satisfy Rosamond, it did little to ease Falcon's disquiet. Something was wrong. He could feel it in his bones, hear the warning in the air.

Mariah prayed feverishly for deliverance from this latest threat to her and Robbie. She rose up from her knees when she heard the key turn in the lock. Osgood burst inside, his face red, his fists clenched. Walter hovered behind him, looking no less threatening than his father. Mariah waited with bated breath for Osgood to tell her whether or not Robbie had been found.

"Where is he, Mariah?" Osgood blasted. "How could one small boy disappear into thin air?"

Mariah's relief was so enormous, her legs turned to jelly and she collapsed into a chair.

Osgood grasped her arms and pulled her to her feet. "You know where he's hiding! Tell me."

Mariah shook her head. "Nay. I opened the gate to you in good faith. I had no idea you intended harm to me and mine. How could I have hidden Robbie when I was on hand to greet you in the courtyard?"

"What about the healer? She could have taken the boy away."

"Nay. We both saw Edwina was in the hall, remember?"

"Someone fled with the brat through the postern gate. Perhaps one of the servants. I made a mistake, but it won't happen again. The gate is well guarded now. No one else will leave without my knowledge."

"We went from house to house in the village," Walter growled. "If the boy was hiding there, we would have found him."

Father Francis pushed into the chamber. "Did you harm any of the villagers?"

"Bah, they knew naught," Osgood sneered. "A dumber lot I've never seen."

"How long do you intend to keep me imprisoned?" Mariah asked.

"You are free to leave the solar to work in the kitchen. You and the healer are all we have until the servants can be persuaded to return."

"You must allow me to travel back and forth to the village to administer to my flock," the priest pleaded.

"I have no intention of preventing you from doing God's work, Father," Osgood replied piously. "You may continue to administer to the sick and dying in the village.

"While you are performing your duties," Osgood continued, "you can tell the cotters that I mean no harm to their lady or to them. Inform the servants that they can return to their duties without fear."

Mariah's hopes soared. Father Francis would be a link to the village and thus with Robbie, for she knew with a certainty that her son was in a place no one would think to look for him. It worried her, however, that she did not know how long he would have to remain hidden. She prayed it wouldn't be long.

"Go down to the kitchen, lady," Osgood ordered, "and help the healer prepare the evening meal."

"Where are my men? Have you harmed them?"

"They will come to no harm," Osgood promised. "Once you and Walter are wed, he will have need of them. Henry won't interfere once you and Walter are husband and wife, but slaughtering your men would bring his wrath down upon me and mine."

"Do you give your word as a knight of the realm not to harm my men or servants should they return?" Mariah asked.

"Aye, you have my word. We need the servants as well as the guardsmen, for doubtless they will remain to serve you after you wed Walter. I shall release your steward, to prove my good faith."

Head held high, Mariah brushed past Osgood and Walter and descended the stairs. Father Francis followed close on her heels. Now that Osgood had sworn not to harm her people, she would send word through Father Francis for the servants to return. Despite her distrust of him, she hoped Osgood would keep his word.

Mariah entered the kitchen, her mouth watering when she saw a haunch of venison roasting over the fire, bread baking in the hearth oven and various pots hanging on hooks suspended over the fire.

Then she spied Edwina, basting the venison as it turned on the spit. Mariah flew to the healer and hugged her. "Where is Robbie?" she whispered into the old crone's ear. "Is he well?"

"He is well. Fear not, Osgood will never find him, but the lad cannot remain hidden in the alewife's cellar forever. I made arrangements for Robbie to be transported to London with the next shipment of ale that leaves the village."

"London! Robbie will be lost there; 'tis a big, wicked city. All kinds of bad things could happen to him there."

"Becca promised to take him to the king and explain your predicament."

Panic-stricken, Mariah cried, "I cannot let them go alone! I need to go with them. If Becca cannot gain the king's ear, I know not what will become of them. Becca is a country lass—she knows naught of London."

"Mayhap there is something I can do to help," Edwina confided. "I will think on it and confer with Father Francis. He is allowed to travel freely between the castle and the village."

"I wish . . ."

"What do you wish, Mariah?"

" 'Tis fanciful of me to think Falcon might learn of our

predicament and send help. But now that he has Rosamond, I fear Robbie and I are naught to him."

"You should have told him that he is Robbie's sire," Edwina scolded.

Mariah shook her head. "To what purpose? Falcon's future is with Rosamond. He already distrusts me for lying about my relationship to Edmond. Robbie will always be a bond tying me to Falcon, but I can never tell him about his son. I would die if he took Robbie away from me. I cannot bear the thought of Rosamond raising him."

"You don't know Falcon would take Robbie away from you," Edwina chided.

Mariah's answer was forestalled when Osgood stuck his head into the kitchen and barked, "What plot are you two hatching? My men and I are hungry. Get to work."

"We are planning your demise," Mariah said sweetly. "Are you sure you trust us around food?"

Swearing violently, Osgood summoned one of his mercenaries to watch over the women, warning the guard that he was to be the taster, so he had best make sure naught poisonous was added to the food.

The women exchanged amused glances as they turned their backs to Osgood.

The day following Osgood's occupation of Mildenhall, Father Francis passed on Osgood's promise that the servants would not be harmed if they returned. By midday, a few hardy souls had straggled back, relieving Mariah and Edwina of kitchen duty.

Edwina had managed to speak at length with Father Francis early that morning before he left, and together they'd arranged a precarious escape for Mariah.

After the priest left, Edwina explained the details to Mariah while picking herbs in the kitchen garden, where they couldn't be overheard.

"Father Francis is arranging your escape as we speak," Edwina murmured.

Mariah bent close to Edwina, glanced around to make sure no one was about and asked, "Am I to leave with Robbie?"

"Aye. If all goes well, you, Robbie and Becca will be smuggled out of the village today."

A mixture of pleasure and fear suffused Mariah's face. "If you can make that happen, you are a miracle worker. Tell me more."

"Father Francis is the miracle worker, not I. He and the alewife are arranging for a shipment of her best ale to be delivered to the keep today while the men partake of the midday meal. The ale will be welcomed, for Osgood's men have depleted the stock on hand. Among the kegs will be one large enough to hold an adult, one that has never contained ale. While Horace unloads the filled kegs, Malcolm will help you into the empty one.

"When they return to the village, they will reload the wagon with ale to be delivered to a village south of here. Two of those kegs will hold Robbie and Becca. To anyone who asks, Malcolm will say that he is making a regular delivery to the alehouse in the neighboring village, but instead, he will be taking you, Becca and Robbie to London. Once you arrive, you can seek the king's help."

Mariah worried her bottom lip with her teeth as she imagined all the things that could go wrong. If they were caught, Robbie would become Osgood's pawn, and she would be forced to wed Walter in order to protect Robbie.

But if everything went as planned, she and Robbie would be free to seek the king's help.

Another alternative was to let Robbie and Becca leave without her. But they would be like two lost lambs in a wild and lawless town. She might never see her son again.

"What are you thinking, Mariah?" Edwina asked. "I know the plan Father Francis and I have hatched is a dangerous one, but 'tis the only one that has a chance of working."

Mariah stared at the old woman who had befriended her when she'd arrived at Mildenhall as a young girl. After her parents' deaths, when Edmond had become her guardian, Edwina had assumed the role of mother. She would trust both Edwina and Father Francis with her life. "I will do it," she whispered.

"Take naught with you but a change of clothing and whatever coin you can lay your hands on."

"Sir Martin has hidden away some gold coins; I know where to find them."

"Malcolm and Horace will deliver the ale while Osgood and his men are eating, so you won't be missed. When Malcolm brings the wagon around to the kitchen, you are to sneak out the door and climb into the keg. God go with you."

"I will need God to pull this off," Mariah muttered.

Jamie reached the village with a powerful hunger. He made straight for the alehouse and ordered a meat pie, hoping to get some information along with his food.

The serving girl greeted him enthusiastically, having made his acquaintance during his stay at Mildenhall keep. "Jamie, what are you doing back here? I thought you left with Sir Falcon's party."

"Falcon was uneasy after leaving and sent me back to inquire at the keep. I stopped here first for a bite to eat, and information. Is all well at the keep, Callie?"

Callie glanced about the crowded taproom and whispered, "Not here. Osgood has placed men throughout the village. It wouldn't do for you to be recognized or be seen talking to me."

"Sir Osgood occupies Mildenhall?" Jamie gasped. "What happened?"

"Come around to the kitchen after you've eaten and I'll explain."

Jamie gobbled his meat pie and left. Cautiously he worked his way around to the kitchen entrance. Callie was waiting for him.

"How did Osgood get inside the keep?" Jamie asked without preamble.

"He used trickery. Now Father Francis is the only one allowed outside the gate. Since Sir Osgood thinks him harmless, he's been our only source of information. Osgood is pressuring Lady Mariah to wed Walter."

"Has a marriage taken place?"

"Nay. Our lady refused, but only because Robbie has disappeared and Osgood cannot use him to force Lady Mariah to his will."

"Do you know what happened to Robbie?"

"Nay, no one does. We believe, but cannot be sure, that he's on his way to London with his nursemaid to seek the king's help. Osgood's mercenaries searched the keep, the village, everywhere a lad could hide."

"What about Lady Mariah? Is she well?"

"According to the priest, she is."

Jamie gave Callie a swift buss on the cheek and hurried off.

"Where are you going?" Callie called after him.

"To London, to report to Falcon. Take care, Callie."

Chapter Twelve

Upon his return to London, Falcon heard on the street that King Henry had taken his army to France to lay siege to Normandy. If the gossip proved true, Falcon needed to be with the king.

Though Rosamond wanted Falcon to secure a special license from the bishop so they could wed immediately, Falcon resisted the pressure of her constant nagging. He refused to do anything until Jamie reported back to him. The feeling that all was not well at Mildenhall intensified with each passing hour.

Soon after their arrival, Falcon escorted Rosamond to her father's town house.

"Papa, you look ill!" Rosamond cried when her father met them at the door. "Come, sit down. I have some news to impart. Falcon and I are betrothed and are to be wed soon."

Lord Norwich, once a robust man, did indeed look ill. His face was pallid, his skin sagging. He was not the same man Falcon had known five years ago.

"Where have you been, daughter? I came up to London despite my illness, hoping to find you here."

"I was at Mildenhall, visiting Lady Mariah. Falcon happened to be there on the king's business."

"Are you sure marrying Falcon is wise, daughter? You can do better than a landless knight."

Falcon shifted uncomfortably, unaccustomed to being talked down to.

"You agreed to the match once," Rosamond said, pouting. "Now that I am a widow, you have no say in my choice of husband. I have an estate and wealth of my own, and I want Falcon."

Lord Norwich stared at Falcon with intense dislike. "Do you promise not to leave my daughter at the altar? I cannot bear for her to be disappointed again."

"What happened before was unavoidable," Falcon retorted.

"So I was told," Norwich bit out.

Falcon deliberately changed the subject. "I heard on the street that King Henry is in France. Is it true?"

"Aye, so I've heard, but I cannot say for sure."

"If it's true, I intend to join him as soon as I can. Perhaps it would be best to postpone the wedding until I return."

Norwich sent Rosamond an "I told you so" look. Rosamond, however, was having none of it. Glaring at Falcon, she stamped her foot. "I like this not! We will be wed before you leave or not at all. I have waited too long to be your wife."

I prefer we not wed at all, Falcon thought but did not say. But he knew he might never get another chance to wed an heiress. "Very well," he agreed. "Once my business affairs are in order, we can be wed."

A catlike smile curved Rosamond's mouth. "Make it soon, Falcon. I don't like waiting for what I want."

Falcon decided to leave before he said something he'd regret. He had always known Rosamond was spoiled and demanding, but the size of her dowry had made him overlook those qualities. Perhaps he should have examined her faults before agreeing to marry her.

"I must leave," Falcon said. "There's a great deal to do before we can be wed. I will be in touch, Rosamond."

Rosamond grasped his arm. "I'll walk you to the door."

Once out of sight of her father, Rosamond stopped, twined her arms around Falcon's neck and pulled his head down to hers. Her lips were soft and plump, and for a moment Falcon allowed himself to explore them, probing between them with his tongue to taste her.

The kiss did naught to arouse him. If Rosamond were Mariah, his cock would be in full rut and eager for consummation. Rosamond's kisses left him cold. He broke off the kiss and took his leave, much to Rosamond's vexation. He had a great deal to think about. Marrying Rosamond would be for the rest of his life. Was that what he wanted?

Falcon returned to his rented rooms above the Fox and Hound Inn near Whitehall. The rooms were comfortable and had proved adequate during his years of service to the king. Besides, the inn had a fine cook and the quality of the food was excellent. And the inn's stableman took good care of his horse.

After bathing and eating an excellent meal, Falcon took himself off to Whitehall. It didn't take long for him to learn that the king, having set his sights on Normandy, had sailed across the channel with his army three days earlier. Falcon heard the details from Lord Humphreys, one of the king's advisors.

"Did Henry leave any instructions for me?" Falcon asked.

"None that I am aware of. You have just returned from Mildenhall, have you not?"

"Aye."

"Is all well there? Henry was fond of Lord Edmond and wanted to help his widow."

"All was as it should be when I left," Falcon hedged.

"I assume you want to join the king as soon as possible."

"I do, but not until I settle my affairs in England."

Falcon left Whitehall soon after their conversation. At loose ends, he dropped in at the Cock and Crow, where he knew he'd find his friends enjoying their leisure time. He wasn't disappointed. Falcon joined Sir Dennis and several others; they spoke at length about the king's return to Normandy and their desire to join him. Falcon promised to inform them when he was ready to depart, and then took his leave.

Falcon was worried about Jamie. If the lad didn't return tomorrow, Falcon intended to send someone to see what was keeping him . . . or go himself, no matter how strenuously Rosamond objected.

Falcon was spared a journey to Mildenhall when Jamie showed up at his rooms the next day.

"There's trouble at Mildenhall," Jamie cried the moment Falcon opened the door to him. He had to stop and draw a deep breath before continuing. "Osgood used trickery to gain entrance to the keep."

Falcon's heart thudded against his ribs. "Sit down, lad, and catch your breath." He led Jamie to a chair. "Now tell me what happened."

"I decided to stop for a bite to eat at the alehouse in the village before continuing on to the castle," Jamie explained. "What I learned in the village changed my mind about going on to the castle. Sir Osgood is in control of Mildenhall. He used some sort of trickery to gain entrance. The castle guards were overpowered and are under lock and key."

Falcon's stomach clenched. He should have turned back when his gut warned him that something was wrong. Had the phantom voice he'd heard calling for help been Mariah's?

"Did you learn anything about Mariah and Robbie's fate?"

"Walter intended to force Lady Mariah to wed him, but that plan failed when Robbie disappeared."

"Disappeared? What do you mean? How did the boy escape the trap Osgood set for him and Mariah?"

"No one seems to know what happened to the lad," Jamie explained. "Both he and his nursemaid went missing. Father Francis is the cotters' only source of information. The priest is allowed to come and go in order to serve his flock. I think Osgood fears that God will punish him if he interferes with the priest's work."

Falcon began to pace, his face a mask of fury. "If Osgood were wise, he would fear God *and* me."

"What are you going to do?"

"I'm not sure yet. I wish I knew whether Robbie is safe. Where could he have gone?"

"The consensus was that his nursemaid took him to London, to seek the king's help."

His fists clenched at his sides as Falcon's face hardened. "If Osgood has hurt the boy or his mother, he will suffer for it. You've earned your rest, Jamie. Go find your bed. We'll talk later, after I decide what's to be done."

Jamie left. Falcon dropped into the chair Jamie had vacated. He needed to think through all he had just learned. He wished Sir John hadn't taken his new wife home to meet his family. John had never failed him when a cool head was needed. Falcon was inclined to be hotheaded, acting first and thinking later. But with Mariah's life at stake, he couldn't afford to act impulsively.

Without the king's help, storming the castle could bring disastrous results. Possibly even endanger Mariah's life. That thought was almost too painful to bear. Why had he ever left Mariah? Why had he thought marrying Rosamond would bring him everything he'd ever wanted?

He was a fool, that's why.

Land and wealth didn't bring happiness.

On the other hand, could a woman who had lied to him for unknown reasons make him happy? Falcon didn't know. What he did know was that he couldn't leave Mariah to Osgood's machinations. Tomorrow he would gather his men and outline his plans to return to Mildenhall. But first, there was Rosamond to contend with.

Not one to put things off, Falcon called on his betrothed at her father's town house later that day. She received him in the drawing room.

"Falcon," she gushed, "I've been waiting for you to return. If you hadn't called today, I was going to send a messenger to your quarters. Papa is most anxious to see me settled. His illness progresses each day."

Falcon cleared his throat. "There's trouble at Mildenhall, and I'm worried about Mariah and Robbie."

Rosamond reared back as if struck. "You're worried about a woman and child who should mean naught to you? Let Walter have the witch. 'Tis what Osgood wants, is it not?"

Falcon narrowed his eyes as Rosamond's words sank in. "I never mentioned Osgood or Walter. Why would you think the trouble involves them? We both saw them leave Mildenhall. Do you know something I do not, Rosamond?"

"N-nay! I just assumed . . ."

Her denial did naught to assuage Falcon's suspicion. "As it happens, your assumption is correct. Osgood used trickery to gain entrance to Mildenhall. He and his mercenaries have seized control of the keep."

"How do you know this?"

Falcon shrugged. "I had a premonition and sent Jamie back to investigate. He returned today with the news of Osgood's takeover. I cannot allow Osgood to have his way in this. I am still under the king's orders to protect Lord Edmond's widow and son."

"What Osgood wants is to wed his son to Mariah. He means her no harm."

"What about Robbie? Does he mean the lad no harm?"

Rosamond shrugged and looked away. "Unavoidable things happen to children. Only a lucky few live to maturity. My mother bore three sons; none of them lived past the first year."

Falcon blew out an angry breath. "Admit it! You knew about Osgood's plans to return to the keep."

"Nay, you accuse me unjustly! I swear to you, I knew naught of what Osgood planned."

He backed away from her, convinced she knew more than she was admitting.

"What are you going to do?"

"Return to Mildenhall, of course. I cannot sit idle while Osgood forces Mariah to his will, or poses a threat to Robbie. We will talk after I return."

"Papa is not going to like this," Rosamond warned.

"I will settle with your father when I return—*if*," he stressed, "you still wish to marry me and I still wish to marry you."

"Do not count on my being here when you return," Rosamond threatened.

"The choice is yours, Rosamond."

Fire lit the centers of her eyes, and her face screwed up into an ugly sneer. "My choice, Sir Falcon, is to deny you the wealth and land you desire just as you continue to deny me your heart. You care naught for me; you proved it once and you're proving it again. Papa was right. I *can* do better than a landless knight. Go sniffing after Mariah, but heed me well, Falcon. She'll put horns on you just like she did her husband. Good-bye, Sir Falcon. You can let yourself out."

Turning on her heel, she flounced off, leaving Falcon standing in the middle of the drawing room. The only feeling he could muster was relief. He was free. Free to help Mariah and protect Robbie. Though he might never be more than a landless knight, he still was in possession of his honor. If all heiresses were as spoiled and demanding as Rosamond, he wanted naught to do with them.

Falcon left the house without regret. There was a great deal for him to do before he returned to Mildenhall.

While Falcon was making plans to return to Mildenhall, Mariah, Robbie and Becca were on their way to London. Well out of sight of Mildenhall, Malcolm had pulled the wagon to a stop to help his passengers out of the kegs. When Robbie saw his mother, he gave a cry of gladness and flung his arms around her neck. Then he began to sob.

"Where were you, Mama? Why didn't you come for me? I was so afraid."

Near tears herself, Mariah said, "We're together now, my love. No one will ever take you from me again." She turned to the nursemaid. "Are you all right, Becca?"

"I'm fine, my lady. Both Robbie and I are glad to be out of Dame Bertha's cellar."

"Where are we going, Mama?"

"To London, Robbie, to seek the king's help. Henry needs to know what Sir Osgood has done."

"London? Can we visit Falcon?"

"I . . . don't know. Falcon and Lady Rosamond are planning their wedding. It wouldn't be right to interfere."

"I want to see him," Robbie demanded between sobs.

"I will think on it, Robbie," Mariah said without meaning it. The king had the power to see justice done for her and Robbie; there would be no need for Falcon.

Mariah settled Robbie and Becca in the wagon bed and turned around to speak to Malcolm.

"I've been thinking, Malcolm, perhaps I should rent horses for Becca and myself when we reach the next village. It would be safer for all of us. A long absence from the village might be noticed and bring trouble to you and your family. And Becca, Robbie and I can reach London faster on horseback."

Malcolm nodded. "Your logic is sound, my lady. We are nearly in Cambridge. 'Tis a good-sized town; buying horses should be no problem."

"'Tis settled, then," Mariah said, scooting down beside Robbie.

Mariah's small group spent the night at the Traveler's Haven in Cambridge. The inn offered clean, comfortable rooms at modest prices and served tasty food. Robbie was already asleep in Becca's arms when they arrived at the inn. Mariah engaged two rooms, one for Becca and Robbie and one for herself. Then she ordered baths and meals. She planned to make it an early night, for she hoped to reach London the following day.

Mariah woke early the next morning and bought horses to carry them the rest of the way to London. They set out shortly after breaking their fast and reached London before the city gates closed that evening. Since Mariah had been to London several times with Edmond before he took ill, she knew exactly where to stay and engaged two rooms at the King's Arms.

The following morning, Mariah rose before Robbie and Becca were awake and left early for Whitehall. She wanted to be the first in line to see the king.

When she arrived, she spoke to Henry's secretary and learned that the king was in France, and that his return was not expected anytime soon. Mariah felt as if her world had just spun out of control. If she remained in

London to await the king, her funds might run out before he returned. She could probably survive a few weeks, but the longer she remained away from Mildenhall, the stronger Osgood's hold would grow on her home and people. What if she were never able to return to Mildenhall? Whatever would she and Robbie do then?

She could wed Walter.

She shuddered, the thought was too horrible to contemplate.

She could try to find Falcon and ask for his help.

Rosamond would never allow it, and Mariah had no right to ask. But desperate times called for desperate measures. Even if Falcon refused, she had to ask. But finding him would be near to impossible. London was a big city. Then she recalled that Lord Norwich kept a town house in London. Though Rosamond might not like her inquiring about Falcon, it was a place to start.

Before she left Whitehall, Mariah asked everyone she encountered in the reception hall for directions to Lord Norwich's residence. The third man she spoke to directed her to the earl's home.

When she arrived, her knock was opened by Rosamond herself.

"What are *you* doing here?" Rosamond asked.

"Please forgive me for arriving unannounced, but it's imperative that I find Falcon. Is he here? If not, can you tell me where I can find him?"

Rosamond's eyes narrowed. "Why do you want Falcon?"

"I need his help. Osgood has seized Mildenhall."

"Indeed. I'm surprised he let you walk away."

"He didn't. I haven't time for this, my lady. Do you or do you not know where I can find Falcon?"

A sly smile curved Rosamond's lips. "He's making preparations to join the king in France."

"Have you already wed, then?" Mariah knew she had no business asking such a thing but couldn't help herself.

"Aye, we were wed quietly the day after we reached London," Rosamond lied.

A painful silence ensued as Mariah tried to regain her composure. But the agony of Rosamond's words hit her like a blow to the gut. She was lost. No help would be forthcoming from any quarter.

Then, to Mariah's utter dismay, Rosamond slammed the door in her face. Stifling a sob, she turned and fled.

From the pain.

From the hopelessness of her situation.

Mariah walked for what seemed like hours. She walked aimlessly, without direction or purpose. When she finally roused herself from her stupor and became aware of her location, she realized she was standing outside the Fox and Hound. The inn was not far from Whitehall and very close to her own lodgings. She looked around to get her bearings and saw . . .

Falcon!

She gaped at him, unable to believe her good fortune. For a moment she could do naught but let her gaze drift over him, admiring the masculine perfection of his powerful build. He strode purposely toward the inn, the long muscles of his legs strong and shapely beneath his hose. She couldn't take her eyes off him, fascinated by the combination of hardness and softness in his face, the bold

217

angle of his nose, the full curve of his bottom lip, the way his thick lashes cast shadows over his cheekbones. And his eyes . . . how she loved his golden tiger eyes.

A lock of unruly midnight hair bounced against his wide forehead, reminding Mariah of the times she'd run her hands through the thick strands. He was large but not bulky. There wasn't an ounce of fat on his muscular body. He was a warrior with a warrior's body. And she loved every inch of it.

Mariah raised her hand to hail him just as he saw her. He stopped in his tracks. They stared at one another for two heartbeats, and then he seemed to explode as he started toward her, a look of utter disbelief on his face.

"Mariah!"

Mariah met him halfway, but he didn't react as she expected. Grasping her elbow, he dragged her into the inn and up the stairs to his rooms. He slammed the door shut with his foot and pulled her into his arms, kissing her with a desperation that took Mariah by surprise. A married man shouldn't be kissing a woman the way Falcon was kissing her.

Despite that knowledge, Mariah's body softened, yielded, melting against him. She opened her mouth to him, and their tongues dueled in rapturous abandon. His scalding heat seeped through her clothes and spread through her like a blistering fever—the very same way he had entered her life and her heart. His lips left her mouth; he pressed hot, fervent kisses across her jaw, down her neck, until he reached the round collar of her gown.

He looked up then, into her eyes, his arms tightening around her. "How did you get here?"

Mariah had been so caught up in the moment, she could scarcely think, let alone speak.

"Mariah, talk to me. Where is Robbie?"

Mariah found her voice. "Robbie is safe at an inn with Becca. Osgood is in control of Mildenhall. We escaped and came directly to London to seek the king's help."

"The king is in France."

"I know. Rosamond—"

He placed a finger against her lips. "Nay, say naught. I am just so relieved to see you. When Jamie told me Osgood had returned to Mildenhall, my fear knew no bounds."

"Jamie? Your squire? How did he know?"

"I had a premonition that all was not well and had him return to Mildenhall. He reported back to me just yesterday. You must have left shortly after he did."

She stepped away from him so she could think without being distracted by him. "Rosamond—"

"I've thought of naught but you since I left Mildenhall," Falcon interrupted, reaching for her.

Mariah tried to resist, but the moment he touched her, she was lost. His hands sought her breasts. She splayed her fingers against his chest, feeling the rapid pounding of his heart against his ribcage. He acted as if she mattered to him. How could that be?

Then she lost her train of thought as his mouth covered hers in a searing, devouring kiss. Though she knew that what she was doing was wrong, she slid her hands around him to stroke his back, feeling a desperate desire to touch him. With a ragged groan, he deepened their kiss, his tongue plunging and stroking while he filled his hands with her breasts, his fingers teasing her nipples through the material of her gown.

"Too many clothes," he muttered against her lips.

With swift urgency, he removed her cloak and began undressing her, releasing the buttons on her bodice and pushing it and her chemise down over her arms, baring her breasts.

"Falcon, what are you doing? Rosamond—"

"Nay, do not speak her name," Falcon said raggedly. "I want to make love to you. I *need* to make love to you."

Mariah needed it, too, even though she knew she would probably go to hell for sinning with him again. Her first grave sin had been taking Falcon to her bed while she was still wed to Edmond, and this time her sin would be bedding a married man. She had to try one last time to tell Falcon that she knew he was wed to Rosamond.

"Falcon, listen to me. Rosamond—"

"Nay, say naught. Just let me love you. We can talk later."

He lowered his head, his tongue laving swirls around her nipples and then drawing each aroused bud into the velvety heat of his mouth. Try as she might, Mariah couldn't help arching her back in a silent plea for him to taste more of her.

With a hoarse groan, he swiftly undressed her, his hands shaking with need. Then he scooped her into his arms and carried her to the bed. His doublet and boots were quickly shed, leaving naught but his hose full to bursting with his hardened flesh. Apprehension gnawed at her as he stripped off his hose, baring the awesome strength of his desire.

He sank to his knees beside her, trailing wet, open-mouthed kisses along her stomach. She sucked in a breath, inhaling deeply of his erotic musk. His tongue tasted the indentation of her navel; her muscles tensed, quivered.

"Spread your legs, Mariah," he demanded in a raw rasp.

Feeling as if she were being burned to a cinder, she obeyed. He rewarded her by lowering his head and stroking the swollen, wet folds between her thighs. It had always been thus with Falcon, Mariah thought before all coherent thought fled. She had no resistance where he was concerned.

She gasped, a sigh of pleasure falling from her lips in a soft purr as Falcon's mouth delved into her exposed cleft. His tongue traced the swelling bud of her sex, then slipped lower to probe the dewy entrance of her sheath. Mariah felt her body turning liquid, her senses focusing on his mouth and tongue stroking between her legs.

Falcon drew back slightly to blow on her damp flesh, then teased the peak of her sex with the tip of his tongue. Mariah clenched her fists and flung her head back, arching upward, pleading words gurgling in her throat. Just when she thought she could bear no more, he slid three fingers inside her slick channel. The erotic scent of her arousal drifted up to her.

Mariah couldn't move, couldn't think; her body trembled with pleasure. His mouth continued to torture her as his fingers thrust and withdrew, driving her mercilessly toward oblivion. She cried out sharply, her body convulsing in ecstasy as his fingers thrust and withdrew.

As she lay gasping on the bed, Falcon came over her, nudging her legs apart with his knees. The fiery hold of his gaze trapped her as powerful arms engulfed her slen-

221

der form. Mariah's breath caught as he lowered himself, his naked body pressing all along hers. With a strangled cry of surrender, her arms locked around his neck. How she had missed him—the feel of his naked body pressed against hers, the hair-roughened limbs, the stunning weight of his chest, his rippling muscles.

"Take me inside you," he whispered raggedly.

It was a raw plea. She could not deny him, no matter how wrong it might be. Her fingers curled around his rigid length and guided the engorged head of his sex through the damp curls to her entrance. She stared into his eyes as he flexed his hips and thrust deep. She felt the shudder that wracked him as he buried himself to the hilt with a single stroke.

She moaned as he plunged deep inside her, again and again, the forceful tempo driving her higher and higher, until she feared he would pierce her very soul. She arched against him, her inner muscles clenching his hard flesh as he drove her mercilessly, upward and onward, toward excruciating bliss.

Suddenly her body clenched in a massive shudder as contractions ripped through her. Yielding, straining in mindless abandon, she dug her nails into the muscles of his back and exploded. Fire rushed through her veins. She screamed; his mouth covered hers to absorb the sound. Then he lost control, pumping wildly, crying her name into her mouth as he released his seed.

Finally he collapsed against her, spent, trembling, his breathing harsh and grating. Dazed and exhausted, Mariah lay beneath him, contemplating the sin they had both committed against Rosamond, but refusing to regret it.

Falcon rolled off Mariah and dropped down beside her.

"I'm sorry—was I too rough? It seems I can't control myself with you."

"You didn't hurt me," Mariah assured him.

"Good," Falcon muttered, his eyes already closing.

Confusing thoughts whirled around in Mariah's head. Had Falcon truly been concerned about her and Robbie? If he did not care for his wife, why had he married her? Naught made sense where Falcon and Rosamond were concerned.

"Falcon, if you still care so much what happens to me and Robbie, why did you marry Rosamond?"

Silence.

She rose up on her elbow and peered down at him. He was sleeping, his mouth slightly open. She smiled. Falcon was as dear to her as Robbie.

But he wasn't hers.

He belonged to Rosamond.

Mariah had no right to force her troubles on him. Rosamond had warned her away from Falcon. The least she could do after what had happened between her and Falcon today was leave him to his wife.

She had just made love to another woman's husband, and though she didn't regret it, she would never forget it.

Mariah eased out of bed and quickly dressed. She knew what she must do. She had to return to Mildenhall. Somehow she'd find a way to thwart Osgood and gain a measure of peace for herself and Robbie.

Chapter Thirteen

"Don't leave, Mama," Robbie sobbed when Mariah announced she must return to Mildenhall the following morning.

"I have to go, darling," Mariah soothed, hugging him tightly. "Becca will take good care of you while I'm gone."

"Why do you have to leave? Why can't I go with you?"

"Sir Osgood is in control of Mildenhall, 'tis too dangerous for you to return. You'll be fine here with Becca."

Becca sent Mariah a shaky smile. "I won't let anything happen to Robbie, my lady, even though London frightens me. I do not like big cities."

"I know, Becca, and I pray it won't be for long. I'll send for you as soon as I'm able. Meanwhile, I'm placing my precious son in your care."

"Won't Falcon help us, Mama?"

Mariah sought to make her answer to Robbie's question sound reasonable, even though her heart was breaking. "Falcon can't help us, darling. Falcon and Rosamond are married now. It really wouldn't be a good idea to burden him with our problems. We can solve this on our own." Though she had no idea how.

"Did you speak to Sir Falcon, my lady?" Becca asked. "Did you ask for his help?"

"I spoke with him yesterday, Becca, in his rooms at the Fox and Hound. I know his wife would never approve of his getting involved in problems.

"I'm leaving you most of the money we brought with us," Mariah continued. "There's a secondhand clothing store off Bond Street. Buy warm clothing for yourself and Robbie. The days are growing colder. I'm leaving a horse for your use."

Fighting her tears, Becca nodded. "Be very careful, my lady. Sir Osgood can't be trusted."

"I will, Becca. Be good, Robbie. Just remember, Mama loves you and wants you safe. Kiss me good-bye now, for I intend to leave before you wake up tomorrow."

Falcon awoke in the wee hours of morning, surprised that he had slept through the afternoon and far into the night. He reached across the bed to pull Mariah against him and encountered naught but rumpled bedding. The room was dark; an errant beam of moonlight filtering through the window fell across the empty bed. Falcon peered into the darkest corners of the room, softly calling Mariah's name, though his senses told him he was alone—utterly and devastatingly alone.

Mariah had left him. Why? What had he done or said to make her leave before telling him where he could find her? He wanted to help her reclaim Mildenhall. He'd told her they would discuss her predicament later; he had been too eager to have her beneath him again, to be inside her, to show her how desperately he had missed her, to wait. He felt a deep, abiding connection to Mariah, an emotion he had experienced with no other woman.

Falcon had to find her, wouldn't rest until he did. Together they would make plans to reclaim Mildenhall for Robbie. Though Falcon wracked his brain, he could not recall Mariah telling him where she was staying. He chafed at the delay, but realized he would have to wait until morning to hunt for the woman who had insinuated herself into his life and became an integral part of it.

Mariah spent a sleepless night, anxious for daylight so she could begin her journey. At first light, she dressed, kissed a sleeping Robbie and left the inn, taking only bread and cheese from the kitchen to break her fast. To her relief, the first leg of her trip proved uneventful. After spending the night at the Traveler's Haven in Cambridge, she continued on the following morning to Mildenhall village.

Mariah reached the village that evening without incident. The journey, completed so swiftly, had left her exhausted, so she decided to spend a few nights at the small village inn while formulating her plans and learning how things stood at the keep.

Mr. Maypole, the proprietor, gaped at her when she entered the dim taproom. "My lady, why have you returned? 'Tis dangerous for you to be here."

"I've thought this through, Master Maypole, and decided the only way to free Mildenhall is to face the problem. Are my guardsmen still being held prisoner inside the keep?"

"Aye. We all pray for their safety."

"What about Edwina and Father Francis?"

"No one has seen them since you left the keep."

Mariah's heart plummeted. Things at Mildenhall were even worse than when she'd left. She had hoped Edwina and the priest had found a safe haven away from the keep.

"I'll need a room for a few days to rest and make my plans. But I have no funds to pay for my stay."

"Worry not, my lady," Maypole said, "your lack of funds means naught to me. You and Lord Edmond have been good to everyone in our small village. You may stay in our best room and eat our food as long as you like. No payment is required."

"Would a bath be too much trouble?" Mariah asked.

"No trouble at all. My good wife will see to it and prepare you a decent meal."

"Please tell no one that I've returned, Mr. Maypole, for I wish to confront Sir Osgood on my own terms. I left my horse in the courtyard. Would you please see to it?"

"Of course, my lady, whatever you say, but surely you must know that no one in the village would betray you."

"I know, and I am grateful."

"Is your lad with you, my lady?"

"Nay, I left him and Becca in a safe place," Mariah replied. "After a bath, food and a good night's rest, I will decide what I need to do to save Mildenhall."

Mariah didn't venture from the inn while formulating her plan to free the guardsmen. As for keeping her presence in the village a secret, she might as well have stood in the square and announced her return. So many people visited her at the inn, offering help and wishing her well, that she was surprised Osgood himself hadn't heard about her return and sent his mercenaries to fetch her.

Several days passed before a viable plan began to take form in Mariah's mind. It included telling some falsehoods, but she had no compunction about lying to Osgood. As long as Robbie was safe in London, she feared neither Osgood nor Walter.

Aware that delaying a confrontation would solve naught, Mariah walked the short distance to the castle late in the afternoon on the fourth day of her stay at the inn. The portcullis was firmly in place when she arrived, but her presence did not go unobserved. One of Osgood's mercenaries peered down at her from the wall walk.

"Who goes there?" he asked in a booming voice.

"Mariah of Mildenhall. Raise the portcullis."

The guard's head disappeared behind the wall. A long time passed before Mariah saw Osgood and Walter striding across the courtyard toward the gate. She waited patiently for them to arrive, rehearsing in her mind what to say.

"What do you want?" Osgood growled. "Mildenhall belongs to me now. You have no business here."

"Let me in," she answered. "Mildenhall is my home, and I wish to return."

Osgood stepped closer to the portcullis, peering through the bars at Mariah. "Where's the boy?"

"Robbie is safe. Isn't it enough that I am here?"

"What good are you without the boy?" Walter barked.

"I thought you wished to marry me," Mariah ventured.

"Aye," Walter replied, "but not until the boy is delivered to us. He needs to be where we can keep watch over him. Where is he, Mariah? I will fetch him myself and bring him home."

"I see no reason to bring Robbie into a hostile environment."

"Robbie belongs at Mildenhall," Osgood argued. "Fetch the boy, and the portcullis will be opened to both of you."

"I cannot do that," Mariah countered. "How do I know your intentions toward Robbie are honorable?"

"Because I have given my word."

Mariah snorted. "How can I trust the word of a liar and bully? Nay, Osgood, Robbie will stay where he is, unless you prove you can be trusted. The only proof I will accept is an act of good faith."

"I owe you naught," Osgood bellowed. "Mildenhall is mine whether or not you wed Walter. Possession is nine-tenths of the law."

"If I appeal to the king, he will send troops to reclaim my home. His decision has already been made concerning Mildenhall's heir. The earldom belongs to my son. 'Tis his legacy."

Osgood gave a bark of laughter. "I doubt Henry will make the effort."

Mariah detected a note of uncertainty in Osgood's voice. She searched for a way to use his weakness to her advantage. "You are deliberately flouting the king's decision. Is that wise?"

"Bah! The king could be chasing Welshmen, or Scotsmen, or even in France, seizing territory to add to his kingdom. He has no time to waste on a widow with little standing. And Falcon is out of your reach; you no longer have a champion."

How true, Mariah thought, but that wouldn't stop her

from exploiting Osgood's tenuous position. "You could be wrong. Falcon could be on his way to Mildenhall even as we speak."

Osgood paled. "Is he?"

Though her insides were roiling, she said calmly, "He could be. You won't know until he arrives. But if I am inside the keep, he will be reluctant to attack."

While Osgood mulled this over, Walter expressed his disbelief. "Falcon won't come, Mariah. He is wed to Rosamond and unlikely to leave her for the likes of you and your son. You can enter Mildenhall, but only with Robbie."

"And I repeat," Mariah replied, holding firm against the evil pair, "I cannot and will not entrust my son to someone who wishes him harm. You must prove yourselves worthy of my trust before I will consider your request."

"I would never hurt the lad," Walter lied, pasting a false smile on his face. "I will raise him as my own, alongside the children we will have together."

Mariah suppressed a shudder but gamely continued. She had a purpose in mind and prayed that it would come to fruition. "Prove it," she said.

"Stop this foolishness!" Osgood demanded. "Tell us what you want."

"Allow Edwina, Father Francis and my guardsmen to leave Mildenhall."

"Are you mad?"

"I'm being reasonable. Let my people go or prepare to face the king's wrath."

"If I let them leave," Osgood said, "will you fetch Robbie and bring him to us?"

Mariah crossed her fingers behind her back and asked God to forgive her lie. "Aye, you have my word."

"I will go with you to fetch him," Walter offered.

Mariah groaned. How was she going to get out of this? She was digging herself deeper into a hole. "Very well, I agree to your terms, but not until you send out my people."

"I need the servants and your steward; they will remain with us," Osgood argued.

Mariah decided she had pushed her luck as far as she could. Besides, Osgood needed the servants and Sir Martin; she doubted he would harm them. "As you wish," she agreed.

"Stay here and keep an eye on Mariah while I arrange for the release of her people," Osgood ordered his son.

While Mariah had been making plans in her room in Mildenhall village, Falcon had been searching London for her. Both Jamie and Sir Dennis offered their help, which Falcon gratefully accepted. Since inns abounded in London, Falcon feared he would never find Mariah. But he wasn't about to give up. He purchased a map of London, assigning different streets to Jamie and Dennis so they wouldn't overlap one another.

Falcon returned to his lodgings on the evening of his second day of fruitless searching and ordered supper in his room. Weary and despondent, he spread out the map and pored over it while he awaited his supper. There came a rap on his door. Thinking it was his meal, he called permission to enter. The door opened.

"Set the tray on the table," Falcon said.

"Falcon!"

A small body hurtled forward, colliding with Falcon's knees and nearly toppling him. Robbie's little arms clung tightly, as if he were afraid Falcon would disappear should he let go. Falcon looked past Robbie at Becca, who stood on the threshold, wringing her hands.

Falcon lifted Robbie in his arms. The lad began to sob, wetting Falcon's shirt front.

"Where is your mama, Robbie? Has something happened to her?"

"M-M-Mama went away," Robbie stuttered between sobs.

Stunned, Falcon stared at Robbie. "She left?" He looked at Becca for confirmation. When she nodded, Falcon invited her in and closed the door. "Tell me what happened."

"My lady returned to Mildenhall, sir. She left Robbie in my care because she feared Sir Osgood would hurt him. She said she would send for us as soon as she reclaimed the keep from Sir Osgood."

Falcon cursed beneath his breath, mindful of the young lad clinging to his neck. He couldn't imagine why Mariah would return to Mildenhall without apprising him of her intentions. Had their passionate encounter meant naught to her? Why hadn't she confided in him? Did she think he would deny her request for help? Naught made sense to him.

"How did you find me?" Falcon asked.

"My lady mentioned where you were staying before she left, but said she didn't want to burden you with her problems. I took the chance that you would still be here."

"Burden me!" Falcon shouted, causing Becca to flinch. "Damnation! I cannot believe what I am hearing. You should have come to me the moment Mariah left. What finally brought you here?"

"I do not like London," Becca whispered. "I'm afraid to leave the inn for fear we'll be accosted on the streets. Robbie cries nearly every day for his mother; I could think of naught to do but try to find you and beg your help. We both want to go home."

"You were wise to come to me, Becca," Falcon said. "I've been searching for Mariah and Robbie since the day she visited me in my rooms. Your lady explained that Osgood had invaded Mildenhall, but she left before I could offer my help. I didn't know where to find her, because she didn't tell me where she was staying."

"You'll help us, then?" Becca asked in a trembling voice.

"Help us, Falcon," Robbie begged. "I miss Mama. What if Osgood hurts her?"

Falcon's heart went out to the lad. "Of course I'll help, Robbie. Did you doubt it? Where are you staying?"

"At the King's Arms," Becca replied.

"Damnation! That's just around the corner! I spent two days looking for you while you were but a stone's throw away. I'll send Jamie to fetch your things as soon as he returns. Meanwhile, I'll engage a room for you and Robbie here, where I can keep an eye on you until we leave for Mildenhall."

"You're going to take me home!" Robbie crowed. He sent a superior look at Becca. "See, Becca, I told you Falcon would help us."

Becca dashed away a tear. "That you did, Robbie lad, but your mother said Sir Falcon's wife wouldn't approve."

"My wife?" Falcon nearly strangled over the word. "Why would Mariah think I was wed when I said naught to her about having a wife?"

"I know not, sir. Are you saying you're not wed?"

"That's exactly what I am saying."

"When can we leave, Falcon?" Robbie asked.

"Tomorrow, if at all possible, Robbie, my lad. It will take but a few hours to gather my men, and then we will leave London to reclaim Mildenhall for you and your mother."

True to his word, Falcon and his party left London the following day, riding full tilt for Mildenhall. He prayed he wasn't too late, vowing to rid Mildenhall of Osgood's vile presence once and for all.

As Falcon neared Mildenhall, Mariah waited at the portcullis for her guardsmen to appear, pacing back and forth while Walter watched her.

"Marrying me is a wise choice, Mariah. I swear you won't be sorry," Walter said. "You have naught to fear from me as long as you remember your place."

"Like your mother and Elizabeth have naught to fear from your father?" Mariah goaded. "You could have helped both of them had you shown some gumption. Instead, you stood by while your father abused them."

Walter's expression turned sour. "At least Mother knows her place, which is more than I can say for you. So did Elizabeth until you turned her against us." His expression softened. "You'll learn soon enough, Mariah. And when you do, you'll realize I'm not the ogre you think me. All I need from you is a son."

"Over my dead body," Mariah muttered beneath her

breath. She knew exactly what would happen to Robbie once she bore Walter a son.

"What did you say?"

"I said naught."

Walter's reply was forestalled when Osgood appeared, prodding Edwina and Father Francis before him.

Edwina's face drained of all color when she saw Mariah. She stopped in her tracks. "Mariah, what have you done?"

"Move," Osgood snarled, giving Edwina a vicious shove. She stumbled, and then sprawled on the ground at Osgood's feet. Father Francis helped her up.

"Hurt her and our agreement is off," Mariah warned.

Edwina, leaning heavily on Father Francis, hobbled toward the gate, her gaze fixed on Mariah's face.

"Raise the portcullis!" Osgood shouted.

The portcullis cranked open. "Go," Osgood ordered; "both of you."

Edwina and the priest walked through the gate. "What is this about?" Edwina whispered so only Mariah could hear. "Why did you return? Are the king's troops on their way?"

"I know what I'm doing," Mariah replied. "Father Francis, take Edwina to the village. Tell Mr. Maypole I sent you, that you're both to be given rooms in his inn."

"Mariah," Edwina pleaded, "please tell me you're not going to do anything foolish."

"Don't worry. Robbie is safe," Mariah whispered. "He's with Becca; they're staying in London at the King's Arms. It's near Whitehall. Take care of him if I'm not able. Please go now; my work here isn't finished."

Mariah watched as the pair hurried down the path toward the village; then she turned to confront Osgood.

"Where are my guardsmen? Not all my terms have been met."

Osgood muttered a curse and raised his arm. It must have been a signal, for immediately a line of men, possessing neither armor nor weapons, emerged from the keep and proceeded under guard to the portcullis.

"Never let it be said that Osgood Fitzhugh didn't keep his word. As you can see, your guardsmen are unharmed." He laughed. "They will be of little use to you without weapons or horses."

"At least they are free to seek employment elsewhere," Mariah maintained.

Each guardsman stopped before her to bow over her hand and renew his fealty as he walked through the portcullis.

"Sir Maynard," she whispered as her captain of the guard paused before her, "meet me in the stables behind the inn at midnight tonight."

The men moved on.

"Well, Mariah, I kept my part of the bargain. The rest is up to you. Walter will go with you to fetch Robbie."

"Walter may call for me tomorrow at the inn," Mariah replied with false bravado. "You've kept me waiting so long, 'tis too late to leave tonight."

Osgood kept his rage well in hand, though Mariah could tell he was eager to vent it.

"What nonsense is this? Are you not a woman of your word?"

How easily lies slipped from her mouth. "It grows late; we will leave to fetch Robbie tomorrow and not before."

"Is he not in the village?"

"Nay, he is not. Your men made a thorough search of

the village, so you must know he is not there. He is nowhere near Mildenhall."

"Then you will abide the night here with us."

"I will await Walter at the inn," Mariah insisted.

Osgood scowled at her. "Walter will accompany you. I trust you not, Mariah."

"Then we are even, Osgood. Walter may come if he wishes, but I doubt he will find room at the inn."

"I'm not going to sleep in a stable, Father. I enjoy my comforts too much. Send one of our men to keep watch over Mariah until I fetch her in the morning."

"Very well, but if she tricks us, I'll retaliate in a way she won't like. Sir Martin and the servants will suffer the consequences if she does not keep her word."

A chill settled deep in Mariah's gut. How in God's name was she going to get out of this mess without harming those she cared about? She would set Father Francis to praying for deliverance from this impossible situation.

Spinning on her heel, Mariah set off for the village before Osgood could change his mind. Moments later, a mercenary, having received hasty orders from Osgood, jogged after her.

Dame Helen, the innkeeper's wife, rushed forth to greet Mariah when she arrived at the inn. "My lady, you've returned. Are you all right?"

"I am well, Dame Helen."

"Who is that?" Helen asked when Osgood's mercenary placed himself between her and Mariah.

"Osgood sent one of his men to make sure I don't flee. Did Edwina and Father Francis arrive?"

"Aye, they occupy our last two rooms."

Mariah started toward the stairs.

"Where are you going, lady?" the mercenary asked.

"I need to speak to Edwina and Father Francis."

"Nay, 'tis not allowed. Sir Osgood ordered me to stand guard outside the door until Walter arrives in the morning to fetch you. You are to confer with no one."

"What harm can there be in talking to a priest and an old woman?" Mariah argued.

"I know not. I have my orders, lady, and dare not disobey them. Sir Osgood deals harshly with failure."

Mariah had no choice but to climb the stairs, enter her room and fume in impotent rage as the door slammed behind her. After pacing the length of the room and back several times, Mariah opened the door and peered into the hall.

To her consternation, the guard prowled outside her door. "Is there something you wish, lady?"

"Naught from you," she replied, closing the door and leaning against it. How was she to slip out to meet Sir Maynard with a guard watching her?

Later that evening, Dame Helen arrived with Mariah's supper. "Are Edwina and Father Francis all right?" Mariah whispered.

"Aye. They tried to visit you, but your guard turned them away."

"I'm to meet Sir Maynard in the stable at midnight, but I don't know how I'm to accomplish it without alerting the guard." She ran to the window, disappointed that no sturdy tree existed for her to climb down. Despondent, she sank onto the bed. "How will I ever get out of this? Naught Osgood could do will make me give up Robbie to him."

"Don't lose hope, my lady. Your guard was yawning when I passed him. Mayhap if I offer to send up a chair for him to sit on and feed him tea laced with soporific herbs, he will fall asleep so you can sneak out to meet Sir Maynard."

Mariah clasped Dame Helen's hands in hers. "Thank you, Dame Helen. Any help would be appreciated."

Mariah ate her supper without really tasting it. Would her problems never end? She worried about Robbie and Becca, alone and friendless in London.

To make matters worse, her thoughts kept straying to Falcon. The man must be a total degenerate if he could make love to her so passionately just a few days after marrying Rosamond. Had he no conscience, no morals?

Was she any better than he for allowing a married man to make love to her?

Thrusting Falcon from her mind, Mariah worried about how Osgood would react when she refused to lead Walter to Robbie. Her remaining hope for rescue rested with Sir Maynard and her guardsmen. If she was able to meet with them tonight, she intended to send them to seek help from Edmond's neighbors, men who had been friends with her husband. But would that help arrive in time to save her?

Mariah awakened from a light doze as the chapel bell tolled Matins. The hour of midnight had finally arrived. She rose from her chair and tiptoed to the door. Holding her breath, she opened the door and peeked out. If God was good to her, she'd find the guard sleeping.

To her utter delight, the guard was sprawled in a chair that Dame Helen had provided, a cup sitting on the floor and his head resting against the wall. His mouth was open, emitting loud snores. Mariah stepped out into the hall, closed the door behind her and tiptoed past him. In a trice she was down the stairs and out the door, racing around to the stables.

The comforting scent of horses and hay greeted Mariah. There was no light, no sound, just utter silence and obsidian darkness.

"My lady," someone whispered.

"Sir Maynard, is that you?"

"Aye, we're here, my lady."

"I don't have much time, so listen carefully."

Though she saw naught but shadows, Mariah felt the reassuring presence of her loyal men.

"Tell us what you wish us to do, my lady," Maynard said. "We are too few to storm Mildenhall, and have no weapons, armor or horses."

"We need help, and quickly. I want you to make your way with the greatest haste to the estates of Lord Edmond's friends. I know Lord Branbury to the east of here and Lord Thornhill to the west would help if they were made aware of my predicament. Both estates lie but a short distance from Mildenhall. Beg the lords to lend you whatever you need in the way of weapons, armor and mounts. And most important, bring men to help reclaim Mildenhall for Edmond's heir."

"We are afoot, my lady," Maynard reminded her.

"Take six horses from Master Maypole's stables. Ride double if you must. Do not attempt to reclaim Mildenhall until you have sufficient weapons and help to succeed. Arrange to meet and coordinate your efforts the day after tomorrow at the huge willow tree near the brook in the forest beyond the village."

"What about you, my lady?" Sir Maynard asked. "Come with us."

"Worry not about me. Reclaim Mildenhall for Robbie. If something happens to me, Edwina knows where to find him. She and Father Francis will see him restored to his rightful place at Mildenhall."

"But, my lady—"

Suddenly a light appeared in the stable yard. "Lady Mariah! I know you're out here somewhere." The light swung in a wide arc.

"Go," Mariah hissed as she stepped aside to allow her men access to the horses. "I'll keep the guard occupied while you lead the horses out of the stable. Make as little noise as possible."

The men melted into the darkness. Mariah heard movement in the stalls as she strode off to waylay the guard. She met him in the courtyard. He grasped Mariah's arm, hauling her back toward the inn.

"You have caused me a great deal of trouble, lady," he growled. "What are you doing out here?"

"I felt in need of some air," Mariah fabricated.

He shook his shaggy head. "I must have fallen asleep; Sir Osgood will have my head for this." His grip tightened on her. "Did that old witch you call a healer give me something to make me sleep?"

"Do not blame my friends for your incompetence."

The guard stopped abruptly beneath a tree, his face red with anger as he turned to confront Mariah. "We will both suffer for this, lady."

Mariah knew a moment of fear as the guard's rage escalated. Would he strike her? Then something behind the man caught her eye. A shadowy figure moved stealthily toward them. She watched in disbelief as the figure hovered behind the mercenary, lifted something large and heavy and brought it down on the man's head.

The rush light dropped from his hand as he made a slow spiral to the ground. Mariah snatched up the torch and lifted it high. Stunned, Mariah saw Dame Helen standing over the mercenary, a heavy iron skillet dangling from her hand.

"Are you all right, my lady?" Helen asked.

"Aye, and I thank you, Dame Helen. But you shouldn't have done that. You could be in serious trouble."

"Nay, my lady. The brute here"—she nudged him with her toe—"didn't know what hit him. I heard him stumbling down the stairs, grabbed my skillet and followed."

The sound of horses' hooves pounding away from the inn brought a smile to Mariah's lips. Her guardsmen had gotten away; help would be on its way soon.

Helen must have heard them, too, for she said, "You must leave with your men before the guard awakens."

"I cannot. The people at Mildenhall will suffer if I leave."

"Don't be foolish, my lady. Leave now, while you still can. Robbie needs you."

Mariah was torn. "I cannot leave Sir Martin and the servants to face Osgood's wrath. I fear he will kill them."

"You must leave regardless. You alone, can petition the king for help. If you are imprisoned, there will be no one to make Sir Osgood pay for what he has done and may yet do."

After much soul-searching, Mariah agreed to leave. She could do more for her people if she was free than if she was locked up inside the keep.

Chapter Fourteen

Falcon drove his men relentlessly toward Mildenhall. When darkness made travel unsafe, he called a halt a short distance south of the village and led his men through the forest to a clearing well back from the road. They took care of their horses and ate a cold meal of bread and cheese. Then everyone but the guards posted as lookouts rolled up in their cloaks on the ground, resting their heads on their saddles.

Falcon did not join them just yet. Strapping on his sword, he set off to scout the immediate area. He had no idea why he felt uneasy. Perhaps it was Mildenhall's towers, which rose like sentinels against the night sky, that drew him from the safety of the campsite. Or perhaps it was thoughts of Mariah imprisoned inside the keep, at Osgood's mercy.

No matter how long or hard Falcon thought about it, he could not figure out what had made Mariah leave his bed and flee to Mildenhall. Her actions did not make sense. What did she think she could accomplish on her own?

Falcon paused when he emerged from the forest onto

the road. The little-traveled dirt track was deserted, just as it should be at this time of night. He knew he should return to camp and try to sleep, but being this close to Mildenhall and Mariah made him anxious to do something . . . anything. Sighing in resignation, he decided to return to camp, but stopped in his tracks when he heard what sounded like a horse carefully picking its way down the rutted road.

Falcon melted back into the shadows, eager to learn who would risk life and limb traveling on a moonless night well after Matins. The horse and rider approached from the village, that much Falcon knew. When the horse drew abreast of him, he unsheathed his sword and stepped in front of the startled animal.

"Halt!"

Fright pounded through Mariah's breast when she realized she was being challenged. She had no idea Osgood had posted guards this far from the keep. For a moment she considered digging her heels into her mount and risking injury or worse to escape her challenger. But the man holding the sword looked big and burly enough to drag her from the saddle as she dashed past him. When he grasped the horse's reins, Mariah knew she had hesitated too long. She had been caught. Her fate was now in Osgood's hands, for she would not lead Walter to Robbie no matter what they did to her.

"Dismount!"

Mariah hesitated, but in the end had no choice but to obey. She slid from the horse's back. When she turned to confront her nemesis, she heard a loud gasp. And then the man whispered her name.

"Mariah?"

Mariah's heart pounded furiously as the man slowly lowered his sword. *Nay, it couldn't be.* "Who is it?"

The man grasped her arm and dragged her against him. She recognized his scent as a familiar heat enveloped her, and nearly collapsed in relief. What was Falcon doing here? How did he know she had returned to Mildenhall?

Mariah clung to him; a myriad of emotions raced through her brain, a hundred questions were on the tip of her tongue. But she could do naught but repeat his name, over and over.

"It's all right, Mariah," Falcon soothed. "I'm here. You're safe now. I'm not going to let anything happen to you."

Mariah opened her mouth to ask how he'd known where to find her but the words froze in her throat when Falcon claimed her lips. His kiss stole not only her words but her senses. Her arms circled his neck as he pulled her closer, his mouth ravishing hers with such passion, Mariah feared her bones would melt.

When Falcon finally broke off the kiss, Mariah went limp. His arms tightened around her and he held her close to his heart.

"Foolish woman," he said. "You cannot begin to know how worried I was about you. Why did you leave my bed without a word of explanation? Why did you leave London before I had time to muster my men? I thought you understood that I would help you reclaim Mildenhall."

"I hoped you would, but realized it was a foolish dream after I spoke with Rosamond."

"You called on Rosamond?"

"Aye. I didn't know where to find you and hoped she would tell me where you were."

"'Tis too dangerous to stand in plain sight, even though it is the middle of the night," Falcon said as he grasped the horse's reins and led Mariah and her mount into the forest. When they came to a small clearing, he tethered the horse to a sapling and grasped her hand. Then he seated her on a grassy mound, unbuckled his sword, leaned it against a tree and dropped down beside her.

"What did Rosamond tell you?"

Mariah hesitated. Though she didn't feel comfortable in disparaging Falcon's wife, she didn't want to lie to Falcon. "She told me about your marriage."

Falcon cursed beneath his breath. "Go on. What else did Rosamond tell you?"

"She said you intended to join the king in France."

"That much was true. Did she tell you where to find me?"

"Nay, she refused. She told me to stay away from you."

"But you did find me. We met outside my lodgings."

Mariah sighed. "Our meeting was a coincidence. I happened to be on my way to my own lodgings at the time. With the king away and unable to help me, and you married, I realized I had to depend upon myself to outwit Osgood and reclaim Mildenhall for Robbie. I left Robbie with Becca in London and returned to Mildenhall."

A slim beam of moonlight pierced through an opening in the clouds, revealing Falcon's features. His expression was hard, angry. Shivering, Mariah leaned away from him.

His arms circled her shoulders and brought her closer against him. "You're cold."

"Nay. Your expression is . . . frightening. Are you angry at me?"

"When I awakened and found you gone, I was furious. I couldn't imagine why you would sneak away like that. I had no idea where to find you, or what I'd said or done to make you angry."

"You did naught, 'twas I. I realized I had no right to burden you with my problems. You are wed; you owe me and Robbie naught."

"Damn Rosamond! She lied. I didn't marry her, Mariah. I decided I couldn't live the way she wanted me to."

Joy surged through Mariah. He wasn't married! Then another thought occurred. "Oh, Falcon, how could you give up everything Rosamond had to offer, everything you've ever wanted?"

"'Twas easy. I've gotten along just fine without land or wealth. Forgive me for not telling you in London, but I assumed you'd know I wasn't wed when you found me in my bachelor lodgings. I searched for you after you left, and would have continued the search if Becca hadn't come to me."

Shock shuddered through Mariah. "Becca came to you?"

"Aye, she brought Robbie to my lodgings. Being alone and friendless in London terrified her."

"I knew she didn't like London, but she assured me that she and Robbie could fend for themselves for a while. I did what I thought best to keep Robbie safe. I'm on my way to rejoin them now."

"There's no need, Mariah. Becca and Robbie are staying at the Traveler's Inn in Cambridge. I took them there myself. Cambridge is a small, quiet town; they will be safe until things are settled at Mildenhall. I left a man to guard them, so you have naught to worry about."

Mariah nearly collapsed in relief. "Thank you. Now I can concentrate on reclaiming my home without worrying about Robbie."

"Tell me everything that's happened since you left London."

Mariah hesitated a moment to gather her thoughts. "I reached the village without incident and stayed at the inn a few days to formulate my plans before confronting Osgood." Then the rest came tumbling out—how she'd gained freedom for her men and sent them to fetch help. She tried to gloss over the part where she'd promised to bring Robbie back to Mildenhall, but Falcon would have none of it.

"You what?" Falcon gasped. "Repeat what you just said."

"I lied to Osgood. I would never place Robbie in Osgood's keeping. I lied to free my guardsmen. I needed them to fetch help from Edmond's neighbors."

"What did you think would happen to you when you refused to return your son to Mildenhall?"

"I hoped Sir Maynard would return with help before I had to admit that I'd lied."

"Finish your story. You said Osgood's mercenary was ordered to keep you imprisoned in your chamber at the inn until Walter arrived. How did you escape?"

Mariah related all the details to Falcon's satisfaction, including her meeting with Sir Maynard and her instructions to him. She also related Dame Helen's part in her escape.

"Good for Dame Helen," Falcon said.

"I didn't want to leave," Mariah said. "Osgood threatened to kill Sir Martin and the servants if I tried to trick him. I shouldn't have listened to Dame Helen. Fleeing as I did places my people in danger."

"Have you any idea what Osgood might have done to you when you refused to reveal your son's location?"

Mariah shrugged. "It didn't matter as long as Robbie was safe. And I held to the hope that Edmond's friends and neighbors would come to my defense. I know the king would have intervened if he was in London, but I didn't have the funds to remain in the city until his return. His absence could have been a lengthy one."

Falcon glared at her. "Your thinking was faulty, Mariah. Your first mistake was leaving my bed without telling me where to find you. Everything you did after that placed your life in danger."

Mariah bristled. "You should have told me you weren't married before we . . . before we . . ."

"Before we made love? I had no idea you'd spoken with Rosamond. I intended to tell you that Rosamond and I had parted ways, but my need for you was immediate. Forgive me, Mariah. We both did things we shouldn't have; neither of us was thinking clearly that day. Admit it—you wanted me as badly as I wanted you."

"Mayhap I did, but I suffered for it. I believed I'd made love to a married man. Guilt weighed heavily upon me."

He touched her face, letting his fingers slide down her cheek and lower. The pulse in her neck jumped when his fingers lingered there.

"It will be dawn soon," Falcon murmured. "We have so little time."

He rose and spread his cloak on the ground, then grasped Mariah's hand. "Lie with me, sweeting."

"Here?"

"I can think of no better place."

He knelt on his cloak and pulled Mariah down beside him. She resisted but a moment before following her heart's desire. Refusing Falcon anything was impossible.

Gently he laid her down and covered her with his body. A pale sliver of moonlight filtered through the trees, illuminating the tense, drawn lines of his face. Mariah was surprised to realize just how deep his concern for her had been.

She melted into his kiss, stroking his cheek. His stubble of beard rasped against her palm. How dearly she loved this man. How desperately she wanted to tell him the truth about Robbie—that he was Robbie's father.

Falcon couldn't get enough of Mariah's kisses. Her mouth tasted sweeter than honey; her body, so familiar to him, was dearer than life. Why had it taken him so long to realize that everything he'd ever wanted rested right here in his arms?

He wanted her naked, but the night was too cold. Danger surrounded them, he could smell it in the air. Come dawn, he would take Mariah to Cambridge, where she would remain safe while he won back Mildenhall for her and Robbie. But tonight, before dawn parted them, all he could think about was making love to her.

He found the hem of her skirt and slid his hand beneath it, raising the material as his fingers skimmed along her leg and thigh.

"I want to make love to you, Mariah."

251

He caressed her stomach as he lifted her skirt higher, baring her lower body to his avid gaze. "I wish I could see you more clearly. One day soon, sweeting, I will have you naked beneath me in a soft bed where no one will disturb us."

Mariah gasped when he sifted his fingers through her feminine hair, seeking the tender folds of her womanhood.

"Lower your bodice for me—I want to taste your breasts."

Mariah didn't hesitate. Once she'd freed her breasts, Falcon's mouth fastened on a nipple, sucking, licking, teasing the tender bud fully erect. Then he shifted his attention to the other nipple, lavishing the same attention on it. When she moaned and arched against him, Falcon's mouth left her breasts, gliding over the smooth skin of her belly to her weeping center.

His tongue slid between the succulent folds, savoring the sweetness of her passion. He could taste her forever, but fear of discovery and lack of time made that impossible.

"Falcon . . ." His name whispered from her lips on a long sigh.

With great reluctance, he lifted his head from the vee between her legs. "I know, love, I feel the same things you do. I'd like to draw this out longer, but we cannot linger here."

He scooted upward, lowered his body flush against hers and kissed her. She responded eagerly, her mouth opening beneath his, tongues tangling, breath mingling.

Falcon broke off the kiss; she looked up at him. The planes of his face were taut with passion, his eyes stark with need. He fumbled with his hose, and then his rampant sex sprang free. "Open your legs for me, love." His voice was harsh, grating, his breathing erratic.

Her legs fell apart; he settled between them, fitting his loins in the cradle of her thighs. "Take me, Mariah. Take me now."

Shaking with need, Mariah felt the rigid length of his sex pressing against her thigh. She wanted him inside her, needed to feel his strength. Reaching between them, she clasped his staff and brought it to her throbbing center. She felt the tip penetrate her, but it wasn't enough. She needed all of him.

Grasping his buttocks, she arched upward, forcing him deeper. But he still wasn't deep enough. "Falcon, please."

"Aye, love, we shall please each other."

Flexing his hips, he drove himself to the hilt, filling her completely. Mariah gave a satisfied sigh as she moved in tandem with his forceful thrusts, raising her hips high to take everything he had to offer, just as she gave him her all.

Mariah soared, heat seared her; she was afire, from her breasts to her loins. Her breath caught, nearly stopped altogether as her body grew rigid. Then the contractions started, followed by pleasure so physically powerful, so glorious, that she cried out Falcon's name.

Falcon covered her lips, taking her cries into his mouth as his own climax exploded through his body. He stiffened, shuddered, and emptied himself inside her. Mariah accepted the comfort of his weight as he collapsed against her, holding him tightly, never wanting to let him go.

Falcon lifted himself away from her. "As much as I would like to lie here with you, I cannot, love. If I don't return to camp soon, Sir Dennis will send out a search party. You'll come with me, of course."

He rose, lifted her to her feet and adjusted his hose. Then he helped her fasten her bodice and smooth her skirts into place.

"I cannot go with you," Mariah said, startling Falcon.

"What in damnation are you talking about?"

"I must return to Mildenhall. Osgood holds Sir Martin and my people hostage. Their lives are at risk."

A mixture of anger and frustration made Falcon's voice harsh. "I won't let you return. You can't go backward, only forward."

"Listen to me, Falcon," Mariah pleaded. "I instructed my guardsmen and allies to rendezvous nearby to plan their strategy for reclaiming Mildenhall. If I return to the keep, it won't be for long. Now that you're here, our victory is assured. Once my guardsmen arrive with reinforcements, Osgood cannot hold Mildenhall. He will be forced to surrender."

"I know that, but have you considered what might happen to you in the meantime? Don't you realize Osgood will take his anger out on you, and might even kill your people in retaliation? Nay, Mariah; you're coming with me and that's final."

Though Mariah saw the wisdom of Falcon's words, she still felt as though she were abandoning those she'd left behind at Mildenhall.

"Stay here while I fetch your horse and my sword," Falcon ordered.

Consumed with guilt and worried for her people, Mariah turned away from Falcon and began fidgeting with her hair, smoothing it into some semblance of order. If she had to face Falcon's men, she wanted to look presentable. A slight noise behind her did not trouble her. Nor did approaching footsteps, for she assumed they belonged to Falcon.

She whirled to confront him; she wanted to try one last time to convince him to let her return to Mildenhall. "I still think I should—"

Rough hands seized her shoulders. "You've caused me a lot of trouble, lady," a gruff voice growled into her ear.

Panic-stricken, Mariah flinched away from the man whose punishing grip dug hurtfully into her soft flesh. "You!"

"Aye, me," said the mercenary. "Did you think I wouldn't find you? I told you before that Sir Osgood wouldn't accept failure. I know not who struck me, but I am convinced it was your guardsman—the man I just killed." He grinned. "He'll never raise a sword to anyone again."

"Where is . . ." Color drained from Mariah's face. Was he referring to Falcon? "What did you do to him?"

"Never mind him. He's dead. He cannot help you."

Mariah screamed, pounding him with her fists. "You killed him, you scurvy beast?"

"'Tis no more than he deserved." He covered her mouth with his hammy fist, stifling the screams she had hoped would alert Falcon's men. "Sir Osgood was wrong to free your guardsmen. Trusting you was another of his mistakes."

As he started to drag her back toward the road, Mariah saw Falcon. He was sprawled on his stomach on the ground, as still as death, a trail of blood seeping from beneath him. A kind of madness seized her as she tried desperately to free herself. But the mercenary merely laughed at her puny efforts. She did, however, manage to free her mouth.

"Wait! Maybe my man is still alive. Let me tend to his wounds."

"Nay, lady. If he isn't dead, he soon will be. My blade pierced his heart."

Nay, Falcon couldn't be dead. "How did you find us?"

"I have good ears. I heard voices."

Though Mariah struggled fiercely, she was no match for the mercenary. He dragged her through the forest to the road where he had tethered his horse. He pitched Mariah into the saddle, untied his mount and leapt up behind her.

"Where are you taking me?"

"Back to the inn. You'll be there when Sir Walter arrives to fetch you. Say your prayers, lady, for he will deal harshly with you."

"How will he deal with *you* when I tell him you fell asleep on guard duty and let me escape?"

The man's jaw clenched. "But you haven't escaped, have you?"

Mariah had no answer to that. Inside she was crying for Falcon. He couldn't be dead. Wouldn't she feel the loss in her heart if he no longer lived and breathed? Sadness overwhelmed her. Was Falcon to die an ignominious death alone, without a friend beside him to lend comfort? Nay! Sir Dennis would find him, she had to believe that. And if God was good, Falcon's injury wouldn't prove fatal.

The one thought that cheered her was the mercenary's failure to correctly identify Falcon. He thought Falcon was one of Mildenhall's defenders, and she hadn't corrected him.

If Falcon died, a part of her would die with him. She would never forgive herself for not telling him the truth about his son. Ruthlessly she drove the thought of Falcon dying from her mind. He would live—she refused to believe otherwise. He was strong, his strength and her prayers would save him.

Dawn was breaking as they reached the inn. Dame Helen's mouth flew open when the mercenary dragged Mariah inside. Master Maypole held his wife back when she would have gone to Mariah.

"My lady, what happened?"

Mariah warned Helen with her eyes to say naught.

"The witch escaped from her room," the mercenary spat. "I don't suppose either of you know anything about it?"

"How could we? My good husband and I were in our bed. We just arose to begin our day."

"Has Sir Walter arrived?"

"Not yet," Maypole answered.

"Did I hear my name?"

Mariah groaned as Walter entered the inn.

"What's going on?" Walter asked.

"Lady Mariah attempted an escape," the mercenary replied. He sent Mariah a smug smirk. "She didn't get far."

"I thought you were smarter than that, Mariah," Walter chided. He shoved Mariah toward the door. "Shall we go fetch Robbie now?"

"Wait!" Helen cried. "Lady Mariah hasn't broken her fast."

Walter sent Dame Helen a sour look. "Very well, you may prepare food if you do it with haste."

Helen scurried into the kitchen. Walter shoved Mariah into a chair and addressed the mercenary. "Is there anything else I should know before you return to the keep, Hugo?"

"Lady Mariah made contact with her guardsmen; I killed one of them. I doubt they will cause any more trouble."

"I know they won't." Walter smirked. "I brought an escort along. Father was wrong to free Mariah's guardsmen. You may leave, Hugo. Tell Father I'll return soon with the boy."

Mariah said naught as Helen arrived with fresh bread, butter, ham and eggs. Mariah pushed her plate aside; concern for Falcon had stolen her appetite.

"Eat," Walter ordered. "We need to be on the road. I want to have your brat safely returned to Mildenhall by nightfall."

Mariah picked at the eggs and ham, spread butter on a thick slice of warm bread and nibbled. *Are you alive, Falcon?* she silently lamented. *Please be alive.*

"Eat, my lady," Helen urged as she set a pot of tea before Mariah. "You need your strength."

Heeding Helen's words, Mariah chewed and swallowed without really tasting the food. After drinking two cups of tea, she settled back in her chair and folded her arms across her chest. She might as well get this over with.

"You're mad if you think I'm going to take you to Robbie," she said with a calmness that belied her racing heart.

Walter rose so abruptly, his chair fell to the floor with a

clatter. "What the hell are you talking about? Of course you're going to take me to your son. You promised."

"I lied."

Walter was so furious that all he could do was sputter and shake his fist at Mariah. "Bitch! Lying bitch!" When he raised his arm to strike her, she didn't flinch, expecting violence from him. No matter what he did to her, she wouldn't risk her son's life by placing him in Osgood's hands.

Father Francis, bless his soul, appeared at the bottom of the stairs, saw what was about to take place and cried, "Stop! God will punish you if you strike her."

Walter wavered, but Mariah could tell by his expression how badly he wanted to hurt her. The priest hurried to Mariah's side, placing himself in front of her. He stuck out his chin.

"You'll have to strike me first. 'Tis the only way I'll let you hurt Lady Mariah."

Walter's fist remained clenched; he didn't lower it. Mariah feared he would hit the priest and tried to push him aside, but he remained steadfast.

"Father, please—he'll hurt you if you don't move away."

"He'll hurt you if I *do* move away."

"I'll give you one more chance, Mariah," Walter warned. "Take me to Robbie."

"Nay, she will not!" the priest answered in her stead.

"Never!" Mariah echoed. "How do I know you don't mean Robbie harm?"

"You don't," Walter snarled. "Move away, priest. I'm taking Mariah to my father. He'll deal with her more harshly than I will."

"I shall accompany Mariah," the priest argued.

"Nay, Father, I'll be all right," Mariah assured him. "I'd rather you checked on my wounded guardsman. You'll find him about a mile south of the village, lying in a small clearing in the forest, a short distance from the road. He may be dying."

Walter laughed. "Aye, priest, go minister to the man Hugo killed. 'Tis what you do best. Mariah's fate is in my father's hands."

Father Francis searched Mariah's face. He must have seen the desperation in her eyes, for he stepped aside. "Very well, but I'll expect you and your father to treat Mariah like the lady she is."

"Please, Father, go," Mariah begged. "Take Edwina with you."

The priest watched helplessly as Walter dragged Mariah from the inn, lifted her onto his horse and mounted behind her.

"Master Maypole, may I borrow a horse?" Father Francis asked.

"There's not a horse left in the stables," Maypole apologized. "Mildenhall's guardsmen took them."

"Then Edwina and I shall walk. Mariah was determined that we help her defender. Would you please fetch Edwina for me, Dame Helen?"

He strode out the door, surprised when he saw a saddled horse calmly walking into the stable yard. "Master Maypole," he shouted, "whose horse is that?"

Maypole came running from the inn. "That's Lady Mariah's horse. I did wonder what happened to him. My wife told me my lady was mounted when she left."

"Ask and God will provide," the priest said piously, making the sign of the cross.

Maypole collected the horse's reins and brought him to the priest.

"I am here," Edwina cried as she left the inn carrying a small wooden chest. "Dame Helen provided me with her medicine chest in case the poor man is merely wounded instead of dead."

The priest mounted the horse and nodded toward the innkeeper. "Edwina can ride behind me. Would you please help her mount, Master Maypole? It seemed important to Mariah that we find the wounded man."

Edwina handed the chest to Father Francis, and then Maypole helped her scramble up behind the priest. A nudge of the priest's heels set the horse into motion. As they cantered down the road, the priest told Edwina what Mariah had said about the wounded man's location.

Though they could not pinpoint the precise place where Mariah had last seen the wounded man, Edwina's keen sense of intuition told her they were close.

"Stop, Father!"

"Are you sure this is the place?"

"Every instinct I possess tells me that something foul took place near here." She slid off the horse's rump. Father Francis dismounted and handed Edwina the chest. Edwina entered the forest as if she knew exactly where she was going. The priest tethered the horse and followed.

They found the clearing that Mariah had described. Edwina spied blood on the ground and stooped to inspect it. The sound of swords being unsheathed warned her scant seconds before they were surrounded.

"Edwina, Father Francis! Thank God you've come," Sir Dennis cried, sheathing his sword. "Our prayers have been answered. Come quickly. Sir Falcon has been sorely wounded and hovers near death."

Chapter Fifteen

Edwina and Father Francis followed Sir Dennis through the forest to Falcon's campsite. Edwina spied Falcon immediately. He was lying on the ground on a blood-stained cloak.

"What happened?" Edwina asked, falling to her knees beside Falcon.

"We don't know," Sir Dennis replied. "When Falcon failed to return after he left camp to take a look around, I organized a search party. We found him lying in a pool of blood at the place where we encountered you and the priest. He was alone, though there was some indication that a horse had been tethered nearby.

"After we brought him back to camp and made him comfortable, we returned to the place where we found him, hoping the culprit would return. Then you and the priest arrived. Can you help him?"

"Remove his shirt," Edwina ordered. "I can't tell you anything until I examine the wound."

Sir Dennis carefully removed Falcon's bloody shirt, revealing a knife wound on his left side, just below his heart.

"I need hot water. Does anyone have a pot?" Edwina said.

"I have a kettle," a man said. "I'll fetch water from the brook."

"I'll build a fire," Sir Dennis offered, "even though Falcon forbade it."

Edwina probed the wound; it was still bleeding but not excessively. "'Tis not so bad," she said. "Falcon's rib deflected the blade from his heart. No vital organs were damaged."

When the water was heated, Edwina removed a wooden bowl and clean cloths from Dame Helen's medicine chest. Then she filled the bowl with water and dipped the cloth into it. As she cleaned the blood and meticulously picked bits of material from Falcon's wound, he remained blissfully unconscious.

"Shouldn't he be coming around?" Sir Dennis asked worriedly.

"Falcon has suffered a shock to his body," Edwina replied. "He'll regain his senses soon enough."

While Edwina worked over her patient, Father Francis remained on his knees to pray for Falcon's life.

Once the wound was cleansed to Edwina's satisfaction, she rummaged in the chest for needle and thread. After dipping the needle in boiling water, she threaded it and painstakingly sewed the edges of the six-inch-long wound neatly together. Then she smeared a generous amount of marigold salve over it and bound it with strips of clean cloth, blessing Dame Helen for having a well-stocked medicine chest.

After she had finished caring for Falcon's wound, she

placed her hand over it, closed her eyes and listened to the drone of the priest's prayers until her hand began to tingle. When she opened her eyes, she found Falcon staring at her.

"Edwina?" He glanced around, suddenly aware of the anxious faces watching him. "What happened?"

Sir Dennis dropped to one knee beside him. "We hoped you could tell us."

Falcon's brow knitted. "I was with Mariah; I encountered her on the road not far from our campsite." He tried to rise. "Where is she?"

Edwina placed a hand on his chest and gently pushed him down. "Is that all you remember?"

"Aye. I was going to bring Mariah to our campsite and went to fetch her horse. I heard a twig snap behind me and turned. That's all I remember. Is Mariah all right?"

Edwina exchanged a speaking glance with Father Francis. The priest must have understood what she wished him to do, for he said, "The man who stabbed you was Sir Osgood's mercenary, my son. He mistook you for one of Lady Mariah's guardsmen. Apparently, Sir Osgood believes you are still in London."

"Where is Mariah?" Falcon's gaze shifted between the priest and Edwina, fearing the answer.

"At Mildenhall. Walter returned her there early this morning," the priest said gently.

Falcon struggled to sit up. "We cannot leave her there. She may be in grave danger. Prepare to storm Mildenhall immediately."

No one moved.

"Sir Dennis, help me to my feet. I will lead the assault myself."

Dennis shook his head. "Nay, you are too weak. We will wait until you are able to sit a horse."

Falcon was unaccustomed to being thwarted; his pale face flushed with anger. "I can do this without your help," he growled.

But it was not as easy as Falcon thought. His arms collapsed beneath him when he tried to lift himself. "Edwina, do something. Brew one of your concoctions to return my strength."

"You need two days and mayhap more to recuperate; even longer than that if fever sets in," Edwina replied. "And a rich meat broth to straighten your blood, and herbal tea to ward off fever." She glanced at Sir Dennis. "Are there hunters among you, sir?"

"Aye, Dame Edwina. Fear not, Falcon shall have his broth."

Immediately several men fetched their bows and arrows and fanned out into the forest.

"You must return to the keep," Falcon begged Edwina. "Mariah has no one to protect her."

Edwina gazed off into the distance, her eyes clouding over. When she returned her gaze to Falcon, her eyes had regained their natural sharpness.

"You need me more than Mariah does right now. Osgood won't hurt her, for she holds the key to his legal occupation of Mildenhall. He knows the king will intervene once he learns what has transpired here, so he is eager to find Robbie and wed Mariah to his son. If you wish to save Mariah and your son, you must regain your strength."

"What did you say?" Falcon's ears perked up.

Father Francis cleared his throat. "She said you need to

recover if you wish to save Mariah and her son from the fate Osgood has planned for them."

Falcon knew his thinking was still fuzzy, but he could have sworn Edwina had called Robbie his son. Nay, he had heard wrong. Father Francis was a man of God; he wouldn't lie.

"I pray you are right about Mariah's safety," Falcon muttered, "for I shall never forgive myself if she is harmed because of my failure to protect her."

Mariah refused to believe that Falcon was dead despite Hugo's insistence that his blade had struck a fatal blow. She had to believe that he lived in order to survive Osgood's plans for her. Mariah had no idea what direction Osgood's anger would take. She doubted he would kill her, at least not until he found Robbie. But he certainly could make her life miserable for refusing to place her son in his keeping.

Walter had been so angry with her that he had thrown her upon his horse, mounted behind her and raced his mount toward the keep. The ride was a short one. Minutes later they rode through the portcullis and into the courtyard. Mariah's blood froze when she saw Osgood standing on the steps to greet them.

"I'm glad I'm not in your place," Walter goaded. "Father isn't going to be pleased. This little rebellion of yours will only prolong the inevitable, for in the end we'll find Robbie and our marriage will take place as planned. Once you are my wife, you will learn obedience or pay the consequences."

"You will never have Robbie, no matter what you do to me," Mariah defied.

"You are naught but a willful bitch. My mother would never defy my father like this. She knows better."

"What is this?" Osgood roared when Walter reined in before the steps. "Where is the brat?"

"Mariah lied, Father. She won't tell us where he is," Walter said.

Reaching out a long arm, Osgood pulled Mariah off the horse. She fell with a thump, bruising her hip. Grabbing her long hair, Osgood pulled her upright.

"Hugo said he found you speaking to one of your guardsmen in the forest. He didn't tell me how you got there, but he's been severely punished for letting you escape."

Mariah stumbled and righted herself as Osgood shoved her up the stairs. Sir Martin saw her enter the hall and immediately came to her aid.

"Release Lady Mariah," he ordered Osgood.

"Keep out of this, Martin. 'Tis none of your affair," Osgood snarled.

"It's all right, Sir Martin," Mariah soothed. "Sir Osgood won't hurt me. He and Walter need me."

Osgood flung Mariah into a chair while Sir Martin hovered nearby, wringing his hands. "You lied to me!" Osgood shouted.

Mariah's chin rose defiantly. "I had to do something to free my people. You were stupid to think I would place my son in your vile hands."

Osgood backhanded Mariah so fast she was unable to avoid a direct strike. She reeled sideways and would have pitched from the chair if Sir Martin hadn't rushed forth to steady her. She clutched her cheek, feeling it swell beneath her cupped palm. But she could take Osgood's abuse. She could survive anything to keep Robbie safe.

"Take her to her chamber, steward," Osgood ordered. "I cannot stand the sight of her. Being deprived of food should go a long way to quell her recalcitrance. If you change your mind, Mariah, let me know and food will be forthcoming immediately."

Sir Martin helped Mariah to her feet and escorted her up the stairs to the solar. Two burly men trailed behind.

"I'll try to protect you as much as I can, my lady," Sir Martin whispered. "Trust me to see that you don't starve."

"I believe that Falcon and his men are camped in the forest nearby," Mariah whispered so only Martin could hear. "He plans to attack Mildenhall."

Martin barely managed to contain his joy. "When can we expect him?"

"There's more. Hugo found us together in the forest. He attacked Falcon and left him for dead; fortunately, Hugo didn't realize it was Falcon he'd stabbed. Though I saw Falcon lying on the ground in a pool of blood, I cannot believe he is dead. I sent Edwina and Father Francis to help him."

"Pray God he is still alive," Martin said piously.

"What are you two whispering about?" one of the guards asked.

"Naught that would interest you," Mariah replied.

Martin opened the door. Mariah walked inside. "Stay strong, my lady," he murmured. "I am sure Sir Falcon is alive and well."

"Tell no one that Sir Falcon is camped nearby."

"Get out," the guardsman ordered Martin. Martin had scarcely cleared the threshold when the door slammed behind him. Mariah didn't need to be told that both burly mercenaries had remained in the corridor to guard her door. This time there would be no escape.

One day without food didn't bother Mariah. The huge breakfast Dame Helen had forced on her at the inn would stay with her the rest of the day. She walked to the washstand, looked into the water pitcher and found it full. At least she wouldn't die of thirst. Not for a few days, anyway.

She sat down on the bed, her thoughts returning to Falcon. Would Falcon's men attack Mildenhall if he was too hurt to lead them?

What if Falcon was dead?

Falcon was alive—she had to believe that or go mad. And Robbie was safe. Edwina and Father Francis knew where to find him and would take care of him if she . . . Nay, she had to remain positive.

The day progressed, and night came creeping in through the windows. Mariah had no choice but to try to sleep.

She didn't feel hunger pangs until late on the second day of her captivity, but she ignored them. No one had entered her chamber since the day before, not even a maid. Never had she felt so alone, so abandoned. The solitude left her with too much time to think and fret.

She missed Robbie. Did he miss her, cry for her? Was Becca taking good care of him? She tried not to dwell on Falcon, for thoughts of him only brought tears, and she couldn't afford to give in to grief. She needed to concentrate on getting herself out of this mess.

But no matter how hard she tried, she could not banish

from her mind the image of Falcon lying on the ground, blood seeping from beneath him. Falcon had provided a miracle for her when he had given her Robbie; perhaps another miracle would occur, one that would give him life.

If Falcon lived, Mariah swore she would tell him the truth about Robbie. She dropped to her knees and fervently begged God to spare Falcon. She was still praying when Osgood entered her chamber a short time later.

"Praying for your supper, Mariah?" Osgood goaded.

Mariah opened her eyes. "Nay, I'm praying that you and your evil son will be banished from this earth forever."

Osgood moved away from the door; a servant bearing a tray of food entered the chamber and placed it on a table. Mariah eyed the food with misgivings. What kind of torture did Osgood have in mind now?

"Are you hungry, Mariah?"

"Not really."

"I thought you might like to share your supper with Walter in your chamber. Starving you is futile; you are too stubborn to admit you are hungry. This could go on for days, and your death would solve naught."

A tantalizing aroma drifted up from the dishes arrayed on the table. There was roasted game, fish, vegetables simmered in cream, thick slices of warm bread accompanied by a pot of sweet butter, and a jug of ale to wash down the food. Mariah's mouth watered, but she was made of sterner stuff. A few skipped meals weren't going to sway her.

"Ah, here's Walter now," Osgood said as Walter strode into the chamber. "And look, the lad has cleaned himself up for you. You could do worse than casting your lot with my son, Mariah."

"And I could do much better," Mariah retorted.

Though Walter wore clean clothing and appeared to have shaved and bathed, he still didn't appeal to her. The thought of any man but Falcon touching her made her stomach roil.

"You can leave now, Father," Walter said. "And take the guards with you. Mariah and I wish to be alone."

"Like hell we do!" Mariah cried. "Take the food away, I don't want it."

Walter ambled over to the table. Mariah felt a shimmer of fear when Osgood left and closed the door behind him. Walter appeared not to notice her skittishness as he pulled chairs up to the table and piled food on two plates. Then he sat down and invited Mariah to join him.

"I'm not hungry," Mariah said.

Walter picked up a haunch of venison and bit off an enormous chunk. Mariah grimaced in disgust at the rivulet of grease that ran down his chin. He wiped it on his sleeve.

"The venison is excellent, Mariah. Your cook has a way with wild game." He poured ale in her mug and offered it to her.

Thirst almost made Mariah grab it, but her willpower won out. "If I accept the food, you will expect me to fall in with your plans for me and Robbie."

He shrugged. "We will have our way in the end, and well you know it. You can save yourself a lot of pain if you tell me where to find Robbie. Once he's home where he belongs, you and I can be wed immediately."

"Father Francis won't marry us if I'm unwilling," Mariah replied, "and there is no other priest within miles."

Walter tossed a bone on the floor, wiped his hands on his shirt and leaned back in his chair, a smug smile curling his lips. "I intend to bed you tonight. Once the priest learns I have known you, he will have no choice but to perform the rites. You wouldn't want to bear another bastard, would you?"

Mariah leapt to her feet, grabbed a meat knife from the table and slowly edged toward the door. "Touch me and you'll regret it."

Walter laughed. "That puny knife can't hurt me." He grabbed for her. She ducked away.

Her gaze slid over him, searching for a vulnerable spot, one where the knife would do the most harm. She decided to aim for his face, for it was the one place the small blade would inflict serious damage. If the guards had left as they had been ordered, she could escape her chamber and hide until help arrived from either Falcon or her own guardsmen.

Walter stalked toward her. "You don't understand, Mariah. If I don't succeed with you, Father will punish me. He wants Mildenhall, and you and Robbie hold the key to everything he desires. Don't you see? I have to marry you."

"And what of Robbie?"

Walter refused to meet her gaze. "You'll have my children to love, many children, for I intend to be a diligent husband."

A chill slid down Mariah's spine. It was just as she suspected: Osgood intended to do away with Robbie once she bore Walter a son.

"Stand aside. I'm leaving."

"You're not going anywhere, Mariah, so you may as

well accept the fact that I'm going to plant my seed in you tonight. If it doesn't happen tonight, it will tomorrow night, or the next, or however many nights it takes."

Mariah moved a shaky step backward. As if aware of her intention, Walter grasped her arm and swung her toward the bed. She twisted from his grip and raised the knife in a threatening manner. "I swear I'll use this if you touch me again."

Walter's gaze narrowed on the blade. "That toothpick isn't even capable of puncturing my skin. Give it to me."

"Nay!"

He lunged for her. Grasping the handle firmly in her fist, she brought the knife downward, aiming for Walter's face but willing to accept anywhere it chose to land. Her aim was true. The blade dug a jagged gash down his left cheek. Caught off balance from his forward lunge, Walter staggered and fell, slamming his head into the bedpost. Mariah stepped aside just in time to avoid him. His eyes widened and then rolled back in his head.

Mariah couldn't move, couldn't think. Had she killed Walter? That hadn't been her intention. But she'd been willing to do anything to keep from being raped by him. Gingerly she bent over Walter's prone form and looked for signs of life. Relief washed over her when she saw the steady rise and fall of his chest. His left cheek was a bloody mess of ripped skin. Though the wound wasn't fatal, his face was going to be permanently scarred.

Mariah backed away. Had she just written her own death sentence? She needed to leave, now, before Walter awoke and wreaked vengeance on her. Despite her precarious situation, her legs refused to move. It was as if they were frozen in place.

A knock on the door roused Mariah from her state of shock.

"My lady, Sir Osgood asked me to bring wine from Mildenhall's private stock to your chamber."

Sir Martin! Mariah nearly collapsed with relief. "Are you alone?"

His voice sounded puzzled. "Aye."

"Come in, then, and quickly."

Sir Martin opened the door and stepped inside. The wine decanter rattled on the tray when he spied Walter lying on the floor. He set the tray on a chest and hurried over to examine Walter. "What happened?"

"He tried to force me," Mariah whispered. "I couldn't let him do that to me and struck him with the meat knife. He's not dead, nor is he badly wounded. He hit his head on the bedpost when he fell." She wrung her hands. "Whatever am I going to do?"

"You cannot stay here. Follow me."

"Where are you taking me? Osgood will leave no stone unturned to find me."

"To the nursery," Sir Martin replied as he opened the door and peered into the corridor. "Good, the guards haven't returned. We cannot delay, for I must return before Walter awakens and gives the alarm."

Mariah didn't argue as she followed him into the corridor and up the stairs to the nursery. Her heart was beating an erratic tattoo when she entered the suite of rooms and closed the door firmly behind her. Once she caught her breath, Mariah said, "Osgood's men are sure to find me here."

"Fear not, my lady. Follow me," Martin said.

The nursery consisted of three small chambers—

Robbie's bedchamber, Becca's bedchamber, and a schoolroom. Mariah followed Martin into Becca's bedchamber. She frowned when Martin went to the wardrobe and opened the door. "This won't do, Sir Martin. 'Tis too obvious."

Martin didn't bother with explanations as he pressed a panel at the back of the wardrobe. Mariah was startled when it slid open. "Step inside, my lady, quickly!"

"What is this room?" Mariah asked warily. "Why didn't I know about it?"

"There was never a reason for you to know," Martin explained. "The room was built before Sir Edmond's time. He showed it to me because he thought the steward of the keep should know."

Mariah had to stoop to get through the panel. Sir Martin followed her. "I'll bring clean linen for the cot and smuggle food for you whenever possible. And look, the room even has a window. 'Tis not easily discernible from the outside, for the window can only be seen from the rear of the keep. Anyone looking up would think it a part of the nursery."

"Why was this room built?" Mariah wondered.

Sir Martin shrugged. "The reason was lost over the years. The keep is very old; perhaps the room was used to hide an enemy of the Crown. The room was used by neither Lord Edmond nor his father before him. From time to time I make sure the panel still opens and clean the cobwebs from the room."

Mariah shuddered. There were indeed a few cobwebs decorating the corners. "Let's pray I won't have to stay here long," Mariah said.

"I will show you how to open the panel from the inside,

and then I must leave. I see no reason why you cannot leave the room during the night to stretch your legs, as long as you confine yourself to the nursery. After Osgood's men search here, 'tis unlikely they will return."

Mariah watched closely as Sir Martin showed her how to open the panel. He left with a promise of clean sheets and food.

Walter was staggering to his feet when Martin let himself back into Mariah's bedchamber in the solar.

"Walter, are you ill?" Martin asked solicitously. "What happened? Where is Lady Mariah?"

"What are you doing here?" Walter asked shakily.

"Your father asked me to deliver wine to you and Lady Mariah." He grabbed a napkin from the tray he had brought earlier and dabbed it in the pitcher of water. "You're bleeding. Let me help you."

Walter pushed him away. "Where is Mariah? That bitch stabbed me. She's going to pay dearly for this."

"You were alone when I arrived a few moments ago," Sir Martin ventured.

"Mariah!" Walter shouted. "You're not going to get away with this!"

"Damnation! What is going on in here? Your bellowing could be heard below stairs."

Walter's gaze swung to the doorway, his expression a mixture of relief and fear when he saw his father.

"Look what that bitch did to me!" Walter roared.

Osgood glanced around the chamber before returning his furious gaze to his son. "Where is she?"

"I know not. Look at my face! She ruined me. I'm going to kill her when I find her."

"Wipe the blood from your face," Osgood ordered.

Walter plucked the wet cloth from Martin's hands and dabbed at his cheek.

Osgood walked over to inspect the wound. "'Tis no more than you deserve," he sneered. His beady gaze settled on Sir Martin. "What do you know about this?"

"Naught, sir. I arrived with the wine as you instructed and found Walter on the floor. He was just coming around."

"You passed out from a paltry wound like that?" Osgood said disparagingly.

"Nay, Father." He rubbed the lump rising on his forehead. "The suddenness of Mariah's attack surprised me. I staggered, fell, and hit my head on the bedpost. I was still groggy when Sir Martin arrived with the wine."

Osgood's eyes were as cold as death as he stared at his son. Walter must have felt the rejection, for he immediately said, "I'll find her, Father. There's no way she can leave the keep without our knowing. And when I do find her, I will take her roughly, on the floor, against the wall, it matters not. Trust me, I will not spare her; she will suffer. I *will* plant my seed in her."

Sir Martin flinched at Osgood's answer. "If you don't get a son on her, I will. And if you fail to find her, your punishment will be severe. You may be my son, but I do not accept failure." He turned to leave.

"Fetch the healer," Walter ordered Sir Martin. "My wound needs stitching."

Osgood spun around. "That witch is gone, and well you know it. You're going to have to live with the scar. Ask the cook to clean the wound and apply salve. I'm sure she can find something in her cupboard to suffice. I expect you to initiate a thorough search of the keep for Mariah. Don't fail me in this, Walter." He strode from the chamber.

Cursing roundly, Walter stalked after him. Left alone, Sir Martin gathered up the salvageable food from the un-eaten meal and placed it and a pitcher of ale on a tray. The corridor was still deserted as he crept up the stairs to the nursery. It took but a moment to gain entrance to Mariah's hidey-hole. She rose from the cot when he en-tered, a hopeful look on her face.

"I didn't have time to find sheets, but I will bring them the first chance I get," he said. "This is all I could salvage of the feast you were supposed to share with Walter."

Mariah eyed the food hungrily. "Thank you. It will help enormously. What happened when you returned to Walter?"

"He was just coming around when I arrived. No one suspects me of aiding you. The search for you will begin soon, so I came up here straightaway."

"Does Osgood know what I did to Walter?"

Martin rolled his eyes. "Oh, aye, he knows. I wouldn't want to be Walter when he fails to find you."

"How does Walter's face look?"

Martin grinned. "Like he's been mauled by a wild boar. He wanted Edwina to stitch him up, but Osgood re-minded him that she was gone. I have to go, my lady. If I'm discovered here, it would be disastrous for both of us. I hope you can make do with what I've brought until 'tis safe for me to return."

"Thank you, Martin, you may have just saved my life. Go now, I will be fine."

Will I be fine? Mariah wondered after Martin left. What if he wasn't able to return? She might die of thirst, or hunger. What if her guardsmen failed to recruit help from Edmond's neighbors?

What if Falcon was dead?

Chapter Sixteen

Impatience plagued Falcon, even though he knew he was still too weak to lead a siege against Mildenhall. As much as he wanted to be up and about, his body refused to cooperate. He was more than grateful, however, that Edwina had kept his fever to a minimum with potions and herbal teas, and prevented any infection with salves and sheer force of will. Though Falcon appreciated Edwina's excellent care, his concern for Mariah was the catalyst that hastened his recovery.

Three days after his near-fatal injury, Falcon rose from his pallet before dawn and began practicing with his sword, testing his strength by hacking at an imaginary enemy. Twinges of pain shot up from his injured left side, but he stoically ignored them.

Sir Dennis joined him. "Are you sure you're well enough for this? I can lead the men without you."

Despite the cool air, Falcon was sweating. His strength was nowhere near capacity, but he wasn't going to let that stop him.

"I know you are capable, Dennis, but I need to be a part of the assault. Though we have enough men to win the battle, I am concerned about Mariah's well-being. I know not what Osgood will do to her when we attack. Will he use her against us?"

"Osgood doesn't dare harm Mariah," Edwina said as she joined them. "He needs her to bear Walter a son. Once that's accomplished, they can get rid of Robbie and claim Mildenhall and the title."

"He'll never get Robbie," Falcon vowed fiercely.

"You should be resting," Edwina maintained. "Look at you. You're weak as a babe."

"I'll never regain my strength by resting," Falcon replied. "I owe you a great deal, Edwina. This is the second time you've saved my life. I vow your skill won't go unrewarded."

"The only reward I will accept is Mariah and Robbie's safety. Give me that, sir, and I will be happy."

"You have my word. Restoring Mariah and Robbie to their rightful place at Mildenhall is the reason I am here. Has Father Francis returned to the village? He asked permission to leave, and I gave it."

"Aye, his flock has need of him. He will be safe; Osgood doesn't dare harm a man of God."

Just then Jamie burst into the clearing. "Sir Falcon! The sentry has spotted a large number of riders traveling toward Mildenhall."

"Fetch my horse," Falcon said, sheathing his sword.

Dennis laid a hand on his shoulder. "Nay, Falcon, stay here. I will identify the men and report back to you."

"They might be Mildenhall's men at arms. Lady Mariah sent them to neighboring estates for help. I will go myself."

"Nay, Falcon, let Sir Dennis handle this," Edwina advised. "Give yourself one more day to recuperate. I suspect you are right about the identity of the riders, for Osgood has few allies among his peers."

Sir Dennis had already left, so Falcon had no choice but to wait for his return. He didn't like feeling weak and hated being treated like an invalid. He unsheathed his sword and began dueling with an imaginary enemy. With each thrust he felt strength flow into his muscles; if naught else, his fierce will would heal him.

Falcon had been practicing at swordplay for nearly an hour when Sir Dennis returned, accompanied by Sir Maynard, Mildenhall's captain of the guard.

"Falcon, I could scarcely credit it when Sir Dennis confronted us on the road. I thought you were in London."

Falcon clasped Sir Maynard's shoulder. "I was in London, but now I am here to retake Mildenhall. Did you bring reinforcements with you?"

"Aye, Lord Banbury and Lord Thornhill sent men-at-arms to join our ranks and provided us with horses and weapons. If not for Lady Mariah's cunning and bravery, we would still be prisoners inside Mildenhall."

"I wasn't surprised to learn that she had outwitted Osgood," Falcon acknowledged. "The lady is smart as well as beautiful. Where is your army?"

"Right behind me. Let us find a quiet place to coordinate a plan of attack."

"Aye," Falcon agreed as he led Sir Maynard to an isolated spot some distance from the main camp.

Maynard sent Falcon a sharp look. "Sir Dennis said you had been wounded."

"'Tis of little consequence," Falcon replied. "I am well

enough to lead our combined forces against Osgood. Is there aught I should know about Midenhall's defenses?"

"The castle has never been put to the test, never been attacked in its long history," Maynard explained. "Mildenhall has no political value, nor is it located in a place advantageous to the kingdom. The defenses are limited. The walls can be easily breached, and, given the small number of men Osgood has at his disposal, reclaiming the keep should not prove difficult."

"If Osgood were smart, he would surrender without a fight," Falcon mused.

"No one ever said Osgood was smart," Maynard scoffed.

"Lady Mariah is inside the keep, we cannot risk her life."

"Nor should we," Maynard agreed. "Do you think Osgood will harm my lady when we launch our siege?"

"I do not know. Edwina believes Mariah will be safe, for she and Robbie are the key to possessing Mildenhall."

"I pray that Lady Mariah has hidden Robbie where Osgood cannot get his hands on the lad."

"The boy and his nursemaid are as safe as I could make them. They are in Cambridge, protected by two of my men."

"Thank God Lady Mariah has a friend in you," Maynard said. "Together we shall reclaim Robbie's birthright for him."

"Here's what we shall do," Falcon said, outlining the plan he had come up with during his recuperation. "If you disagree with anything I say, tell me, so we can work out any flaws I may have overlooked."

Sir Maynard didn't disagree, and the plans were laid.

* * *

Mariah heard men searching the nursery on two separate occasions. She had held her breath while they opened the wardrobe and searched inside.

Each time she had remained very still, fear clutching at her heart until the men departed. Sir Martin had managed to sneak food and water up to her early this morning, but she ate and drank sparingly in case naught more was forthcoming.

During the darkest part of her second night in hiding, Mariah ventured out of her tiny hiding place. As she crept from the wardrobe, moonlight filtered through the windows, allowing her to view the damage done to the walls by Osgood's men during their search for secret doors or passages.

Mariah tiptoed to Robbie's bed. Tears came to her eyes when she remembered how sweetly Robbie slept. How desperately she missed him. When would this all end?

Sir Martin had told her he had neither seen nor heard from Sir Maynard or Falcon. Surely they hadn't given up, had they?

Mariah lingered in the nursery until dawn sent shafts of daylight through the windows, and then returned to the chamber that had become not only her place of refuge, but also the place where her thoughts threatened to destroy her. She refused to contemplate the possibility of Falcon's death. If there had been even a tiny spark of life in him when Edwina found him, she knew the healer would find a way to save him.

Mariah spent a great deal of time deciding how to tell Falcon he was Robbie's father. And even longer wondering how he would react when he learned the truth. Would he take Robbie away from her?

Lowering her head in her hands, she tried to imagine life without Robbie. It would be bad enough to lose Falcon, but without her son, her life would have no meaning. Despite her misgivings and fears, she vowed to tell Falcon the truth.

Mariah tensed when she heard a noise on the other side of the wardrobe. The panel opened, and Sir Martin stepped through. He had brought food and a jug of water with him. One look at his face told Mariah he brought news.

"What is it, Sir Martin? What have you heard? Does Falcon live?"

"Listen carefully, my lady, for I dare not linger. Sir Maynard has returned with your men-at-arms and reinforcements from neighboring estates. They are outside the walls, demanding that Sir Osgood surrender Mildenhall to them."

Excitement raced through Mariah. "Thank God! Think you Osgood will surrender?"

Martin shook his head. "Nay. A siege is unavoidable. Heed me well, my lady. Do not leave this room until I come for you."

Mariah wanted to ask him a million questions, but there was no time. Sir Martin had disappeared through the panel.

Sir Maynard's small army had approached Mildenhall's outer walls and halted just out of arrow range. Bellowing up to a guard, Sir Maynard demanded yet again the castle's surrender. A length of time had already elapsed while

Osgood was sent for. Now he appeared on the wall walk.

"Surrender!" Sir Maynard called up to him. "You are outnumbered."

"Never!" Osgood returned. "Mildenhall is mine. I will not give it up."

"Heed my warning, Sir Osgood. We have brought reinforcements, all of them prepared for a lengthy siege. Save yourself the agony of defeat and surrender now. Why waste men's lives for a hopeless cause?"

"You forget, Sir Maynard, that we hold Lady Mariah. Attack us and she will suffer."

"Hurt Lady Mariah and you will regret it, that I promise," Maynard replied. "The king will not condone what you have done to my lady."

Osgood laughed. "He will do naught after Walter and Mariah are wed. The matter will be out of his hands."

"That will never happen," Maynard asserted. "No priest will wed Walter to an unwilling bride."

"Not so! No priest will refuse once he learns Mariah is carrying Walter's child," Osgood boasted.

Those words had no sooner left Osgood's mouth than Falcon rode up from the ranks, joining Sir Martin at the wall. He glared up at Osgood, his expression stark in the early light of dawn.

Osgood gaped down at him, as if unable to believe his eyes. "Falcon!" he blustered. "Damnation! What are you doing here? Never say you left your new bride to come to Mariah's aid. I'm surprised Lady Rosamond allowed it."

"I did not wed Lady Rosamond. We did not suit. I advise you to heed Sir Maynard's words. Surrender. Your men are outnumbered; fighting will only bring about their deaths."

"You dare not attack as long as I have Mariah," Osgood gloated.

"Bring Mariah out where I can see her."

Walter appeared at Osgood's side. They whispered together a few minutes before Osgood deigned to answer Falcon's challenge.

"Mariah is . . . indisposed. You'll have to trust me when I say she is unharmed," Osgood said.

Falcon's hands fisted at his sides. He didn't like the sound of that. Just how indisposed was she?

"You have given me no reason to trust you. If you have harmed her, I will personally kill you."

"Mariah has not been harmed."

"If that is true, why do you refuse to let us see her?"

Osgood conferred again with Walter, and the younger man ducked away. "Would you believe Sir Martin?" Osgood called down to Falcon.

"Let me speak with him so I can judge for myself."

"Something is wrong," Sir Maynard said in an aside to Falcon. "Osgood would produce Lady Mariah if she were available."

"Perhaps Sir Martin will convey the truth to us," Falcon replied. He didn't like the present situation any better than Maynard.

At that moment, Sir Martin appeared on the ramparts.

"Sir Martin is here, Falcon," Osgood shouted. "Listen to him. He will tell you that Mariah is unharmed."

Sir Martin peered down at Falcon. "Mariah said you were alive, and so you are, Falcon."

"What's this?" Osgood demanded. "How did Mariah know Falcon was coming to Mildenhall?"

"Ask your man Hugo," Martin replied. "He saw Falcon in the forest, talking to my lady."

Osgood sent Falcon an incredulous look. "Are you saying Falcon was the man Hugo believed he had slain?"

Falcon grinned. "I am that man, but as you can see, I didn't die. Didn't even come close."

Osgood let loose a string of curses. Then he pressed his knife into the back of Martin's neck and hissed, "Falcon wants to know if Mariah has been harmed. He doesn't believe me, Martin, so I want you to tell him what he wants to hear."

Falcon stared up at Martin; he wished he were close enough to see the man's expression, read the truth in his eyes. Instead, he was forced to rely on his instincts.

Martin flinched when the sharp point of the knife drew blood and Osgood ordered under his breath, "Tell him, Martin. Tell Falcon that Mariah is well."

"My lady is well, Sir Falcon, very well indeed. She will be ecstatic to learn you have recovered from your wound."

"Very good, Martin," Osgood muttered.

Falcon still wasn't satisfied. "Where is she? Why won't Osgood produce her?"

Martin chose his words carefully. "I believe the lady prefers to remain hidden until matters are settled here."

"What does that mean?" Sir Maynard asked Falcon. "Martin's answer doesn't make sense. Why would Lady Mariah hide from us? If Osgood wanted, he could force my lady to appear."

Falcon digested Martin's words, took them apart one by one and then reviewed the whole. What was Martin trying to tell him?

"Martin, when was the last time you saw Lady Mariah?" Falcon shouted.

The knife dug deeper into Martin's neck. He flinched but remained true to his purpose. "Why, just this morning, Falcon, when I told her that her protectors were at the portcullis, demanding her release. She said she would remain hidden until Osgood and his men were driven from Mildenhall."

"That's enough!" Osgood blustered, shoving Martin into a mercenary's arms.

Now Falcon understood what Martin had been trying to convey to him. Osgood didn't know where Mariah was. Somehow, Falcon's wonderful, resourceful Mariah had found a place to hide, allowing him time to recover from his wounds and her loyal guardsmen to seek help.

Maynard must have come to the same conclusion. "Osgood has no idea where Lady Mariah is. Somehow she managed to hide where he can't find her. We can attack Osgood without fear for my lady's life."

"I agree," Falcon replied. "I will give Osgood one last chance to surrender. If he refuses, prepare to breach the walls. Our numbers are superior; we will take the day."

"Osgood," Falcon called. "Surrender while you still can."

Suddenly a body came hurtling down from the ramparts, landing with a sickening thud not far from Falcon and Sir Maynard. Falcon dismounted and turned the body over. It was Sir Martin. His throat had been slit.

"That is your answer, Falcon!" Osgood shouted. "Come and get me if you want me."

Rage simmered inside Falcon. Sir Martin was a good man, loyal to the end. He didn't deserve to die like this. Falcon glanced up to vent his rage at Osgood, but the villain had ducked out of sight.

"The cowardly bastard," Maynard hissed.

"Osgood has given us his answer. Now we will give him ours," Falcon said through clenched teeth.

Almost immediately, arrows showered down upon Falcon's party from above. Only a few found a home, for the majority of Falcon's army remained out of range. Falcon raised his sword as a signal to begin the assault.

"Bring the ladders!" he shouted over the din of whizzing arrows and the cries of the wounded. He had wanted to do this without loss of life, but Osgood had refused to listen to reason.

Falcon called encouragement as men rushed forth with ladders they had been building while Falcon lay recuperating from his wound. Dodging arrows, they set the ladders against the wall and scrambled up while their comrades loosed their own arrows at the enemy. Falcon was one of the first on the ladders, the first to crest the wall. What he saw, or rather didn't see, stunned him.

Osgood's men had left their posts. All he saw of them were their backs. Apparently, they had the sense to realize that defending Mildenhall was impossible. They were outnumbered. They knew, even if Osgood did not, that they were defeated before the battle had begun, and were unlikely to receive pay for their services. Being mercenaries, they had fled to seek gainful employment elsewhere.

"They're escaping through the postern gate!" Falcon shouted. "Stop them!"

With Sir Maynard in the lead, Falcon and half the army raced around to the postern gate. Just as Falcon had suspected, the gate gaped open. Some mercenaries had fled on horseback while others had just run for their lives.

"Shall we give chase?" Sir Maynard asked.

"Nay. The mercenaries were doing what they were paid to do. Doubtless Osgood has seen the last of them."

"What about Osgood and his son? Are we going to let them get away?"

"There is nowhere they can go but to their manor in Southwold. I know where to find them when I am ready. And so will the king. He will learn of Osgood's treachery when he returns to London."

The servants poured from the keep to greet their deliverers. Falcon searched among them for Mariah.

"Where is Lady Mariah?"

The servants looked at one another in confusion. Horace stepped forward as their spokesman. "No one has seen her since Osgood confined her to her chamber without food or water."

"What!" Falcon exclaimed, his face taut with rage. "I should have killed the bastard."

"My lady disappeared from her chamber," Horace continued. "Osgood's men searched everywhere for her."

"Did they find her?"

"Nay, they did not. My lady slashed Walter with a meat knife," Horace said. "Caught him in the cheek, she did." The man's smile told Falcon just how much he and the others hated Osgood and his son.

"Damnation! Did Walter hurt Lady Mariah?"

"Nay, though he probably would have had she not disappeared while Walter lay unconscious. You'll have to ask Sir Martin to show you her hiding place, for he's the only one who knows. We all knew that he carried food and water to her."

Relief combined with a measure of dread slammed through Falcon. "Thank God Lady Mariah was unharmed." He paused, reaching for words to reveal Sir Martin's fate. "It saddens me to say that Osgood killed Sir Martin."

A great deal of wailing and wringing of hands followed Falcon's words. A few women sobbed openly.

"Does anyone have any idea where Sir Martin could have hidden Lady Mariah?" Falcon asked hopefully.

Blank faces met his words. Apparently, no one knew where Mariah was hidden.

"Sir Osgood won't return; you have naught more to fear from him," Falcon assured them. "Spread the word. The crofters are free now to come and go as they please."

"What about our lady and the little earl?" Horace asked.

"Robbie is safe. I intend to send a man to fetch him and his nursemaid home immediately. Lady Mariah *will* be found, you can depend upon it."

The search for Mariah began immediately after Falcon and Sir Maynard thanked their allies and bade them farewell.

Mariah had sat in her tiny room, listening to the sounds of battle. Though she could see naught from the window but trees and hills, she could hear far more than she wished. She wanted desperately to leave her sanctuary but remembered Sir Martin's warning about remaining concealed until he came for her.

Later that day she heard men moving about in the nursery and Becca's chamber. Someone opened the wardrobe door. She held her breath, fearing discovery. Then the wardrobe door closed, and Mariah forced out the breath she'd been holding. If Osgood had been driven from Mildenhall, where was Martin? Why had no one come for her?

Mariah paced . . . and waited. She munched on an apple and drank the last of the water Sir Martin had provided. Darkness filled the tiny chamber. Looking out the narrow window offered scant comfort, for she could see naught of what was happening inside the keep. Mariah shivered. The chamber was cold; she wrapped herself up in a blanket and lay down on the cot. Finally she fell asleep.

The next day was much like the one before. She heard movement in the nursery, but no matter how much she wanted to reveal herself, she could think of a hundred reasons why she should wait for Martin.

The worst scenario was that Falcon was dead, and Osgood still held the keep. Martin hadn't actually seen Falcon, which worried Mariah. If Osgood still held Mildenhall, he might be preventing Martin from coming to her. Would she know in her heart if Falcon were dead? That horrible thought nearly doubled her over in pain. Nay! She could not relinquish her faith. Falcon was alive and doing all in his power to reclaim Mildenhall for Robbie.

Mariah heard the church bell chime Sext. It was noon,

her stomach rumbled. She was hungry and thirsty. The last of her food and water was gone.

Mariah paced endlessly, fretted endlessly. Thirst plagued her. She could bear the hunger, but not the thirst. Where was Martin? Darkness invaded the chamber. Martin hadn't supplied her with candles for fear the light would be seen from the outside, so she sat in the dark and imagined the worst.

Mariah couldn't sleep. Intuition told her that something terrible had happened to her steward. He would not leave her without food or water unless something dire had transpired. It was late, very late, no noises filtered up from the hall below. Unable to stand another moment of not knowing, Mariah slid open the panel and emerged from the wardrobe into stygian darkness.

The sound of silence was music to Mariah's ears as she felt her way around the furniture to the door. With utmost caution, she opened the door and peered into the dark corridor. No one lurked about. Hugging the wall, she inched along the corridor to the stairs.

She heard naught, saw naught to indicate who held the keep.

Step by careful step, she made her way down the staircase, hoping that her midnight foray would help her discover whether friend or foe held the castle. And she was desperate to find food and water.

Mariah reached the solar and stopped to gather her courage before continuing.

Falcon burned with frustration. Two days of frantic searching had yielded no sign of Mariah. The crofters hadn't seen her; she was nowhere in the village. Edwina had returned to the keep and appeared as perturbed as Falcon. She knew of no secret place Mariah could be hiding. Falcon had been sleeping in her chamber in order to be on hand should she decide to return on her own.

Falcon believed the answer to Mariah's whereabouts rested with Sir Martin in the cold grave they had dug for him. Falcon had scarcely slept since he had reclaimed the keep for Mariah. He had searched every wall in the castle for secret passages and found naught.

Where are you, Mariah?

Falcon sat in the chair before the hearth, but the blazing fire did naught to warm the chill in his heart. He had to find Mariah. Robbie needed his mother.

Falcon stared into the flames, fingers tented, his mind whirling in all directions when he heard a sound, barely audible: it was more an awareness, or expectancy. Anticipation slammed into him. He rose, snatched up his sword and approached the door. Someone was creeping toward his chamber.

He heard the sound again, this time identifying it as the soft shuffle of footsteps. His senses raced to high alert as he flung open the door. A shadow shifted, halted. He heard a small, breathless sigh as he pounced on his hapless victim. His arm curved around a slim waist, his fingers sinking into tender feminine flesh. Her hair brushed against his face as he dragged her into his chamber. He'd recognized her scent immediately.

He closed the door with his foot and dropped his sword, turning her in his arms so he could look at her.

She met his gaze with unbridled joy. "You're alive! I prayed so hard for it to be true."

"Where have you been? We've looked everywhere for you. God's eyes, Mariah, I've been worried sick about you. Why did you wait so long to show yourself?"

She touched his face. "It really is you. Sir Martin found a hiding place for me after Walter attacked me. He told me to remain hidden until he came for me."

Falcon's face showed a myriad of emotions. "Did Walter hurt you?"

"Nay, he did not. I slashed his face with a meat knife. He fell and hit his head on the bedpost, knocking himself unconscious. Sir Martin arrived soon afterward, saw what I had done and found a hiding place for me. We both feared Walter's wrath."

"You are amazing." Falcon grasped her hands, led her over to the fire and guided her into a chair. "Your hands are like ice. You must be thirsty and hungry."

"More thirsty than hungry. What happened to Sir Martin? Why didn't he come for me?"

Falcon left her for a moment to fetch a cup of water. He handed it to her and she drank thirstily. "I'll send for some food."

"Nay, do not waken anyone now. I can wait until morning. Something terrible has happened to Sir Martin—I can feel it in my bones."

Falcon knelt beside her and folded her hands in his. "Sir Martin is dead. Osgood killed him. Osgood's mercenaries deserted him when they realized they were outnumbered. Your enemy had no choice but to flee with them. They left through the postern gate before we could seal it."

Mariah swallowed hard. "How did Sir Martin die?"

"He died a hero's death, Mariah; that's all you need to

know. If not for him, we wouldn't have known you were unharmed and out of Osgood's reach. Without that knowledge, we could not have begun the siege for fear that Osgood would harm you. We buried Sir Martin in the family plot. I hope you approve."

Mariah nodded, wiping tears from her cheeks. "Aye, I do. He was a good and loyal man."

Falcon lifted her to her feet. "You're still shaking. You're safe now, love. Osgood will never return. He might find it expedient to leave the country before the king returns."

"I thought you were dead," Mariah whispered. "I was afraid I would never see you or Robbie again."

"I sent for Robbie and Becca. They'll be here tomorrow."

They stared at one another. Tension radiated between them, a tension born of desperate need, a need that relentlessly drew them together despite all adversity. Then she was in his arms. He was not sure who had taken the first step; it didn't matter. He only knew they needed each other, and that need was too explosive to wait.

Mariah shuddered and closed her eyes. Wanting was such a fierce emotion. She wanted Falcon, but would he want her after she told him the truth about Robbie?

Chapter Seventeen

"Falcon, there's something I need to tell you," Mariah said.

Falcon didn't want to hear it. Not now. Mariah filled his senses. He felt the immediate reaction of his body to hers, the swirling whirlpool of desire that overrode speech. No words were necessary at a time like this. He felt her quickened breath, and his body grew rigid. He wanted to touch and be touched. He wanted to love her.

"Words can come later, love."

His mouth claimed hers; his tongue prodded her lips, urging them to open to him. As she readily acquiesced, he explored and teased, overwhelmed by urgency. He broke off the kiss and placed her hand over his heart.

"Can you feel my heart pounding? I cannot begin to describe how desperate I was to find you, or how afraid that I never would. With you in my arms I can think of naught but carrying you to bed and making love to you."

Taking both of her hands in his, he led her to the bed.

"Falcon, I want that, too, but first I must tell you—"

"Nay, later, sweeting; my need is too great."

He swept the rich thickness of her hair from her shoulder and pressed his lips against the silken flesh of her neck, and then against the pulse beating at the base of her throat. His lips plied their magic on her while his hands made short work on the lacings of her gown. The gown tumbled to her feet and her shift followed as his lips claimed hers. He reveled in her response; the growing pressure of her hands on his shoulders and her glowing eyes proved she wanted him as ardently as he wanted her.

He kissed her passionately as he edged her backward. When the back of her knees hit the bed, he urged her down and knelt at her feet to remove her shoes and stockings. Then he stood and removed his doublet and shirt.

"Oh, your wound," Mariah cried when she saw the puckered raw edges of Falcon's healing wound. "It must have hurt terribly."

"You sent Edwina to me. Without her I might have died. But I didn't. You can see for yourself how well I am healing."

Mariah watched in awe as he finished undressing, revealing splendid muscles and rippling bronzed flesh. She knew she should try harder to make Falcon listen to her confession, but her mouth was too dry to repeat the words. She would tell him later, once their desire for each other had been sated. All the fear and hesitancy she felt concerning Falcon's reaction to what she was going to tell him exploded in raw need. She wanted his love. She wanted his heart. She wanted him deep inside her. They would be at one with each other for perhaps the last time before he learned the truth and turned away from her.

Falcon joined her on the bed. Leaning over her, he licked her stomach, his lips moving lazily upward to nuzzle her breasts and suck her nipples. Mariah trembled like a leaf in a freshening wind. The peaks of her breasts had hardened into pebble-hard buds, exquisitely sensitive to the touch of Falcon's mouth and tongue. Her nails curled into her palms as his tongue laved and teased and caressed the elongated nubs.

There was a brief moment when he claimed her lips that Mariah wanted to stop him and blurt out her secret, but all thought ceased when he plundered her mouth with his tongue, delving, seeking, demanding.

A pulse pounded in Falcon's head and in his groin as he pursued his purpose with unrelenting passion. Mariah was his. How dare Walter assault her! How dare he try to force her to wed him against her will!

He tore his mouth from hers. Positioning himself between her sweet thighs, he used his mouth to begin a slow exploration of her body, tasting every hidden crevice, every tempting curve. He strung kisses along the inside of her inner thigh to the plump petals of her sex. He parted her gently and bent his head to take the firm little bud between his lips and suckle it.

He kept up the pressure until Mariah clung to him, beseeching him, demanding that he fulfill the promises his hands and mouth had made.

"Do you mean to devour me?" she cried.

"Aye, in tiny morsels. Do you object?"

"Nay, not if you let me do as I please to you."

Lust rolled through him. "I can hardly wait, sweeting."

Then he returned to his luscious feast. His lips found the soft hollow of her throat. He could feel the pulse throbbing excitedly beneath his mouth. His pulse marched to the same cadence as hers.

He rolled onto his back, drawing her atop him. His

301

hands caressed the length of her, brushing over sensitive flesh. Then he grasped her waist and lifted her up so that her breasts hung over his face. Raising his head slightly, he licked and nipped at her nipples. A tiny moan slipped from her lips, followed by a gasp as he sucked hard upon them, each in turn.

He rolled again, bringing her beneath him. He smiled into her eyes as he opened her cleft with two fingers and stroked down the sides, teasing her nether lips before thrusting his fingers deep inside her. Moisture dampened his hand; she moaned and arched up against him.

His fingers left her. She could feel the heat of his rigid flesh probing her weeping center. The same heat blazed in his eyes as he gazed down at her. It intensified as he entered her, gliding easily into her yielding wet flesh. Mariah drew in a sharp breath, his kiss scorching the arch of her throat as he flexed his hips and thrust hard and deep.

He lifted his head and smiled down at her. "You flow all around me like warm honey."

Anticipation screamed through her senses. She hadn't realized how desperate she was for this, for Falcon. She arched her back against him and clutched his shoulders. "Please," she gasped.

He withdrew slowly, filled her again, thrusting in long, slow strokes. She struggled against him, desperately wanting more than he was giving her. With his hands on her hips, he pressed her down when she tried to arch up, preventing her from controlling the pace or taking what she needed.

"Falcon . . . please . . ."

"Please what, sweeting?"

"Let me come," she begged.

He thrust deep and held, grinding his hips against her pelvis, pumping into her again and again. She rocked forward against him, intensifying the pleasure. The tension gripping her body suddenly exploded. She screamed his name. He caught it with his mouth and held it captive while she thrashed wildly beneath him. He continued the steady thrusting until she went limp beneath him. She felt his muscles clench and gazed up at him. His head thrown back, his neck corded, he drove into her one final time. A moan escaped him as his orgasm burst forth in a powerful stream.

They clung to each other in the aftermath, gasping for breath. An eternity later, he pulled away and rolled onto his back. Another eternity passed before he spoke.

"I didn't hurt you, did I? I seem to lack control when I am with you."

Mariah brushed a lock of hair away from his damp forehead. "Nay, you didn't hurt me."

"I'll try to be gentler next time. It's just that . . . the thought of you here at the mercy of Osgood and Walter while I was recuperating and could do naught about it nearly drove me insane." He paused, then asked, "Are you sure Walter didn't hurt you?"

She placed a finger against his lips. "Very sure, though he might have if Sir Martin had not hidden me."

"Thank God he didn't find you. You'll have to show me your hiding place. Had Martin not taken the secret with him to his grave, you would have been found immediately."

"I am here now—that's all that matters."

Mariah lay relaxed in Falcon's arms, fully aware that

she had to tell him about Robbie before they left this chamber. But not yet; dawn was still hours away. Raising herself up on her elbow, she began tracing a finger down Falcon's chest and nuzzling him with her lips. She heard him gasp, and smiled when she saw his sex stir and begin to rise. Then she used her lips, mouth and hands to tease him, until his manhood grew rigid, pulsing against his stomach with renewed need.

She sent him a shy smile before lowering her head and covering the tip with her mouth.

Falcon jerked upright. The feeling of her mouth on him was so intense he feared he would explode. Afraid that she would stop, he held her head in place and guided it up and down his engorged length until she learned the rhythm.

Apparently, Mariah needed no lessons, for she began an erotic exploration of his cock with her tongue, from the tip to the root, while her hands caressed the sacs at the base.

"Mariah, I can't . . . Dear God, you have to stop!"

Grasping her waist, he pulled her on top of him and thrust deep inside her, driving them both to a volatile climax. Falcon held her close while her body convulsed and then stilled. Moments later, she fell asleep splayed on top of him.

Dawn lay heavy on the horizon when Falcon woke Mariah. She stirred, yawned and snuggled closer against his chest.

"Wake up, sleepyhead," Falcon murmured. "I want us to be downstairs in the hall when everyone congregates for breakfast. Your people need to know that you have returned to us."

Mariah raised her head and glanced out the window. Though the day promised to be gray and dismal, daylight was indeed creeping over the horizon. And she still hadn't told Falcon about Robbie. She crawled off of him and sat beside him on the bed, hugging her knees to her chest.

"There's something I need to tell you. Something I should have told you a long time ago. I lied to you, Falcon."

Concern creased Falcon's brow. "What untruth did you tell me this time? Were you afraid to tell me that Walter raped you? It doesn't matter. It wasn't something you wanted. Try to put it out of your mind."

"Nay, that's not what I lied about."

Falcon sat up and pulled her into his arms. "Tell me. We're friends, aren't we?"

Friends. Was that all she was to him? "I hoped we were more than friends."

Falcon looked chagrined. "Of course we are. We've been lovers for years. I care about you, Mariah. If I didn't, I would have wed Rosamond instead of rushing off to defend you and Robbie. You should know that by now."

"Have you forgiven me for lying about my relationship with Edmond?"

"Aye, I've forgiven you, though I still don't understand why you lied. Was Edmond aware that you were bedding me? I deserve the truth, Mariah."

"Telling the truth is exactly what I intend to do. If you promise not to interrupt, I will tell you everything."

Falcon sat back against the headboard and nodded, though his eyes remained wary. "Very well, I promise to be attentive; I've been waiting a long time for this. When I returned to Mildenhall and learned that Lord Edmond was your husband and not your father, I was angry enough to wring your lovely neck. A man doesn't like being lied to, nor does he enjoy cuckolding a man he respects. I'm most eager to learn the reason for your lies."

Mariah inhaled sharply, then let her breath out slowly. She knew this wasn't going to be easy, but it had to be said, even though Falcon might hate her afterward.

"I'd better start at the beginning," she said.

"By all means."

"In the beginning, I was Lord Edmond's ward. He was an old family friend; my father named him my guardian in his will. I was thirteen when my parents died in a boating accident. My parents weren't wealthy, I wasn't an heiress. After their funeral, I came to Mildenhall to live with Lord Edmond.

"He was like a father to me. I loved him dearly. When the king wanted me to wed a man Edmond knew to be cruel, he married me himself. I was seventeen.

"I felt more like Edmond's daughter than his wife, and Edmond felt the same. Consummating our vows was awkward for both of us. But because Edmond needed an heir for Mildenhall, we both endured the process a few times.

"Eventually, Edmond took ill and lost the ability to . . . to sire a child. He hated the thought that Osgood would inherit if there was no heir. He knew Osgood would bankrupt Mildenhall, and that our people would suffer under Osgood's heavy hand.

"Both Edmond and I feared that Osgood would force me to wed Walter after Edmond's death. If I refused, I would have had to leave the only home I had known since I was thirteen."

"Then I arrived at Mildenhall," Falcon said quietly.

"Aye, you were the answer to our prayers. At first I was appalled at Edmond's suggestion that I seduce you for the son you could give me. He saw his plan as a chance to thwart Osgood and his evil machinations. Edmond genuinely liked you and saw you as his last hope to save Mildenhall. Edwina told us that your memory would return in time and you would leave Mildenhall."

"You wanted a child from me," Falcon said through clenched teeth.

"Aye, but our relationship came to mean much more to me than that. I began to care for you. I wanted you to stay at Mildenhall forever. I was heartbroken when you found your memory and returned to London. Shortly after your departure, I learned I was carrying your child. Edmond was ecstatic. He loved me enough to want me to experience what he could not give me. With you, I learned what it meant to be a woman."

"You used me." His words were clothed in bitterness. "Robbie is my son—*my* son!"

Mariah could not meet his eyes. "Aye, Robbie is yours."

"When did you intend to tell me?"

"Never. Our futures were at stake. No one could know that Robbie wasn't Edmond's son. Everything would have gone as planned if Osgood hadn't challenged Robbie's legitimacy and seized Mildenhall. I never expected you to arrive when I asked for the king's help."

Falcon's words dripped with sarcasm. "You must have been terrified to see me walk in the door as the king's representative."

307

"I despised the lies I told you, but the truth would have left me and Robbie without a home and naught but my widow's portion to sustain us. Telling you the truth would have given Osgood everything he desired."

"Telling me the truth was the honorable thing to do," Falcon rejoined harshly.

"You would have taken Robbie away from me," Mariah said in a trembling voice.

"Could you not have trusted me?"

"Too much was at stake. Please try to understand—"

"I understand very well," Falcon spat. "You seduced me, told countless lies, and kept my son from me."

"You weren't even around!" Mariah charged. "You were in France. Robbie and I were alone and unprotected but for a few loyal guardsmen who had remained after Edmond's death."

"You could have told me when I returned to Mildenhall on the king's business. Think you I didn't know Edmond was incapable of siring a child? I was here for weeks, I saw his weakness, knew how ill he was. You even lied about Robbie's age; I assumed you had taken a lover after I left. How old is Robbie? The truth, Mariah."

"He'll soon turn five. Edmond worshiped him. He is as much Edmond's son as he is yours."

Falcon rolled out of bed and stood over her, his eyes cold, his expression unreadable. "I don't want to hear how much Edmond adored my son. Get up." She stared at him for several heartbeats before obeying. "I'll order a bath for you. Come down to the hall when you're ready."

"Falcon, do not condemn me. Edmond and I needed a son to save Mildenhall."

"Lies. Lies. Lies. That's all I've heard from you since

the first day I arrived at Mildenhall, near death and vulnerable to your intrigues."

"What are you going to do?"

"I don't know. I need to think this through before I make a decision."

"If you tell the king that Robbie isn't Edmond's son and heir, you'll be playing right into Osgood's hands. Does that mean naught to you?"

"Did it mean naught to you?" he flung back at her.

"It did." She looked into his eyes, offering him her heart and soul with that single glance. "I . . . I love you, Falcon."

Falcon laughed; it was not a comforting sound. "So you say, but you have a strange way of showing it. I am an honorable man, Mariah. It took me a long time to work through my anger after I learned Edmond was your husband and not your father. But through it all I never forgot how it had been between us. I didn't want to care for you, to make love to you, but I couldn't help myself.

"But this . . ." He shook his head. "I compromised my honor, took another man's wife while I thought I was making love to his widowed daughter. You took something precious from me, Mariah. I have a son who can never take my name. I admired Edmond, but now I'm not sure how I feel about him. The man is dead and cannot answer for himself, but you could have told me weeks ago."

"I'm sorry," Mariah said, "so very sorry."

With a snort of disgust, Falcon stormed from the chamber.

Heartbroken, Mariah fought back tears. She'd told Falcon the truth and had paid the ultimate price. He hated her, just as she'd feared he would. Did he hate her enough to take her son from her? She didn't know. He had changed from passionate lover to virtual stranger during the course of her tale. He hated her, and she had no one to blame but herself.

She rose and donned her chamber robe. A knock sounded on the door. Unless it was her bath, Mariah didn't wish to see anyone right now.

"Who is it?"

"Edwina. May I come in?"

Mariah opened the door to her friend and found herself enfolded in arms that were so very dear to her.

"Where have you been?" Edwina asked. "Falcon was nearly out of his mind with worry."

"Falcon knows about Robbie, Edwina. He hates me now."

"You told him?"

"Aye, I couldn't live with the guilt any longer."

"'Twas time," Edwina said sagely. "How did he take it?"

Mariah collapsed on the bed. "Not well. He is an honorable man. My lies have hurt him. From the first, I knew those lies would return to haunt me. Mistakenly, I thought having Robbie made everything right. Why did Falcon have to return? Though I missed him dreadfully, yearned for his return, I knew 'twas best for me and Robbie if he never came back."

"You love Falcon, Mariah. I knew it from the beginning."

Mariah nodded miserably. "His return left me in panic, but after a while we seemed to reconnect. He helped defeat Osgood and advised the king to accept Robbie as the new Earl of Mildenhall even though he knew Edmond couldn't have been Robbie's father.

"I thought Falcon had decided in Robbie's favor because he realized he cared for me. We shared a bond. But then Rosamond arrived, offering Falcon everything I could not give him."

Edwina patted Mariah's shoulder. "But he didn't wed Rosamond, did he? The man has strong feelings for you, Mariah. You're the mother of his son. You have a great deal to offer him."

"Apparently, not enough. I can give him neither land nor wealth. Mildenhall belongs to Robbie, unless Falcon decides to expose his illegitimacy to the king, in which case Osgood will claim it."

"Calm yourself, lass. Look at me."

Mariah turned her head toward Edwina. After several moments of staring into Mariah's eyes, Edwina nodded complacently. " 'Tis just as I thought."

Mariah had no idea what Edwina was talking about. "What do you see?"

"Do you not know?"

"Nay. Why are you acting so strangely?"

Whatever Edwina meant to tell Mariah had to wait; a knock on the door announced the arrival of Mariah's bath. When her bath had been prepared and everyone had left, Mariah looked for Edwina, eager to continue the conversation, but the healer had disappeared.

Falcon arrived in the hall before Mariah, his mind still trying to accept the fact that he was a father, had been for nearly five years. Mariah could have told him the truth any time during the past weeks but she had not. Could he forgive her lies? Did he want to?

Sir Maynard joined Falcon at the head table. "The men

are ready to resume the search for Lady Mariah after they break their fast."

"That won't be necessary," Falcon said stiffly. "Lady Mariah is no longer missing. She left her hiding place during the night. I found her wandering about in the corridor outside her chamber."

A combination of relief and joy suffused Sir Maynard's face. "Thank God! Will you make the announcement?"

"Aye, I will," Falcon replied. He stood and pounded a cup on the table to gain attention. The hall took on an expectant silence as Falcon searched for the right words.

"The search for Lady Mariah is officially over. She left her hiding place last night and is in her own chamber as I speak. I expect her to arrive in the hall momentarily."

A rousing cheer followed Falcon's words, but he did not share the general joy. He felt sorely used and badly deceived. The drone of happy chatter failed to lift Falcon's dour thoughts. He welcomed the interruption when Sir Dennis joined him.

"What wonderful news!" Dennis exclaimed. "Think you Osgood will present a danger to Mildenhall in the future?"

"I doubt it. Osgood is a broken man. He has no friends to back up his claims, and after this defeat, he'll have a hard time recruiting mercenaries to his cause."

"What are your intentions now that Osgood is no longer a threat to Lady Mariah and little Robbie?"

"Since I have unfinished business at Mildenhall that needs resolving, I intend to remain for a while."

"I'm certain the men won't complain; they like it here. Have you given any thought to appointing a new steward to take Sir Martin's place?"

"That's for Lady Mariah to decide."

A rousing cheer and vigorous clapping announced Mariah's arrival. She acknowledged the accolade with a smile and a wave of her hand.

Falcon stood to seat her on his right. "Your people are thrilled to see you," he said as he resumed his seat. Dennis sat down next to Mariah. "Sir Dennis and I were discussing the fact that you need to appoint a new steward."

Falcon could tell by the poignant look on Mariah's face that she was still mourning Sir Martin. He hardened his heart against the crush of compassion that threatened to overwhelm him. He didn't want to feel anything for Mariah. His emotions were still too raw.

"I can't think about that right now," Mariah replied. "Sir Martin will be sorely missed."

Servants streamed in from the kitchen, bearing bowls of porridge and platters of ham and eggs. "You must be starving," Falcon said. "It's been a while since you've eaten."

Sir Dennis cleared his throat. "My lady, you are the most courageous and resourceful lady I've ever met. We are grateful you survived Sir Osgood's evil plans."

"Thank you, Sir Dennis. It didn't take much to outwit Osgood."

Sir Dennis bowed and left to join his men.

From the corner of his eye, Falcon watched Mariah pick at her food. She should be hungry, so why wasn't she eating? Why did he even care?

He jumped when Mariah's fork clattered against her plate. "What's wrong?"

She shook her head. "Food doesn't appeal to me." She started to rise. He grasped her wrist; she resumed her seat.

"Eat, Mariah."

"How can I eat with you glowering at me?"

"I'm not glowering."

"I want you to leave Mildenhall. Your hatred will be easier to bear if you are not here."

The barb went straight to Falcon's heart. Was it hatred he felt for Mariah? Last night, as she lay in his arms, he would have given his emotion another name.

"Fear not. I will leave in my own good time. But I've missed too much of my son's life to leave without greeting him when he returns."

Her face took on a greenish cast.

Alarm slammed through Falcon. "Are you ill?"

She clutched her throat. "I . . . don't feel well. Excuse me."

She tried to rise, but Falcon's hold on her wrist increased. "Are you afraid of me?"

She lowered her head. "Not of you. I fear that you will destroy my life. If you leave Robbie with me, I will go to the king, admit my wrongdoing and leave Mildenhall to Osgood. My son is more important than material things. Please don't take Robbie away from me."

He released her wrist, alarmed to see a darkening bruise where he had applied pressure. "I am not a monster, Mariah."

Mariah's head shot up, her gaze burning into his. "Are you not? Then prove it. Leave Mildenhall. Now. Today."

Falcon shook his head. I need time to think. I want to see Robbie before I decide anything."

"Do you intend to inform the king about Robbie?"

"I told you, I've decided naught. Now eat, don't let your people see you distraught."

Though Falcon thought she still looked a bit pale, he was gratified to see her begin to eat. No matter what she had done to him, how many lies she had told, he still cared about her and knew she cared for him. Mayhap even loved him, if that wasn't another of her lies.

Whatever was he going to do about Mariah?

Should he take this mess to the king?

What about his own dreams and aspirations? He had a son, and he wanted his son to be proud of him. But the way things stood now, he was doomed to remain a knight forever, a man without land to call his own or wealth to provide for his son.

Even if Henry offered him another heiress, Falcon doubted he would marry her, because Mariah had ruined him for any other woman. Would his honor allow him to forgive her for the lies she had told him?

He had a son! A son!

Very soon he could hold his son in his arms and tell him . . .

Tell him what?

Damnation! What a coil.

Chapter Eighteen

Robbie arrived home later that afternoon. He came bursting through the door and ran straight into Mariah's arms. Falcon forced himself to wait to greet his son, even though he wanted to tear Robbie from Mariah's arms and hold him close. He'd been denied too long.

After waiting impatiently for Robbie to notice him, Falcon cleared his throat and called out a greeting. Robbie's face lit up when he saw Falcon standing nearby. He left his mother's arms and went straight into Falcon's. Falcon scooped him up and swung him high.

"You're still here!" Robbie chirped. "I'm glad. Are you going to stay at Mildenhall with me and Mama?"

Mariah arrived hard on Robbie's heels. "Sir Falcon must return to London to serve the king," she said before Falcon could form an answer.

Falcon sent Mariah a quelling look. "I don't intend to return to London just yet, son, so I'll be around for a while."

"I thought—" Mariah began.

"I know what you thought, my lady, but you were

wrong. I have yet to decide what I will do or where I will go. I suspect the king will return to London very soon, so haring off to France will serve no purpose."

"Does that mean you will stay forever?" Robbie asked.

"Robbie, Becca is waiting to take you to find something to eat. You're hungry, aren't you?"

"Aye, Mama, very hungry."

Reluctantly Falcon relinquished Robbie to Becca.

"It's not going to work, Mariah," Falcon warned.

"I don't know what you're talking about."

"I think you do. There's no way you're going to keep my son from me."

The color drained from Mariah's face. "What are you going to do? I'll deny Robbie is yours if you petition the king for him."

Falcon shook his head. "Mariah—"

"Don't do this to me, Falcon. I beg you—"

"That's enough, Mariah! I don't know what I'm going to do. I'll let you know when I make up my mind. Meanwhile, don't even try to keep Robbie away from me. I'll see him when and where I please."

"You can't stay here! You have to leave!"

God, he hated this. He wasn't a monster; he just wanted to get to know his son. Mariah was being unreasonable. She'd had his son to herself while he was out of the picture, now it was his turn to play a prominent role in Robbie's life. The lad needed a father.

"Go to our son; he's missed you."

Falcon took note of her tightly clenched fists as she stormed off. He wanted to comfort her, but couldn't bring himself to reach out to her. Too many lies stood between them.

* * *

During the following days, Falcon spent a great many hours with Robbie despite Mariah's attempts to curtail their time together. He took his son up on his horse and rode around the courtyard, enjoying Robbie's squeals of delight. He played toy soldiers with him and told him stories of legendary knights and battles.

One day Sir John and his new wife arrived unexpectedly at Mildenhall. Mariah hugged Elizabeth while Falcon greeted John enthusiastically.

"I learned in London that you were at Mildenhall," John said.

"We were on our way to Southwold to visit Elizabeth's mother when I suggested we stop at Mildenhall first and see where things stood with Osgood. I admit I was surprised to learn you were here. Did Rosamond come with you? I cannot believe she'd let you leave so soon after your marriage."

"I didn't wed Rosamond," Falcon replied. "Things didn't work out between us. As for Osgood, he's gone for good." Then he went on to explain everything that had transpired since John and Elizabeth had left to visit his parents.

"What an incredible story," John said when Falcon finished. "Obviously, you recuperated from your wound. Thank God it wasn't serious."

"Edwina and Father Francis saved my life, one with herbal concoctions and the other with prayers. Robbie and Becca returned to Mildenhall a few days ago."

"Mother is alone at Southwold with Father and Walter," Elizabeth said in a voice fraught with fear. "Father must have been in a rage when he was driven from

Mildenhall. I'm afraid that Mother will suffer the brunt of his anger. Oh, John, we must go to her."

John took Elizabeth into her arms. "We'll leave for Southwold first thing tomorrow."

"Fetch Martha and bring her here," Mariah insisted. "She has a home with us for as long as she wishes."

"Thank you, Mariah," Elizabeth said gratefully. "John and I planned to take Mother to John's family home in Devonshire and hoped Father wouldn't be there to stop us."

"Your father had no place to go but home once he fled Mildenhall," Falcon said. "But his mercenaries have deserted him; I doubt he has the men to stop you."

Elizabeth looked unconvinced. "I hope you're right. Father is a brutal man, and Mother is defenseless against him. Walter is no help, for he's afraid to cross Father."

"Don't fret, sweetheart, I will not let your father hurt your mother," John said.

"Choose two men to take with you in case Osgood causes trouble," Falcon offered.

"I'm taking Elizabeth to her chamber; she looks exhausted," Mariah said. "She'll have plenty of time to rest before the evening meal."

"I have a skin of fine wine in my chamber," Falcon said to John. "Will you join me?"

"I'd be delighted." John followed Falcon to his chamber and accepted a goblet of wine from him. Falcon idly swirled the red liquid in his glass as John surreptitiously studied him.

"You look troubled," John said. "Do you want to talk about it?"

"I have a son," Falcon blurted out.

John choked on the wine he had just swallowed. "You

have a son? I know you, Falcon. You've been careful to sire no bastards; you didn't want to embarrass your family. How did it happen?"

A bitter laugh escaped Falcon's lips. "It happened when I had no memory and was vulnerable to Mariah's seduction."

"Lady Mariah? You mean . . . Are you saying that Robbie is your son? You made a cuckold of Lord Edmond?"

Falcon drained his goblet in one gulp. "She lied to me. She said she was a widow, and that she was barren. I believed her because I wanted her. Little did I know she wanted me for one thing: to give her the child Lord Edmond couldn't. They plotted together to get an heir for Mildenhall."

"I cannot believe Lady Mariah would do such a thing," John said, shaking his head. "How long have you known?"

"A few days. Mariah finally admitted she had lied about Robbie and everything else. I didn't learn she had lied about being a widow instead of a wife until the king sent me to Mildenhall to investigate the matter of Robbie's legitimacy. Had I not returned, I never would have known I had a son."

"What are you going to do about it?"

"I don't know. Though I want my son to know his father, I don't want him to lose Mildenhall, for I have naught but my name to offer him."

John searched Falcon's face for several long minutes before offering a solution. "You could wed Mariah."

Falcon turned on him. "Wed a liar, a deceiver? Never!"

John grinned. "You protest overmuch, Falcon. You cannot hide the truth from me. I am no fool. I knew you and Mariah were lovers long before I left with Elizabeth."

Falcon's expression turned sour. "That was before I learned about Robbie. We are like two strangers now, with little to say to one another."

"I would think you'd have a great deal to say to one another. You share a son. How could you not have suspected that the lad was yours?"

"I thought about it a lot when I first saw Robbie, but Mariah lied about his age. Though I knew Lord Edmond wasn't capable of getting Mariah with child, I assumed she had taken a lover after I left."

John rose. "Well, my friend, I can see you have some decisions to make, so I will leave you to your solitude. I want to look in on Elizabeth. I know how worried she is about her mother."

"You love her very much," Falcon stated.

John smiled. "You have no idea."

"I envy your happiness."

"You could have the same thing if you weren't so damn honorable. No one is without fault, Falcon. No one is perfect. Remember that while you're making your decision." He clasped Falcon's shoulder. "Thank you for the wine, it was excellent."

Falcon brooded long after John left. If John thought Falcon should forgive Mariah, he was bound to be disappointed. There was no room for forgiveness in Falcon's heart, no place for anyone but Robbie. He wanted his son with a fierceness that overrode every other emotion.

Whatever was he going to do about Mariah?

* * *

Mariah got Elizabeth settled in her chamber, then stopped to look in on Robbie. She found him sitting on the floor, all freshly bathed and scrubbed clean. The sudden need to hold him in her arms, to hug him fiercely and never let him go, overwhelmed her. She couldn't bear the thought of losing him to Falcon.

Why couldn't Falcon believe she loved him? Why couldn't they raise their son together? Had that thought never occurred to him? Had her lies killed whatever tender feelings he'd had for her?

Driven by the sudden need to cling to Robbie, she picked him up, sat down in a chair and cuddled him in her lap. He snuggled against her, his little arms curving around her neck.

"I missed you, Mama. I don't want Sir Osgood to come back. He's a bad man."

"I know, my love, but we don't have to worry about him ever again. Falcon sent him away, this time for good."

"Falcon is a good man, isn't he, Mama?"

Mariah gave him a wistful smile. "Aye, a very good man. He came to Mildenhall when we needed him."

"I'd like it very much if you asked Falcon to stay."

"Falcon has duties elsewhere," Mariah replied.

"Mayhap he'd stay if you asked him to be my papa," Robbie said. "I don't remember much about my own papa, except that he was sick a long time."

Mariah had no idea what to say to that. Though Falcon was Robbie's father, the child could never know that. If the truth came to light, Robbie would lose Mildenhall and the title Edmond had wanted for him. "I know you like Falcon, Robbie, but what you are asking is impossible."

"I want Falcon to stay," Robbie persisted.

"I'd like to stay, Robbie," Falcon said from the doorway. "For a while, anyway."

Dismayed, Mariah stared at Falcon, surprised to see him leaning against the doorjamb, arms crossed over his chest, an unreadable expression darkening his eyes. Then he pushed himself away from the wall and stalked toward her.

"What are you doing here?"

"The same thing you are, I suspect."

Robbie grinned up at Falcon. "Will you be my papa?"

"Robbie!" Mariah chided.

"Naught would please me more, Robbie, and I intend to visit you as often as I can in the future," Falcon replied.

"Why can't you stay forever? Mama said Mildenhall belongs to me, so I can invite anyone I want."

"Robbie, I think you've said enough," Mariah warned. She kissed his forehead. "It's past your bedtime. I'll tuck you in."

Reluctantly, Robbie climbed into bed. "Can Falcon tuck me in tonight?"

Hurt by Robbie's preference for Falcon, Mariah turned away, unwilling to let Falcon see her anguish. Her stomach was churning; she felt like spewing her guts out. This feeling was occurring too often of late, and she didn't like it. Terror was her constant companion; she feared Falcon would take Robbie from her.

"Of course I'll tuck you in," Falcon said, moving past Mariah to kiss Robbie's forehead and tuck the blanket around him. "Sweet dreams, son."

Robbie was almost instantly asleep, and Falcon left the chamber without uttering a word to Mariah. What could he say? The tension between them had not abated. It still burned hot. He sensed the invisible bond drawing him to her, felt the warmth of her body when he brushed past her. It was tugging him into her spell, and he fought against it. Mariah had hurt him, hurt him badly. Her lies had robbed him of something precious.

Despite the fact that Elizabeth and John were present at the evening meal, the tension between Falcon and Mariah was palpable. No one was more relieved than Falcon when the meal ended and the women retired to the solar.

To relieve his tension, Falcon played at dice with his men. When the game broke up a few hours later, Falcon sought his bed. The moment he entered the room, he knew he wasn't alone.

Edwina rose with difficulty from a bench near the fireplace. "I've been waiting for you, Sir Falcon."

"I'm tired, Edwina. Can't this wait until tomorrow?"

"Aye, but I am here now."

Falcon sighed. "Very well; say your piece, then leave me to my rest."

Edwina wasted no words on preliminaries. "Mariah is increasing."

Falcon's mouth dropped open. "What?"

"I am being blunt, Falcon, but this is something you should know."

Falcon dropped down on the bench Edwina had just vacated. "How do you know? Did Mariah tell you?"

"Nay. I'm not sure she realizes it yet. I looked into her eyes and saw what others cannot see."

Stunned, Falcon's mouth worked wordlessly before he gained the wits to say, "I saw no sign of it."

"You are a man," Edwina said as if that explained Falcon's lack of perception. "I'm telling you this because you cannot leave Mariah and your children without protection. Though you cannot claim Robbie without stirring up a hornets' nest, you can wed Mariah and claim the second child she carries."

Falcon fought the urge to agree to Edwina's demand without offering a fight. "How do I know the child is mine?"

Edwina drew herself up to her meager height. "You, sir, know better than anyone that you are the only man who can claim Mariah's child."

"Aye," Falcon admitted grudgingly. "You have said what you've come to say; now leave."

Edwina's chin rose stubbornly. "What do you intend to do about this matter?"

"That is between Mariah and me. Good night, Edwina."

Apparently, Edwina felt there was naught more she could say, for she took herself off, but not before sending Falcon a look that spoke volumes about her feelings concerning his duty to Mariah.

Falcon stared into the dying embers in the grate, aware that he should build the fire up for the night but unable to focus his mind on anything but Edwina's words. *Was* Mariah expecting his child? Would she admit she was increasing, or let him leave without telling him?

Falcon rose and walked to the window. The night was as black and unfathomable as his emotions. He could not bear the thought of losing another child.

Damnation! Did Mariah truly not know she was increasing? He punched his fist against the window embrasure, the violent act an expression of his anguish.

Falcon had a great deal of thinking to do. This night would bring him little rest.

Mariah entered the hall the next morning with Robbie hard on her heels and Becca trailing behind them. Mariah smiled down at her son. He had been reluctant to let her out of his sight since he'd returned home.

Mariah didn't see Falcon in the hall and hoped he had already left for the training field with his men. She couldn't bear his animosity. His coolness made her sad. She loved Falcon; just looking at him sent her pulse racing and blood pounding through her veins. His beauty of face and form were without compare. No other man of her acquaintance possessed Falcon's strength of body and spirit.

Mariah had to accept the fact that she had lied to an honorable man and must now pay the consequences. But did the consequences have to be so painful? When she had agreed with Edmond to seduce the unknown knight, she'd never expected to fall in love with him, never thought she would see him again after he recovered his memory and left Mildenhall. But fickle fate had given her a man she could not forget, a man she could not help loving, an honorable man who could not forgive her.

Falcon entered the hall. Robbie saw him first and ran to greet him. Mariah's heart nearly broke when she realized that the bond Falcon had forged with his son was becoming stronger.

Mariah fixed her gaze on Falcon's face, surprised to see how haggard he looked. Had he not slept well last night? What had kept him awake? Fear settled in her heart. Had he reached a decision about Robbie? Holding tightly to Robbie's hand, Falcon approached Mariah. Ignoring her, he motioned to Becca.

"Take Robbie to see the new kittens in the stable. I need to speak privately with your mistress."

Becca nodded and took Robbie off. Mariah watched in trepidation as Falcon finally met her questioning gaze. His harsh expression was not comforting.

"Have you eaten?" Falcon asked.

Not trusting her voice, she shook her head.

"Neither have I. We'll eat first and then talk."

"I'm not hungry," Mariah whispered.

Falcon's gaze probed deep into her soul. She looked away.

"That's not acceptable; you must eat something."

He filled her plate with eggs and ham and pushed it toward her. Mariah's stomach protested as she stared at the runny eggs and greasy ham. She pushed the plate away. "Some dry bread and tea are all I require this morning." She reached for a slice of bread, forcing herself to nibble on it. What in the world was wrong with her? Her healthy appetite seemed to have deserted her.

While Falcon demolished his own breakfast, he watched her closely. Mariah rose abruptly. "I cannot take this. Just tell me what you have decided and get it over with. I want you to know, however, that I will fight you tooth and nail if you try to take Robbie away from me."

"Not here," Falcon said coolly. "I will accompany you to your chamber, where we can speak in private."

Her head held high, Mariah preceded Falcon out of the hall and up the stairs to the solar. Though her knees were quaking, pride kept her from stumbling. She refused to let Falcon turn her into a cowering mass of fear, even though that was exactly how she felt.

Mariah entered the solar, walked to the middle of the chamber and spun around to confront Falcon. Falcon closed the door and leaned against it. He stared at her for several heartbeats before pushing himself away from the door and prowling toward her. Mariah held fast, refusing to retreat.

With a slight tremble in her voice, she asked, "What is it you wish to say to me?"

Falcon clasped his hands behind his back and began to pace. After several turns around the chamber, he stopped in front of her. "I'm not going to take Robbie from you."

Mariah's knees wobbled and she feared she would collapse, so great was her relief. Falcon must have seen how close she was to fainting, for he grasped her shoulders, led her to the nearest chair and eased her down.

"Are you all right?"

"I am now."

"Then perhaps I should finish."

"There's more?"

"Aye, a great deal more. Though I'm not going to take Robbie from you, relinquishing him to you is out of the question. My son means a lot to me. I've come to love him and will not let you cut him out of my life."

Mariah's fear returned. "What do you mean?"

Falcon cleared his throat. "I've thought about this all night before reaching a solution that should satisfy both our needs."

Mariah held her breath as she waited for Falcon to continue. What possible solution had he come up with that would satisfy both their needs?

Falcon stared into Mariah's eyes, recalling Edwina's words. He saw naught in her gaze to indicate she was increasing, but Edwina often saw things others did not.

"We shall marry immediately. I've already spoken with Father Francis, and he's agreed to perform the ceremony this very day."

Falcon watched the play of emotions on Mariah's face. He saw surprise, which he had expected, followed closely by disbelief. He also noted her hesitation and wondered if she would refuse.

"You want to marry me?"

"Did you not hear me? I put it as plainly as I could."

"Why? Marrying me will gain you naught. I have no land, no wealth; naught but my widow's portion. Edmond's estate belongs to Robbie."

"Think you I don't know that?" Falcon growled. "Robbie needs a father more than I need land and wealth. And Mildenhall needs a protector. I'm willing to act in both capacities."

"But . . . you don't love me. You don't even like me."

"You said you loved me," he reminded her. "Have you changed your mind?"

She shook her head.

"Then mayhap we can build on that."

Though Falcon's words gave no hint of his feelings, he realized he wanted this marriage to work. He and Mariah had been lovers a long time. He had one child with her and perhaps another on the way. He loved making love to Mariah, loved everything about her except her lies. Even now he desired her. He felt his body swell with need; he wanted to make love to her again.

"Why are you doing this? If you cannot love me as much as I love you, marriage makes no sense," she said.

Falcon wasn't about to let her refuse. "Would you rather I claimed Robbie and took him away? My family would be happy to raise him. My brother's wife loves children."

Falcon could tell by Mariah's pained expression that he had struck where it hurt most. Though he didn't feel good about it, his words had the desired effect.

"You wouldn't!"

"Aye, I would. Think very carefully before you answer this question, Mariah. Are you carrying my child?"

Mariah turned so pale, Falcon knew he had shocked her. He watched her closely as she placed her hand over her stomach and gaped at him.

"Did you not know?" Falcon asked.

"How could you know when I've only just began to suspect it myself?"

"Is it true?"

"It could be. With everything that's happened, I haven't kept track of my—" Her eyes widened. "Sweet Mother of God, 'tis true—I'm going to have a babe!"

She looked so miserable, Falcon wondered if she hated the thought of bearing him another child.

"How did you know?" she demanded.

"Edwina told me. Apparently, she suspected before you did."

Mariah's head shot up and her shoulders squared. "If that's what prompted your proposal, I must say you nay. I can take care of my child without you. We are so remote here, no one will ever know or care."

"I will know and I will care," Falcon replied. "Father Francis agreed to perform the ceremony in the chapel today before Vespers. I'll ask cook to prepare a wedding feast and dispatch a messenger to the village with an invitation to any of the cotters who wish to attend."

"I haven't said yes," Mariah whispered. "This is all going too fast for me."

"You have no choice, Mariah."

"Can you forgive my lies?"

Falcon looked torn. "I do not know." Grasping her hands, he lifted her to her feet and took her into his arms. She stiffened and then melted into him. "Look at me, Mariah." She raised her eyes to his. "We'll always have this."

Then he kissed her, and all Mariah's doubts fled. Falcon was the only man for her, the only man she'd ever want, so why fight her feelings? She loved him enough for both of them. And one day, mayhap Falcon would return her love. If he was willing to give up his dreams of wealth and land to marry her, it was possible that he already loved her and either didn't know it or refused to acknowledge it.

Falcon's kiss deepened, grew more demanding. Mariah's arms circled his neck as his hands roamed hotly over her back. Reaching down, he cupped her buttocks, pulling her hard against his arousal. She felt the rigid proof of his need and reveled in it. Falcon could lie to himself, but he couldn't lie to her.

His kisses tasted like more than simple lust.

Connie Mason

He cared about her, mayhap even loved her.

Her conviction grew firmer when Falcon swept her into his arms and whispered against her lips, "I want to make love to you." His voice held a note of desperation. "Nay, I *need* to make love to you. This was meant to be. *We* were meant to be."

Mariah felt no need to argue.

Chapter Nineteen

Mariah's gown and shift disappeared so quickly, she was left breathless. Falcon shed his own clothing as swiftly as he had rid her of hers. Desire softened his mouth as his gaze burned a trail of fire down her body. Then he kissed her, fusing their mouths and bodies together as if they were one, as if he wanted to devour her. He eased her onto the bed and followed her down.

Mariah sighed as he reached between her thighs, found the delicate petals of her sex and slipped two fingers inside her aching cleft. She moaned and parted her legs wider, opening herself to his intimate caress. When he lowered his head and blew gently on her wet flesh, she shivered and arched up against him. Then he placed his mouth where his fingers had been and used his tongue to arouse her, sucking and licking her swollen sex.

She felt a rush of heat and wetness flood her, but before she reached a climax, Falcon grasped her waist and pulled her on top of him. "Take me inside you," he murmured raggedly.

Mariah eagerly obliged. The need to be filled by him

was overwhelming. She straddled his hips and positioned herself over him, barely grazing his arousal with her hot, slick center. It was as if every nerve he'd just aroused had been slumbering, aching to be taken to new delights. Gazing into his eyes, she placed her hands flat against his chest and sheathed him in her wet heat.

Falcon groaned and lifted his head until he could reach her mouth, driving his tongue deep inside. Mariah kissed him back, then broke the kiss, gazing down at him as he thrust into her, awed by the sight of his naked body, his strength, his blatant masculinity. Naught existed but Falcon and the thrill of having him inside her.

Falcon tried to slow down in order to savor the beauty of the creamy skin of her shoulders, her breasts and rosy nipples hanging just out of reach above him. But desperate need drove him. He wanted to make this last, wanted it to go on forever, but his body was clamoring for completion. Inserting a hand between them, he began to stroke the nub of pleasure hidden in the sleek folds between her legs. Her breath caught, then disintegrated into frantic little moans as he filled and caressed her at the same time.

She began to move faster atop him, in turn making him thrust deeper, harder. He wanted to remain joined to her forever, wanted to spill himself into her and forget the past that lay between them. Despite her history of lies, Falcon wanted to make a life with Mariah and their children. In bed they were perfect.

His frenzied thrusts into her body grew frantic. Falcon wanted to slow their pace, to hold her against his pounding chest while he regained a semblance of control, but the pleasure surging through him was unstoppable. Suddenly Mariah cried out, stiffened and then rocked frantically against him, his name on her lips. He couldn't hold back. He drove into her again and again, releasing his seed into her in a rush of scalding heat.

She collapsed against him, her breath erupting in harsh puffs against his shoulder. Her hair fell in a tangled mass of gold across his chest, and her sheath still gripped him tight. He wrapped his arms around her, pulled out of her and eased her onto the mattress beside him.

Rising over her, he kissed her, claiming ownership with his mouth and tongue, as if making love hadn't been enough to place his brand upon her. He licked and nipped and tasted. He kissed her long and hard, and then slow and deep. He wanted to prove to her that she needed him, for this if for naught else.

He broke off the kiss and rolled away. Then he rose and began to dress. "There's a great deal to do before our wedding," he said distractedly.

Mariah wasn't sure what had just happened. Falcon had gone from blistering hot to cool and preoccupied in a matter of minutes. Was this the kind of behavior she could expect in their marriage?

"I . . . I'm not sure we should wed," she stammered. "I don't know if I could live with a man who feels naught for me."

Falcon whipped around, his eyes dark with an emotion she couldn't read. "You are mistaken, Mariah. You know I value honor above all else. If I disliked you, I could not have made love to you as I just did. Tell me my lovemaking was cold and emotionless and I will call you a liar."

Mariah lowered her eyes. "Nay, I cannot. You were as involved as I was."

"Then clear your mind of such thoughts and prepare for our wedding." He strode to the door.

"Falcon, wait!"

He halted at the door and turned to look at her. She was sitting up in bed with the sheet pulled up to her neck. "Before we are bound forever, please tell me you feel something for me. Give me hope for a happy future."

Falcon didn't move, didn't bat an eyelash. A shudder ran through him, and then he moved swiftly to the bed. Grasping her hands, he brought them to his lips. "I wouldn't wed you if I didn't want to. That should tell you something."

"It tells me you are an honorable man, but naught of what I truly want to hear."

He inhaled sharply. "Damnation, Mariah, what do you want from me?"

Mariah knew what she wanted and wasn't afraid to ask for it. Her heart told her Falcon loved her, and she would settle for no less. "Your heart; I want your heart. You've always had mine."

"*Do* I have yours, Mariah?"

"Aye, you are the only man I've ever loved. 'Tis a difficult thing to admit when you've given me no reason to believe my love is returned."

Falcon sat on the bed. "I've done a great deal of thinking lately. I understand why you lied, I can even understand why Lord Edmond encouraged you. You needed an heir to keep Osgood from inheriting, and I was handy."

"It was more than that, Falcon. I wouldn't have made love with you if I hadn't had feelings for you even then. You weren't just a man who walked in and out of my life, a man who left an heir for Mildenhall.

"I wanted you to stay, but once you regained your memory, you were determined to leave immediately. 'Twas as if I ceased to exist for you. I wasn't the heiress you needed, nor would I ever be the kind of woman you wanted. But over the years I remained true to you in my heart. Had you not returned, I would never have known love again."

A lump formed in Falcon's throat. Mariah's impassioned words humbled him. How could he not return her love? Had he ever felt for another woman what he felt for Mariah? The answer surprised him. Honor was a part of a knight's oath. He had always been or tried to be an honorable man in all his dealings, but what was honor without love?

What kind of a life would he have without Mariah in it? Without Robbie or the new babe Mariah carried? Was that love? Though he wasn't sure, his feelings for Mariah eclipsed any other emotion he'd ever experienced.

"Tell me what is in your heart, Falcon," Mariah pleaded.

Falcon grasped her face between his hands and kissed her, putting his heart and soul into his kiss. When he finally released her and leaned away, he was humbled by the pure joy shining in her eyes.

"You *do* love me!" Mariah crowed.

Falcon sighed. "I can no longer hide behind my honor, Mariah. What I once considered lies, I now perceive as acts of desperation. I've known that for a long time, but couldn't bring myself to admit it. I've always wanted you; that hasn't changed over the years. Learning that Robbie is my son has been a life-altering experience.

"It's taken a long time and hard introspection to make

337

me realize I love you. I refused to acknowledge that emotion because I believed loving you would compromise my honor."

He snorted. "But you knew all along, didn't you?"

Mariah's smile could have lit the world. "There are some things a woman knows about the man she loves. I had to make you admit how you felt before I could marry you. I know love isn't important in most marriages, but it is to me. Edmond was a father and friend to me, but after his death I yearned for more. I needed a man who would be my lover, my friend, my husband, a man who loved me as much as I loved him. That man is you, Falcon."

"I will be all of those things to you, my love. Forgive me for being so stubborn, for hiding behind my honor when 'twas you I wanted, only you. Will you forgive me?"

"Only if you forgive me."

He kissed her hard and quick. "Truth to tell, I wouldn't marry you had I not forgiven you." He raised his hand when she tried to interrupt. "Nay, I know what I told you earlier, but I was experiencing so many strange emotions, I didn't know what to make of them. I love you, Mariah, never doubt it. I've been an inflexible ass."

"Aye, you have," Mariah agreed, "but I forgive you." She gave him a push. "Go now and prepare for our wedding."

Mariah couldn't remove the smile from her face after Falcon left. Why did men have to be so stubborn? Lust is a powerful emotion that sooner or later wanes, but love lasts forever. Falcon's need for her had never diminished. That was her first hint that he loved her.

There came a knock at the door. Mariah roused herself enough to ask who it was.

"Edwina," came the muffled reply.

"Come in, Edwina."

A wide smile rearranged Edwina's wrinkles. "I just spoke with Falcon. Today is your wedding day, lass. The whole castle is atwitter."

A frown replaced Edwina's smile. "What are you doing abed? Are you ill? Is it the babe?"

Mariah's cheeks glowed with color. "I am fine, Edwina. Falcon just left my chamber. I wish you had told me I was carrying Falcon's babe before you told Falcon. Though I suspected, I wasn't sure."

Edwina's grin returned. "Falcon was here with you?" She rolled her eyes. "He must have been pleased about the babe."

"I think my pregnancy surprised me more than Falcon. At first I feared . . . well, I feared he would leave me. Then he told me we would be wed this very day. For a while I balked. I . . . I wanted him to admit that he loved me. I want a real marriage, not an arrangement for the sake of our children."

"Falcon loves you. I told you that long ago."

Mariah smiled wistfully. "Aye, he does love me. I can finally be happy."

"Then let's prepare you for your wedding. Your bathwater is heating in the kitchen as we speak."

"Will you fetch Robbie for me? I want to tell him before anyone else does."

After Falcon left Mariah, he issued a string of orders and then went to look for Robbie. He found the lad in the stables, playing with the new kittens. He lifted Robbie onto a bale of hay and sat down beside him.

"Are you going to take me for a ride on your horse, Falcon?" Robbie asked.

"Not today, son. There's something I want to tell you, something very important, something that I hope will make you happy."

Robbie cocked his head, his eyes round. "You're going to leave, aren't you?"

"Nay, just the opposite. I'm going to marry your mother and stay at Mildenhall."

Robbie flung his arms around Falcon's neck. "Will that make you my papa?"

"I'd like to be your papa, but you cannot forget that you're the Earl of Mildenhall, that your . . . father was Lord Edmond."

Though it nearly choked Falcon to say it, those words had to be said. Mildenhall belonged to Robbie, and should the truth about the boy's father reach the king, it would prove disastrous for the boy. Robbie's future depended on remaining the unchallenged heir of Lord Edmond of Mildenhall. One day, Falcon would tell Robbie the truth, but not until he was old enough to understand.

Robbie remained silent for a long time, and then his face lit up. "I know all that, Falcon, but my real papa is dead." His little body stiffened with self-importance. "I am the Earl of Mildenhall. If I say I want you for my papa, you have to do as I say because you are merely a knight."

Falcon suppressed the desire to laugh at Robbie's royal manner. The lad would make a fine earl, and an even finer son.

"I will try to live up to your high expectations, Robbie.

Go find Becca. Tell her to dress you in your finest attire so you can make your mama proud at her wedding."

Mariah felt no nervousness as she walked with Robbie through the deserted hall to her wedding. She felt as if her marriage to Falcon had been preordained. She had even decided to wear the same wedding gown in which she had wed Edmond, because she knew Edmond would approve.

She glanced down at her son. Robbie was happier than she'd ever seen him. She'd been a little disappointed when she learned that Falcon had told him about their marriage, but she supposed he deserved the honor since he'd been denied nearly five years of his son's life.

Sir Maynard intercepted her at the door. "Lady Mariah, since you have no male relative, I would be honored to escort you to the chapel. This is a happy day for Mildenhall; I know Lord Edmond would be pleased to see you wed to such a fine man."

Pleasure suffused Mariah's face. "Thank you, Sir Maynard. I dare say you've earned the honor after your years of faithful service to Mildenhall."

Placing one hand on Maynard's arm and holding Robbie's hand with her other, she allowed them to escort her out the door.

A great crowd spilled out of the chapel into the courtyard. A loud cheer went up when Mariah appeared. The crowd parted, creating a path for Mariah to the chapel door. Her gaze went to Falcon the moment she entered the small chapel. Sir Dennis stood beside him, but it was Falcon who captured her attention.

He looked magnificent in a light blue doublet that emphasized the powerful span of his shoulders, and gray hose that hugged his muscular legs and thighs. Holding tightly to Robbie's hand, Mariah started down the aisle on Sir Maynard's arm.

When Falcon saw Mariah and Robbie walking toward him, he wanted to rush forward and sweep Mariah and his son into his embrace. The only thing stopping him was Dennis's restraining hand on his shoulder.

Mariah looked like an angel in a gown of pale ivory silk with long sleeves, a fitted bodice and an embroidered skirt. A short veil trailed from her shining blond locks, held in place by a gold circlet studded with pearls. His gaze shifted to her face. She was literally glowing, her happiness there for everyone to see.

Then Falcon's eyes descended to Robbie . . . his son, a lad any man would be proud to claim. He was dressed in his finest and looking as pleased as Mariah. They walked side by side, both of them his to love and cherish forever.

A sigh rose up from the assembly as Mariah floated down the aisle. And then she was beside him. Sir Maynard slipped away as Falcon took his place. When Sir Maynard attempted to steer Robbie into a nearby pew, Falcon shook his head.

"Let the lad stay," Falcon said. "He's a part of this family."

Falcon took Mariah's hand and they both knelt as Father Francis began the nuptial mass. When the time arrived for the vows, Mariah and Falcon spoke theirs clearly and without hesitation. A titter went through the assembly when Robbie tossed in an "I do" before Father Francis pronounced them husband and wife.

Falcon turned toward Mariah, smiled and gently kissed

her. Then he lifted Robbie onto his shoulders, grabbed Mariah's hand and left the church amid great rejoicing.

An elaborate wedding feast had been prepared by cook and her staff. Tables had been set up in the hall for the guests, who crowded into the keep behind Falcon and Mariah; nearly everyone from the village had turned out for the event. Falcon seated Mariah at the head table, settled Robbie on her left, then took his place on her right. Moments later, servers brought in the platters piled high with three kinds of meat, fish, oysters, a variety of vegetables and freshly baked bread.

They were halfway through the feast when a guardsman burst into the hall. He skidded to a halt before the head table.

"Sir Falcon, my lady, the king is approaching Mildenhall. A messenger just arrived with the news. King Henry will arrive within the hour."

Falcon leapt to his feet. "The king? Here? Where is the messenger?"

"I am here, Sir Falcon." A knight approached the head table. Falcon recognized him immediately.

"Sir Percy, welcome. As you might guess, we are in the midst of a feast to celebrate my marriage to Lady Mariah of Mildenhall."

"Hearty congratulations, Falcon, my lady. Does Henry know?"

"Nay, but he will soon enough. Why is he honoring us with a visit?"

"You will have to ask him that yourself," Percy said. "He will be here soon."

"How many men accompany him?" Falcon asked, fearing there wouldn't be enough food for all the newcomers.

"He brings but ten of his royal guard," Percy replied. "He anticipated no trouble in this part of England."

"Join us, my friend," Falcon invited. "We shall await the king together."

They didn't have long to wait. King Henry and his entourage showed up a scant forty-five minutes later. Surprise illuminated Henry's face when he walked into the hall and saw a large assembly of merrymakers. Immediately Falcon and Mariah rose. Falcon bowed deeply while Mariah executed a perfect curtsey. Then the crowd went silent, many too awed to react to the sight of their king while others scraped and bowed.

"What's going on here?" Henry boomed. "The celebration cannot be for me, for I sent no word of my impending visit."

"Sire," Falcon said, bowing. "Welcome to my wedding feast. Lady Mariah of Mildenhall has done me the great honor of becoming my wife. Today is our wedding day."

Henry's gaze swept over Mariah before returning to Falcon. "Could you not wait for the heiress I promised you?"

Falcon smiled at Mariah. "Some things cannot wait, Majesty."

"So that's the way of it," Henry replied. "I must say I'm surprised, but who am I to stand in the way of true love."

"Then you approve, sire?" Mariah asked.

"I can think of no reason to object. Are you going to invite me to the feast or must I remain standing?"

"Forgive me, sire," Falcon said, motioning to a servant to set another place at the head table.

The king sat down beside Falcon while his entourage

found seats among the other guests. Fresh food was brought from the kitchen and the feast recommenced.

"What brings you to Mildenhall, Your Majesty?" Falcon asked.

"You did, Falcon. I heard some surprising news when I returned from France. I was told you did not wed Lady Rosamond, even though she was eager for the match, and that Sir Osgood did not remain in exile as I ordered. When I did not hear from you or see you in London, I decided you must be at Mildenhall and came to see for myself what was transpiring."

"Falcon was seriously wounded by one of Osgood's mercenaries," Mariah revealed.

Henry sent Falcon a sharp look. "He looks healthy enough to me. Certainly healthy enough to take a bride."

"Mariah's healer is without compare. And Father Francis's prayers didn't hurt," Falcon explained.

No one saw Robbie slip up to the King until he tugged on Henry's sleeve. Startled, Henry looked down at him and smiled. "Well, if it isn't little Lord Robert. What can I do for you, lad?"

"You're not going to take my new papa away, are you? Mama and I need him."

Henry raised an eyebrow in Falcon's direction. "The lad is well-spoken, Falcon. It seems you have won him over as well as his mother." He ruffled Robbie's hair. "Rest easy, Lord Robbie, I'm not taking Falcon away. Not unless I am forced to war again and need him to protect England."

Becca hurried over to her charge and led him off. Conversation ceased while Henry ate. When he had eaten his fill, he sat back and sighed. "Excellent meal."

"Musicians from the village should arrive soon," Falcon said. "There will be dancing, if you care to join in. If not, your chamber is being prepared as we speak."

"We shall see, we shall see. But first, I would speak privately to you concerning the real reason I came to Mildenhall."

A frown marred Mariah's smooth brow as Falcon rose and led Henry to the guest chamber the king was to occupy. A maid, who was delivering a decanter of wine, dipped into a curtsey and scurried off when they entered.

Henry dropped into a chair beside the hearth and held his hands out to warm them. "Sit down, Falcon; I don't like you looming over me."

Falcon pulled up a bench and perched on the edge. Whatever could Henry want?

"I know you needed to wed for land and wealth, but I suspect you followed your heart. But all is not lost, Falcon."

What was Henry trying to say? Falcon knew the king well enough to know he did not speak idle words. "Sire, I am happy with my marriage. Robbie needs a father who can guide him into manhood. I can teach him how to be a good and just earl."

"Aye, you can, Falcon, of that I have no doubt. Does it not annoy you to know you are a mere knight while the lad you will raise is an earl?"

"It might have at one time. Ambition often drives a man to wish for more than he deserves."

"You are an honorable man, Falcon, and an exemplary knight. You have fought bravely for king and country and are long overdue for the reward I promised you. Did you know that Lady Rosamond's father had died, and that she recently wed the Earl of Kincade, a Scottish nobleman?"

"Nay, I did not."

"Her father's dying wish was that she wed Kincade. She has since settled in Scotland with her husband. After a thorough search, no male heir was found to claim the Norwich title. Your years of faithful service deserve an elevation in rank and circumstance. Therefore, I have appointed you the Earl of Norwich. Norwich lands are extensive and reach to all corners of England. The tithes from the villages and everything that goes with the title now belong to you."

Falcon dropped to one knee. "Sire, I cannot believe . . . Your generosity overwhelms me."

"You deserve it, Falcon. Now you will have something of value to leave to your children with Lady Mariah. Rise, Lord Norwich. We shall return to the hall and inform your wife and guests of your new station in life."

King Henry made the announcement when they returned to the hall. The musicians had already started playing, but stopped when Henry raised his hand for silence. A loud cheer filled the hall after the king publicly bestowed Falcon's new title upon him. Falcon looked at Mariah; she appeared even more stunned than he had been. He reached for her hand and lifted her to her feet.

"Shall we retire, my love?"

"The king," Mariah whispered. "It wouldn't be proper to retire before His Majesty."

Henry waved them off. "In this instance, I give you leave. It would please me to remain in the hall and enjoy the musicians before I retire."

A toast was made in their honor by Sir Dennis and another by Sir Maynard before Falcon and Mariah were allowed to leave. When they reached the staircase, Falcon paused, took Mariah into his arms and kissed her. The cheering continued long after they reached their chamber.

Falcon closed and locked the door. "Finally," he sighed, pushing himself away from the door. "I thought the day would never end."

The chamber looked magical. Someone had lit an abundance of candles and placed them around the room. A decanter of wine awaited them, and the bed had been turned down.

Mariah stared thoughtfully at Falcon. "I cannot believe the king came all the way to Mildenhall to bestow a title on you. At last you have everything you've ever desired—a title, wealth, several estates. The king is a generous man."

Falcon reached for her. "Forget the king, this is our wedding night."

"We already had our wedding night this morning, or have you forgotten?"

"How could I forget? We did more than make love this morning. We both revealed what was in our hearts." He pulled her into his arms. "Are you too tired to let me love you again?"

She pressed herself against him, lifting her face up to his. "I'm never too tired for you, Falcon."

His mouth was smiling when he lowered his head and claimed her lips. One kiss was all it took to set off a firestorm inside them.

"I love you in that dress, but I prefer you without it," Falcon whispered.

Mariah turned her back so Falcon could undo the row of tiny buttons down the back. "'Tis the same dress I wore when I wed Edmond. I hope you don't mind."

"Not at all; you are mine, naught else matters."

The dress slid off her shoulders. Falcon lifted it up over her arms and tossed it aside. Her shift followed. He knelt, rolled down her stockings one leg at a time and removed them along with her shoes.

"Now your turn," Mariah said, reaching for him. Once she had him naked, he took her hand and led her to the bed. Moments later, she found herself lying flat on her back, not quite sure how she got there. She reached up her arms to draw him down with her. Passion flared between them. He kissed her face, her throat, her breasts. Her fingers tangled in his hair as she lifted herself to rub against him, bare skin to bare skin.

He kissed and caressed her breasts, rubbed his thumbs over her nipples and then suckled her until she moaned with mingled pleasure and need. She could smell soap, his body heat, his masculinity, and went wild beneath him.

He worked his way back to her mouth and kissed her again and again as his hand found her core and teased through the folds to stroke her. She could feel her own wetness. His fingers pressed inside her while he used the heel of his palm to stimulate the sensitive bud of her desire. His fingers pressed deeper; her muscles clenched around them. And then his fingers left her.

She braced her feet against the bed and waited expectantly as his erection probed her entrance. She tilted her hips; he came into her with a single powerful stroke. He withdrew to the brink of her, then entered again, over and over, until she could hear the liquid heat of their joining, smell the scent of their passion.

Their coupling lacked the frenzy and sense of urgency of this morning; this time it was slow and sweet and thorough, engaging all the senses. It was not just a man taking his pleasure from a willing woman. It was the joining of two people in love, sharing excitement, need, sensation and pleasure.

That knowledge raced along her nerve endings and pooled in that place where Falcon was embedded, until love overflowed and she felt herself shattering, sending her spiraling to the stars.

Falcon drove inside her in a frenzy of need; he thrust deep and then held. She heard him call out her name, felt him release inside her, and then he came down heavily on top of her, panting.

They fell asleep in a tangle of arms and legs.

Epilogue

The king did not leave Mildenhall immediately after the wedding feast, but decided to avail himself of a few days of hunting. On the final day of his stay, Sir John returned from Southwold, accompanied by Elizabeth and her mother. Dame Martha, supported between two guardsmen, was barely able to walk. When John saw the king sitting in the hall with Falcon, he dropped to one knee before him.

"Your Majesty," John said. "I didn't expect to find you here."

"Rise, Sir John," Henry said. His gaze was riveted on Martha. "What happened to the lady?"

Mariah entered the hall at that moment, saw Martha and let out a heart-wrenching cry. "Martha! Oh, you poor thing. What happened to you? Who did this to you?"

"That's what I'd like to know," Henry roared. "Who abused that poor woman, Sir John?"

Mariah could tell that Martha was in pain by the way she held her ribs. Her left eye was swollen shut, and purple bruises marred her face. Mariah sent a servant after

Edwina and ordered the guardsmen to carry Martha to a guest chamber.

Elizabeth stepped forward, her face a mixture of anguish and anger. "Sire, the lady is my mother. John and I traveled to Southwold to remove her from Father's influence. Father is a vicious man, and I feared for her life. When I lived at home, I was able to protect Mother and myself from Father's brutality in a limited way, but after I married John, she had no one to protect her. I knew I had to return for her. John felt the same way."

"We found Dame Martha as she is now," John said, placing a comforting arm around Elizabeth. "Osgood had beaten her. My mother-in-law said Osgood took his frustration out on her after Falcon defeated his forces and sent him fleeing from Mildenhall."

"When John and I arrived at Southwold, I told Father we were taking Mother with us," Elizabeth said, continuing the tale. "Of course he refused to let her go. Walter was no help. Though he didn't condone Father's treatment of Mother, he did naught to protect her."

"I couldn't leave Dame Martha with Osgood," John said. "I feared he would kill her." He paused to catch his breath.

"What happened next?" Henry asked impatiently. "How did you manage to pry Dame Martha away from Sir Osgood?"

"I asked the men who had accompanied me to find a cart, pad it with blankets and place Dame Martha in it. No matter what it took, I wasn't going to leave Elizabeth's mother with that madman."

Henry shook his head. "I knew Sir Osgood had a mean

streak, but I never thought he would take his frustration out on a defenseless woman. Did he put up a fight?"

John sent Falcon a sidelong glance before replying. "Aye, he did. We fought. He lost. I am a much better swordsman than Osgood, thanks to Falcon's training."

Henry's eyebrows arched upward. "You killed him?"

"Aye, sire. I didn't want to, but he gave me no choice."

"John speaks the truth, sire," Elizabeth cut in. "Father drew his sword, forcing John to defend himself. We left immediately afterward. Walter promised to see to Father's burial."

"The kingdom is better off without Sir Osgood," John said.

Henry gazed thoughtfully at John. John held his breath, waiting for the king's verdict. Would he punish or praise him?

"After learning of Sir Osgood's misdeeds from Falcon, I intended to dispatch my royal guardsmen to Southwold to arrest him," the king said. "He would have been charged with treason. No one deliberately disobeys my orders without paying a price. The way I see it, his death was well deserved."

John expelled the breath he had been holding. "My wife was distraught when she saw the condition her mother was in. I'm glad you understand my predicament and approve."

"Thank you, sire," Elizabeth said. "Please excuse me; I must go to my mother." When the king nodded, Elizabeth executed a clumsy curtsy and made a hasty exit.

"Join us, John," Falcon invited. "You look like you could use a drink."

A servant approached with foaming mugs of ale and placed them on the table. John sank down into a chair. "I knew Osgood would protest if we tried to take Dame Martha," he said, "but I never expected him to draw his sword. He must have been desperate."

"You did what you had to do," Falcon replied. "Dame Martha is safe now, and in good hands. Edwina will heal her. As for Osgood, he was indeed a desperate man. He had disobeyed his king and faced punishment."

The three men fell silent, each thinking his own thoughts about Osgood and his demise. They didn't look up until Mariah joined them.

"How is Dame Martha?" Falcon asked.

"She'll survive," Mariah replied. "Edwina found three broken ribs and painful bruises on her back and hips. Fortunately, she wasn't damaged internally. You all saw her face; Osgood was a monster. If he were here now, I'd kill him myself."

"You are nearly as fierce as your husband, lady," Henry crowed. "Methinks you will suit."

Falcon grasped Mariah's hand. "You have no idea, sire," he said with a twinkle.

Her cheeks blooming with color, Mariah squeezed Falcon's hand.

Much later, the king and Falcon sat in Henry's bedchamber, discussing Falcon's new title and the castle at Norwich.

"What do you intend to do about Norwich Castle? If you don't move there, you'll have to find a suitable steward," Henry advised. "Have you made any plans yet?"

"Aye, I have," Falcon replied. "I hold fond feelings for

Mildenhall, and so does Mariah. But since I am now the Earl of Norwich, I should make Norwich Castle my primary residence and appoint a steward for Mildenhall until Robbie comes of age. I already have a man in mind, if he will accept."

"I shall leave that in your capable hands, Falcon."

The following day, the entire household except for Dame Martha, who was still recuperating, gathered in the courtyard to bid the king farewell.

"Well, my lord," Mariah teased once Henry had departed, "what is your first order as Earl of Norwich?"

"I told Henry we would move to Norwich," Falcon revealed. "I'd like to accomplish that as soon as possible. The people there need to meet their new lord and know that they will be taken care of."

Dismay colored Mariah's words. "You want us to live at Norwich?"

"Does that upset you, love?"

"A little. What will happen to Mildenhall?"

"Good things, I hope. Ah, here comes Sir John. I'll know more after I speak to him."

"Well, my lord," John said, grinning. "It seems as if you've finally gotten everything you wished for. I hope you will accept my offer to remain in your service. Elizabeth and Martha need a home, and they are both fond of Mildenhall."

"Join Mariah and me inside, John," Falcon invited. "There's something I wish to discuss with you."

Falcon pulled up three chairs before the hearth.

"What is this all about, Falcon?" John asked once they were seated. "If you decide you no longer need me, I will understand and seek a new lord."

"Nay, never that, John," Falcon said. "I want you to be Mildenhall's steward until Robbie is old enough to take over the reins of his estate. I am moving my family to Norwich; it's where I belong now. If you accept, Elizabeth and Martha will always have a home here."

Mariah clapped her hands. "What a wonderful idea! Mildenhall will fare well in John's hands, and Elizabeth and Martha are familiar with the keep. What a perfect solution, Falcon. What say you, Sir John? Will you take care of Mildenhall for Robbie?"

"Your generosity overwhelms me," Sir John replied. "I gratefully accept, and promise that Mildenhall will prosper under my care. I swear Robbie will find no fault with my stewardship."

After John left to tell Elizabeth the good news, Falcon grasped Mariah's hand and led her up the stairs to their chamber. He took her into his arms the moment he closed the door behind them.

"I haven't paid proper attention to my wife during the king's visit," Falcon said. He reached over and latched the door. "I intend to change that, starting now, sweeting."

Mariah wound her arms around Falcon's neck, pressing her body against his. "It's the middle of the day."

"Any time is a good time to show my wife how much I love her. Ah, Mariah, whatever would I do without you? When I first arrived at Mildenhall, I was badly injured and without a memory; I left healed in both mind and body. And somewhere along the way, you bewitched me."

She planted a soft kiss on his lips. "I seduced you, my lord, plain and simple; no witchcraft involved."

He began to undress her, letting her clothes fall where they might. "I was willing to be seduced, if you recall. It took little effort on your part."

She tugged at his shirt, and soon he was as naked as she. Together they tumbled onto the bed. The first time they came together, it was fast and frantic. The second time was slow and leisurely. They had just finished and were dozing in each other's arms when Robbie pounded on the door, demanding entrance. Falcon didn't have the heart to turn him away. He rose, slipped into his hose and shirt, waited until Mariah dressed, and then opened the door to their son.

"I've been looking all over for you," Robbie said. He stared from one to the other. "What have you been doing? Your hair is all messed, Mama."

Falcon choked back a laugh. "We were discussing our move to Norwich," he replied without missing a beat.

"We're leaving here? I don't want to go. Mildenhall is my home."

Falcon knelt down to Robbie's level. "Mildenhall will always be yours, son, but the king has honored me by making me the Earl of Norwich; moving there is the right thing to do. Sir John will take care of Mildenhall until you're old enough to accept the responsibility of the earldom."

Robbie seemed to mull that over in his mind. "Can I come back to visit?"

"Of course," Mariah said. "Your father didn't lie to you, Mildenhall is yours; Sir John is merely its keeper until you come of age."

"Then I suppose it's all right," Robbie said, apparently

appeased. He grasped Falcon's hand. "Will you take me up on your horse today, Papa? The sun is shining; it's a good day for a ride."

Mariah and Falcon exchanged glances over Robbie's head. Hearing Robbie call him Papa made Falcon's heart swell with love. It was a good day to begin the rest of their lives.

AUTHOR'S NOTE

A Knight's Honor is for those readers who keep requesting Medieval Romances, but I hope all my readers will enjoy Sir Falcon and Lady Mariah's story.

I'm taking my readers on a different path with my next book. *A Taste of Paradise* takes place on the tropical island of Jamaica, where hot days and sultry nights set the scene for Sophia and Christian's story.

I have visited Jamaica several times and enjoyed the lush setting, never realizing the island was infamous for its slave trade. During the 1800s, dealing in sugarcane, rum and slavery became a booming business. My story takes place in 1831. Its hero, Christian, wins a Jamaican plantation in a card game and intends to become a planter. He differs from other planters in that he plans to free his slaves and pay them to work for him. This, of course, causes a rift between him and other planters.

Chris, a ship captain, is trying to escape a painful past in which he killed his best friend during a duel over a woman. As Chris prepares to sail from London, a stowaway sneaks aboard his ship.

The stowaway is the woman who caused the rift and duel between Chris and his friend seven years earlier, the woman Chris claims to hate. *A Taste of Paradise* is a story that never slows down. The love between Chris and Sophia, despite Chris's reluctance to let her into his life, becomes the focus of a story that involves a hurricane and the slave rebellion of 1831, a true event.

I enjoy hearing from readers. For a newsletter and autographed bookmark, please send a long self-addressed stamped envelope to me at P.O. Box 3471, Holiday, FL 34692. I can also be reached at conmason@aol.com. Visit my website at www.conniemason.com to read the first chapter of *A Taste of Paradise*.

ATTENTION
BOOK LOVERS!

Can't get enough of your favorite **ROMANCE**?

Call **1-800-481-9191** to:

✳ order books,

✳ receive a **FREE** catalog,

✳ join our book clubs to **SAVE 30%!**

Open Mon.-Fri. 10 AM-9 PM EST

Visit **www.dorchesterpub.com**
for special offers and inside
information on the authors you love.

We accept Visa, MasterCard or Discover®.
LEISURE BOOKS ♥ LOVE SPELL

Carnival Pride^{SM}
April 2 - 9, 2006.

7 Day Exotic Mexican Riviera Itinerary

DAY	PORT	ARRIVE	DEPART
Sun	Los Angeles/Long Beach, CA		4:00 P.M.
Mon	"Book Lover's" Day at Sea		
Tue	"Book Lover's" Day at Sea		
Wed	Puerto Vallarta, Mexico	8:00 A.M.	10:00 P.M.
Thu	Mazatlan, Mexico	9:00 A.M.	6:00 P.M.
Fri	Cabo San Lucas, Mexico	7:00 A.M.	4:00 P.M.
Sat	"Book Lover's" Day at Sea		
Sun	Los Angeles/Long Beach, CA	9:00 A.M.	

ports of call subject to weather conditions

TERMS AND CONDITIONS

PAYMENT SCHEDULE:
50% due upon booking
Full and final payment due by February 10, 2006

Acceptable forms of payment are Visa, MasterCard, American Express, Discover and checks. The cardholder must be one of the passengers traveling. A fee of $25 will apply for all returned checks. Check payments must be made payable to **Advantage International, LLC** and sent to: **Advantage International, LLC, 195 North Harbor Drive, Suite 4206, Chicago, Il. 60601**

CHANGE/CANCELLATION:
Notice of change/cancellation must be made in writing to Advantage International, LLC.

Change:
Changes in cabin category may be requested and can result in increased rate and penalties. A name change is permitted 60 days or more prior to departure and will incur a penalty of $50 per name change. Deviation from the group schedule and package is a cancellation.

Cancellation:
181 days or more prior to departure	$250 per person
121 - 180 days or more prior to departure	50% of the package price
120 - 61 days prior to departure	75% of the package price
60 days or less prior to departure	100% of the package price (nonrefundable)

US and Canadian citizens are required to present a valid passport or the original birth certificate and state issued photo ID (drivers license). All other nationalities must contact the consulate of the various ports that are visited for verification of documentation.

<u>**We strongly recommend trip cancellation insurance!**</u>

For complete details call 1-877-ADV-NTGE or visit www.AuthorsAtSea.com

---

For booking form and complete information
go to www.AuthorsAtSea.com or call 1-877-ADV-NTGE

Complete coupon and booking form and mail both to:
**Advantage International, LLC,
195 North Harbor Drive, Suite 4206, Chicago, IL 60601**